ALSO BY SHELBY BACH

The Ever Afters: Of Giants and Ice

The Ever Afters: Of Sorcery and Snow

THE EVER AFTERS

# of Witches AND Wind

SHELBY BACH

Simon & Schuster Books for Young Readers
NEW YORK   LONDON   TORONTO   SYDNEY   NEW DELHI

SIMON & SCHUSTER BOOKS FOR YOUNG READERS
An imprint of Simon & Schuster Children's Publishing Division
1230 Avenue of the Americas, New York, New York 10020
This book is a work of fiction. Any references to historical events, real people, or real places are used fictitiously. Other names, characters, places, and events are products of the author's imagination, and any resemblance to actual events or places or persons, living or dead, is entirely coincidental.
Copyright © 2013 by Shelby Randol Trenkelbach
Cover illustrations copyright © 2013 by Cory Loftis
SIMON & SCHUSTER BOOKS FOR YOUNG READERS is a trademark of Simon & Schuster, Inc.
For information about special discounts for bulk purchases, please contact Simon & Schuster Special Sales at 1-866-506-1949 or business@simonandschuster.com.
The Simon & Schuster Speakers Bureau can bring authors to your live event. For more information or to book an event, contact the Simon & Schuster Speakers Bureau at 1-866-248-3049 or visit our website at www.simonspeakers.com.
Also available in a Simon & Schuster Books for Young Readers hardcover edition
Book design by Chloë Foglia
The text for this book is set in Usherwood.
Manufactured in the United States of America
0918 OFF
First Simon & Schuster Books for Young Readers paperback edition May 2014
4 6 8 10 9 7 5
The Library of Congress has cataloged the hardcover edition as follows:
Bach, Shelby.
Of witches and wind / Shelby Bach.
pages cm.—(The Ever Afters ; [2])
Summary: Rory Landon continues to attend Ever After School and participates in another Fairy Tale.
ISBN 978-1-4424-3149-2 (hc)
[1. Characters in literature—Fiction. 2. Magic—Fiction. 3. Fairy tales—Fiction. 4. Adventure and adventurers—Fiction.] I. Title.
PZ7.B1319Oi 2013
[Fic]—dc23
2012026025
ISBN 978-1-4424-3150-8 (pbk)
ISBN 978-1-4424-3151-5 (eBook)

To Angela, Dana, Ems, Kaitlyn,
Katie, Martha, and Will—the friends
who made middle school awesome

1

You would think, if you were battling ice griffins, you would want your best fighters on your side. Or at least someone with experience. These creatures—half bald eagle, half snow leopard—weren't exactly a picnic. Most kids could avoid their giant hooked beaks, the talons on the feathery front legs, and the claws on the furry hind legs, but what you really needed to worry about was their breath. Each griffin could breathe out air so cold that it would freeze puddles into ice slicks under your feet.

But the eighth graders wanted to fight this flock all by themselves.

The ice griffins herded them together in front of the soccer goal. If an eighth grader tried to stab one, the griffin just flapped its wings a couple times and dodged into the sky. Our guys were completely trapped.

"Wow. This is going to end so well," I said.

"We should really follow the Director's orders," said Lena, my best friend. "You know, keep looking."

"Just a sec. Seeing this gives me a warm fuzzy feeling inside," said Chase, my other best friend. His dad, Jack, a big-deal warrior, kept track of how many dragons, griffins, and trolls Chase slayed on every mission. So getting demoted to backup was harder on him than it was on most of us seventh graders.

We all attended Ever After School, a program for fairy tale Characters-in-training, which met every weekday after school let out. We would all survive our own Tale someday, but in the meantime, we trained. Sometimes we even went on missions to make sure magical creatures didn't attack any innocent bystanders. Usually, that meant fighting dragons or ice griffins sent to kill some Character EAS hadn't discovered yet.

Like now. Earlier this afternoon, the Director of EAS had received a report that ice griffins had attacked an all-girls boarding school on Lake Michigan, and she'd given the eighth graders the mission. We lowly seventh graders were just supposed to find the new Character who was under attack.

Seniority was stupid.

A roar thundered across the field. The lion head of the chimera, the flock's three-headed captain, had given an order. The griffins stopped herding, but it didn't matter. The eighth graders were completely surrounded. The snake head wiggled a little, another signal—three griffins shrieked straight at the ground. The puddle underneath them turned to ice, and suddenly the tight knot of warriors twisted and wobbled like they were all simultaneously trying on roller skates for the first time.

I groaned. This was actually painful to watch.

Normally, some people from the boarding school might have come out to investigate all this noise on their soccer field, but we were lucky. Lake Michigan was extremely foggy. We only caught a glimpse of their brick buildings every few minutes. If any students or teachers heard all this shouting, then they probably just thought someone was having an extra-epic soccer game. I wasn't sure what they would think of all the roaring, shrieking, and bleating.

Two eighth graders slipped and landed facedown on the ice.

The chimera's goat head bleated. A half dozen griffins leaped into the air and swooped down at their victims, talons and claws outstretched. A few eighth graders screamed.

"Can we help yet?" Chase yelled at Hansel, EAS's sword master. He was also our chaperone for this mission, but, lounging by the bleachers, he didn't look too concerned that the eighth graders were losing.

"Bryan, you're the smallest, fastest, and tastiest. Use that to your advantage!" Hansel shouted. The eighth grader whose Tale had turned him into a fawn darted out of the ring. He squeezed between two griffins and cantered as fast as his hooves could carry him. The walking, talking venison was obviously too snackworthy for three griffins to resist. They broke rank and swooped after him, despite the chimera's protesting roars, bleats, and hisses. The eighth graders started fighting their way out.

In all the commotion, one eighth grader in a bright red blazer was too busy not slipping to get his spear up. Seeing the opening, an ice griffin closed its talons over his shoulders and lifted him bodily away from his classmates.

"Crap!" Chase said, and Lena gasped and clutched my arm. My hand closed over my sword hilt, like that would help.

"Go after Ben," Hansel told us, pointing. The kid in red screamed as the griffin carried him across the field toward Lake Michigan. "Make sure he doesn't drown."

And so we were demoted to lifeguards.

We sprinted forward before we lost Ben in the fog. Lena pulled out in front. The grass under our feet gave way to sand. We scrambled down a dune toward the shore.

Ben yelled again.

"Poor sucker," Chase said. "His second day at EAS and he gets kidnapped by an ice griffin."

The kidnapper in question glided straight past the beach and over the lake.

"We can't follow them over water!" Lena cried.

The fog was thicker here. All we could see now was a silhouette of ten-foot wings and kicking legs. Plus one long pointy thing. "Ben! You still have your spear! Use it!" I said.

"Aim for the wing joints!" Then Chase added, much more quietly, "And hope you don't break your neck hitting the lake."

I didn't think of that. Maybe he hadn't heard—

Ben grabbed his spear with both hands and jerked it upward into the feathery chest. The ice griffin shrieked and released him. I gulped hard, watching Ben drop. I hated heights more than most people.

"He has a better chance of surviving that fall than—" Lena winced, interrupted by a huge splash. Ben was in the water. The fog made it impossible to see exactly where he fell in. "—the griffin taking him back to her nest."

"Ben!" I said. We sprinted across the sand to the water. "Ben! Shout back if you can!"

No answer. I put a finger on my nose and glanced at my friends. I didn't want to be the one who went in after him. It was cold here.

Lena caught on, her finger on her nose. "Not it!"

"Awesome. Thanks, guys." Chase kicked off his sneakers.

He was moving so slowly. I'd seen him muzzle dragons faster than he was unbuckling his sword belt. "Ben could drown, you know. If he's unconscious," I said.

"Nah. He probably just had the wind knocked out of him." Chase shoved his sword, jacket, and shoes into my hands and waded into the lake.

"I'll check this way," I told Lena, heading left.

She ran right. "Ben!"

For anyone looking for a kid who might have swum to shore on his own, fog doesn't really help. It muffled my shouts, and every slap of waves sounded like Ben splashing back onto the beach. I nearly ran into a boulder, but I didn't find him.

I had just started wondering if the others had had any luck, when Chase called from the water, "Let me know if you've got him!"

"He's not here!" Lena shouted, so far away that I could barely hear her.

"Ben! BEN!" I hadn't meant what I'd said about drowning, but the idea didn't seem so crazy suddenly. Trying not to panic, I listened harder, past the chimera's roars, the griffin squawks, and the waves.

"Here." The voice came from behind me. It definitely wasn't Ben—it belonged to a girl. I turned around, listening again, and the voice said louder, "Here!"

I ran back, and near a clump of stones I'd searched a minute before, I spotted two figures. But by the time I reached them, only Ben was there—his jacket covered with wet clumps of sand.

"Found him!" I shouted happily.

He vomited water, on his hands and knees, eyes squeezed shut. He had also lost one shoe. His rescuer had disappeared.

"Thank gumdrops!" Lena cried, through the fog.

"So, I got all wet for nothing?" Chase shouted, but he sounded relieved too.

Ben wiped his mouth and drew a shaky breath.

"Anything broken?" I asked him anxiously.

"My lungs, maybe," Ben wheezed without looking up. Then he threw up some more.

Chase splashed out of the water beside us. "Sense of humor's intact. I bet this one's going to live."

"Who rescued you?" I asked Ben.

Ben frowned. "A girl. Long dark hair. Great swimmer."

That didn't sound like anyone on this mission. "Did you recognize her?"

"Not precisely," Ben said. "She might be a student here."

"Give him a break, Rory." Dripping, Chase squatted down beside the eighth grader. "The kid was busy drowning."

"Well, that explains the huge splash," said someone behind us. Adelaide, one of my least favorite seventh graders at EAS. "We were wondering."

Four figures marched down the beach, their bows and quivers slung over their shoulders—Adelaide, Daisy, Tina, and Vicky. They were the seventh-grade archer squadron. I liked the last two the best. Tina's dad and Vicky's mom had just gotten married in January. They spent a lot of time bickering over who would be Cinderella and who would be the ugly stepsister. Daisy just did whatever Adelaide said.

"We heard all the shouting and came to see what was up." Tina whirled around suddenly, bow raised, like she'd heard something behind her. But it was only Lena, sprinting along the water.

Chase carefully peeled Ben's red blazer away from his shoulder. "Just two talon punctures. Your shoulder pads took the brunt of it. Once we get back to EAS, we'll get you fixed up before you get home."

"Did you guys find the Snow Queen's target?" Vicky asked.

Lena shook her head and glanced at me. She knew my stomach always flip-flopped whenever that name came up.

The Director had never mentioned it, but every Character at

EAS knew: Only one villain commanded armies of ice griffins and dragons—Solange, the Snow Queen. During the war that had lasted half of the twentieth century, she'd almost wiped out everyone who opposed her, including all Characters. These days she was locked up in the Glass Mountain, but apparently that didn't stop her from sending monsters after defenseless kids.

"Ooooooh! I forgot!" Lena started digging in the tiny electric-blue backpack she carried everywhere.

It always worried me when she did that. Since she was a magic inventor, Lena's bag of tricks was more unpredictable than the average seventh grader's. Once, in the Boston Common park, when we were flushing out the troll that lived under the bridge, she whispered a spell to a painted dragon scale, and a phoenix as big as a limo flew across the sky, a riot of flame and feathers. She told us it was the most beautiful light show she could whip up on short notice. Since trolls can't resist pretty things, she guaranteed that the trick would lure the troll straight to us. Which it did, but every other troll in a ten-mile radius came too.

Humans can't do magic. That was one of the first things the grown-ups told you when you joined EAS.

But every rule has exceptions, and Lena was one of them.

Lena becoming a magician was the weirdest thing that had happened since we'd climbed the beanstalk last May. Melodie, the golden harp we took from the giant's safe, had taught Lena a whole bunch of spells, where she could use dragon scales, phoenix feathers, or unicorn hair like magic batteries. Usually, Lena enchanted them to power new inventions.

All Lena's searching woke up Melodie. She stuck her golden head out of Lena's backpack and yawned. "What is it you're looking for, Mistress?"

"Got it!" Lena waved a fabric-covered square triumphantly in our faces. It kind of looked like an e-reader cover, but I knew from experience that the hard casing held a square mirror. An M3, to be exact—the EAS version of a walkie-talkie. "My mini magic mirror."

"Big whoop." Adelaide never missed a chance to criticize us. She had been Chase's closest friend before Lena got the Beanstalk Tale, so we definitely knew why. "You invented those back at Thanksgiving. You can't expect us to still be impressed."

"When was the last time you invented something, Adelaide?" I snapped.

"I've been modifying the mirrors." Lena's eyes gleamed behind her glasses. She was obviously too excited to get her feelings hurt. "I'm trying to give them new capabilities, so they can do anything smartphones can do."

"Text?" Tina said, interested.

"Tetris?" Vicky asked, impressed.

"No, not those," Lena said, in a smaller voice.

The others looked disappointed, so Melodie sniffed. "All practical uses."

Lena just opened the M3 and muttered something in Fey. Chase, the only other kid in earshot who spoke that language, burst out laughing.

I sensed a joke. "What?"

"Don't you dare translate, Chase Turnleaf," Melodie warned. "If you do, Lena and I will turn you into something small and slithery. Like a salamander. We just perfected that potion."

For someone about a foot tall and attached to a golden harp without legs, Melodie could be really scary when she felt like it. Chase abruptly stopped laughing.

"Tell me later?" I whispered to him.

"Do I look like I want to turn into a salamander?" Chase whispered back. "If she'd said frog, I would've considered it. 'The Frog Prince' isn't a bad Tale."

Ben laughed, but then he choked a little and brought up another round of puke. My chest squeezed in sympathy.

"Wow," Adelaide said mildly. "Did you swallow half the lake?"

Lena angled the M3 at Ben and his watery bile. His face was nearly as red as his jacket.

"Geez, Lena." I pushed the magic camera down with maybe more force than was necessary. The paparazzi had recorded enough of my ugliest memories for me to know that it sucked. "Do you have to film this?"

But Ben perked up. "You filmed it? Did you get the whole thing?"

"I wish." With a sigh Lena swung the M3 around, toward the eighth graders' fight. The wind thinned the fog, and past the lumpy dunes and half the soccer field we caught a glimpse of feathers. "I just turned it on."

"How far did I fall?" Ben asked eagerly.

"Fifty feet or more," Chase said.

"Really?" Ben sat up with a wince. He actually sounded pleased with himself.

Adelaide and Daisy both rolled their eyes.

"You're gonna be one big bruise tomorrow," Chase said, with the air of someone bequeathing bragging rights.

"I don't think it's very funny." The voice came from the lake, so soft that you could barely hear it. "He was underwater for a long time."

We all turned. A girl splashed to shore, water dripping from her plaid skirt and jacket. Her long black hair was the kind that got very wavy when wet—but it made her look elegant, not scruffy.

She had the beginning of a tan, which gave her skin a golden sheen, and her light blue, long-lashed eyes took up most of her heart-shaped face.

She was beautiful. Not just normal beautiful, but too pretty to feel real. Like a sculpture, or a painting, or an airbrushed photo.

She didn't seem to notice that everyone was staring at her with dumbfounded expressions. Even Ben's mouth hung open. We weren't used to kids outside EAS approaching us on missions, and definitely not ones who looked like models for school-uniform catalogues.

"Who are you?" Adelaide shook her blond hair back. She only did that when she felt threatened.

"My name is Mia," the dripping girl said uncertainly.

"You're the girl who saved me!" Ben burst out.

I did a double take. Mia didn't seem like the rescuing type.

Encouraged, Mia slipped out of the water and glided to Ben's side. She held out something oblong and leather—his missing loafer. "You lost this."

"Right," Chase said. "Because that makes sense. Diving back into Lake Michigan to rescue his shoe."

I personally thought this was a fair point, but Ben shot to his feet in knight-in-shining-armor mode. "She saved my life. That doesn't happen every day."

Poor new kid. After he spent more time at EAS, somebody saving his life wouldn't impress him so much.

"She might be the Character we've been looking for," Lena said distractedly. She was busy glaring at her M3. "It's too foggy. We won't be able to record anything this way."

"Maybe if we got a little closer, Mistress," Melodie suggested.

"Good idea." Lena hurried toward the dunes between the shore and the soccer field.

Adelaide turned to the other archers. "Who has the mirror the Director gave us? For the test?" Tina and Vicky both pointed at Daisy, who pushed her arrows aside and reached into her quiver.

The chimera roared extra loud, and I glanced back toward the battle—all I saw were dunes, fog, more fog, and a soggy stretch of grass.

But Chase tensed too. He took his sword belt back and buckled it on.

"Test?" Mia asked, drawing closer to Ben.

"It's not hard. You just look into a magic mirror and tell us what you see in it," Ben explained.

I was sure Mia would never suspect that he had just taken the test himself three days ago. "We need to know if you're a Char—"

"Incoming!" one of the eighth graders called.

The chimera galloped across midfield as fast as its lion paws could carry it, all three heads focused straight on us.

I dropped Chase's stuff and hurriedly drew my sword.

"Oy! Monster!" cried Ben.

Snorting, Chase unsheathed his blade. "Did you seriously just say that?"

Only one Character stood between us and the charging chimera, and she was too absorbed with her updated M3 to draw her sword.

Lena.

Chase and I erupted forward. The second my hand curled around the sword hilt, my body seemed very far away, like someone else was moving for me. This was normal. I had an enchanted sword. This runner's-high feeling happened every time the magic kicked in.

"I got it." Chase ran so fast he practically skimmed over the sand. "You go cover Lena."

The sword's magic sent me weaving through the dunes to Lena's side, right at the edge of the soccer field. Her eyes were still glued to her M3. "Rory, you have to see this!"

"The image is so clear," Melodie added.

They clearly hadn't noticed the chimera barreling over the grass, twenty-five feet away and closing.

"Lena, we've got company!" I tried to tug her back through the dunes. She would be safer behind the archers.

"No, I can't move—" Then she glanced up and found herself practically face to face with a three-headed monster. "Oh!"

"Don't worry. I'll take care of it." Chase charged out, and, seeing him on the field, the chimera slowed. Its snake head hissed. "Yeah, you know it's all over for you—don't you, ugly?"

Lena dashed back through the dunes and behind the archers before Chase and the chimera even came to blows. She wasn't the fastest runner in seventh grade for nothing.

When I was halfway to the others, Chase said, "Crap!"

I whirled around and raised my sword, its magic thrumming.

But Chase wasn't hurt. The chimera leaped from the edge of the grass to the nearest dune. It had gotten past him.

He sprinted after it. "I still got it, Rory!"

The chimera glanced at Adelaide, Daisy, and the stepsisters, their arrows notched to their bows, and then closer to the water, where Ben just watched. His mouth was open. Mia peeked nervously around him.

The new kid didn't even have a weapon.

"It's after Ben and Mia!" Lena cried, panicky, but I was already running, racing the monster as it bounded over the sand.

The stepsisters recovered fastest. They loosed their arrows. The chimera's lion head yowled as it dodged, but it gave me the extra two seconds I needed.

I tackled Mia and Ben, knocking them to the sand an instant before the chimera pounced.

Somebody's bare elbow struck my cheekbone, right outside my eye, but the three-headed monster sailed over us—so close that its tufted tail brushed my neck.

I scrambled to my feet as the chimera landed half in the water. Its goat head bleated angrily, and the back legs bent. It was ready to attack again.

"Rory, I said I got it," said Chase, somewhere behind me. He still wasn't close enough to do any slaying.

The chimera leaped.

My body knelt, and the sword's magic guided the blade straight into the monster's heart. Chase's sword flashed above, and the beast gave a wet sort of roar-bleat. Two somethings thumped to the sand with a squish.

The chimera collapsed on the beach, a couple feet away from its goat and lion heads. Gross, but definitely dead.

I straightened slowly. "Is everybody okay?"

"Do you recall those talon punctures?" Wincing, Ben reached into his red jacket. "I'm almost positive they have sand in them now. But," he added hastily when I opened my mouth to apologize, "better sand than a chimera bite."

Mia gingerly sat up. Her skirt had a palm-size rip out of the hem, stained black at the edges, but otherwise she seemed all right.

Lena ran over, biting her lip.

Chase scowled at me. "What part of 'I got it' do you not understand?"

I knew what he was really upset about. Whoever slayed the chimera got the most bragging rights. I smirked. "You were too slow."

"Still my kill," Chase said.

"No, this round goes to Rory. When you're beheading a chimera, you have to make sure you get all three heads. You missed one, Chase. It took a bite out of Mia's clothes." Melodie pointed a golden hand at the body. Between the fangs of the viper head, a plaid patch flapped in the breeze.

"But it was two-thirds dead by the time Rory got it," Chase protested, and I snorted.

"Who are you people?" Mia said, voice shaking.

"It's okay." Ben squeezed her hand. I bet the gesture would have been ten times more comforting if his fingers hadn't been streaked with blood. "The chimera's their leader. Hansel told us earlier that the ice griffins always scatter after the chimera is killed—"

Something Jeep-size swooped down out of the fog, shrieking. Everybody ducked automatically. Except for Chase, who leaped up and sliced once at the monster's white throat.

The ice griffin thudded onto the sand beside the chimera. Its spotted tail twitched once and then was still.

Chase grinned. "That one was definitely mine."

"They're coming!" Adelaide aimed her bow straight up. A dozen griffins sailed across the soccer field toward us. "God. Didn't the eighth graders kill any of them?"

"They're supposed to scatter. Why aren't they scattering?" Ben said, eyes wide.

"The snake head wasn't trying to bite Mia," I said, realizing. "It was marking her."

Mia gasped. Ben shoved her behind him, which seemed equally gallant and useless.

"Archers, aim for the wings!" Chase said. "Where are the spears when we need them?"

"Coming!" cried someone down the beach.

It is extremely hard to run with a spear and not stab the guy running next to you, but the seventh-grade spear squadron—the Zipes triplets and Paul Stockton—managed it. Very impressive, considering Paul had only been at EAS a couple months.

"I want two of you defending them." Chase pointed to Ben and Mia. "She's the Snow Queen's target. Rory, you help them. The other two, help me finish off the griffins our archers bring down."

"Got it." Something flapped behind me. I whirled around, heart sinking. "Three more incoming! Lakeside." They were close, just a hundred feet away, fifty, moving so fast the fog rippled away from their wings.

I lifted my sword, but at the last second all three griffins plowed into the lake at once and sent an enormous wave crashing over our heads.

I choked on a lungful of water.

When I opened my eyes, my throat raw with coughing, the griffin was ten feet from me. It knelt down, breathing its icy breath across the puddle. I darted forward, swung my sword two-handed like a baseball bat, and sheared its head from its feathery shoulders, but I was too late—the beach was already frozen. The griffins were trying to screw us up the same way they'd dealt with the eighth graders.

Unfortunately for the griffins, we seventh graders had more experience fighting on ice. And we had a magician.

"I'm on it!" Feet planted far apart, Lena dug through her backpack again.

With quick measured slides, like I was wearing ice skates, I hurried back toward the fight, three times slower than normal.

The archer's bows twanged. From the shrieks above us, I guessed their arrows were hitting their marks.

"Okay, raise your hand if you want spikes on your sneakers!" Melodie shouted over the griffin cries. "We need to know how many dragon scales to use!"

"We all do." Chase leaped on the back of a griffin as it frantically flapped its arrow-riddled wings ten feet above the sand. He stabbed its neck and hopped off before the dead griffin hit the ground. Someday he would have to teach me how to jump that high. "And what kind of idiot is going to raise his hand during a battle?"

Ben sheepishly dropped his raised hand.

Lena held out what looked like three mini CDs, colored green and gold, and shouted another Fey spell. As the dragon scales crumpled in her hands, spikes sprouted on the soles of every seventh grader's shoes.

"Thanks, Lena." I could run again. I sprinted straight for the new kids.

Kevin Zipes's spear was pinned under a dead ice griffin. He struggled to free it, glancing back anxiously at Ben and Mia, but three more flockmates closed in.

The runner's high came back. I ducked under the closest one and slashed at the belly, where the brown feathers gave way to leopard spots. It screamed above me, but by the time it turned around, I had already moved on. I stabbed the next griffin in the ribs, but when it clawed at me, I dodged at the last second. The blow fell on the first griffin.

The third one bit toward me and pinned my blade in its beak. Great. Of course I'd get stuck fighting a smart griffin.

I kicked it in the throat, hoping it would let go, but the spikes on my shoes barely knocked any feathers loose. The griffin tugged, almost yanking me off my feet, but then an arrow thunked into its forehead.

"Yes!" Tina cried behind me, bow in hand, as the griffin keeled over. "Did I get the last one?"

I looked up, surprised. The icy beach was littered with seventeen bodies, arrows poking out of most of them.

"Is it over already?" Ben said, still crouched in front of Mia. Both of her hands were clamped over her mouth, her face white.

Another griffin soundlessly glided up behind them, almost fast enough, but Paul threw his spear, nailing it in the feathery chest. Its wings hit the water with a slap.

"That was the last one," Paul said, smirking.

An eighth grader limped out of the fog. Kenneth, their best fighter. He was furious. "You didn't leave us any?"

I glanced at Mia. Ever since we'd returned to EAS, her beautiful face had stayed calm. Her eyes stared straight ahead, even as a bunch of boys shoved each other for the privilege of walking beside her. Either she didn't notice, or she did a really good job of pretending not to.

She was definitely less freaked out than I had been when a dragon almost killed me my first day. She could have been in shock—or she could have still felt like she was dreaming. Those were normal reactions when people first learned magic was real.

Either way, ever since Hansel had confirmed she was a Character using the mirror test, she hadn't seemed all that curious about finding herself at a magic after-school program.

She barely glanced at the Tree of Hope, the three-story live oak whose branches swooped low to the ground and twisted skyward again. She didn't even look at the hundreds of doors lining the courtyard's outer walls, each one a different color. Maybe they would seem more interesting after she found out that they were EAS's Door Trek system. Almost every door led to a different city in North America.

But she'd only asked one question on our way here from Wisconsin: "What does this Snow Queen want with me?"

Nobody had answered her.

Lena and I stationed ourselves next to Vicky on an overstuffed leather couch underneath the Tree of Hope. A griffin had clawed Vicky's forearm. She was the only seventh grader to lose any blood, but the wound wasn't that serious—just painful. Her face was pinched behind her freckles, and she didn't even touch the chocolate cake we had grabbed her from the Table of Never Ending Instant Refills.

"The nurse is coming." Tina dropped into the armchair beside her stepsister. "Geez, the guys are still fawning over that new girl? She's an eighth grader. It's not like they have any chance with her."

All three Zipes triplets and Paul Stockton had joined the crowd around Mia. Only Chase was missing. He'd gone to tell the instructors that we'd found the new Character.

Lena couldn't have been happy about it—she'd had a crush on Kyle Zipes for as long as I'd known her—but she kept her voice light. "What do we think Mia's Tale will be?"

"Snow White, maybe." I gestured to Adelaide. She hovered beside the boys, shook her long hair back, and scowled when no one looked away from Mia. She obviously hated losing her title as prettiest girl in middle school. "Adelaide will play the role of her evil stepmother."

The girls laughed, even Vicky, but she immediately winced and clutched her gauze-covered arm. Whoops.

"Hey." Chase perched himself on the arm of the couch. His T-shirt and his hair were soaking wet. "It could take a while. Another new Character showed up about ten minutes back. She doesn't talk. She can't write. The Director thinks she has a mute Tale from one of the other continents. We get all sorts of weirdos here." Chase pointed to the chocolate cake. "Anybody going to eat that?"

Vicky shook her head.

Chase reached across me and Lena to grab the plate. Something dripped on me. I made a face. "Why are you all wet?"

"I suggested we call the other new girl Chatty," he said.

I hoped she didn't think we were all as rude as he was. "Chase," I started.

He shoveled a ridiculously large bite in his mouth. "She didn't like it either. She used some water from the Director's fountain to tell me so."

Lena and I grinned. We would have definitely started teasing him, but the amethyst door to the Director's office swung open, and Ellie strode out. You would have never guessed that she had been a Cinderella, not with her frizzy brown hair and the grease marks on her apron. She was kind of EAS's housekeeper. She basically made sure all the day-to-day stuff ran smoothly.

An odd girl with a tiny smile wandered out behind Ellie. Her damp blue dress was all ripped up, trailing lace from its skirt like bits of seaweed. Her dark hair hung down to her waist, very straight, except for slender braids and random seashells that ran through it—the kind of hairstyle five-year-olds gave each other. Her black eyes widened as she took in the courtyard. She moved a little bit like a sparrow, running forward with a flurry of steps and freezing, head tilted. She kept darting off to inspect a pretty door, or an interesting armchair, or the bark on the Tree of Hope.

Mia looked a little stunned when Ellie clamped both hands on her shoulders and steered her out of the crowd. Ben watched her go. "Gooey-eyed" was the word that came to mind.

Chatty took three swift steps toward him and peered into his face—way inside his personal bubble. Ben jumped back so fast he jarred his injured shoulder and winced. She grinned kind of apologetically, her teeth extremely white in her tan face.

"Chatty!" Ellie called from the doorway of the Director's office, and the new girl rushed off.

Chase stuffed the last cake crumbs in his mouth. "See! I knew the name was catchy."

"Wait, Rory killed the chimera?" someone shouted.

The crowd backed out of his way. He always wore sleeveless shirts, because they showed off two things: His muscles were as big as a high schooler's, and his armpit hair had grown in early.

I braced myself. It was Kenneth.

Kenneth stomped to our couch, his pimply face sneering. "It doesn't count. You're not strong enough to fight on your own. Without that sword, you're nothing."

Shame flamed across my cheeks. I couldn't argue. Everybody at EAS knew my sword was enchanted. I could keep up with Chase, but only when the magic was turned on. Without it I was a pretty average fighter. My sword had really slain the chimera and those griffins, not me.

Chase stood up. "Says the kid who face-planted on griffin ice. Rory didn't have any trouble staying on her feet. She's worth ten of you."

Darcy scowled. "How are we supposed to learn how to fight on ice if you seventh graders keep taking over our battles?"

"Yeah. So shut up before I head-butt you," added her brother, Bryan. It would've sounded a lot more threatening if he hadn't looked like a fawn. The scariest thing about him was his spiked collar.

Paul snorted. "Bring it, Bambi."

"My name is Bryan," snapped the fawn, and Bryan did head-butt Paul, knocking him to the ground and trotting across Paul's chest with sharp cloven hooves. The triplets shoved through the crowd to help.

But somebody else was faster—Hansel. "That's enough."

Directly behind him stood Gretel, his sister and EAS's top nurse. One of her feet was made out of iron, and that combined with her slate-gray hair and her usual *don't even think about misbehaving* frown made her three times as intimidating as Hansel. She cupped pale green ointment in her palm. "Eighth graders with injuries, line up here in front of me."

Ben shrugged off his blazer. His blue button-down shirt was spotted with blood.

"But aren't you going to punish them, sir?" Kenneth asked.

Every seventh-grade head whipped to Hansel. He was known for punishing kids with gingerbread jacks. Trust me, you don't want to know what those are.

"No," said the sword master. "You don't learn how to fight on ice in a middle of a battle. You train for it here, out of danger. When the Director sent you today, she assumed that you'd already put extra time in, like the seventh graders."

Jaws dropped across the courtyard, including mine. Hansel had just taken our side.

What he'd said about our extra practices was true. When Chase has started giving me private lessons last spring, the other seventh graders had joined in pretty fast. But Hansel never took sides.

"Luckily for you, we've arranged some extra training for you eighth graders. Right now." Hansel pointed to a heavy wooden door studded with iron—the entrance to the training courts.

I didn't smile, but I was so tempted.

Throwing us dirty looks, the eighth graders began to file silently out of the courtyard.

Chase smirked. "They won't be our biggest fans for a while."

"Except for me. You saved my life today," Ben told me and Chase cheerfully. Gretel had finished with his shoulder fast. He pushed his shirt aside. The talon punctures had already scabbed over, the edges pink with newly healed skin.

"Well," Chase said, "it probably won't be the last time."

Yeah, Chase was always this modest.

"Excuse me!" Tina said, irritated. "We need a nurse too!"

"I am here," said a quiet, musical voice behind the couch, and we all jumped.

Rapunzel, EAS's resident seer and backup nurse, stood over Vicky with a small smile. "The deepest wounds cause the most pain."

Vicky gulped.

Rapunzel was kind of a startling sight: pale silver braid hanging down to the ground; slim body of a sixteen-year-old ballerina; wide, unblinking eyes that looked too wise and dark for her face. She also happened to be my favorite grown-up at EAS.

She held out what looked like a metallic toothpaste tube.

I had seen it three times before: when Chase had gotten a dragon bite up the beanstalk last spring, when Adelaide had busted her chin running away from a troll around Thanksgiving, and when I had sliced my arm capturing a dragon for Lena in February.

"It's the ointment of the witch whose power is in her hair, the same one Gretel is using," I explained to Vicky. (Yes, that was its technical name.) "It'll heal you fast."

Vicky surrendered her forearm reluctantly. Rapunzel squeezed out a pea-size drop and dabbed it on the claw mark. The ointment smelled like mint and peppercorn.

Before he followed his students into the training courts, Hansel turned to Rapunzel and said something that lost him all the awesome points he'd won a few minutes before. "Leave the black eye. Rory needs something to help her remember her little stunt."

EAS has some weird justice.

The stepsisters, the triplets, and Paul quickly skulked away. "Homework," Tina mouthed apologetically.

"What stunt?" I asked.

"You can't punish just Rory," Lena said. "It's not fair."

"Not that we're volunteering," Chase said. "But come on. The griffins came to us."

But Hansel ignored them. "How many times have I told you, Rory? You don't tackle people you're rescuing—not when you have a weapon in your hand. You sheathe it first."

I scowled. Sure, Hansel had told me this before, but what were the chances he would have seen me from all the way across that foggy soccer field?

I didn't look forward to explaining a black eye to my family. I couldn't tell my mother a damsel-in-distress had accidentally elbowed me in the face when I rescued her. My mom didn't know much about EAS. Not about chimeras or griffins, or about magic, or that I used my sword for more than just fencing class. She didn't even know that I got to see Chase and Lena every day. She still thought that they lived in North Carolina. That was where I'd been living when I met them last April.

I knew what would happen if I told my overprotective mother the truth. Mom would either commit me to a kiddie loony bin or never let me out of her sight again.

"Hansel, she was saving lives," Rapunzel said quietly. "If you punish her for every life she saves, our doom will come faster."

Rapunzel was a little weird. She was about two hundred years old, and all the time in her tower made her a little . . . off. She also saw the future. It was hard to understand exactly what she was trying to say, but if you did, it just might keep you from meeting a gruesome end.

So I immediately started worrying that lives depended on how I explained my black eye to Mom and her assistant, Amy. No pressure.

Hansel smiled, tight-lipped, like he guessed what thoughts were sending me into a panic, and closed the iron-studded door behind him.

"Is it just me, or does he hate me more than the other seventh graders?" I asked Rapunzel.

"That is the wrong question," Rapunzel said. "He does not view it as picking on you."

From her pocket she drew out an ice pack and pressed it against my eye. Apparently, she had known about Hansel's punishment beforehand too. "I will tell you a secret. We are all a bundle of wishes, but sometimes one desire can drive a person as an engine propels an automobile. You can understand such a person by learning what desire pushes him."

Lena and Chase exchanged glances. From the bag on Lena's shoulder Melodie said, "Rory, we'll meet you in the workshop."

They usually cleared out when Rapunzel started talking like a fortune cookie.

I was a little bit better at understanding what she meant than the average EASer, but only a little. "Um . . . you want me to ask myself what Hansel wants most in the whole world?"

Rapunzel smiled her tiniest smile, the one she wore when she thought I was funny but didn't want to hurt my feelings. "To understand him better, yes."

It was obvious what he wanted—to humiliate me in front of the whole seventh grade. "To make us into awesome warriors he can brag about to other grown-ups."

"No," Rapunzel said. "You should ask Gretel. His sister will know."

I turned around. "Gretel, what does Hansel want most?"

Gretel smeared the last of the ointment over a tiny scratch on Bryan's furry shoulder, and he trotted off.

"To keep you kids safe. His life mission. He never stops talking about it." Gretel shot a warning look at Rapunzel.

Rapunzel put the ice pack in my hands. "Your friends are waiting for you."

I was clearly dismissed. I jogged over to the workshop. Knowing the punishment was for my own good only made it more annoying.

I wasn't stupid.

I knew Hansel was right. My sword could have caused serious damage in that tumble. I could have gotten myself killed. I could have gotten Mia or Ben killed.

My stomach sank all the way down to my toes.

It would have never happened if I'd really been a fighter as experienced as Chase. He would have diverted the chimera, or shoved Mia and Ben out of the way—

"Rory," Rapunzel called, and I turned back. "If you had not acted when you did, the new Characters would surely have died." Rapunzel couldn't read minds. She had told me that more than once, but sometimes it was hard to believe. "Most mistakes can be corrected. Inaction cannot."

I half smiled. She was obviously trying to make me feel better.

Then she pointed to the workshop. "Extinguish the match in Lena's hand."

Uh-oh. Lena had a bad habit of burning stuff accidentally, and some of Rapunzel's warnings came just in time.

The workshop's steel doors slid open from the middle like an elevator, and I rushed through. The Shoemaker's elves were busy covering picnic tables in red and gold paint. The paler elves had veins showing green through their skin, but besides that, they could have been miniature humans in canvas work suits—no wings, no pointed ears. A few of them waved as I passed, but most of them looked stressed. I skirted between them and the tables, saws, chisels, mallets, hammers, sanders, and screwdrivers pushed to the wall.

They were enchanting the Tables of Plenty with the menu for tomorrow's feast. This was the first one I'd ever been to. All I knew was that a new Red Riding Hood was joining the Canon, the big group of Characters in charge of the rest of us. Everyone at EAS was invited—including some representatives from chapters on other continents.

I spotted Lena in the back, where the Shoemaker had let her set up a permanent station. Fortunately, she wasn't on fire yet. She was hanging long strips of green paper from an aluminum frame about the size of a garage. When she tacked the fourth wall to the floor with masking tape, it looked like she had created a room within the workshop.

I opened my mouth to ask what was going on, but Melodie pivoted around inside the bag on Lena's shoulder and pressed a finger to her lips.

Okay, so this was a spell. To a clueless observer like myself, it just looked like Lena was talking to herself in Fey as she threw green-gold glitter on each wall of the paper room.

Sometimes I wished we'd never found Madame Benne's golden harp.

No, that wasn't exactly true. I mean, I was definitely glad that we'd kept Melodie from the Snow Queen. Otherwise she would have used the harp to free herself from prison. Just the thought made me shudder.

And I was glad that through Melodie, Lena had access to Madame Benne's knowledge. It helped Lena invent stuff. If my best friend had a desire that drove all her actions, it was this— becoming the best magical inventor in the last thousand years.

I stepped back, out of the way, past a line of anvils to the furnaces burning in the back wall. Wistfully, I watched Melodie whisper something in Lena's ear, and Lena repeated it in a loud clear voice. In Fey, of course, so I couldn't understand.

At times like this, it felt like Lena and Melodie were in a private inventors' club of two. All the rest of us could do was watch from the sidelines. Even Chase had apparently gotten bored and wandered off.

I could use someone to talk to. I knew what the Snow Queen wanted with Mia.

Despite the heat from the furnaces, goose bumps prickled my arms.

The Snow Queen was targeting all the new Characters closest to my age, anyone who might become my friend, and she was sending out her ice griffins and dragons more often than ever. In fact, in the past three months, the only new sixth, seventh, or eighth grader EAS had found in the regular way—by sending a recruiter to schools to perform the mirror test—was Ben.

She wanted to make sure I had as few people on my team as possible.

I didn't really know why. Last year, when I'd first come to EAS, scarily important people had been interested in me. During the

Fairie Market we'd overheard the Canon discussing my arrival. When Jack had visited the Glass Mountain a few days later, the Snow Queen herself had asked him about me.

No one would tell me anything, though. The only hint we had was what we'd overheard Genevieve Searcaster, the Snow Queen's giant general, telling her son: *They haven't seen anyone like her since Solange's first arrival. Years before she became the Snow Queen, of course. The arrival of this new Character has forced Her Majesty's hand. War is returning.*

Chase and Lena thought this meant I had a Great Destiny— that some prophecy foretold me taking down the Snow Queen. When I'd asked Rapunzel about it, she'd said something like *Keep your fear, and you will do what must be done.* I was pretty sure that was her way of saying, *Stay alert, but don't worry about it too much now.*

So I didn't think about it very often.

It felt the same as thinking about graduating from high school. It was big and vague and scary and far away, and I couldn't really do anything to get ready for it. But some days I wondered if I should be doing something, something better than accidentally stabbing the kids I was trying to rescue.

I took a deep breath to steady myself, and then I wondered where that burning smell was coming from—

Alarmed, I spun around.

The paper room was on fire, flames eating the long strips from the ground up. Lena watched, a little to the side, arms crossed, a match still alight in her fingers. The flame was dangerously close to her sleeve.

I rushed over, plucked it from her hand, and blew it out.

"Oh, hi!" Lena grinned, like I'd just shown up. She noticed the match smoking in my hand. "Thanks for that. I'm making a carry-all. See?" She waved at the flaming paper room. She always talked this fast when she got excited. "Remember my deal with the Director? She lets me keep a dragon in the menagerie and gives me all the scales; I make her fifty new carryalls."

I nodded. She had told me about it at least a hundred times before we captured the dragon and dragged it down to the dungeon.

"Well, the Director told me that if I don't hurry up and produce a few carryalls by the end of next week, then the deal's off." Lena sighed. "She said something like, 'recreating the carryall spell should take priority over your own inventions.'"

"So, why are you burning the paper?" I asked quickly when she paused for breath.

"Oh, I need the essence of the space. This is how big it'll be on the inside. It's easiest to get an essence of something by burning a small piece of it, like fingernails or spit or leaves, but with space it's tricky because you need the whole space. Madame Benne's original recipe for a carryall tells you to burn down a whole hut, but Gran brought out the fire extinguisher when I tried to do that in our backyard. I think I can get away with just this." She pointed at the aluminum frame. The last of the paper waved from the top bar, like a banner edged with orange flame.

Now we could see clear to Lena's worktable, strewn with her notes. Behind the table a huge vial rose from floor to ceiling, the glass several feet thick and embedded with black iron bits shaped like strange symbols and letters.

"But the scales are turning out to be a problem," Lena said. "Madame Benne preferred to work in phoenix feathers, but the elves needed all the spare ones. Unfortunately, it's harder to burn scales, so we're trying powdered scales instead—"

I nodded seriously, pretending I followed all that.

The last of the paper burned up.

"Mistress!" Melodie pointed to the floor. The ashes glowed slightly green.

And then the inventors' club was back in session.

"Yay!" Lena knelt on the floor next to the pile of ashes. "What's the next step?"

"We need to bind the ashes to the inside of the backpack—" Melodie began.

I could only stand so much of this. Before they got too carried away, I interrupted, "Where's Chase?"

"Um . . ." Lena glanced around the room, puzzled. The ashes had turned her brown hands gray and glowing. "He was just here a second ago. . . ."

Metal clinked against glass, and we both turned toward the vial. A pewter hand gripped the cylinder, and a metallic face peeked out from behind it, light reflecting dully from his hooked nose, his wide full mouth. His eyes were in shadow, the metal skin covered in reddish brown hair.

Iron Hans. The Snow Queen's most deadly warrior.

My heart lurched with panic, but I forced myself to stay where I was. I even folded my arms over my chest.

This Iron Hans was too short to be a full-grown villain. In fact he was exactly Chase's height, and he held his huge ax—the double-headed blade as big as a steering wheel—the same way Chase held his sword.

He took a step toward us, and I grabbed him, feeling a boy's T-shirt rather than the hairy old dude's shoulder it looked like I held.

"Not funny, Chase." I shoved hard.

Chase went sprawling and dropped the illusion, laughing.

It had been a few months since he'd tried this last. The first time he'd done it, right after my first sword lesson, he'd been friends with Adelaide, and they'd scared a squeak out of me with this same trick. I'd gotten better at not flipping out, but I didn't understand why he kept trying it.

"I couldn't resist," Chase said, grinning.

Maybe he was still upset that I'd killed the chimera instead of him. He always needed to be the best—that was the desire that drove *him*. It was pretty annoying, actually.

"Wow." Lena appeared beside us. "That was a glamour, wasn't it?"

Chase picked himself up off the floor. "Nah, just an illusion."

"But when Gretel does an illusion spell, you can see it coming out of her," Lena said. "How did you hide it so well?"

"Secrets of the trade." But for once, Chase sounded a lot more uncomfortable than smug.

"Can you teach me?" Lena asked, grinding up some more dragon scales.

Chase was an expert at changing the subject. He tapped the vial. "What is this thing, anyway?"

"It was once the East Wind's prison," Melodie said.

All of Lena's excitement rushed back. "It contained his essence, the same way the Glass Mountain contains the Snow Queen's essence. We're going to recreate that after we sort out the—are you okay?" she asked me anxiously.

When she'd mentioned the Snow Queen, something had twisted in my stomach. The freak out must've blazed across my face.

I shook it off. I was being stupid, worrying like this. There wasn't exactly an instruction manual to tell seventh graders how to defeat the worst villain the world had ever seen.

All I could do was train even harder to improve my griffin-slaying skills.

Outside the workshop a bell clanged—first of the evening. That meant it was six p.m. where my mom was—time for everyone in Eastern Standard Time to go home.

Lena, who lived in Milwaukee, an hour behind New York, and Chase, who lived there at EAS, didn't need to go anywhere yet.

I hopped off the stool. "Chase, swear you'll give me a lesson tomorrow."

"You think we'll have time before the feast?" He clearly disagreed.

"I'm coming early, remember? Half day at school," I said happily, weaving back through the elves' Tables of Plenty. Tomorrow was also the first day of spring break. Chase, Lena, and I were going to hang out at EAS all week—plenty of time for training. "Mom's going to drop me off at the airport, and Ellie is going to set up a Door Trek gateway there." Mom and Amy thought that I would be flying down to North Carolina to visit Lena. I chose not to think about that.

"What time are you coming again?" Chase asked.

"Around one." I wondered why Lena looked so distracted. It was impossible to tell what invention was on her mind.

"Rory, did you think of an excuse for your black eye yet?" she asked.

I had completely forgotten. I couldn't even remember where I'd left Rapunzel's ice pack. Dread curled up in my stomach. "Help me think of something!"

Unfortunately, Mom was in the front hallway closet when I returned to the house we were renting. I couldn't warn her before she saw me.

"Rory, what happened?" She threw her coat over the stair rail and rushed toward me.

"Some kid threw a ball at her." Amy only sounded that disapproving when she was worried about me.

Ever since I'd gone up the beanstalk, Amy had been suspicious of EAS. Mom would've been too, but Gretel had enchanted her to think that I had taken a five-day-long field trip to Raleigh. Unfortunately, Amy had noticed I didn't remember taking any of the pictures saved in my camera.

Amy knew something about EAS didn't add up, which made my life slightly more difficult. When Mom had first realized that she would be stuck promoting one of her films during my spring break, she'd given me a choice—visit Lena or visit my dad. It was an easy decision—spend a week hanging out with my friends, or spend a week trailing after my famous director father, stuck in boring meetings. I'd picked Lena. But Amy had spent the rest of the day asking, "Are you sure?" She'd obviously hoped I would change my mind, which—considering that she wasn't my dad's biggest fan—was really saying something.

"No, they didn't throw it at me." It took all my willpower not to wince when Mom tilted my chin and examined my eye. "Some eighth graders were playing catch, and I walked right into the baseball." This lie came compliments of Lena. I held my breath to see if it would take.

With a sigh, Mom steered me into the kitchen. "You are so accident-prone, Rory."

Lena's lie had worked. I hid a smile as Mom guided me through the swinging door and straight to the kitchen table.

Amy scurried around unpacked boxes to grab ice out of the freezer. "I have a dream, kid. Of picking you up in your cleats and your shin guards and you telling me all about soccer practice, free of black eyes and other mysterious bruises."

"They had tryouts two weeks before I got here. It wouldn't be fair if I walked on," I reminded her. Our crazy moving schedule gave me a lot of excuses. I pulled out my homework, hoping that would end all discussion about injuries.

Amy passed me ice wrapped in a kitchen towel. "You have three different options, but I'm afraid I couldn't find any stylists you've seen before. Do you want to try someone new, or do you want me to keep calling around?"

At first I thought she meant a stylist for me. I didn't need a haircut, except possibly long bangs to cover my black eye.

Mom sighed. "Let's keep looking. I would normally be okay with someone new, but I have too many interviews. . . ."

Oh. They had completely changed the subject. I was never this lucky. Usually, I had to spend half an hour reassuring Mom I was fine.

"Wait. What happened?" I asked. Mom's hair looked completely normal to me—short, blond, and full of weird tufts.

"Maggie's on-set stylist found some gray hair this morning." From the look on Mom's face you would have guessed that Amy had said that my mother had a poison-ivy rash in underwear territory or something equally embarrassing. Amy didn't notice.

My mom was an actress, kind of a big-deal one. She was only in her mid-thirties, but if she looked too old, it limited the kinds of roles she could get. I'd overheard her and Amy discussing it the week before.

Mom changed the subject. "Have you packed yet?"

"Um, kind of," I said. "I just need to put everything in a suitcase."

"Good. That means you still have room for these." Amy patted a shoe box I hadn't noticed. The designer's name seemed vaguely familiar.

Mom scooted the box toward me with a too-bright smile. "I got you something for your trip."

Not sure what to expect, I lifted the lid. Inside lay . . . shoes. They were very pretty, made with poppy-colored silk, stitched all over with golden beads. Each shoe probably cost over a hundred dollars. Any of the girls at school would have killed for them. Maybe have killed me for them.

"Thanks." I wondered if she really expected me to wear these. "But I have shoes."

Mom hesitated.

"Rory, you couldn't get those any rattier even if you sprayed them with mud and then threw them in the garbage disposer," Amy said.

My sneakers were stained with dirt and grass, the laces were fraying, and there was a hole at the ankle. I would probably outgrow this pair soon anyway, but they had sentimental value. They had survived almost as many battles as I had.

Even my family thought I needed to improve my look. The girls at school usually told me so, but this was the first time I'd ever heard about it from Mom and Amy.

"Your tennis shoes are fine for visiting Lena," Mom added. "But you need something to wear if Mrs. LaMarelle wants to take you someplace nice. I just don't want you to be uncomfortable."

I didn't mind wearing flats every once in a while, but if I wore them at EAS, they would fall off if I had to do something intense . . . like dodge an ice griffin or slay some dragons. I tried a different tactic. "But isn't this kind of overkill? Couldn't we have started out with sparkly shoes from Target or something?"

"Is that all? Your mom wore them during filming. Wardrobe comes as a bonus. Those were free," Amy explained.

"It's nice that you and I are the same size now," Mom added. "I get more samples than I know what to do with."

We were only the same size in shoes.

My feet had shot out in the last year, forcing me out of kids' sizes forever. My hands had also gotten huge, but I didn't mind that so much—I could grip my sword hilt easier. Mom and Amy both swore that this meant I was going to be tall, but so far I just had clownishly big hands and feet. And that Mom forced some of her hand-me-downs on me.

Sometimes you have to pick your battles. I wasn't getting out of town without the shoes. "Okay. Thanks, then."

Amy and Mom both smiled, and then the phone rang. "Ooh! Maybe someone had a cancellation!" Amy said before answering. "Hello. Assistant to Maggie Wright speaking."

The rest of the evening passed in a blur of last-minute packing. When I said good night, Mom was standing in front of the mirror, tilting her head in a million different directions, looking for what her stylist had seen. Climbing into bed, I vowed to never go into any business where finding gray hair turned into a career emergency.

That night, I dreamed of satiny black hair flowing around a beautiful face. Her eyes were closed, the long lashes casting spiky shadows over her cheeks. Her lips were perfectly shaped, tinged with a delicate pink, like they belonged on a painted figurine. I started to wonder what Mia's deal was, and why her hair was spread flat over the table, and if maybe she was practicing for a Tale where she got kissed. Then my gaze fell below her chin.

It was Mia's head—and only her head—resting on the table.

he next day at school was a totally different nightmare.

Somebody thought we kids needed to bond before we left on break for nine and a half days, so they scheduled an extra thirty minutes of homeroom after last period. Clearly, the principal had never been a twelve-year-old girl.

My homeroom only had five kids. It was easy to understand why if you met the other four girls in it. Everyone else had transferred out rather than spend extra time with Madison and the KATs.

I was first in the class, even before the teacher. I shoved away the urge to hide in the bathroom for the next half hour, and I glanced out the window. The red door of the house across the street could take me to EAS. Ellie had set it up as part of the Door Trek system when I first started school here.

Geez, I had faced down a flock of griffins yesterday without much fuss. I could handle homeroom.

All four girls in Madison McDermott's little group glided in and filled the room with this week's designated scent: strawberry splash. My stomach turned. It smelled more like chemicals than fruit.

Madison marched to the chair across from me and dropped

magazines on the table with an ominous slap. I didn't look up, but my whole body tensed. Madison had clearly gone tabloid shopping. Out of the corner of my eye I could see that my mother's face was on the cover of one. That meant that if our teacher, Mrs. Lapin, didn't come soon, this would suck more than usual.

The paparazzi stalked anyone related to Hollywood royalty. Most of the time I could survive it.

Unfortunately, all of Mom's recent films had only shot on location, and that made things tough. It meant that she, Amy, and I moved three or four times a year—whenever Mom started work on a new movie. A new city always meant a new school, which made me a new kid. Usually, I could fly under the radar until school let out and be fine. I was an expert at keeping my head down.

But every few schools, I got singled out. Controlling my temper was harder than walking on griffin ice, but if I didn't, I would make a huge scene, one probably destined to end up an article in those same tabloids.

The four girls sat at once, like a group of synchronized swimmers, and four hands reached for a magazine, each set of fingernails painted the color of yellow highlighter. It must have been the nail polish of the week.

I knew about the scents and colors of the week because when I'd first come to the school, Madison had invited me to be part of their little troop. The others' names were Katie, Arianna, and Taylor. I'd started thinking of them as the KATs because it helped me remember their names. They all looked and acted the same. Madison had all these weird rules that told the rest of us which color to paint our nails, how many notes we could take in geography class and with what kind of pen, who we could talk to and who we couldn't, etc. I avoided getting sucked in as much as I could. Then Madison tried to invite herself to my house.

I knew what she wanted—to meet the famous Maggie Wright. But the idea of watching her suck up to Mom made me feel simultaneously like throwing up and punching a hole in the wall. So I said no.

Now all Madison wanted was to punish me.

They flipped through their magazines.

I sat on my hands to keep from biting my nails.

"There's a really great interview in here with Brie Catcher," Arianna said.

Brie Catcher was my dad's girlfriend. They had been going out for about a year. I hadn't met her yet, but Dad wanted me to—he brought it up every time I called him.

That might have influenced my decision to go see Lena instead—just a little.

But when I'd told Dad what I'd decided about spring break, he'd said, "You're not coming?" The hurt in his voice had made me feel as if someone had dropped a ton of bricks on my head. When I'd tried to explain how tagging along on Dad's busy schedule was the opposite of fun, he'd said, "I can cancel some meetings—a whole day. No, two days."

That hadn't lessened the guilt any, but Dad would never cancel all his meetings. Even if he tried, someone would call, last minute, and it would be too tempting for him to ignore. So I'd just said, "We're still going to Prince Edward Island in June, right? Just you and me?"

"And Brie," Dad said, sounding more cheerful, and finding out Dad had invited her without asking me had done wonders for my guilt.

Katie said, "I like Brie Catcher so much more than that last person Eric Landon was with. That Maggie Wright."

I bristled, but I bit my tongue.

I wished Lena was with me. I knew exactly how she would react to this—she would look at me and roll her eyes in a way that clearly said, *Don't they have anything better to do?* Then she would lean forward and tell me what she was going to invent with her dragon scales next.

Madison didn't look up. Translation: *Keep going until you bring me something good.*

Taylor sighed. She was reading the magazine with Mom's face on the cover. "I used to like Maggie Wright, but recently . . ." She sighed again.

"I know," said Arianna. "She's just—"

"Over the hill," finished Madison.

I snorted. I couldn't help it. It was such a lame insult. Despite her recent gray-hair emergency, my mom was years younger than all of theirs, and much prettier—I had seen that on Parents' Night a couple weeks ago.

Definitely a mistake.

Katie, Arianna, and Taylor all drew toward Madison like a flock of ice griffins looking to their chimera captain before they tore their prey apart.

Madison just flipped the magazine to one of my least favorite things in the world, the celeb candids. The paparazzi surprised actresses, directors, singers, or their families when they least expected it, and magazines paid them for that torture.

"Ugh, I hate it when they publish pictures of the celebrities' kids," Madison said.

"Yeah," Taylor said. "Who cares?"

It was a picture of me. Me and Mom, actually—just outside

the coffee place up the road, between school and my house. We'd never seen a photographer there. Mom looked polished and pretty, with enormous sunglasses covering most of her face, but the picture had caught me at an awkward angle, my face tilted up toward Mom. I was obviously talking, so my mouth was in a weird twisted lemon shape.

"It's like celebrity kids feel like they should get special treatment. This one thinks she doesn't need to worry about personal hygiene," said Madison.

The KATs nodded, murmuring "ewwww" and "gross" and "definitely, Madison" at nearly the same time.

The photo showed mud caked down my whole right side, turning half my shirt and jeans dark brown and staining my dark brown hair a shade darker. I remembered that: the Director had sent us to capture a red cap infestation in Newport, Rhode Island, at some old mansion-turned–tourist attraction. It had been raining, and I'd slipped in the mud trying to catch a two-foot-tall elflike creature with a scarlet hat. Chase had laughed so hard that he'd slipped too, trying to help me up.

On the way home, I'd told Mom that I had gotten muddy in an epic game of soccer.

Madison stabbed a finger down at the photo. "She's not even that pretty. What a huge chin."

"And her mouth. It's enormous." Katie tossed her straight locks over her shoulder, and the smell of burned hair wafted over.

"The only thing that could make her look uglier," said Madison, "is a black eye."

I willed myself not to press my lips together or touch the bruise around my eye. They would just get worse if they knew they were getting to me.

"And her nose—" started Arianna.

Just then, our homeroom teacher strode in. The box in her hands smelled like cinnamon and powdered sugar. "Hello, girls!"

My shoulders slumped with relief.

"Hello, Mrs. Lapin!" chorused Madison and her KATs. They slapped their magazines shut and shoved them into their backpacks.

"Sorry I'm late! I wanted to bring you a treat." Mrs. Lapin dropped the box on the table and opened it—donut holes. The other girls reached in with murmurs of appreciation, clearly famished after a hard day of bullying.

"Don't you want one, Rory?" Mrs. Lapin asked.

She had taken me aside a few days before, worried about my social skills. *You have plenty of nice girls in your homeroom, but you're so . . . quiet all the time,* she'd said.

So even though I was sure that anything I ate in front of Madison would taste like tissue paper, I took one.

"Now, then." Mrs. Lapin slipped into a chair at the end of Madison's table. "What is everyone doing for spring break?"

She pointed at me. I told them what Mom thought: I was going to visit my friends Lena and Chase in North Carolina.

Then the other girls chatted away about the weeklong sleepover they were having at Katie's house, glancing my way like this was supposed to bother me. Madison, it turned out, wasn't joining the KATs sleepover either. Instead she was flying out to L.A., because her agent (more commonly referred to as her mother) wanted her to audition for a role at Nuthatch Studios.

Another reason to be glad I was spending the break at EAS.

Mrs. Lapin said, "Congratulations, Madison! What an honor. That's where Rory's from. Maybe she can suggest a few places."

Thankfully, the bell rang right then. School was over, and I didn't have to stop and recommend restaurants to Madison.

"Thanks for the donuts, Mrs. Lapin!" I jumped to my feet, threw my backpack over my shoulder, and sprinted for the door. "Bye!"

Vacation had officially begun.

"Please commence saying your good-byes now." Amy steered the car toward an exit labeled with a plane icon. "We'll be there in approximately four minutes."

Mom turned all the way around in her seat and clasped my hand tightly. Suddenly, all her worry shone out of her eyes. She didn't want me to leave.

"I'm really glad you get to see your friends again, Rory. I know how close you three are," she said, like she was trying to convince herself. "When I talked to Mrs. LaMarelle yesterday, she said that Lena's been talking about this visit nonstop for weeks."

I half smiled. Guilt scrambled the contents of my stomach. Someday, I would stop lying to my trusting mother.

She wouldn't let me go unless she'd cleared it with Lena's grandmother, but Mrs. LaMarelle had almost refused to play along. "You won't be staying with us, Rory. You'll be staying at EAS. I don't want to lie. Get Jack to cover for you," she had suggested.

But as the champion of the Canon, Chase's dad had been away on EAS business, like usual. Even if he'd been around, he wouldn't exactly have come across as responsible over the phone.

Lena had finally had to promise to stop experimenting in the family kitchen before her gran would agree to such a sneaky arrangement.

"I'll be fine, Mom. I've traveled by myself before." Pretty much every time I'd visited Dad since we'd moved out of L.A.

"Our little Rory. Almost a teenager," Amy added.

Mom sighed. "I guess you did have to grow up sometime, Rory.

But I want you to call me every day—right before dinner. I need to know you're okay."

"I promise," I said.

A plane roared above us, and the control tower loomed straight ahead. I leaned forward, my hand on my seat belt, ready to unclick as soon as we braked.

Amy laughed at my enthusiasm as she found a spot to park. "Easy, Rory—you're not getting out of here without a hug."

Mom climbed out with me. Out of the corner of my eye I saw some other travelers do a double take (having famous parents had trained me to spot the warning signs), but Mom just grabbed me in a tight squeeze. "Who's my favorite daughter?"

I smiled into her shoulder. Same-size feet or not, she was still a head taller than me. "But I'm your only daughter."

"Then it's a good thing you're my favorite." Mom kissed the top of my head. "You take care of yourself, Rory. My life would never be the same if anything happened to you."

I would definitely miss her, but it would be a relief to have a break from her overprotectiveness.

"Did you want me to ask them if they'll let me walk you through security?" Mom asked hopefully.

And a break from the babying.

"Just in case you need me," Mom continued.

Bad idea. Mom's presence would screw up my real travel plans. "You mean, like the way you already printed out my boarding pass for me? 'Just in case' all the machines were broken, and 'just in case' the people at the desk weren't around to help?"

Grinning, Amy ran around the car and hugged me, too. "Touché. Besides, Maggie, we don't have time. We need to get you to that hair appointment. It'll take too long to get you out of the airport." Amy nodded at the crowd behind her.

Walking me to the gate wasn't the problem. Signing autographs would slow her down. Already she'd drawn a crowd—their camera phones poised and ready. Mom donned her "business face"—a smile that showed all her teeth—and waved. The gesture was welcomed with a flurry of flashes.

I hoped those pictures wouldn't make it into one of Madison's magazines by the time I got back.

"Okay, okay." Mom gave me another quick hug, and Amy handed me my duffel. I promised again to call when I got there. I looked back once as I passed through the sliding doors: Mom looked about as tragic as she had in her last movie, when her character had found out that her beloved husband had cancer. Amy squeezed her shoulder sympathetically and pointed to the passenger seat at the same time.

Sometimes it felt like Mom didn't want me to grow up, but I couldn't help it. No one could stay a little kid forever.

Security was shockingly fast because I didn't have a computer. I didn't even bother to tie my shoes before collecting my bag from the conveyor belt, and I shuffled off toward the bathroom marked on the map Ellie had given me.

When I found the bathroom, it was easy to tell which stall door would take me to EAS. The one on the end was red. Every portal door Ellie had ever set up for me had been that color. An OUT OF ORDER sign was taped to it.

Poor Ellie. I knew that setting this up had been pretty involved. First she'd needed my signature, so she could bind the Door Trek to me—that part of the spell made sure no one else could come through accidentally. Later Ellie had come back for a copy of my itinerary so she could enchant the airline, its computers, and its flight attendants to think I was flying over to North Carolina as scheduled.

Her map only gave me one last instruction: *WAIT UNTIL YOU ARE ALONE TO USE THE DESIGNATED STALL*—with lots of stars. I figured if Ellie had broken out the all caps, then I'd better pay attention.

I washed my hands five times in a row. The teenager doing her hair—the last person in the bathroom—finally stuffed her brush back in her ginormous purse and sauntered out. I sprinted for my exit before anyone else could come in.

I pushed the red stall door open. A familiar tunnel stretched out in front of me—cool and dark after the fluorescent brightness of the bathroom. I walked forward, my fingers brushing along the familiar grooves and bumps on the wall.

My hand found the doorknob, and then I stepped out into the courtyard.

It was so quiet. I had never seen it so empty. The doors that lined the outer wall were still. The Tree of Hope seemed bigger than usual, without its usual swarm of EASers, and underneath it the Table of Never Ending Instant Refills was bare, looking naked without all its platters.

The courtyard was beside an ocean today. The air was full of seagulls and wind, and the Tree's leaves swished back and forth, like they were keeping time with the waves. The beach started about twenty feet beyond it. The sand sparkled cobalt in the sun, like someone had sprinkled blue glitter all over it.

The landscape magically changed every few days. Last week we'd had a maze of trees, and then some awkward swamp land had driven Ellie crazy trying to supply each door with the right number and size of rain boots.

I'd heard my dad say this in an interview once: Walking onto a movie set was like walking into the very best dream of your life. You could become anyone, make anything happen.

That probably described EAS much better than any studio lot.

At EAS, I didn't need to be pretty or fashionable. I'd slain a chimera the day before. I was one of the best fighters in the whole North American Chapter.

At least . . . when I had my sword.

I needed to find Chase. I pushed through the iron-studded door that led to the training courts. The old hinges squeaked, echoing over the mats, and the training mirrors reflected my face.

I sighed. My right eye was even more purple than yesterday.

"Chase?" I called, but the room was still.

Not here.

I dumped my duffel and went to search.

An orange-gold door in the courtyard led straight to another smaller courtyard, where the walls were lined with instructors' apartments, including the one where Chase and Jack lived. Unfortunately, EASers couldn't get through it anymore—ever since some tenth graders had TPed Hansel's house on All Hallows' Eve.

But Chase had shown me and Lena a shortcut. I remembered the first part: The door beside the weapons closet led to a corridor where two pigs were carved, huddled in a hut made out of sticks, and a wolf stood on its hind legs, getting psyched to huff and puff and blow the house down. When I reached it, I passed silver doorways numbered one through seven in scarlet ink.

But I couldn't remember where to go after I turned left and found myself on a torch-filled corridor. I remembered the spinning wheels inlaid on the floor, but not which of the twelve doors I needed to go through.

Making a mistake might take all afternoon.

EAS was a lot bigger than it looked from the outside. Sometimes if you closed a door behind you and opened it again, you might find yourself in a completely different hallway.

If Lena had been there, she would have reminded me that this was a magic building, one where we kept dragons in the dungeon. Unsupervised areas could be dangerous.

But I had never explored EAS on my own before, and I might never get another chance.

Behind the first door I found aquarium tanks big enough to hold small whales. Most of them were empty, but in one a goldfish as big as my mother swam in circles. Its long, drooping tail had stitches.

In the next room, behind a plain oak door, I stumbled straight into someone. In the dark all I could tell was that he was tall and unyielding—and human.

"Sorry!" My voice must have activated the torches. They sputtered on, and I saw the dude I had run into: at least six and a half feet tall, dressed in some sort of soldier uniform centuries out of date, and covered with a dull gray sheen from the top of his hat to the tips of his pointy shoes.

Other people surrounded us, so lifelike that at first I thought I had stumbled into a meeting. But none of them were moving. Three girls in fifties skirts and bobby socks stood in a circle, their hands linked, their faces looking outward, scowling fiercely at some unknown bad guy. A little bronze dog stood, paw up, frozen mid-bark. A bunch of stone statues looked like they were running, including one guy wearing a baseball cap and shorts who had fallen on his side. A woman wearing a bustle, a muffler, and a hat as big as a car tire hunkered down awkwardly, her hands pressed over her eyes, hiding from something.

The uniformed guy had been turned to stone. Enchanted.

They were *all* enchanted.

The stone soldier was looking sidelong, a sad smile forever frozen around his mouth, his shoulders hunched forward—he'd been protecting something when the spell had hit him, something precious. Or maybe someone.

I circled the soldier, eyeing the long old-fashioned rifle, the brittle stone bayonet. He wore a tag around his other wrist. I stepped closer to read it, and my hip grazed something—a weird wooden pedestal. It toppled.

"Crap!" I automatically steadied it, but when my hand brushed the object on top, something crackled up my arm—like static electricity, if static could smell and taste like a ball-point pen exploding as you chewed on the end. I nearly dropped it in surprise. Magic.

I put it back on its pedestal and stared at it, rubbing my fingers. It looked like some sort of old-fashioned heavy metal can, with holes in the top, kind of like a saltshaker but dented—clearly ancient. I thought about shaking it to see what was inside, but it didn't seem like a smart idea. It could be the saltshaker of doom, a weapon that could turn whole armies to stone, or wood, or quartz.

Instead I turned back to the stone soldier and read the tag around his wrist, yellowed with age: WOLFGANG SEBASTIAN BRUHM, 1788–1804.

He was only sixteen when he got enchanted.

A shudder ran through me. It would suck so much to get trapped in an unmoving body for two centuries—never breathing, or speaking, or growing up. To be frozen while the whole world changed around you.

Maybe he could even sense me staring at him, the way they say people in comas can hear you talking.

I took a step back. Being all alone at EAS was getting creepy.

I hurried out and closed the door behind me.

And two more tries later, after a sky-blue room empty except for three chandeliers made out of spoons, and a black door that opened into an obsidian wall, I finally found the garden in front of the EAS apartments. Relieved, I wove through the tulips and Japanese maples and headed straight for the brownstone with a flashy red-and-gold door—Jack and Chase's place.

But someone was singing, a lone voice rising in high trills, a few notes away from shattering glass.

It was Chase. He was standing in the gazebo, which looked like a wrought-iron wedding cake, surrounded by fairies. With their backs to me all I could see were bright wings and long skirts. Then Chase met my gaze, and his voice dropped a couple octaves.

Well, I'd finally found him.

But Chase didn't smile, or wave, or stop singing, or give any sign like he was happy to see me. He just stared at me hard and kind of angry. He obviously would have preferred me waiting for him in the training courts.

I veered toward the gazebo, grinning.

The tallest Fey woman—the one with white wings threaded with palest pink—noticed where Chase was looking and turned around. Weird gray dots lined her face in horizontal rows. She sprang into the air, and in two wing beats she latched her hand over my wrist.

The dots on her face weren't tattoos. The blackish freckles were slightly raised and circular, and her skin had a silvery sheen. "He's nearly finished."

Then she dragged me across the garden. I was kind of too shocked to pull away.

The appearance of one fairy was enough to keep EASers talking for weeks. I hadn't seen three together since the Fairie Market.

The cobalt-skinned Fey and the third, very short one didn't glance our way when we came up the gazebo steps. Chase sang a long note that sailed out into the garden. I hadn't known he'd had it in him.

When his voice died away, the three Fey clapped, and so did I. "That was really impressive," I told him.

"I didn't actually have a choice." He glared at me. Not his *don't tease me right now* glare. It was the kind he shot me as a warning when I'd run straight into a dragon's lair or something else dangerous.

The Fey *were* known to be touchy.

I made a mental note not to call them fairies to their faces. "Fairy" was technically slang. Characters had started calling the Fey that about a thousand years ago, and the nickname caught on. The Fey had been known to enchant a kid stupid enough to say "fairy" in their presence.

"Yes. Let's all remember: I gave him that voice," said the cobalt fairy.

"Yes, but I gave him these curls." The smallest Fey grabbed a fistful of them, like she would like to cut them off and pocket them again. Chase flinched.

"No, you gave him grace of movement," said the fairy with dots on her face. "Remelda gave him the curls."

"Oh. You're right. But I suggested the curls to Remelda. She did not know which blessing to bestow upon the babe," she added with a wide smile.

"It is the custom." The Fey with dots had very green eyes, slightly too large for her face. It made her look constantly surprised. "Each of a child's godmothers bestows a gift upon the child at the time of his christening,"

So they were Chase's godmothers. That had happened to a Character three grades above us. Her father had had an extra boon from a Fey, left over from his days at EAS. He'd used it to make the fairy his daughter's godfather. Pretty much everyone expected her Tale to be "Cinderella."

This was too weird for me to start teasing Chase with glass-slipper jokes. Jack hated the Fey. He wouldn't have asked any of them to be his son's godmothers.

Chase said something in Fey to the fairy with dots, something that started with "Amya" and ended with "Rory."

"Chase, my dear, don't be rude. Speak English for the guest's sake." But her eyes widened even more.

The shortest Fey glided closer. "Rory?"

"Aurora Landon?" The cobalt fairy stepped nearer too, and suddenly I was surrounded.

The hairs on the back of my neck stood up.

Even here, among magic people who had never heard of Eric Landon and Maggie Wright, I was more famous than I liked to be. Maybe we were in danger. Maybe they were allies of the Snow Queen, and—

The Fey with dots—Amya? Was that her name?—let out a laugh. "I meant no offense! Chase has told us so much about you. I could not help being curious."

Chase didn't give me any clues on how to react, so I pretended I was Mom. She was always good with strangers, whether they happened to be fellow mothers at Parents' Night or up-and-coming actresses on set. She looked them straight in the eye and put on a megawatt smile like she'd wanted to meet them for months.

The Fey with dots on her face shook my hand. "I am Ayalla Aspenwind."

I smiled my most charming and Mom-like smile. "Nice to meet you, Mrs. Aspenwind."

The other two Fey hissed a little.

"It's Lady Aspenwind, actually," Chase whispered to me.

That was the problem with the Fey. You never knew what would insult them.

"I'm really sorry, Lady Aspenwind," I said, eager to apologize and change the subject before she turned me into a dove or something. "What brings you to EAS?"

"Today is Chase's birthday," said Lady Aspenwind.

"It is?" My voice rose about a million times too loud for the little garden. It couldn't be his birthday. If it was, Chase would have talked about it for weeks beforehand. He would have dropped a thousand hints about the presents he wanted—

Chase wouldn't meet my eyes.

"Of course. That is why we are here to visit." The huge smile vanished from her face, and her eyes glittered brightly. "Chase, he is growing so old."

Old was clearly a tragedy to her.

"Amya," Chase said softly. There had to be a reason he kept calling her that. Maybe that was Ayalla's nickname.

She smiled again. It was a little forced now. "A happy occasion. A happy birthday."

"A happy birthday," echoed the other two Fey mournfully.

"Thank you," Chase said, clearly relieved. "Don't you need to head back now?"

Hurt flashed in her eyes. She *had* come all this way to see him. She turned to me, like she hadn't heard. "Rory, he speaks of you so highly, but my son did not mention his birthday to you?"

"No, he—" Then I realized what she'd said.

Son.

This weird fairy was Chase's mother.

If you ignored all the dots on her face, you could see the resemblance. The broad, high cheekbones. The smile that took up half her face. They even had the same sunshine-yellow shade of blond hair.

"Clever human," whispered the shortest fairy. "Now you've discovered it."

Nobody knew much about Chase's mom—except that his parents weren't together anymore, so she didn't live with Chase and his dad. Chase almost never mentioned her. Now I knew why.

Chase was half Fey.

I closed my mouth. This was why he didn't want me here. This was the secret he wanted to protect.

I glanced at Chase. His face was turning red, a sign he was really mad.

"We should return, Lady," murmured the cobalt-skinned Fey.

Lady Aspenwind nodded, her eyes on Chase. Her mouth quivered. I was just thinking how weird it would be to see a fairy cry, when she actually started sobbing. So loud it echoed in the small chamber.

Her tears were green, solid, and shaped like tiny aspen leaves.

I froze. Watching grown-ups cry in public always made me feel panicky, like I should join in.

"You are turning out just like Cal. You shouldn't grow up so quickly." She buried her face in Chase's neck, which looked awkward since she was taller than he was. With a huge sigh, Chase patted her back lightly and murmured something in Fey.

The other two fairies looked faintly embarrassed for her, like she had sneezed and a big undignified gob of snot had come shooting out.

"Come, milady. We have no time for this." The cobalt fairy tugged on Lady Aspenwind's arm until she gave one last shaky sob, kissed Chase wetly on the forehead, and let herself be drawn away.

"You will think about what I said? If you want to live with me again?" she asked Chase.

Live with her? As in move? He couldn't leave.

"I'll think about it," Chase said.

Lady Aspenwind half smiled, comforted.

The two Fey steered her over the garden's gravel paths and through a midnight-blue door with silver hinges. Then they were gone.

I wanted to ask Chase if his mom always cried when she told him good-bye, but he was scowling at me.

So of course I blurted out exactly what came to mind. "Is it really your birthday?"

"Yeah." Then he turned and strode away. "You coming? You wanted to train, right?"

Sure, I wanted to train, but at the moment I wanted to address the strange development that one of my best friends was half fairy and that he'd never told me. I hurried after him.

He slammed through the door I'd just exited, stalked down the hallway, and stomped around the corner to the Three Little Pigs corridor without looking back once.

I trotted past the scarlet doors, trying to keep up and wondering what his problem was. I had caught him keeping a major secret from everyone. I had every right to be mad, but Chase acted like *I* had done something wrong.

I turned to Chase, all set to tell him off.

But he shoved a hand through his hair. Sweat had gathered at his temples. The last time he'd looked so freaked was when we'd gotten trapped in a skeleton-filled bread box with human-eating giants having dinner right outside.

I could relate, I guess. Last year I'd made a point of not telling anyone at EAS who my parents were. I hadn't wanted people to judge me differently just for being related to famous people. I probably would have done the same thing even if my mom had been a fairy instead of an actress.

Plus, his mom had outed him—whether he liked it or not. On his birthday.

We stepped inside the training courts, and Chase immediately disappeared into the weapons closet to grab our swords. Without a word he came out and passed me mine. We'd been together when I'd found it—in a Yellowstone cave, cornered by a dragon. My first day at EAS. We had been enemies them, but hurling insults at each other had never left much room for awkward silences.

If it had been me with the fairy mother, Chase would just have made some sort of stupid joke by now—eased the tension a little.

So I stepped away and stared—very obviously—at the side of his head.

"What?" Chase said.

"Just checking to see if your ears are pointed," I said. They weren't—they had the same human curve as anybody else's—but they did turn slightly red.

I worried that I'd insulted him instead of cheering him up, but then Chase grinned. "Nah. That's a myth. Only a few Fey clans have pointed ears."

I wished Lena had been here. She would have known what Chase meant by clans. I might have asked Chase, but I was too relieved he'd started acting like his normal self.

"I do have wings, though," he said.

"Yeah? Where are they? Detachable?"

"No." Chase looked a little grossed out. "They're invisible—most of the time."

"Can I see them?"

Chase smirked. "No way. I'm saving that for something really impressive."

Still awkward, but not as bad. Neither of us made any move to get out the practice dummies, though. Maybe Chase didn't want to spend his birthday training me.

My big mouth struck again. "I can't believe you didn't tell me."

His smile vanished. "Really, Rory? You can't figure out why I wouldn't want anyone to know I was only half human?"

"No, I did work that out, thanks," I said. "I was talking about your birthday."

"Oh." Chase shrugged, slightly abashed. "It just didn't occur to me."

I rolled my eyes. "It didn't occur to you to throw a huge party, or tell us what kind of presents you wanted, or—"

"No, that's not how it works among the Fey," Chase said. "For birthdays it's the mother who is celebrated. She gets the presents. She invites her friends. That's why she came to visit today."

"You mean, that was your birthday party?" I didn't mean to sound so pitying, but come on—there hadn't even been any cake.

"She did all the work when I was born. Why wouldn't we celebrate her achievement every year?" he said. I must have looked kind of shocked, because he added, "That's what she says, anyway."

I suddenly wanted to hug him, or give him an awesome present, or explain what birthdays were supposed to be like. But I just changed the subject. "So how old are you?"

Chase paused. "How old are you?"

I didn't stop to guess why he asked. "Twelve."

"I'm thirteen," Chase replied. "Thirteen today exactly."

"You're lying! You turned twelve today, didn't you?" He would be really tall for his age, but it was still possible. I would love to be older than him. It might cut back on his bossiness.

"Trust me, Rory—I've got you beat on this one."

The silence stretched out between us. Chase still didn't look me in the eye. I knew what he was really upset about.

"I won't tell anyone," I said quietly.

"Yeah?" Chase looked more fierce rather than less. Bringing it up clearly wasn't helping. "Will you swear it?"

I nodded.

"On the sword? On its enchantment?"

"If you want." If it would stop him from flipping out any more. I raised it between us, my hand on the hilt.

Chase wrapped his hand around mine. "Repeat after me: I do swear upon this sword . . ."

"I do swear upon this sword . . ." The hairs stood up on my arms, kind of like static but without the stinging crackle. This felt warm and ticklish in a bubbly way, like immersing myself in a soapy bath. I was pretty sure this didn't happen every time two people held the sword.

"Not to tell anyone that the person I see before me, Chase Turnleaf, is half Fey, half human. Not by voice, or written text, or insinuation . . ."

I repeated all this after him, more and more ticked off with every word.

"Not even Mom, Dad, and that scary woman Amy. Not even Lena."

I hesitated. "Lena's really smart. She's going to figure it out." And get really mad at me for keeping such a big secret from her.

Chase shook his head. "No, her head is full of her inventions. She won't solve a mystery she's not looking for. Finish repeating it."

He was being kind of a jerk.

I was tempted to stop repeating right then, but . . . he was just so freaked out.

I sighed. "Not even Mom, Dad, and that scary woman Amy. Not even Lena."

Something invisible rushed over my arms and into the sword, like warm water swirling down a drain. I didn't know why I was even surprised. Of course he could do magic. He was half fairy.

"That was a spell?" I said sharply.

"Yeah. A Binding Oath." He sagged. At first I thought the spell thing had taken more out of him than I expected, but when he smiled at me, his biggest grin, the one that took up half his face, I realized it was just relief.

"Why didn't you tell me you were casting a spell?" I said, but that wasn't what I really wanted to know. I wanted to know why my word wasn't good enough for him—why he felt like I needed to be enchanted to keep his secret.

His relieved smile shrank.

Then the door flew open, and someone launched herself at me so fast I staggered back. "I knew I would find you here!" Lena said triumphantly.

I hugged her back, glad she had interrupted. I wasn't sure if I was ready to know Chase's answer. "Don't you have school?"

"Not really. But I did it! You have to come see." She tugged me back to the courtyard.

"Lena, please tell me that you're skipping class," Chase said, following us outside. His voice gave me the creeps. He sounded so normal—teasing, cocky—like the last half hour hadn't happened. "That would make my day. It would mean I've corrupted you forever."

"No, just study hall. I don't know who scheduled that—a

study hall last period on Friday before spring break. But"—Lena stamped her foot on the grass impatiently—"you guys aren't looking."

About twenty feet from the Tree of Hope, a doorway-size rectangle hung in the air. The edges were on fire, the inside darker than the rest.

"Crap! You made a portal!" Chase yelped, and Lena looked very pleased.

I'd never heard of a kid making a portal. Actually, I'd never heard of any Characters making a portal into EAS besides Ellie—and she only did it using the Door Trek doors that ringed the courtyard, and only when the Director said it was okay.

Beside the flaming doorway Melodie stood on Lena's humongous duffel, scowling. She clearly didn't appreciate being left behind. "Lena, you really need to invent me some legs."

Lena nodded, but I couldn't tell if she was agreeing with the harp or just excited. "I got the idea last year, up the beanstalk. If the Snow Queen could make one from the Glass Mountain to Matilda Searcaster's desk using just a letter, then technically you should be able to make one into EAS the same way. It's a simple spell if you're not linking it up to an existing Door Trek system. It just takes a lot of power."

The breeze wafted some of the doorway's smoke toward us, and I wrinkled my nose. Only dragons and their scales could stink like a hot bowl of sulfur.

Chase sounded impressed. "You're not supposed to be able to do that, you know."

Melodie nodded. "The campus is designed to reject foreign and/or unapproved magics. I've seen it before. We had to take extra precautions."

"Instead of introducing something foreign, we took some dirt that was already here. Right there, to be exact." Lena pointed to the spot below the flaming rectangle. "And then I just substituted it for the pillar in the regular old portal spell. So that's all you need: some dirt, a doorway, and about twenty dragon scales."

I squinted into the dark inside it and spotted old mops and brooms. Probably a janitor's closet in her school.

"Wait, let me get this straight," Chase said. "Nobody knows that you did this?"

"Well, you two. And George and Jenny. They would worry otherwise."

"But none of the grown-ups? Not the Director?"

"No, I didn't want to bother them. I wasn't sure it would work," Lena said uncertainly. "Why?"

"We need to go tell them," Chase said, "unless you want all the instructors running around going, 'Security breach! Security breach!'"

Lena laughed, but then the amethyst door to the Director's office banged open. Lena and I both jumped.

Grown-ups filed out—Hansel and Gretel first, wearing identical tunics of golden chain mail, swords raised. Then came Stu, the Shoemaker, sunlight glinting off his silver breastplate, spear at the ready.

Another door opened on the other side of the courtyard, and iron figures marched out—evil fairies, giant wolves, ugly trolls, and wizened witches. The enchanted dummies we practiced on in the training courts apparently doubled as EAS's army.

An army that was surrounding us.

Mildred Grubb, the Director of EAS, walked out last, her shield engraved with roses. Her long blond hair hung in shining waves down her back, and her blue dress sparkled with silver embroidery. She spotted us.

"Do I even need to say I told you so?" Chase muttered.

All four marched our way, a scowl on every face. We were definitely in trouble.

ou three don't understand the seriousness of the situation," said the Director.

Maybe we didn't understand the situation, but we could all tell it was serious. Lena's eyes were huge, her shoulders hunched up around her ears.

"Security sweep, please." The Director gestured to the other grown-up Characters. Behind her shield she was wearing dainty fingerless lace gloves. Gretel, Hansel, and Stu each disappeared behind a separate door. Dozens of metal dummies split up and clanked after them.

"Um," I said. "Isn't that overkill? You caught Lena already."

For some reason the Director whirled around to glare at Lena instead of me. "Did you bind the portal to your essence so that none but you could pass? Use your signature, or your blood, or all ten fingerprints?"

Lena shook her head.

"Did you at least stand here and guard to make sure no one else entered after you?" the Director asked.

Lena glanced at me, stricken. She clearly regretted coming to find us.

"I thought not. Our Door Trek system is spelled to allow

only approved persons through approved gateways at approved times." The Director obviously liked to have approval over things. "Whether or not you children are aware of the fact, we do this for your safety. We are the second largest chapter of Ever After School in the world, with the highest success rate for completed Tales," the Director continued. "It stands to reason that we would be targeted by the largest number of villains."

Lena stared at her feet, her head bent so low that all her braids slung forward, the beads at their ends clacking together. I knew how much she hated being in trouble.

"Anyone could have entered through your portal and wreaked havoc upon the Characters who seek refuge here," the Director went on. "The Big Bad Wolf, the trolls who cut off Evan Garrison's fingers, General Searcaster—"

"Personally, I don't think General Searcaster could fit," I said before I could stop myself, and Chase snickered. Lena peeked at me through her hair.

"Aurora," the Director said in a warning way, but she really couldn't expect Chase and me to stand there and not say anything.

"I'm just saying—she's like four stories tall." I didn't usually try to push the Director's buttons, but this lecture was going too far.

"And she's not skinny, either." Half Fey or not, Chase caught on and backed me up. We were still a team.

"Enough!" the Director snapped. "Not another word from you, Aurora. I know you put Lena up to this."

Put Lena up to what? Inventing? No way. Everybody knew that Lena obsessed over her inventions even more than the rest of us obsessed over our Tales.

Chase and Lena looked just as confused as I was.

"What? It was me and Lena! We worked it out!" Melodie hated

it when other people took credit for her work.

"Got one, Director!" another voice rang out. Stu, the Shoemaker in charge of all the elves in the workshop, emerged from the steel double doors, escorting a girl in a plaid uniform. Mia.

I remembered her head on that table and shivered.

"Found her in the back of the workshop," Stu told the Director, and Lena glanced up, frowning.

"I'm sorry," Mia said in her too-soft voice. "I just got lost. I was looking for the room where I could read the Tales. I wanted to prepare myself."

A pair of heavy wooden doors swung open across the courtyard, and Bryan and Darcy trotted outside, both of them glaring at Hansel, whose double-handed broadsword was sheathed at his back. Their scowls looked surprisingly similar, considering one of their faces was furry and deer-shaped. "What's your problem?" the fawn demanded, as the sword master escorted them across the grass.

"Ellie told me the reference room got some more books on animal enchantments. I was checking to see if they could tell me how to break Bryan's," said Darcy. "Is that such a crime?"

"I told you," Hansel said. "It's just EAS protocol—for your own security."

Gretel stepped through the amethyst door. "All clear."

One by one, the iron dummies all marched into the courtyard and back toward the training courts. Mia's eyes widened, but I couldn't tell if she was impressed or freaked out.

"So, no bad guy," Chase said. "That means we're free to go, right?"

"Absolutely not." The Director narrowed her eyes at me, Chase, and Lena. "I believe we'll break up your little triumvirate for the afternoon."

Mia's eyebrows lifted. The corners of her mouth went up too. If she thought us getting punished was funny, her getting beheaded seemed slightly less tragic.

"What's a triumvirate?" Chase whispered to me.

Remembering the dream about Mia made me queasy. "Three of something, I think?" I said, distracted.

The Director surveyed us. "Lena, you'll go with Ellie to the workshop and gather all the notes and materials that led up to the invention of the spell. If I hear of you attempting such a portal again, you will appear before the Canon, and we will seriously consider your expulsion. Have I made myself clear?"

Lena stared, wide-eyed, caught between relief and guilt. She had a photographic memory. She didn't need her notes to recreate the spell. The part of Lena that compulsively followed rules wanted to tell the Director this, but she didn't. "Yes, ma'am."

She was an inventor before she was a Goody Two-shoes.

"And Lena, I want you to know—I nearly decided to break our deal about keeping the dragon. The scales have led you into mischief," said the Director.

Lena tensed. This would be a much worse punishment.

"But I've decided instead to allow you only enough scales to make carryalls and no more for the next three months. Is that clear?"

Lena nodded, biting her lip, and Ellie ushered her out.

Then the Director dismissed Stu and Hansel, then Bryan, Darcy, and Mia. She sent Chase to help the Shoemaker and the elves set up the courtyard for the feast. He went, muttering about how we were getting punished just for being Lena's friends.

She ordered Gretel to take me to the kitchens. When she explained that they were overwhelmed with making Red Riding

Hood's favorite dessert for the feast, Mia actually volunteered to help instead of following Bryan and Darcy to the reference room. The word "suck-up" crossed my mind.

Ugh. She shows up beheaded in my dream, and then she can't even talk without annoying me? I didn't want to know what that said about me.

"Come on." Gretel's iron foot gave her a weird limp. She shuffle-hopped away with the same determination and enthusiasm as Amy going to the dentist for a root canal. Mia and I hurried behind her to a plain white door with a big window, all fogged up.

Then Gretel threw the door open. I barely registered the smell of butter and sugar.

So much noise. So many strange witches. They *had* to be witches.

People assumed their ugliness was a stereotype, but Lena had told me once that all witches were cursed with it. Literally, cursed by the Last Mage. Apparently, they were born looking like hags.

Beaky noses, fingernail-size warts, and only three kinds of hair—black and stringy, or gray and strawlike, or bald with spots on their scalps. Several had hunchbacks. One even had green skin.

They stared at us with the same eager hunger a cat gives an unsuspecting goldfish.

Awesome. The Director's villain-rehabilitation program. This would be fun.

Gretel stepped aside, her back hugging the door frame, and waved us in.

One witch in front had a thin-lipped, wide-mouthed smile like a snake. "I still remember how your foot tasted, Gretel dear—faintly of licorice, more of pepper."

Gretel went rigid. I promptly lost my appetite.

"Kezelda, that's enough." One slender, straight figure moved in the crowd toward us, her silver braid brushing the floor. Rapunzel.

I'd been at EAS long enough to know that Rapunzel had good days and bad days. On some days, talking to her felt like shaking a Magic 8 Ball, and on others she spoke and acted like any other teacher.

I guessed today belonged in the second category.

"What? Mother gave her another one." The snake-lipped witch pointed at Gretel, whose skirt flew up several inches, exposing her feet. Gretel's metal foot was much smaller than the other—child-size and bare. No wonder she limped.

I'd never known how she'd gotten it. I kind of wished I still didn't know.

"And we know how Gretel repaid her," added the witch. We did know. Gretel had shoved the gingerbread witch into her own oven to save Hansel. That was how the Tale normally went.

"Kezelda!" Now that Rapunzel was closer, I could see how stressed she looked. A thousand stray hairs had escaped from her braid, and egg slime streaked the front of her dress. "I assure you that your mother was no fool. She knew the danger of allowing a Hansel and a Gretel into a gingerbread house."

Oh. I guessed witches could read the Tales too—same as Characters.

To the rest of the onlookers Rapunzel said coldly, "You have work to do, witches."

The kitchen filled with the sound of chopping knives, metal sifters, and scraping spoons again. Only Kezelda muttered to herself.

"Reinforcements," Gretel told Rapunzel before making her escape.

Rapunzel looked at me and Mia for a second too long. I expected some sort of cryptic warning to pop out of her mouth, but all she said was, "Would you mind keeping an eye on Kezelda, right there by the window?"

I sighed. I was stuck making a hundred Fey fudge pies with thirteen angry, "reformed" witches. Spring break was off to a great start.

Kezelda stirred the molten mixture in a sauté pan almost as big as a cauldron. When she wanted us to add more, she just stabbed a crooked finger at one of us—me for another stick of butter, the green-skinned witch for another handful of Fey fudge chunks.

The heat from the ovens was brutal. Sweat glued my collar to my neck. Even worse, the witches chucked food at us if we kept our backs turned for too long. The witch beating a big bowl of eggs nailed me in the elbow once, but otherwise I got a fair amount of dodging practice.

Mia pretended not to notice, like I did around Madison and the KATs. She just bent over the counter and cut up the fudge. Floury bits of dough and butter collected in her long dark hair.

My skin crawled every time I glanced at her.

Nightmares sometimes came true at EAS. I'd started dreaming about falling off a beanstalk the weekend before Lena got her Tale. If someone at EAS had a nightmare about my head on a table, I would definitely want to know. But maybe I was worrying for nothing. You had to dream it three times to be sure it would come true.

"You, girl. I need more butter." The first words Kezelda spoke to me.

I resentfully unwrapped another stick and dropped it in Kezelda's pan. "My name is Rory."

"We know who you are," Kezelda snapped.

I flinched. My mysterious fame struck again. Mia looked up

curiously. The knife in her hand was speckled with chocolate dust.

"We have all heard your name linked with the Snow Queen's," the witch continued. "Do not give yourself airs, just because—"

With a grunt Kezelda made a weird face like she'd seen something shocking, like a rooster covered in scales rather than feathers. She looked as if she almost swallowed her own tongue. Obviously, she had just remembered that she wasn't supposed to tell me anything.

Kezelda didn't speak to me again.

When a hundred crusts were filled, and all the pies were in the oven, Ellie came to escort the witches to their seats.

"So. The Director wants the results of her villain-rehabilitation program right in front of the foreign delegates," said the green-skinned witch.

"Doesn't work as well when you have to shackle us to our table," grumbled Kezelda.

Seeing the mess the witches' food fight had made of Mia's hair, Ellie ushered the new girl off too—to get her cleaned up.

That left me and Rapunzel to watch the ovens until the Shoemaker's elves took over kitchen duty. I was trying to figure out a polite way to point out it wasn't exactly a job for two people and ask if I could please go, when Rapunzel said, "Today you met his mother?"

I was kind of used to her seeing the future, but it was weird how much of *my* life she seemed to see. "You knew I'd meet her today?"

She shrugged. "Once or twice I have seen your face when you beheld Lady Aspenwind for the first time. But as with your dreams, and the dreams of Tales that all Characters have, I often don't recognize how the past, the present, and the future fit together until what I have foreseen is upon us." I must have given her a blank look, because she added wryly, "I knew that it would happen, but not that it would happen today."

She didn't usually talk about her prophecies. "So, instead of just dreaming about your Tale, you dream about everyone else's? Every night?" I asked.

"Not always at night, not always in sleep," she said. "But you have not told me about the introductions. How you feel."

I scowled. "Weird."

She just waited. Her eyes were startlingly dark beneath her pale gray eyebrows.

"I'm mad," I said. "I know why he did it, but it's like he doesn't trust me at all. And he cast a spell on me." He hadn't even asked. For all I knew, he'd cast dozens of spells over us without us even suspecting.

"A Binding Oath?" Rapunzel asked.

I nodded. "On my sword."

I was sure Rapunzel would be sympathetic, but she only sounded amused. "Then he must have trusted you a little. Or prized your friendship over his secret."

"This is one of those times when I can't tell if you're being accidentally cryptic or if I'm just not paying enough attention to piece together everything you're saying."

Rapunzel pulled her long braid over her shoulder and brushed pieces of butter from it. "He arrived here seven years ago. He had not learned to hide his wings yet. They fluttered when he was anxious. You could see nothing of Jack in him. He could have been any Fey child. But he was so bold, rather reckless, just as he is now. He demanded that the whole Canon swear to keep his secret, a Binding Oath on our lives."

I could definitely believe that Chase had bossed around the most important Characters on the continent at six years old. Thinking of Chase as a tiny fairy kindergartner was harder to swallow, but what *really* weirded me out was finding out Chase hadn't lived at EAS his whole life. I couldn't imagine him anywhere else.

I didn't know Chase as well as I'd thought I did.

"A Binding Oath is like a bargain with magic itself, a deal made with the force that manipulates and compels us. The most basic is to swear on your life. Life itself is a bit like magic—there is something fantastic about it. With it, we are a person; without it, we're only a mass of bones and organs and skin," Rapunzel said, and personally, I thought this was a creepy way of thinking about it. "If you fail to meet the requirements of the oath, if you tell, even by accident, magic will slip into you and rip the life from your body. Such a Binding Oath doesn't take much magic of your own, only an extreme determination. But Chase was so small. I was the only one of us who believed that such a little person could bind seventy-two adults at one time. But he did. Jack included. Chase always had a strong will, Rory—as strong as yours and Lena's. He just doesn't yet know what to do with it."

At least the Characters in the Canon knew what they were getting into. It was a dirty trick to play on your best friend. "So if I accidentally tell, I'll die?"

Rapunzel sighed, almost impatiently. "No, Rory. I have just told you this. You didn't swear on your life, though he could have asked this of you. You would not have known the difference, and he knew that. But a person of little magic can perform a Binding Oath in another way—he can anchor it onto a permanent spell, even one cast long ago."

"Like my sword," I said, understanding.

Rapunzel nodded. "So he must trust you some. More than the entire Canon, more than his father."

"He still should have told me before he did it." But I wasn't as mad as I had been a minute before.

"Yes." Rapunzel untied her chocolate-streaked apron. "But do not cling to your anger, Rory. You need Chase's friendship, the way you need Lena's, the way he needs yours. You three will not survive without it."

I didn't like the ominous way she said that, or the way she narrowed her eyes at the ovens.

"I am concerned, Rory," she said. "I dreamed of Solange, here, in this room, on this day, preparing this dish. She drew a pie out of the oven and presented it to me, smiling, the way she does when she has impressed herself."

My stomach churned. Prophecies about the Snow Queen invading EAS seemed a lot more important than explaining what a Binding Oath was, but I resisted the urge to say so. "How many times?"

"At least once every day this week," Rapunzel said mournfully.

So definitely enough times to come true. I wished she'd told me earlier.

Rapunzel shook out her apron and folded it, frowning. "I may be wrong. I saw no sign of her, no sign of foul play, and I watched the witches carefully. But take care, Rory."

"ow mad are you?" Chase asked impatiently, as soon as I crash-landed in the seat across from him.

Chase had found a spot near the front of the courtyard. A long wooden platform sat right ahead of us on the beach, its red curtain fluttering in the breeze, and the Tree of Hope loomed on our right. Fifteen rows of tables stretched all the way to the wall of doors, the tablecloths very yellow against the grass. Half of EAS was saving seats, and the other half was talking, laughing, and trying to find their friends.

I shoved my phone in my pocket—the call I'd just finished had lasted barely long enough for Mom to tell me that she loved me and that she was late to dinner—and I shot him the dirtiest look I could muster. "On a scale of one to ten? We're looking at maybe twelve and a half."

Chase scowled back. Over his shoulder was a long section with gold cloth—the high table. "I didn't do anything wrong."

Now we were at fifteen and a half on the how-mad-is-Rory scale. "You cast a spell on me without telling me. You don't do that to your friends."

"If I'd told you, would you still have taken the oath?" He clearly thought the answer was no.

"Yes!" I said, so loudly that Darcy, Bryan, and some other eighth graders grabbing seats behind us looked over. I lowered my voice. "I mean, it would have still freaked me out, but I would have done it anyway. It could have been my birthday present for you this year. Instead you tricked me."

I didn't care that I hadn't sworn on my life. I'd trusted him, and—

"I'm sorry." That was the last response I expected. Chase even looked kind of guilty.

A bell rang, and the courtyard filled with the slams of Door Trek doors and the hum of a hundred new voices. School must've gotten out on the West Coast.

"You have to swear never to do it again, or—" I was about to say something really mean, like how we couldn't be friends anymore if he tricked me like that one more time. But you don't just replace your best friends. "Or you'll have to back off during the next hunt—let me have first dibs on the next ice-griffin flock."

Chase glanced at me, and seeing me smile, he knew he was in safe territory again. "That price is too steep," he said, mock-horrified, but now he was grinning back.

"What price?" Melodie asked, as Lena set the harp on the table.

I froze, not sure what to say.

"The price of dwarf-made swords in Avalon," Chase said. "I'm thinking about asking for a new one for Christmas."

He could think up a believable lie in less than a second. Great. Now, I had to worry about how many times he'd done that.

"It doesn't matter. This is important," Lena said, sitting beside me. "What do we think about the new girl?"

"Chatty?" I asked.

Chatty stood in front of the gold table, her hands fisted at her sides, her toes curled in the sand. Beside her the Director folded her arms over a ruffly dress even pinker and puffier than usual. A man wearing a tuxedo squatted down to peer in Chatty's face, and a woman in a kimono embroidered with cranes scowled. They must have been delegates from the chapters on other continents.

"No, Mia. She's been poking around my workshop twice in the past two days," Lena said. "Yesterday, after you left, she came over to my section while the Director was giving a tour of the workshop. And today she was in my section. It's all the way in the back. You can't just accidentally wander in. And . . ." Here Lena glared at Mia with the pure loathing she only reserved for villains who tried to kill her friends, and Characters who dog-eared book pages. Mia was too far away to notice. "The elves said she was looking through my papers. So what do we think? Spy?"

I had a hard time picturing it. No spy would let witches pelt her with butter.

"Don't mind me," said someone standing over us—a very bald someone, with tufted gray eyebrows, a rumpled suit, and a wooden cane with a frog carved on top. The Frog Prince. His name was Henry. "The Director assigned us seats. Two adults to every table."

"Who's the other one?" Chase asked, horrified.

"Rapunzel." Henry sat, his bones popping. "Have I wished you happy birthday yet, Chase?"

"Oh, is it your birthday? Happy birthday!" said Lena.

"Happy birthday." I couldn't remember if I'd told him yet or not.

Chase went pink, all the way to the tips of his nonpointy ears. I wondered how many times he'd actually heard "happy birthday" in his life. "Thanks." Then he added, much louder, "Please don't sing."

Rapunzel slipped into the seat beside Henry, wearing a gray silk dress I'd never seen before. Clearly, this was a dress-up day for the grown-ups. Then Hansel appeared at the table next to us, and Chase's horror multiplied by a thousand.

"Here, Mrs. Taylor—best seats in the house." Hansel smiled, tight-lipped, at a lady I didn't recognize. She was very petite—Ben towered over her as he pulled out her chair. She wore a red suit and some ugly jewelry that looked like silver rope. I was pretty sure I'd seen the same outfit on some female politicians.

"These will be perfectly adequate, thank you," said Mrs. Taylor, as Ben eased the chair forward under her. Either she was naturally snooty, or she was a little freaked out by the fawn arguing with his sister at the next table.

"I still think we should try the shirt of stinging nettles," Bryan said. "Like in 'The Six Swans.'"

"I'm the one who would have to be mute. So I'm the one who gets to make the decision," Darcy replied. "Besides, we don't even know for sure it'll break your enchantment."

The word "enchantment" pushed the woman over the edge. Wide-eyed, she clutched her purse and half rose from her seat, like she was ready to leave.

"Not to worry, Mother," Ben said with a reassuring smile. "I would need a brother or sister for that Tale. I doubt I'll turn into a deer." Then, taking a seat across from her, he leaned over the six inches dividing his table and ours so he could introduce us as "the fine seventh graders who saved me from the griffins yesterday."

Lena stared at him, like she couldn't understand why an eighth grader was talking like a stodgy old man with patches on his elbows.

"I'm sorry your husband couldn't join us," Hansel told Mrs.

Taylor, probably hoping to distract her. "He attended EAS with my niece."

Mrs. Taylor opened her mouth and hesitated, but Ben didn't bat an eye. "I'm sorry to be the one to tell you this, Hansel, but my father passed away. Four years ago. Heart attack."

Lena and I glanced at each other, not sure if we were supposed to say anything. Even Chase looked a little stunned.

"I'm so sorry—" Hansel started.

But Ben spotted a distraction, passing his table in her plaid uniform. "Mia!"

The new girl looked up slowly—definitely not alert enough to be a good spy—and Ben busied himself introducing Mia to his mom.

"Rapunzel, there you are." Gretel strode toward us, propelling Chatty so forcefully that the mute girl winced with every step. "Can you take her?"

"Say no. Say no. Say no." Chase probably thought Rapunzel filled the weirdo quota at our table.

"Still mad about her water-fountain trick, Chase?" I asked, and Chatty grinned at me.

Rapunzel examined her thoughtfully. "Have we figured out which chapter she came from?"

"Probably South America. Their representative is late. The rest of the delegates don't recognize her," Gretel said.

Chatty rolled her eyes as if to say, *Yes, by all means, talk about the mute girl like she's not here. She won't stop you.*

Then she spotted Ben, who pulled a chair out for Mia the same way he'd done for his mom and said, "Any girl who can fish me out of Lake Michigan on a school night is a girl I want to know."

Chatty clearly disapproved of the display. Scowling, she stomped over to the bench and dropped into the seat beside Lena, so hard that the whole bench shuddered.

"Hey! Nobody said you were staying!" Chase said.

Chatty stuck her tongue out at him halfheartedly, her chin in her hand.

Just as Kenneth took the seat next to Mia, the Director stood up at the high table and raised both arms for silence. The sun was setting in a fiery way behind her, backlighting her dress. She looked as airy and fluorescent as pink cotton candy. Probably not the look she'd been hoping for.

"EASers, juvenile and grown, foreign and domestic, parents, guests, instructors, and Canon members, we gather today to welcome the new Red Riding Hood to the Canon." The Director gestured to two ladies sitting side by side at the high table. One wore a Sunday hat so giant that the African delegate seated at her other side leaned slightly out of the way. She waved, but the other Red Riding Hood, wearing a more manageable baseball cap, looked nervous.

Then the Director explained that the ninth graders had prepared a skit depicting the history of EAS. We were free to talk throughout the performance, but she expected absolute silence during the ceremony. Then, finally, she added that to begin our meals, we each needed to tell our Table of Plenty "chicken" or "pasta," depending what we wanted for the main course.

As soon as she said "Enjoy" and sat back down, we turned back to our places.

"Pasta," I said. Chatty waved her hand in my face, pointed at the steaming bowl of Alfredo that appeared in front of me, and then at her spot. "Pasta," I said for her too, and a second bowl appeared.

Chase immediately sliced into his chicken with gusto. "Feast meals are always the best," he told Ben.

Melodie grabbed Lena's sleeve and mine, and we both bent down. "Did you want to do something for him?" the harp asked, too low for Chase to hear. "It's too late to throw him a party today, but—"

I wondered why I hadn't thought of this first. "Yeah! Maybe on Monday! We can invite the triplets!"

On the beach, the stage curtains were pulled aside to reveal a forest. Not like a set of painted trees, but an actual forest, with oaks as big around as our table and dappled green light shining through the leaves. It stretched back and back, even over the water, like someone had placed a strip of trees right on top of the ocean.

Shocked, I stopped twirling my fork through my pasta.

On the sand beside the stage, Gretel's mouth moved. She was a sorceress, so her magic worked a little differently than Lena's. A rainbow blur of light spilled from her cupped hands and crawled outward across the stage.

The actors gathered around a campfire among the trees Gretel had conjured. An old woman gestured hugely with fingers crooked as sticks, and the others—who also looked a lot older than ninth graders—listened intently. I waited for a giant to come pulling up trees, or big bad wolves to howl, but the actors just kept talking.

The skit didn't even have any sound. Kind of a letdown.

Kenneth decided to make the skit more exciting and get rid of his vegetables in one swoop. He loaded his spoon with peas and pulled it back, aiming at the stage. He might have gotten away with it if he hadn't checked to see if Mia was watching (she wasn't).

Hansel snatched the spoon catapult away—peas and all. "We have guests, Kenneth. Three strikes and I will take you out. That was one."

Kenneth slid a fraction closer to Mia. "Yes, sir," he said with so much sarcasm I hoped Hansel would count it as strike two.

Rapunzel nodded at the figures onstage. "The first meeting of the Canon."

"But no one called it that. Maerwynne just called everyone together to exchange stories. She's the one in the red cloak." Melodie pointed to the dark-haired woman sitting alone on a stump. Gretel's illusion made her taller and her face a little more lined, but it was still easy to recognize her—Gwen, the best friend of Lena's sister, Jenny. "She wore it until her death. It reminded her of her eleven sisters. After the 'Twelve Dancing Princesses', nine Failed their Tales, and five died as Red Riding Hood before Maerwynne took the cloak and slew the wolf. She called this meeting so no family would be ravaged as hers had been."

"Nine Failed their Tales?" I said. Failing your Tale was pretty much as embarrassing as flunking out of school, except it was usually life-threatening. "Nine?"

"Back then, fairy tales weren't collected in books. In fact there weren't very many books," Melodie said. "You depended on word of mouth for all your news, but Maerwynne and her sisters were princesses. They didn't meet many travelers, and they spent half their time underground, dancing with Queen Titania's court. They'd never heard of Red Riding Hood."

"Lena, imagine that you find a beanstalk in your backyard, instead of here," Rapunzel said softly. "Imagine you know nothing of beanstalks. Imagine you climb it, and you know nothing of giants. You know not even that they eat humans. Do you see how easily you could be devoured?"

Lena didn't answer. She was made uncertain by creepiness.

Chase snorted. "Nobody needs to convince Lena that knowledge is power."

Suddenly, some weird noises came from the witches' table, all the way in the back—squawking and screeching and cawing. I thought for a second that they'd been enchanted to sound like birds of prey, but then they stood and started clapping. They were cheering.

"What set them off?" I asked.

"Madame Benne," Lena breathed, staring at the stage.

"The witches feel that as a fellow magical being," Rapunzel explained, "Madame Benne was their voice in the Canon."

Onstage, Jenny played the role of her ancestress. Her hair had grown four feet, into a long black braid wound with leather and ribbons, but the biggest change was her skin—it was gold.

"Ummm," I said. "Is there a reason she looks gold-plated? Did that happen during her Tale or something?"

"She didn't have a Tale. She was the only Canon member who never had one," Lena said.

"Honorary founding member," said Melodie smugly.

"Gold skin," I pointed out again, in case they missed what I was shocked about.

"She was only half human. And a quarter Fey, and a quarter mermaid." Henry frowned at me, probably wondering exactly what EAS was teaching us these days.

"The mermaid's blood on Madame Benne's paternal line helped her raise and quell storms. She was famous for it." Lena sounded so proud I couldn't believe she'd never brought it up before.

"Lena, you're part fairy—" The word "too" almost slipped out, but my tongue tripped, getting magically snagged in my teeth. I guessed it was the Binding Oath's way of reminding me not to go there.

Chase went uncharacteristically still.

Lena shrugged. "Madame Benne was over twenty generations back. This is like a drop of fairy and a drop of mermaid. Nothing to brag about. Most Characters have a bit of nonhuman way, way, way back in their family tree. That's why most of us can study to be magicians."

"I have a drop of mermaid," Rapunzel said. "On my mother's side."

"My wife used to joke that I was part dwarf," added Henry. "Because I'm so short."

From the sly look on Chatty's face right then, I guessed even the mute girl had a goblin grandfather or something. I was the only person at that table who was completely human.

Chase decided to change the subject. He pointed to a dark-haired boy with broad cheekbones sitting near Maerwynne. He wore leather chaps so embarrassing they begged to be mocked. "Ben, that's Rikard Longsword, the last of the great Hungarian horsemen. They say he rode a Dapplegrim into battle and slew fifty-seven giants before he turned forty."

Ben looked intrigued. "Dapplegrim?"

Chase grinned. "Just wait. There's a Dapplegrim cameo in about four minutes."

Onstage, Madame Benne moved through the crowd, handing out golden apples.

"Where is Jenny's harp? I was with Madame Benne then! I am forgotten by history." Melodie plucked her strings in a pathetic-sounding minor scale, which was probably her version of bringing out the sad violins. "And they weren't actually apples! That was just the code name for the object that held the antiaging enchantment. This is so inaccurate."

Lena's eyes followed her sister. "I could use a golden apple. Not for too long," she added hastily, seeing my face. "I don't want to live forever exactly. Just maybe another century. Do you know how many more inventions I could perfect if I had an extra hundred years?"

"Lena, you sound kind of creepy and obsessive when you say that," Chase said. "Mad scientist in a bad way."

Normally, this was where I told Chase not to insult Lena, but he had a point.

Lena's jaw jutted forward. "Are you saying you wouldn't want to stop aging?"

"No, I wouldn't. I'm going to live to be an old man and die in my sleep. An extra hundred years aren't worth it if you live long enough to bury all your grandchildren." Then, clearly relishing Lena's shocked expression, Chase picked up his lemonade and raised it to his mouth.

Chase's mother was Fey. Most fairies stayed the same age for years and years. Of course Chase would think about this more than the regular kid.

"Anyway, I helped Madame Benne develop the formula, derived from some ancient Fey magic—" Melodie started, but Chase's cheeks bulged, like a blowfish. Then he made a choking sound, which gave us a half-second warning before he turned his head—away from me, fortunately—and sprayed the whole bench next to him.

It amazed me how much lemonade could fit in Chase's big mouth.

"Crap! Sorry." Chase wiped his tongue down with a napkin.

Because Ben had bent over to tie his shoes, Kenneth got the worst of it. His face looked decidedly purple. The Director didn't seem too pleased either when she saw what a commotion our table was making, and the way the delegates from other chapters had turned to stare. She shot Hansel a glare that clearly said, *Take care of it*.

"Strike one, Chase Turnleaf—" the sword master started.

"It wasn't my fault. It tastes salty. Really bad, like the ocean." Chase moved his glass in front of Hansel. "Here. Taste it if you don't believe me."

Chatty shook, both hands pressed over her mouth. For a second I thought something had happened to her lemonade too, but she was giggling, madly but silently. The saltshaker was in front of her—unscrewed and empty.

"Wait—you put the salt in his drink?" Hansel asked Chatty.

She nodded gleefully.

"Ooh, a prankster in our midst," said the Frog Prince, like he was welcoming a long-lost friend.

"You always have to watch out for the quiet ones," Ben said.

"Wow. You really are corny. We need to introduce you to Ellie," Chase told Ben. He wasn't looking when Kenneth rose from his seat, his soda in hand, and started to pour it over Chase's head.

"Watch out!" I said, pointing.

Chase knocked the soda away before it tipped, which sucked for Kenneth and Mia right behind him. They both got sloshed.

Kenneth jumped to his feet, cursing. Mia blinked at the brown liquid running down her arm, as Ben tossed napkins her way, eager to help.

"Not my fault, Hansel," Chase said swiftly.

"Kenneth, those were strikes two and three." Hansel stood up, grabbed Kenneth's shoulders, and forced him toward the dungeon door, ignoring the eighth grader's protests.

"The bathroom's there if you want to get cleaned up," Henry

told Mia. Without a word she swung off her seat and wove her way through the tables.

"Silent but deadly. No one sees her pranks coming," said Ben, and this time everyone laughed, even Chatty.

Hooves clomped onstage.

Chase nudged Ben. "The Dapplegrim."

Hearing him, five boys whipped their heads toward the stage. Even Henry peeked over his shoulder. You would have thought some sort of fancy car or superhero were about to show up.

"A real one?" asked one kid.

"No. Just a horse wearing Gretel's illusion," said his friend regretfully. "Like anyone would use up a boon from a Dapplegrim just for some dumb skit."

"But Gretel's actually seen one," Chase said. "This might be as close as you ever get to the real thing."

"What's a Dapplegrim?" I asked.

Chase looked exasperated. He always gave us that look when we reminded him his best friends were girls. "Only the biggest, most awesome horse to ever stand on four hooves."

"They talk. They have their own herd," Lena explained.

"They're freaking endangered. They only live in the south of Atlantis," Bryan said.

"If there's an awesome talking horse in a fairy tale, it's usually a Dapplegrim," Chase added. "Now where is it?"

Onstage, a horse the size of an elephant walked through the forest, Rikard on its back, with Maerwynne walking beside them.

The Dapplegrim's coat was glossy black, reflecting the lamplight from Maerwynne's lantern in every muscle. Its mane and tail hung in coal-black waves. With every stride, sparks flew up from the ground.

I sneezed. Yep, definitely a real horse underneath the illusion. I knew from experience that horses being magic didn't stop me from being allergic to them. And I was really allergic.

"Seriously?" Chase said, like my sneeze had messed up an awesome fake-Dapplegrim sighting. "Even from twenty feet away?"

Then, when the air filled with silvery streaks ("Elf shot," Lena whispered) and Rikard swung Maerwynne up into the saddle in front of him, the Dapplegrim opened its stride. Flames puffed from each nostril, and the trees slid away in a green blur, nauseatingly fast.

Practically every guy sprang to his feet, stamping, clapping, and whooping all at once. They were even more excited about the Dapplegrim than the witches had been about Madame Benne.

A wolf howled, loud and sudden, onstage. Maerwynne yanked the reins, the Dapplegrim whirled, and Rikard grabbed Maerwynne's waist to keep from falling off.

The Dapplegrim plunged through the woods and stopped in front of a log cabin. Scary movies had taught me to be wary of these.

Maerwynne jumped off the Dapplegrim's back and drew Rikard's sword from the saddle. A gray blur leaped through the door. Maerwynne struck. The wolf's head fell to the ground.

"Oh," Lena said anxiously. "I forgot about this part."

Gretel's illusion brought us and Maerwynne into the cabin, and Chase whistled. "That's a lot of magenta."

It flooded the floor, splattered the walls all the way up to the ceiling. Blood. Gretel must have turned it pink to make it less scary. If it had been its normal color, every Character at the feast probably would have lost their appetite.

"What did I miss? Not dessert?" Hansel reappeared at his place, Kenneth-free. Seeing Mrs. Taylor's horror, he added, "Don't worry.

This happened a very long time ago. Characters rarely confront this today."

But it had happened. And Hansel was talking about it so calmly, like it was a movie we'd gone to see.

On the floor was an old woman's nightgown, ripped to bloody pieces, and a magenta-smeared girl, wrapped in a red cloak—barely alive. She was younger than we were.

Maerwynne fell to her knees at the girl's side.

Lena clutched my arm so tightly it hurt. "All these years later, she still wishes she could have saved her sisters."

Maerwynne stretched out her hand, and a golden apple rested on her palm. The wounded Red Riding Hood reached for it. When the girl's fingers closed around it, Maerwynne disappeared in an explosion of silver, finer than glitter.

"If the apple keeps you alive past the day you would've died, then you turn to dust as soon as you give it away," Melodie said sadly, like she was apologizing for the one thing Madame Benne couldn't perfect.

I glanced at Lena, who bit her lip. That would happen to her if she got that extra century.

The magenta-covered Red Riding Hood onstage stood up, apparently unhurt.

"But it can also heal you instantly, as you take the apple and a place in the Canon." Rapunzel twisted around and pulled her braid aside. A thick scar wrapped all the way around her neck. "Even if the wound is fatal."

Mrs. Taylor gasped. "What gave you that?"

"Yeah, what—" Lena started, but she remembered. "Oh right, the witch in your Tale."

Rapunzel ignored Hansel's glare, the one that clearly said, *Don't bring that up during a parent visit*. "The golden apple can even regrow limbs, if the wound is fresh. And a limb regrown by magical means would make a person into a sorcerer."

At the high table, the Director stood and raised both hands.

"Finally!" Chase muttered.

"Silence now, if you please," the Director said. "I've ordered the elves to deny pie to anyone who fails to obey this instruction. The time for the ceremony has come."

Threatened with no dessert, the courtyard grew eerily quiet.

Beside the Director, the two real Red Riding Hoods stood up together, side by side, in unison.

The woman in the old-fashioned red Sunday hat passed something to the woman in the red baseball cap. I couldn't see what it was. Her hand kept it hidden from view.

The second their hands fell back to their sides, the one in the Sunday hat suddenly looked thirty years older, her makeup folded into her new wrinkles. She stared at the age spots on her hands with horror, and the new Red Riding Hood, the one in the baseball cap, squeezed her arm in sympathy.

I didn't want that. I didn't want to stop aging if the price was losing decades in a second.

The Director clapped loudly to get our attention back. "Thank you. And now, our guests . . ." She gestured to the witches' table. Many witches leered back, and one waved. Kezelda scowled—she didn't feel like much of a guest. "Our guests have prepared a special treat for you tonight: Fey fudge pie."

The elves streamed among the tables. Each piece of pie had a perfect dollop of whipped cream. When they delivered plates first to the tables closest to the kitchens, Chase said, "Ugh. It'll take forever for them to reach us."

"What is Fey fudge?" asked Mrs. Taylor.

"Think of the best chocolate you've ever had in your life, and then times that by a thousand," said Lena.

"I guess it's too much to ask for it to be gluten-free, huh?" Ben said sadly.

I shook my head. I'd watched the witches put the flour in myself.

Ben sighed. "Wheat allergy."

"Better not chance it then, dear," said Mrs. Taylor.

We all felt sorry for him until Ben said, "It's all right. I'm watching my girlish figure."

Chase turned to me, trying so hard not to comment that he looked like he was in pain.

At the high table, the Director lifted her fork, laden with a dainty bite, and closed her eyes with satisfaction. The witches dug in, spearing the chocolate-mousse-y goop. After that first taste, a lot of compliments passed from witch to witch.

The table just behind us got their plates, and the eighth graders dove in without hesitation. Well, except for Darcy.

"It's almost too pretty to eat. Where's my camera?" As soon as she stuck her head under the table to look, her brother darted forward and gobbled up her slice. "Bryan!"

"What?" said the fawn, chocolate stuck to the fur on his nose. "I didn't get one. And I'm sick of eating grass."

"Yeah, well, I just hope it doesn't kill you." Darcy folded her arms over her chest. "I would hate to spend the whole night at the vet again because some stupid baby deer can't control his chocolate cravings."

Then an elf appeared at Lena's elbow, carrying three plates on each arm.

"Rufus, you are a king among elves," Chase told him, completely serious.

Rufus grinned crookedly. Lena and I passed plates down the table.

"Didn't we have spoons?" Henry asked.

When everyone searched the table, peering under plates and around glasses, Chatty started giggling silently once again.

"Chatty," Chase said, annoyed, "the lemonade thing was funny, I admit. But you don't mess with dessert. We're been waiting all night."

Rolling her eyes, Chatty produced the silverware from under the table. We reached for them.

Rapunzel's spoon fell through her fingers, like her hand had forgotten how to grip. Then she whispered, in a low, cracked voice, "Don't let them eat cake."

But she wasn't staring at cake. It was the pie on my plate.

"What?" My spoon halted right over the whipped cream.

"Are you crazy? Did you not see me drooling earlier?" Chase caught the spoon Chatty tossed him.

Rapunzel sprang to her feet with a Hansel-worthy bellow: "Don't let them eat cake!"

Some fifth graders a few tables over laughed, thinking that she was joking, but they didn't see her face. Horror stretched her eyes so wide you could see whites all around her irises.

"What did I tell you? Crazy," Chase said, like he knew the scene was going to get ugly very fast.

Everyone had told me, for almost as long as I'd been at EAS, that Rapunzel was insane, but this was the first time I had seen her act like it.

She lurched up onto the table, swung her leg back and kicked— her plate and mine flew off the table. Both slices fell to the lawn, demolished into brown blobs covered in grass clippings.

I slid out of the way, but Chase, Lena, and Henry grabbed their plates before she could kick those too.

All across the courtyard, heads turned toward us and then questioningly up at the high table, trying to see what to do. The Director forked a big bite of pie and shoved it in her mouth with a flourish. Everyone else followed her example.

I couldn't believe it—they were really going to ignore the warnings of someone who saw the future?

"DON'T LET THEM EAT CAKE!"

"Hansel!" said the Director, smiling in a strained way.

With a long-suffering sigh, Hansel took one last bite of his dessert and rose to his feet. "Come on, Rapunzel. Not now." When she shied away from him, he lifted her bodily off the table.

"NO! DON'T! DON'T LET THEM!"

Mrs. Taylor's mouth hung slightly open. You could see fudge on her tongue.

"Born right after the French Revolution," Henry said conversationally. "Bound to be a little scarred."

Hansel dragged her across the courtyard. Rapunzel struggled so much that the Shoemaker got up to help.

"Easy now, Rapunzel," Stu said, gently but firmly, like she was a kid having a tantrum. "We'll get you to your tower."

Up at the high table, the Director bent her head toward the unnerved ambassadors from other chapters—probably explaining or apologizing.

"She never changes." Then Chase raised a forkful to his mouth.

I batted it out of his hand automatically.

Chase scowled. "Not you, too."

Scowling back, I shoved Lena and Chase's plates into the grass for good measure.

"She dreamed she saw the Snow Queen in the kitchens!" I went for Chatty's next, but she was already on her feet. She dashed to

Hansel's table and knocked Ben's untouched plate to the ground, and his mother's mostly finished one, and Hansel's, and Kenneth's, and Mia's.

"Was that one mine?" said Mia confused, returning from the bathroom.

"DON'T LET THEM EAT CAKE!" Rapunzel shouted one last time, at the edge of the courtyard, before Hansel slammed an orange-gold door behind them.

Henry still held his plate, but when I reached for it, he pulled it out of my reach. "You can't deny an old man his pleasures, Rory. Do you know how many times she has seen the Snow Queen here?"

"Last month she said she saw a 'many-eyed, many-legged monster' lurking in the training courts. We found a spider. This big." Chase made a dime-size circle with his hands.

Now that Rapunzel was gone, and the courtyard slowly filled with murmurs, laughter, and the clink of forks on plates, a tiny bit of doubt crept into me. I didn't know how many times she had seen the Snow Queen. I'd only known Rapunzel for a year, and then only between three and six o'clock on weekdays. Most weeks I didn't even see her two days in a row.

"She saved our lives so many times," I said stubbornly. "All she asked us to do is not eat the pie."

"But it was Fey fudge," said Lena weakly.

Chatty slipped back into her seat, her shoulders hunched forward, uncertain. She was wondering if we had completely over-reacted too.

Then, behind us, Darcy said, "Bryan? Are you okay?"

The fawn's slender legs trembled, and he sank slowly to the grass. "Just don't feel so great."

"It was probably the chocolate. It's too rich for deer." Darcy reached into the pocket of her hoodie. "Hang on. I'll call Mom. We can go to the vet."

Up at the high table, the Director cleared her throat, loudly and uncomfortably, like something was stuck in it.

Across the courtyard, the witches were all in disarray: one vomiting under the table, Kezelda sticking her fingers down her throat to do the same. The rest were clearing their throats in the same slightly panicked way that the Director was. They couldn't breathe.

"Treachery," croaked one.

Kezelda wiped her mouth and stood. "Poison!"

Panic swept across the crowd, Characters wheezing or crying, the two Red Riding Hoods bent double around their stomachs as if something gnawed at them from the inside. Two of the ambassadors fell from their seats, unconscious.

Mrs. Taylor moaned, and Ben rushed around the table. "Mother?" And when she didn't answer, he turned to me, like I knew what to do. "We need a nurse."

"Gretel." I swung out of the bench.

The illusion of Rikard and the Dapplegrim thundering through the trees flickered and faded. Gretel had eaten the pie too.

"We need another, unpoisoned nurse," I said.

Chase jumped to his feet. "Rapunzel."

This didn't feel like good news. If she was still hysterical, I didn't see how she could help us. But it wasn't like we had much choice. "Come on, Lena."

But Lena didn't move. Her breath rasped out of her mouth, her eyes huge behind her glasses.

"Mistress, describe your symptoms," Melodie said desperately. "I probably know the antidote. I must make it."

The fork beside Lena's hand was smeared with chocolate. She had snuck a taste, and I hadn't noticed. "Oh, no."

Lena just pointed at the orange-gold door and shot me a look that clearly said, *Get going*.

Chase and I dashed around tables and vaulted over fallen Characters. We burst through the door to the instructors' quarters. Stu was sitting, slumped, at the base of the stairs.

"I couldn't go any farther," he said apologetically.

We sprinted up the steps. Halfway there we reached Hansel. He clung to the rail, trying to drag himself back to Rapunzel's door, but seeing us, he sank to his knees and raised a key. His voice was weak. "We locked her in. Why couldn't she just shout poison and be done with it?"

Chase grabbed it, and a few seconds later his feet didn't even bother touching the steps. He literally flew up the rest of the way, filling the spiral stairway with a gust of wind so strong I almost tumbled backward.

And then, clutching the rail, I had to stop for a second and try not to think about the fact that I'd almost fallen down the stairs.

Above me I heard Chase turn the lock, and the door squeak open. "Rapunzel!"

"Here. Do not shout."

She was herself again. Relief flooded through me.

"Poisoned!" Chase gasped. "Everyone."

"I understand. This process requires another ninety seconds," said Rapunzel sternly. "I've dissolved and diluted it. It will counteract any poison."

"Oh," Chase said with relief. "The ointment. The witch hair one."

She had a plan. That was what happened when you saw a future no one else did. She could react first. Sometimes she just reacted in a way that was hard to understand.

"It cannot heal them completely," Rapunzel said, like she knew we misunderstood. "It will save them tonight, and for perhaps seven nights to come, but only that. It will buy them time."

Seven days. EAS could lose almost everyone before I went back to school. And an hour ago, spring break had stretched gloriously ahead—so much time to spend free of homework, class, and Madison.

Still breathless, I leaned against the stairway wall, and a door I hadn't noticed behind me creaked open. Copper pots gleamed through the gloom. It was the same kitchen we had been cooking in earlier. This doorway must have been Rapunzel's shortcut.

Chase recovered faster than I did. "It's better than nothing. Has it been ninety seconds yet? Did I mention the dying people?"

As I stepped inside the kitchen, fear shivered up my spine.

Then I saw them, scattered everywhere—over the countertops and the floor, among all the plates, mixing bowls, and measuring cups. A few hung from the ceiling with metallic twine.

Small, round, glittering snowflakes—silver and sharp. Throwing stars.

"Rapunzel!" I knew without counting that there was one snowflake for every person in the courtyard. Only one villain left those with the bodies.

A hand dropped on my shoulder. I hadn't even heard Rapunzel's feet on the stairs. "I know, Rory. She will laugh when she learns she has ruined Mildred's big event."

Chase peeked over her shoulder, and all the blood drained from his face.

The Snow Queen.

She had poisoned everyone.

I woke up in the courtyard the next afternoon and pretended for ten wonderful seconds that last night had just been a nightmare.

Maybe I hadn't really seen hundreds of barbed snowflakes in EAS's kitchen. Maybe Rapunzel hadn't really dragged me and Chase back outside and armed us both with flasks of dark brown liquid, ripe with the smell of burned cheese.

But no. The neat lines of the tables were crooked now, after last night's panic, and Fey fudge pie lay in ruins over white plates. On the beach, past the Tree, the high table's golden cloth—lopsided now—flapped in the breeze with sharp slaps.

The night before, Rapunzel had jumped on it, her long gray braid swinging. "You are Characters! Show calm! Show courage!"

And amazingly, the crowd listened. Rapunzel ordered everyone poisoned back into their seats and everyone not poisoned to report to her for the ointment liquid, assigning them tables when they came for flasks.

I rushed my flask to Lena first. Melodie's face fell when she sniffed it, and after I helped Henry take a sip, he asked, "How long do we have?" His voice was croakier than usual.

"Seven days," I whispered, uncomfortably aware of how Mrs. Taylor's eyes bulged.

"Don't worry," Henry told her, as she drank from the flask. "We're Characters. The magic here is keeping an eye on us. A Tale will start soon and set this to rights. Half of the kids here were bed-ridden with the flu epidemic of 1918, but my father's Tale started and sent him to find a cure from his godfather—a fairy named Death."

All the grown-up Characters spread stories like that after they'd taken a sip. The Director whispered something about a scarlet-fever outbreak and a quest for a flower that only grew on the cliffs of Avalon. Gretel mentioned a kid in the year above her who searched for a unicorn after a witch clan cursed his whole grade with polio.

The idea spread across the courtyard faster than the ointment liquid: Someone's Tale was going to save us.

The infirmary was way too small for all the patients, so Rapunzel instructed us to open the ballroom. The sky blue walls, edged with gold, looked way too cheerful for a hospital.

Jenny assigned me, Ben, and Chatty bed duty, which meant that we dragged hundreds of mattresses, saved from "Princess and the Pea" Tales, out of storage.

The patients filed in faster than we could line their beds up. Some poisoned people could walk on their own, but most could only move if they were leaning heavily on someone who hadn't been poisoned. Rumpelstiltskin had to be carried, and he demanded to go to the library, where he could watch the current volume of ongoing Tales and tell us when the new one started. After helping the Italian delegate into a bed, Chase whispered, kind of out of breath, "You guys got the easy job. These people are heavy."

"Not heavier than mattresses," I hissed back.

"A mattress doesn't yell at you if you drop it," Chase pointed out darkly.

Then, when the last bed was filled, I slipped out to the Tree of Hope before Jenny could give me anything else to do, and I fell asleep, leaning against the trunk.

Of course, I hadn't meant to sleep for so long. I stood up, rubbing a crick in my neck. I didn't want to find out quite yet if I'd get in trouble for napping. I pulled my phone out of my pocket and called Mom. It rang three times, and then voice mail clicked on.

Mom's recorded voice wasn't as comforting as I'd hoped it would be.

So she wouldn't worry, I left a message. Something about how I might not be able to call that evening, because Jenny was having a party and counting on me to help. It was almost true. Except Jenny would be bossing me around the sickroom instead of her house.

The plain pine door to Ellie's storerooms creaked open.

I froze, sure that Jenny was coming to tell me off, or Chase to complain about all the chores that Jenny had made him do while I was sleeping, or Rapunzel to tell me more bad news. But it was just Chatty.

She waved at me, the trash bag in her hand billowing. She stopped and stared at the table so long that I got up to see what it was.

A seagull lay on its back between two glasses, its brown feathers perfect and still, its delicate clawed feet sticking straight up in the air. A dead robin lay a little farther down, and on the next table lay a tiny sparrow.

"What killed them?" I whispered.

Stony-faced, Chatty pointed at an abandoned plate. The fudge on top was riddled with small, cone-shaped holes—like someone had poked it with a pencil. Or maybe a beak.

The Snow Queen had done this, too.

Chatty pushed the trash bag toward me, and while I held it open, she gathered up the ends of the tablecloth. Glass shattered and silverware clinked as she dumped the whole bundle inside the bag.

The Snow Queen was still in her prison. She couldn't have come in person.

The witches. Solange must have sent one of them with the poison. The kitchen had been so crowded. They could have easily slipped it into the crust, or the eggs, or the chocolate. The food fight had been a great decoy.

Up the beanstalk last year, General Searcaster had said, "My queen has a plan for that Ever After School."

This had to be it. I had probably been there when they slipped the poison in. I'd probably been worrying about a stupid dream.

Chatty dumped a fourth tablecloth bundle into my trash bag. Then she waved a hand in my face until I looked at her. She half smiled, her eyes shining with sympathy, and I knew exactly what she was telling me: *It'll be okay, Rory.*

But what if this was how I was supposed to stop the Snow Queen? What if my destiny had been to spot the poison? What if I'd failed already?

Across the courtyard, Lena rushed out from the workshop's double steel doors. "Rory! There you are!" She didn't look like someone who'd been near death the night before.

I frowned. "Aren't you supposed to stay still? Rapunzel said the poison would spread faster if you moved around a lot."

"Yeah, but I just had the teensiest, tiniest bite. Seriously. Like this big." Lena pinched her finger and thumb together so close they nearly touched. In the bag at her hip, Melodie clutched a neon-green backpack and glanced up anxiously at her mistress. The harp was being a lot quieter than normal. "That's barely enough to kill me."

I wished she wouldn't joke. She hadn't heard herself. The

breath rattling out of her throat hadn't even sounded human.

"Rumpel just transferred to the infirmary, and I overheard what he told Rapunzel. The new Tale started—a quest. We have maybe four minutes before everybody comes out here, but I want you to have these." Lena took the neon-green backpack from Melodie and held it out. "First, a brand-new carryall. And this." From her pocket she pulled out what looked like a silvery gumdrop. It was uncomfortably sticky when she stuck it in my hand.

I wrinkled my nose. "Please don't tell me that I have to eat it."

"Of course not. You put it in your ear, like headphones. It's a translator. The other chapters use them—all of them besides us and Australia. None of the other continents share a common language," she explained. "You know, like in Asia it's Thai and Mandarin and Japanese and so on. I improved this one. I added Fey, and Goblin, and most of Elvish and Dwarvish, and some Troll—although I didn't get any Ogre."

Well, that explained a lot. I'd thought Lena had learned Fey kind of fast last summer.

"It turns out they don't have any Ogre-English dictionaries," Lena continued. "That's how you make it. You basically cook the language dictionaries down like fruits for jam, but you add phoenix feathers or dragon scales instead of sugar. And this"—Lena dropped a lunch box on the seat of the nearest chair, the boxy plastic kind that elementary schoolers used—"is a Lunch Box of Plenty. It's the same as a Table of Plenty, but more portable. Instructions are inside."

I stared at the pink ponies on the front, waiting for her to tell me why she was sharing all her favorite inventions. Maybe her brush with death had affected her more than I thought.

"Ignore the sticker. I had to run through a bunch of lunch boxes in the experimenting phase, and this just happened to be one that worked. I would make you a prettier one, but we don't have time before you go on the quest."

I stared at her. I could only think of one reason why I would go on a quest. "You mean it's my Tale?"

I was waiting for my Tale to start, just like almost everyone else, but I didn't want it like this—not with everyone's life at stake.

"No, it's Ben Taylor's," said Melodie.

Poor Ben. He was having an exceptionally tough first week.

Lena spread out a few mini magic mirrors. "I'm volunteering all of these, but I want you to keep one. So we can talk while you're traveling."

She tried to pass me a mirror, but I wouldn't take it. "If it's Ben's Tale, shouldn't you give this stuff to him?"

A bell rang out, echoing through the empty courtyard.

"He'll ask you to be his Companion." Lena shoved the lunch box in the green carryall, the sticky translator in my ear, and the M3 in my hand.

Assuming I would go was kind of like counting your dragon scales before they fell off. Being a Tale's Companion was a coveted honor. I had only been on Lena's. "But Ben doesn't know me at all."

"He barely knows anyone, but you and Chase saved his life," Lena pointed out.

The door to the ballroom infirmary opened. Only thirty people filed out, but just like with a regular Tale, everyone was making guesses about whose Tale it was and what it might be. Ben looked a little paler than normal—I couldn't tell if he knew it was his Tale.

Chase came through the orange-gold door to the apartments, yawning, which meant I wasn't the only one who'd snuck a few hours' sleep.

"Is your dad coming back?" I asked him.

He rubbed his face. "No. He's still in northern Muirland, touring dwarf cities. The Director said not to tell him. The dwarves aren't always friendly and Dad's not great at keeping secrets." That was an understatement. A few glasses of Fey mead in the Glass Mountain and Jack started telling the Snow Queen about every mission he'd been sent on. "We'll be in danger if word gets out."

"Why?" I said. Asking for help seemed like a really good idea to me.

"If you were planning a hostile takeover of EAS, this would be a good time," Chase said. "Now, important question: Why are so many girls healthy? I feel outnumbered."

I glanced into the crowd. Only four people gathered around the Tree were guys: Ben himself, Kenneth, Chase, and a tiny fifth grader who was huddled on the roots, crying but trying not to be obvious about it.

Darcy snorted. "Guess how many of them are on a diet."

Then the library door opened. Out came Rapunzel, carrying something headstone-size and bound in brilliant orange leather. She'd had a hard night: Her silver braid—half-unraveled—trailed along the grass, picking up twigs and leaves. Her lips were parted as if in wonder or fear. My stomach knotted. This was one of Rapunzel's bad days.

She dropped the book in my arms. I staggered. This one book was twice as heavy as my backpack.

"The necessary knowledge is inside," she said.

It was like she'd used up all her making sense-quota for the month the night before, and she'd returned to the regular, slightly insane version. It was hard not to feel abandoned.

"But that's the current volume," squeaked Lena. "It's never supposed to leave the library. None of Rumpel's books are."

"Rumpel is not here." Rapunzel pulled her braid over her shoulder and picked leaves out of it. "Books are mobile. Children are ungainly. A collection of children is a crowd."

There was a stunned silence, and EASers all across the courtyard exchanged freaked-out glances. "Oh, my gumdrops," breathed Lena.

"Is this normal?" Ben asked.

"Yeah. Well, kind of," muttered Chase.

"She meant," I said, feeling as impatient as Rapunzel looked, "it's easier to bring Rumpel's book out here than crowd us all in the library."

"Oh, good," Jenny said, relieved. "Rory, act as translator."

I rolled my eyes. Rapunzel wasn't that hard to understand.

Rapunzel gestured to the book with both hands. "Rory, the necessary knowledge."

"You mean, the Tale? The one that'll save everyone, right?" I asked hesitantly.

"Yes," Rapunzel said.

Kenneth stared hard at the book, like he was trying to develop X-ray vision. Jenny's hands were clasped in front of her, so tightly all her knuckles paled. Even Mia's eyes gleamed.

I struggled to open the book, but it was three feet tall. "Chase, help!" I said, and he grabbed one side. "Lena, you'll need to read. We can't see it from this angle."

"But . . ." Lena's voice was tiny. She glanced toward the library. "Rumpelstiltskin—"

"He ate two and a half slices of pie," said Jenny, "and then he stayed up all night watching the book. He won't be much help to anyone right now."

So Lena reached for the corner of the page and flipped carefully to the current Tale. Her voice trembled. "'Poison snuck into Ever After School and lurked in the most innocuous of food—the dessert. Many fingers were pointed, many enemies named, but in truth the poison was delivered by one hand and one hand only: that of the Snow Queen.'"

Thirty-some voices in the courtyard started asking questions, and Jenny's was loudest. "But how? How did the Snow Queen poison us? When did it happen?"

All eyes shifted to Rapunzel, who shrugged. "These questions lie in the past."

"It's still important. She had to send someone to do it," Jenny said, hands on her hips. "That someone could still be here, waiting to finish the job."

This was a very good point.

"The Snow Queen? Still here?" squeaked a weepy ninth grader.

"The witches," Chase said suddenly.

"But they're just as sick as everybody else," Jenny said.

"Ever heard of a little thing called a suicide mission?" Chase replied.

"Those questions don't interest me now. We must concern ourselves with the future. One week is all we have." Rapunzel tapped the volume Chase and I held, so violently that we nearly dropped it.

"Keep going," I whispered to Lena.

"'Among the poisoned invalids was one Betsy Taylor, and her son, Ben—'"

"Me?" said Ben. So he hadn't known when he'd come out.

"'—vowed at her bedside to do everything he could to save her. And only one thing could be done: He would have to draw the Water of Life from its spring.'"

"Wow. Three days, and it's already your Tale." Kenneth

obviously was torn between being jealous and sucking up. "Congratulations, man."

"I'm glad it is you," Rapunzel told Ben. "Steadiness is strength too."

Ben swallowed hard, trying to keep his cool. "I don't remember the procedure from orientation. I'm afraid you'll need to walk me through the whole Tale process."

But Rapunzel had clearly decided the normal routine wasn't for her. She dropped a hand on my head. "You still know nothing of your future. Listen for what people do not say." A flush crept over my face, the way it always did when I was the center of attention. Geez, Ben hadn't even asked me to be his Companion yet. "Where others see a wall, or a mountain range, you see an escape. She will attack you with words," she added, and I knew she was talking about the Snow Queen.

I wondered if I could ever go on a quest and just have to worry about the quest, not some stupid vague Destiny.

Ben poked Rapunzel's shoulder. "How do I save Mother?"

"Secrecy can be a shield, but it can also slow the arrival of help—and healing," Rapunzel said, looking at Chase.

"Wait. Are you just talking about Chase?" I asked Rapunzel. "Or are you talking about EAS's defenses being down?"

"Yes," she said.

I sighed. These had to be the kind of statements that made sense later.

"But someone should know of Cal," she told Chase, and he paled.

"Well, we shouldn't be telling a bunch of people that we're unprotected," said Jenny. "Ben, pay attention who you tell."

"You don't need to mention the poisoning. The 'Water of Life' Tale always has an illness in it, but usually it's only localized to one person," Lena said thoughtfully. "The mother or father of the Tale bearer. No one should suspect everyone is sick."

"Maybe if you explained this step-by-step," Ben said to Rapunzel.

Jenny answered. "You leave EAS and search for the Water of Life. Before you go, you need to know about the past 'Water of Life' Tales. Do you have them, Rapunzel?"

"History will not help you," said Rapunzel. "The tapestry of the Tales has been ripped apart and restitched."

Jenny put her hands on her hips, so I said quickly, "This Tale will be very different from the others." The Tales were changing. The grown-ups had been saying that ever since I first came to EAS.

Lena's sister had apparently taken it upon herself to be a substitute grown-up. "Rapunzel, did you even look up the five most recent ones?"

"They will not help." Rapunzel sounded just as exasperated. It was hard to be in charge when a fifteen-year-old was bossier than you. "Those Tales Failed."

Everyone stiffened, so much that Ben noticed. "What? What does that mean?"

"EAS is so doomed," Chase whispered to me, and I elbowed him.

"It means the quest will be hard," Jenny said gently.

"Those who quested for the Water never returned," said Rapunzel.

Ben gulped. Chatty patted his shoulder.

"Okay. Lena, what's the textbook definition of the Water of Life?" Jenny asked.

"Substance or Tale?" Lena said.

"Substance first."

"'The Water of Life is pure magic in liquid form,'" Lena said in the tinny voice she used only when she was reciting something from her photographic memory. "'It can be used to power many level-seven spells and enchantments, but its most common function is healing. One teaspoon of the undiluted substance will heal any and all injuries and/or illnesses. It originates only from an enchanted spring, whose location changes every thirteenth moon.'"

"No one knows where it is?" Ben whispered, horrified.

"The lost and fabled continent waits for you, full of Fey and prisons," said Rapunzel.

For a beat, no one said anything. I didn't get that one either.

Lena flipped the page of Rapunzel's book. "'The spring waited for him on the shores of Atlantis. Its path led inland, marked by two crossed pines.'"

"That doesn't sound too terrible," Ben said slowly.

"Uh. Don't you remember how big Atlantis is? As in the biggest hidden continent in the world? One and a half times the size of Australia?" Chase said.

"No," said Ben, disbelieving. "Someone would have noticed. Satellites."

"It's glamoured. If it were glamoured any more, it would be invisible," Chase said. "And it moves all around the Pacific Ocean."

"Isn't there anything else in the book he can go on?" Jenny asked Lena, who shook her head. The rest of the page was blank. The Tale was still writing itself.

"The winds may know more." I thought for a minute Rapunzel was telling Ben to follow the breeze wherever it blew, but then she added, "The West Wind is the friendliest."

"The West Wind is kind of a person. Characters sometimes go ask him stuff," I explained to Ben.

"Lena, what happens in the 'Water of Life' Tale?" Jenny asked.

"Well, there are two major variations. In the first, a king's daughter is dying, and a celebrated physician—" Lena stopped.

Rapunzel was shaking her head so hard that her long braid lashed behind her like a cat's tail.

"Wow, the briefing for this Tale feels exactly like twenty questions," said Darcy.

Only Jenny seemed undaunted. "And the other?"

"A father falls ill," Lena said uncertainly, "and four brothers go on a quest one after the other. They don't come back. The sister takes up the quest."

Now Rapunzel nodded.

"I'm an only child," Ben said.

"Siblings will not fall," said Rapunzel. "Your Companions will."

I didn't need to translate that. Every Character in the courtyard had second thoughts about volunteering.

"What's a Companion again?" Ben asked.

"Since it's a quest, you've allowed to pick other Characters who travel with you," Jenny explained. "They help. You can pick two of them. Anyone not poisoned."

"Four," corrected Rapunzel.

"The Director only lets us pick two—" Jenny said.

"Of the last fifteen quests into Atlantis, none returned uninjured," said Rapunzel. "Ben shall choose four."

"But EAS is only allowed three Characters per quest," Chase said. "The Fey will get cranky if Ben takes more. And by cranky I mean they'll call it an invasion, capture Ben and company, and throw them in prison for seven years."

Ben paled a little more. Yeah, this Tale was sounding better and better.

"No, there's some fine print in the contract the Director and the Unseelie King signed." Lena's voice changed to her tinny reciting one. "'Characters of four or more traveling in Atlantis will have three sunrises to reach the Unseelie Court and request permission to stay longer on the Continent.'"

"Okay, so four Companions," Jenny prompted.

Ben glanced over the crowd.

Lena had a point. Ben didn't really know anyone. It would suck to know that your mom's life—hundreds of lives—depended on your Tale, and only strangers could help you.

"Kenneth," said Ben suddenly.

Kenneth smirked a little, walking forward. He had expected this.

"Chase and Rory," Ben said next.

Lena smiled in a way that clearly said, *I told you so*. Chase propelled me forward, straight to Ben's side.

Kenneth watched us, clearly thinking he thought a rock troll would be a better Companion than a seventh grader. "We don't have to bring Rory. Just her sword."

Chase and I both scowled at him.

"One more, Ben," Jenny said.

"Ummmm . . ." Ben's face went crimson. "Mia."

The crowd parted. Her face was as pretty and still as a sculpture.

Rapunzel drew a ribbon out of her pocket. The rings tied to it glowed neon blue.

"Rings of return," Chase said, for Ben's benefit. "They will bring us back to the courtyard if we put them on."

"One for each." Rapunzel passed the ribbon to me. Which meant that I got the fun task of painstakingly unknotting the ribbon to free each ring. "You shall use it if you are injured. Any injury and you return here so I may send someone else in your place," said Rapunzel.

Kenneth looked like he might protest. Usually, EASers only returned if they were in life-threatening situations.

"Four hundred seventy-three lives depend on this quest," Rapunzel added. "My precautions are necessary."

So she had thought this through, despite how weird she sounded.

Lena gasped. "I almost forgot! The spring Water only works if you've gone on the whole quest and if you seek a cure for a sick blood relative. If someone else does it, the magic might reverse, and it might kill you."

I grimaced. "Got it. Don't touch the water before Ben brings it out."

"So even if he gets hurt, he still gets to keep going?" Kenneth said, like this was unfair.

Personally I thought three trained Companions would be enough to keep him safe. I was more concerned about Mia. This would probably not be a good time to bring up my beheading dream.

Rapunzel regarded Kenneth coolly. "The violence of your temper will be outmatched. Be prepared. For some battles, swords will be no use. Only fire can fight fire. Only wind can fight wind."

That shut Kenneth up.

Closing her eyes, Rapunzel drew in a long breath and then released it just as slowly. When she opened her eyes, her gaze was dark and piercing once again. She had literally pulled herself together. Whatever she said next would make all the other insanity fall into place.

"Now we need something, behind the purple and lilac door on the western side," she told Jenny, who rushed away.

Or maybe not.

"Wait, I have a question," Ben said. "What happens if we take longer than three days and the Fey don't give us permission to stay? Do we just send two people back?"

Jenny returned, carrying an armful of packs and weapons. I recognized my sword belt and took it off her hands. Chase and Kenneth reached for the other two, as Jenny passed a spear to Ben and a staff to Mia.

"It is nearly impossible for a human to get what they want in Fey deals. Allow Chase to negotiate," Rapunzel said. "He has some experience with the Unseelie Court."

My head whipped around. Chase looked grim, but unsurprised. "Not to mention I'm the only one here fluent in their language. And the king kind of likes me."

With a small smirk, Lena met my eyes and tapped her ear, as if to say, *That's right. You'll need that magic translator*.

"The king is touring at the moment," said Rapunzel. "Now on his throne is his son. He owes you a favor, yes?"

Chase said, almost angrily, "No way. I was saving that for something really good."

Rapunzel's dark eyes narrowed.

"Right. Saving four hundred seventy-three lives." Chase sighed dramatically. "Totally worth it."

"Okay, loyal Companions. Ready?" Ben said.

"No!" screamed someone across the Courtyard, and we all turned.

For a second I thought somebody's wicked stepmother was leaning around the doorway, but no—it was the Director. Her hair tufted out in a tangled blond clump above her right ear, and her lips were swollen to twice their normal size. I had never seen her look less than perfect.

It scared me, I realized as Lena drew closer to me, the Director looking so awful. On a healthy day she would never have let people see her like this. She must have eaten a lot of pie.

The Director clung to the doorknob, taking great wheezing breaths. "This is a mistake. Ben's Tale is too important. You need adult supervision. We should call Jack back, or recruit help from other chapters—"

"It's okay. We had an adult." Jenny pointed at Rapunzel.

"Rapunzel will send you into danger—poison—her sister's—" The Director's voice gave out, like her lungs had reached their limit. I couldn't tell what freaked her out more—not having control of the quest or not breathing.

Ben adjusted the straps of his pack self-importantly. "Well, I'm sorry to disobey you, Director, but I'm going. We don't have time to wait. We only have seven days."

Then he opened the nearest door and took a half step forward until he realized where the door led—to a wall of water. Like an actual wall, the same as you see on the ground floor of an aquarium, except without glass. A school of silvery fish swam by.

"That's our special entrance to the MerKing's realm. The door to Atlantis is over there." Chase jerked his thumb across the courtyard.

"Oh, are they different?" Ben said. "I thought that each door took you wherever you wanted to go."

All the fight left the Director at once, and she sagged against the door frame. "You're too inexperienced."

"I would argue with you," Ben said, walking in the direction Chase had pointed, "but my excuses would be all washed up."

My mouth twitched. Kenneth snickered. Chase opened the door to Atlantis, ebony with silver hinges, and said, "Do I even need to tell you how cheesy that was?"

From here Atlantis looked like a creepy forest with black, crooked trees.

Lena hugged me suddenly, squeezing so tightly I felt her bony arms dig into my ribs. I didn't want to go without her. Over her shoulder I saw Ben step through the doorway with a prom-king sort of wave, and Mia hurry after him.

Lena drew back. Her cheeks were wet. "Rory . . ."

It wasn't fair. This spring break should have been the longest, best, most junk-food-filled sleepover in the history of Lena-and-Rory-kind. The Snow Queen had ruined it.

"Do me a favor?" I pulled my phone out of my pocket and pressed it into Lena's hands. "Text my mom every night? Around dinnertime? It'll keep her from worrying about me." Well, for a few days, anyway.

Lena swallowed and nodded. Melodie retrieved a tissue from somewhere in the bag and passed it up to her mistress.

Kenneth shoved Chase out of the way so he could be the next in, and then Chase stomped through too.

Rapunzel firmly escorted me to the door, bending down to whisper, "He'll fall under enchantment."

"Who?" I said, alarmed. I hadn't forgotten the stone soldier from the day before.

"Chase and Ben," Rapunzel whispered. "Chase is easy. Stay close to him. You'll know when. Skin-to-skin contact is best. But it happens twice."

"And Ben?"

She shrugged. "All I see is glass."

The Director roused herself. "What is she telling you, Rory? You can't trust her. She has ulterior motives."

Ulterior motives? Rapunzel, who'd just saved us all? I couldn't believe the Director would stoop so low to keep control of EAS.

"And beware the doll," Rapunzel added.

Chase's head reappeared in the Atlantis doorway. "Rory—you coming?"

"What doll?" I tried to ignore Chase, but he grabbed my wrist.

"I don't know," Rapunzel said sadly, and Chase yanked me into Atlantis.

8

We didn't get the welcome we were hoping for. For one thing, the time difference was crazy. It was *night* in Atlantis, but the moon hung full and low. The forest we'd stumbled into was bathed in silvery light, and we could kind of see branches zigzagging from one tree to the next, tangling together and surrounding us with a fence of black bark. I only spotted two openings. One path wound farther into the forest. The other way—bright with moonlight—led out to a grassy and open meadow.

I knew which path *I* wanted to take, but that was a decision for the quest leader.

"Something's wrong with this forest," Ben whispered. Behind him Mia's eyes were wide.

Chase put his hand on his sword hilt, and I did too.

"No kidding," Kenneth said. "Check out those leaves. Don't they look like they're a weird color?"

"No. I mean, why aren't the birds singing?" Ben hissed.

"We should—" Mia started.

The branch behind her moved. It was so unexpected that I didn't totally believe it, even as the branch snaked across the ground toward Ben's leg.

"Watch it!" Chase shoved the new kid out of the way. The blunt, twiggy fingers snagged on Ben's jeans and tore off a big chunk. The branch whooshed upward and released the fabric about twenty feet up. It seesawed through the air like a feather.

"It thought it had you," Chase told Ben. "It wanted to drop you on your head."

A branch from another tree darted out, its sharp end stabbing toward Ben's back. My runner's high flared, and I slashed down hard. I expected the blade to slice straight through the wood, but it didn't. A terrific clang rang out. The branch pierced the forest floor with a thud we felt through our shoes.

We all backed away.

"Did you hear that?" I asked.

The trees heard it. They must have, because suddenly the whole forest woke up, tree limbs writhing like a mass of snakes.

"We have a few seconds," Mia said, freakishly calm. "The branches are still untangling themselves."

"That way. Now." Chase pointed down the shadowy path.

"What? Who put you in charge?" Kenneth drew his sword.

Ben was skeptical too. "Isn't that way faster?" He pointed to the brighter path.

Chase grabbed a rock on the forest floor and threw it. At first I thought he was just losing his temper, but when the rock hit the moonlight, the meadow vanished. A pit stood in its place, riddled with spikes and full suits of rusted armor.

"Rule number 1 about Atlantis—nothing is what it seems," Chase said, annoyed. He stepped six inches to the side, and a branch whizzed over his shoulder. He pointed down the creepy path with his sword. "Everybody down the middle."

It was like running a gauntlet. As soon as one branch unwound from another, it sped directly at our heads. Kenneth, Chase, and I could dodge, but Mia and Ben . . .

I shoved Ben behind me and deflected a branch away from his face for the third time. "This isn't working!" I told Chase.

"What else do you want to do?" Kenneth slashed at a branch that tried to grab Mia's hair. "Lie down and play dead?"

That was obviously Mia's plan. She'd cowered down and covered her head with both arms.

"We split up. Give them two targets." Chase hacked at an incoming branch, knocking it out of the way before it wrapped itself around Ben's arm. "Rory, get Ben out of here."

Ben opened his mouth, probably to say he wouldn't leave Mia, but I grabbed his wrist and sprinted. The trees didn't come after us. They kept stabbing at the ground Ben and I had just vacated. Only one branch lashed into our path—I just dragged Ben around it and raced to the edge of the forest.

"Trees!" Ben said breathlessly, as I shoved him out of the woods and into a rocky clearing. On the other side were normal-looking oaks. "Trying to kill us!"

"Yep." I ushered him out of branches'—I mean harm's—reach. I glanced back, worried for the others. "Are you hurt, Ben?"

"No. But the trees!"

"Technically, they're not trees," Chase said from somewhere behind us. A second later he, Mia, and Kenneth stumbled out into the open. Kenneth had a scratch on his forehead, but otherwise they were all unhurt. "It's a witch forest. Its sensor spell sucks, though. It takes a while for the trees to notice that you've moved."

"How do you know it was witches? Couldn't it be those Unseelie people?" It was hard to look at Mia with a straight face.

It looked like something had made a nest in her long hair.

"Nah, the branches are made of iron," said Chase. "The Fey can't touch iron. A witch clan set these up to annoy the Fey. We just had the bad luck to find a new one. We'll tell Ellie to move the entrance to Atlantis when this is all over."

"Do you really think it was a coincidence?" I said. "Maybe Kezelda told someone to plant one here. Maybe she knew we'd come to Atlantis for a cure."

Chase just shrugged, but he looked a little worried.

"Witch forests." Ben sat on a German shepherd–size boulder. "Great."

"You need to buck up, man," Kenneth said. "We're going to see a lot worse here in Atlantis."

"Give me a break," Ben snapped. "Four days ago I had no idea magic was real. Since then, griffins attacked me, someone poisoned my mom, and now freaking trees are coming to life. I am not used to stuff trying to kill me all the time. As long as I can still move, I'd say I'm coping pretty well."

I grimaced sympathetically, but Chase said, "I guess I shouldn't tell you trolls set up traps in chair-shaped rocks, right?"

Ben tumbled out of his seat, and Chase and Kenneth both laughed.

"Everybody knows that trolls are too stupid to set up traps," Kenneth said.

Normally, I would've told Chase this wasn't the time for teasing, but Ben laughed too. "Geez, Mia. Stop being so calm. You came to EAS after me, and I didn't hear you scream once."

Mia smiled and tucked some hair behind her ear. She was either really shy or not very smart, but Ben smiled back in a gooey sort of way.

"What time is it here?" I asked, mainly because I was wondering what we should do next.

"A few hours before sunrise," Chase said, so quickly that I wondered if he'd just made an answer up.

"Now, I understand that hundreds of lives are in danger, but I'm going to suggest that we stop for the rest of the night," said Ben. "I could use some R and R."

Chase slung off his pack. "You're in charge."

But Kenneth didn't think we'd had enough adventures yet. "What's the point in sleeping if we'll need to be up in a few hours anyway?"

"If we keep traveling west, we'll get caught smack-dab in Morgian's Glen in the dark," Chase said.

"So?" said Kenneth.

"So, Morgian's Glen is a big pile of moss-covered rocks. If we can't see where we're going, we could easily break a leg." Chase unzipped his bag and rummaged inside.

"Unless you want to get hurt and use your ring of return?" I said. "I'm sure Rapunzel would be happy to swap you out."

"No more of that," Ben told me, as pompously as my school principal. "We're a team. We're never going to survive Atlantis if we fight each other."

"Besides, we have much bigger problems than Morgian's Glen." Chase had been searching our carryalls with growing horror. "I'm pretty sure that Rapunzel forgot to pack us any food."

I found the Lunch Box of Plenty in my bag and handed it over.

"This has to be some sort of sick joke. There can't possibly be enough food in here for five," Chase said.

"It's a Lunch Box of Plenty," I told him. "Lena said she put instructions in it."

"Oooooh." The boys crowded around.

Chase unsnapped the latches and grabbed the folded paper inside. "'Lunch Box, fill yourself,'" he read. "With a double-bacon cheeseburger."

A paper-wrapped, sandwich-size circle appeared in the lunch box—smelling of beef and bacon and grease. Chase picked the burger up and unwrapped it, barely noticing when Kenneth snatched the lunch box out of his hands. "I take back every mean thing I said about Lena being a mad scientist. This is the best invention ever."

We passed the Lunch Box of Plenty around. Then we set up camp, stretched our sleeping bags out side by side, and flopped on top of them. It still felt too early for bedtime, but considering how little rest we'd gotten the night before, it was also kind of necessary.

"Who's going to take first watch?" Chase said. "I'm gonna go out on a limb and suggest it shouldn't be Kenneth."

Kenneth couldn't keep his eyes open. He had pretty much fallen asleep sitting up.

"I'll take it." I probably couldn't sleep anyway. I was too busy trying to figure out whether Kezelda had dumped the poison before or after I'd entered the kitchen.

So I sat down on the rock and nibbled on my grilled cheese.

"I'll help you," Chase said, ordering himself a second burger from the Lunch Box of Plenty. I wondered how many meals he planned on eating. "We should probably have two guards on the first watch tonight. Until we're sure the witches' forest won't pick up their roots and ambush us in our sleep."

Ben laughed briefly—until he saw Chase's face. "Oh. You're not joking."

Kenneth crawled into his sleeping bag. "Fantastic," he said, his sarcasm slurred with drowsiness.

Chase found a seat beside me, and we ate in silence. I thought about EAS, and if Lena was about ready to go to sleep too, and if Jenny was driving her crazy yet. I wondered if getting poisoned was painful, and if it was, whether or not the witches regretted the suicide mission. I wondered if I could have done anything to stop them. I would have loved to distract myself and interrogate Chase, but even though I had a few thousand questions about his mom, I didn't ask. He was too touchy about being half Fey.

For a while the only noise I heard was Kenneth's snores and an owl hooting.

"Chase—" I wanted to know if he needed anything else from the Lunch Box before I packed it up.

"Ben's still awake," he whispered back. Clearly, he thought I wanted to ask something a lot more important.

I glanced over to the sleeping bags. Ben was lying down, but his eyes glinted in the dark, glassy with far-off thoughts.

Chase crossed over to the others and snapped his fingers in Ben's face to get his attention. "You've got to stop worrying, man. It'll be fine. We'll save your mom. You won't lose both of them."

My best friend wasn't exactly known to be sensitive. So I didn't figure out he really meant Ben's father until Ben asked, "Who did you lose?"

Chase hesitated. He knew I was listening. "My older brother. *Half* brother."

If I'd had any grilled cheese left, I would have choked on it.

I'd never even suspected Chase had any siblings.

Family tragedies turned up a lot at EAS. One fifth grader's father had Failed his Tale late—right after she was born. He hadn't made it. But usually, the death of a Character's parents didn't have anything to do with a Tale. Tina had lost her mom to cancer, and Vicky's dad had broken his neck skiing.

I'd learned about Lena's parents in September when someone's father had showed up in a lab coat, and Lena had watched him cross the courtyard with tears in her eyes. "My parents used to wear those." She had been four when they'd died in a car accident and her gran had taken over.

Chase didn't look at me when he came back, and I was kind of glad. I didn't know if I was supposed to say something, especially since he hadn't been talking to me. Especially since he had never even hinted about it before.

After a few minutes, Ben's low breathing joined Kenneth's snores. They were all asleep.

"So." Chase sounded extra hearty. Even he knew this wasn't a normal conversation starter. "What was it like, growing up human?"

I snorted. "Is this supposed to be a philosophical question?"

"No. It was what Ben said." He examined his hands. "I don't remember not knowing somebody might try to kill me. Dad has a great story about convincing a giant to stop halfway down a beanstalk so that he could change my diaper."

Chase had never had a normal kid life. The list of things I didn't know about my best friend just kept growing.

After an awkward silence, Chase said, kind of put out, "Aren't you going to ask me anything?"

"I didn't think you would answer."

"Rapunzel said I shouldn't keep secrets anymore, so . . ." He shrugged.

I dredged up the memory. *Secrecy can be a shield, but it can also slow the arrival of help—and healing,* she'd told Chase.

Ice washed down my spine. I was supposed to help him? But this was too big for me.

I had to say something. I decided to start with the easiest, least emotional question. "Okay, what was this favor the prince dude owed you?"

I expected Chase to get all smug and tell me about the time that he had saved the prince from drowning in an enchanted pool or something, but Chase just got even more uncomfortable.

"Prince Fael locked me in the Unseelie crypt. When they found me, days later, the king—Fael's father—asked me if he had done it. I'd watched Fael literally throw away the key, but I said no. Fael had been in and out of trouble all year. One more thing and he would've either lost his crown prince title, gotten banished, or been turned into a tree. That same night, Iron Hans escaped and stole the scepter of the Birch clan from the mirror vault, so everybody assumed he'd done it. Nobody even suspected Fael. I could be beheaded for lying to a Fey monarch, so they get out of the habit of being suspicious. And since the Fey can't lie, it's usually not an issue. But . . ."

But he wasn't totally a fairy—and now Fael was in his debt. "But why would he mess with you in the first place?" I asked. "Just general evilness?"

Chase scratched the back of his head. "When he turned the lock, he said something about his sister. I was the last one to see her before the Snow Queen killed her and my brother, Cal. They were betrothed."

A memory lurked in the back of my brain. Something about Solange and the Unseelie princess. Lena would have already figured it out. "His sister," I repeated slowly.

An instant later the puzzle clicked into place. Lena had told this story too: The Snow Queen had killed the princess and her betrothed. Their death had angered the Fey so much that they had joined the fight. It had turned the tide of the war.

Lena had told me this last year. Chase had *been* there when she told me.

"You never said anything," I whispered. "You didn't even flinch when Lena was telling the story."

He shrugged again, leaning back slightly, like he was shrinking away from all the emotion in my voice. "I grew up in the Unseelie Court. If you can't hide your emotions, you don't survive."

Lady Aspenwind wasn't just borderline nuts. She was grieving. She was afraid that Chase would die too—

I shoved my sympathy away. Chase didn't want me to make a big deal over it.

I focused on some pretty obvious math. Chase had just turned thirteen, and the war had been a couple decades ago. I was about to ask if his brother had been a time-traveling fairy, but Chase rambled off an explanation. He sounded so matter-of-fact he reminded me of Lena when she recited something from her photographic memory:

"Halflings age like whichever parent they live with. Fey children age whenever their parents decide it's okay. If they cast a certain spell at dawn, the Fey child grows for the next twenty-four hours. If the spell isn't cast, they don't age at all.

"Babyhood and toddlerhood usually go by pretty fast for Fey kids, because even fairies don't like dirty diapers or temper tantrums. Ages four and five last longer.

"Amya really loved five. I turned five the year before Cal died," Chase added, "and Amya had parties for my fifth birthday every year until I lived with Dad. It all kind of blurs together. You don't remember things as well when you don't grow."

I didn't know what bothered me more: the fact that turning a year older every 365 days was apparently a luxury, or that one of my best friends was an old man. Definitely more of a shock than finding out he was half fairy.

If Lena had been here, she could have smoothed this over by asking about all these details: what the components of the aging spell were, if his fingernails grew when he didn't turn a day older. But Chase would have hated that. He would have felt like one of her experiments.

Chase would want me to treat him exactly the same. "If you're so old," I asked, "how come you're so immature?"

When Chase laughed, I felt like I'd won a prize. I'd said the right thing again. Maybe I *could* handle this.

"Thanks, Rory," he said in the voice he used when he was trying to sound sarcastic but he really wasn't.

I didn't tell Chase I was sorry about his brother, but I really wanted to.

So instead I answered his earlier question, the one about growing up human. The story Mom always told about when I was four: She put me down for a nap when I wanted to go to the park, so as soon as she was asleep, I opened the front door and walked five blocks to the nearest playground. On the first day of kindergarten, I was extremely jealous of a little girl with long braided pigtails because she could tie her shoes all by herself and I couldn't. But then she showed me how, by the swings during recess, and Marta and I were best friends for the next four years. How Marta fell out of a tree and broke her arm in second grade, and how I made a pretend bandage out of paper towels when she came back to school, so we could both have casts. How in third grade Mom and Dad couldn't talk to each other at all unless they were arguing. How after they decided they needed a divorce, our house turned as quiet and polite as a museum, where no one spoke at all unless they had a question: "Have you seen my car keys?" or "Will you sign this permission slip?"

It wasn't anything particularly meaningful, just some random memories, but Chase stared out into the witch forest, eyebrows pinched together, even after my voice drifted off. The moon had risen higher while we'd been talking, casting strange shadows, making his face seem more angular, less familiar, less human. It was like—

Well, it was like someone had taken away my best friend and left some weird, distant fairy in his place.

He was one of the best friends I'd ever had, but he'd spent years and years at the Unseelie Court before he'd met me. He'd had a whole lifetime before I was even born. I might not be as important to him as he was to me.

He might leave. He might go back to the Unseelie Court.

I fell asleep leaning against the troll-trap stone, so clearly it didn't bother me too much yet.

I knew I was dreaming as soon as I saw Mia—her eyes closed, her lashes casting long shadows over her cheeks. Her dark hair was still lovingly combed out, her expression serene.

On the table her head stood not on its neck, but on a marble pedestal shaped like shoulders, like she was one of those old-fashioned busts you sometimes see in libraries. My dream self stepped closer, and I could see an arm lying beside the pedestal—Mia's arm. Whoever had cut off her head had also cut up her body into little pieces.

Bile rose in my throat at about the same time as someone shook my shoulder. I opened my eyes and almost threw up all over Chase's shirt.

"You know, there's a sleeping bag over there with your name on it." Chase nodded back at the rows of sleeping figures.

I bolted awake. "The watch!"

"It ended a while ago," Chase said. "I'll wake up Kenneth for the next one. But seriously, your name is stitched on. Lena must have snuck it in there. It's probably an untested prototype. If it starts smelling too strongly of dragon scales, I would get out. It might ignite."

"Well," I said, stepping carefully over the others, "with that cheery thought, I'll sleep really well. Night."

"Night, Rory." Our eyes met. Things were different between us, and we both knew it. We weren't exactly being polite, but we were being careful—like we didn't know what to expect.

I crawled into the empty sleeping bag by my pack, and couldn't help but let out a small, satisfied sigh. I didn't feel one stone, not one bump. It was as soft and yielding as any of the mattresses in the houses Mom rented. Enchanted sleeping bags—definitely a Lena LaMarelle invention.

The worst part about the new Chase was that I couldn't talk it over with Lena. She would know exactly what to think about him. She would be able to guess when things would get back to normal.

We all agreed, the next morning, that we should go find the West Wind right away.

It got a little more complicated after we carefully climbed through Morgian's Glen, a tiny, lumpy valley so green that it looked like it was covered in emerald felt. Beside the dirt path at the glen's bottom, we realized that nobody knew where the West Wind lived.

"I would guess . . . west," said Mia in her quiet way, so deadpan that it was impossible to tell if she was being sarcastic or if she thought she'd said something helpful.

I shook the thought out of my head. I couldn't believe I was so snarky. Her head would end up on a marble pedestal.

"Evan said he passed the West Wing's palace. It was near the Twilfark Hills," said Kenneth.

"Evan spent most of his time in Atlantis in a troll's cage," Chase pointed out in his *you're the biggest idiot on the whole hidden continent* voice. "Do you really think we should follow his directions?"

"I trust his directions more than you," said Kenneth.

"Then you're stupid. My dad—you know, Jack? Champion of the Canon?" Chase said. "He was the one who said it was in the mountains of the western forest."

Amazing. Chase had reverted straight back to his usual bossy, bragging self. I guess he'd recovered from yesterday's talk.

"This could go on for a while," Ben said. "Is there any other way to figure out where to go?"

So I opened the M3's cover, and I was really disappointed to see just my own ginormous chin shining back at me, complete with a zit a little to the left. "Lena?"

Melodie's face appeared. The harp looked away toward someone I couldn't see and called, "Rory's on the mirror!"

"Hey!" Then Lena popped in, her eyes bloodshot behind her glasses. I wondered if this was a new symptom, or if she'd stayed up late reading in the reference room, looking for backup antidotes.

Chase and Kenneth were arguing toe-to-toe now. Ben looked like he might restrain someone, but he couldn't decide who.

"Hey, Lena. We're trying to get to the West Wind's house, but we don't know where it is. Is there a map over there somewhere?" I asked.

"No . . . wait, yes!" All of a sudden her face jumped around in the mirror, like she was running with it. I didn't know where that burst of energy had come from, but I certainly hoped Jenny didn't catch Lena moving that fast. "Rumpel keeps some in the library!"

"Good, because Chase and Kenneth are about ten seconds from punching each other."

Lena's image stilled. "Found it!"

"Great. Now tell these two idiots." Ben plucked the M3 from my hand and marched over to the other boys.

Sighing, I checked my watch. "Wow, we just lost ten minutes. Do you think it's true what they say about guys and directions?"

Mia ignored me. Or maybe she didn't hear me. Or maybe she didn't realize that the comment had been directed at her. Or maybe she just didn't have much of a personality. She just stepped closer to the guys.

It took Kenneth a second to process what Ben was telling him. "Wait, that's Lena? You're not supposed to have contact with EAS during a quest." He kind of sounded like he considered it cheating.

"Are you nuts? We milk it for all its worth," said Chase.

"Those two could wake Snow White from her poisoned sleep." It was an old woman's voice, maybe two feet behind us. I whirled around, my hand on my sword.

Nothing behind me except a tree. I stiffened. Attacking trees were one thing. Talking trees were somehow creepier.

"Down here." The voice sounded irritated now.

The old woman sat hunkered down at the base of the trunk, her limbs so gnarled and knobby that I had mistaken her for the roots. It didn't help that her skin was only a couple shades lighter than the tree, or that her dark linen dress almost perfectly matched the bark's rough pattern. The only feature that didn't blend in was her eyes—dark and narrowed, sweeping over the whole clearing.

Gnome. That was my guess.

"Oh. Hi. Good morning," I said, wondering how much she'd seen and if she could curse us for being so noisy. "I'm sorry if we disturbed you."

"Ever Afters do not disturb me," she said wearily, and I looked at her curiously. "Ever Afters" was an old-fashioned term for Characters. Hardly anyone still used it—usually only people born *centuries* ago. "You humans are like lightning. You're here in brief flashes, and your destruction is always localized."

"We're not trying to destroy anything," I said, a little miffed.

"No?" The old woman smiled, and for a second her face looked kinder—more like someone's great-great-grandmother than a tree. Then that faded. "I lied. They do bother me. They remind me of my sons."

"Do you want me to get them to shut up?" I felt kind of sorry for her. "Kenneth might not listen to me, but Chase—" I pointed him out. "He's my friend. He listens to me about half the time."

"Ah, I see you travel with the Turnleaf," said the gnome.

"Right. But it's just Chase Turnleaf," I said. "Turnleaf isn't a title."

Her gray eyebrows disappeared under the wide brim of her hat. "It is a title. It's what they call a fairy who shirks his heritage and chooses the lifetime of a human. It hasn't happened in hundreds of years. The Fey dislike seeing their gifts scorned, and to a half fairy, immortality is a gift. I believe the human term 'turncoat' comes from Turnleaf."

Only the Fey could be such snots. "But it's not like he had any choice. He was just going to live with his dad. His parents decided—"

"Has he told you that?" asked the old gnome. "Are you sure he wouldn't do such a thing?"

Chase smirked as Kenneth shouted, red-faced.

I wasn't sure of anything. We hadn't covered "Turnleaf" in our talk.

"The home of the West Wind is that way, child." The gnome woman pointed toward a couple peaks looming over us. "You'll find it nestled between the two mountains. He likes to blow figure eights around each summit for his morning workout."

I perked up. We weren't that far away.

"But you will not be able to reach it without aid. It is enchanted to turn away visitors."

That leached all the hope from me. "Oh."

"Here." Suddenly, she leaped onto the branch hanging just beside my face, pretty spry for an old gnome. Before I could react, she reached out and poked my forehead with two fingers. "This will lead you straight there. Do not wait for your friends. Do not attempt to convince them. To do so would break the spell, and they will follow you soon."

"Um, okay." Sometimes a wise old woman would help questers out. I knew that from all the fairy tales I'd read for research. Usually, you did something for them first—like sharing your lunch or something. I didn't think it counted that I had offered to tell off Chase and Kenneth. "Thank you."

The gnome woman disappeared. Her chuckles still hung in the

air. "Do not thank me, girl. I cannot interfere directly in the affairs of my children, but perhaps you can. Perhaps you'll do them a good turn."

I imagined little wrinkly gnomes in diapers and baseball caps.

Then my legs lurched forward—toward the two mountains. Another step, and another. I gulped. I didn't realize that she'd meant that the spell would take over my body.

he spell forced me to move—almost at a run. I gritted my teeth, put my hand on my hilt, and pretended that it was my sword's magic guiding me down a winding path no bigger than a deer trail.

It took a while for the other questers to realize I was gone. I was breathing hard by the time Chase called, kind of panicked, "Rory! RORY!"

"Here!" I shouted back. "I got directions!"

They crashed noisily through the woods behind me.

"Wait up!" said Ben.

My legs moved faster. The spell knew the others were following me now. I vaulted over a boulder in the path, much higher than I ever thought I could jump. "I can't! Follow the sound of my voice."

Chase caught up first. He probably cheated and flew. "Crap."

"Hello to you, too." A tree limb crossed the path ahead of us, and I had just enough control to duck before I walked straight into it.

"What do you mean you can't wait up?" Kenneth had reached us too.

"She's enchanted," Chase explained. "Rory, who did this to you?"

"Some gnome woman." I shrugged. I hadn't even gotten her name.

Chase made an aggravated sound. I could sense him glaring at me, but I couldn't turn my head to glare back. "Gnomes can't do this kind of spell."

"Rory, it's the one that moves against the current," said Ben. I heard two sets of feet with his voice. Mia was with him.

"What?" I asked, confused.

"Rapunzel said to tell you," Ben said. "Well, Lena said that Rapunzel said."

"And you think now's a good time to tell her?" Chase said. "Look at her."

"Wait, what happened to Rory?" asked Ben.

"Enchanted. I think you're going to lose a Companion soon," explained Kenneth smugly. I would have told him off, but then the path turned and I spotted the building straight ahead.

"Rory, you're the most gullible smart person I ever met," Chase started. "Why would you let some stranger enchant—"

"Look." That was all I had breath for.

"I am looking," Chase said. "You can't stop, can you?"

"No, look." Ben pointed. "She found the West Wind's palace."

It looked like a cross between a cliff and a sandcastle, the kind you make when you hold a soup of sand and seawater in both hands and let it dribble out drop by drop. In the front yard was a strange garden—cypress trees and skinny pines, all growing at a tilt, like they were windswept.

"I still want to know who enchanted Rory," Chase said, in a grudging way.

My legs carried me up the rocky driveway. My feet picked out an easy path over the stable stones, like they had walked this way many times before. Behind me I heard the others scurrying after, scattering rocks. I marched right up to the weather-beaten door and put my hand on the pitted wood.

"It's probably locked," said Ben doubtfully.

It *was* locked, bolted shut in three separate places, but after I touched the door, the bolts slid open one by one—clicking two, five, and seven feet above my head. Whatever spell the gnome woman had put on me, it had been very thorough. My hand tugged the handle, and the immense door squeaked open.

It was basically Good Manners 101 not to go into a stranger's house uninvited. It was even more important to be polite when you were dealing with someone as ancient and powerful as the West Wind. I locked my knees and clung to the door frame.

It didn't work. The spell walked me straight in.

"What are you doing?" Ben said, clearly as appalled by my rudeness as I was.

My footsteps boomed in the huge stone corridor. It was glossy and smooth, free of torches or anything else that might block the wind. My heart thudded frantically.

"Stop!" Kenneth hissed.

Through the blood thrumming in my ears, I heard the other four step into the hall.

"I can't." It was definitely time to panic now. Step by step, my body carried me closer to the next door—this one intricately carved, a face in every corner, each with cartoonishly bulging cheeks and wooden wind gusting out in swirls. The spell lifted my hand toward the doorknob.

Then fingers closed around my wrist, and Chase's face was right next to mine, scowling. The spell let me go, and my legs sagged under me. I had to clutch Chase's arm to keep from collapsing to the stone floor in a very dramatic, embarrassing way.

Right. For breaking enchantments, skin-on-skin contact is best.

Lena had explained the mechanics of it once: Enchantments were extremely delicate. You could usually interrupt the spell by touching the person as it was cast. The enchantment intended for one person spread to two, but diluted like that, it couldn't work as well. Unfortunately, if the caster was extremely powerful, the person trying to interrupt the spell could fall under the enchantment too.

So Chase looked pretty relieved himself.

Mia leaned against the open front door, hands over her mouth, and Kenneth and Ben both stared at me. Clearly, they were trying their best not to flip out.

"Wow, you were like the Energizer bunny for a second there," Kenneth told me. "You just kept going and going."

I had to take several deep breaths before I could answer. "I do not recommend that."

"Something's wrong," Chase said, head cocked sideways, like he was listening. "Someone should have stopped us."

"Let's get out of here." Ben turned back. But a powerful gust whipped past us. It slammed the door shut so fast the sound echoed up and down the hall.

A voice came from nowhere, curling around each of us. "Who exactly has stumbled into my brother's house?"

The carved door opened a crack, and out flew a heavy-looking red rug, snapping under the strong wind. Before running even occurred to me, the fabric wrapped around us, throwing me and Chase together and pinning our arms to our sides. Ben and Kenneth thudded into the rug next. Last, Mia was thrown in, and our feet left the floor.

"Crap!" I couldn't see. I couldn't tell how far we were from the ground. We could have been up near the ceiling, forty whole feet above the stone floor. "What if he drops us?"

Chase's voice came from behind my left shoulder. "Rory, one of the four winds just caught us sneaking in the castle. The height's not what you should worry about."

"I'll kill him," Kenneth said in a low voice.

"I would seriously like to see you try," said Chase.

"Noisy little mice, aren't you?" said the West Wind's brother. I wondered where he ranked on the mean-to-friendly scale. Near the *likes to kill EASers for fun* end, probably.

Another door swung open, and another and another and another. Clicks and squeals filled the air, as locks unturned and unoiled hinges creaked. Then we flew, with the sudden terrifying rush of a roller coaster gaining speed.

"Look, Brother. I discovered your rescue party," said the voice from before. "Couldn't you do better than human children?"

We dropped suddenly. We couldn't have been up very high, because we collided almost immediately with the floor. Kenneth and Chase immediately started wiggling free, and in a few seconds the rug slipped off us to the floor. Mia's eyes were wide, her lips parted, her perfect hair sticking out in all directions.

The room was giant, almost as big as EAS's ballroom-turned-infirmary, but bare of any furniture. The only thing that broke up the smooth gray stone was a stained-glass window bigger than the side of our house. The colored panes showed us another bulging-cheek wind, woefully shackled.

"Kenneth, I was joking," Chase said suddenly. "He's a million times stronger than—"

Sword drawn, Kenneth charged at a man in the center of the

room, who looked very out of place on Atlantis. I would have guessed he was going to a Harvard ten-year reunion, or some other event where men wore loafers and argyle sweaters knotted over their shoulders.

"How funny," said the man.

I blinked, and the man swelled from six feet to somewhere around twenty-four. Kenneth's charge didn't falter—I had to give him credit for that. But the man just picked the kid up by his sword arm, pinching Kenneth's right wrist the same way people grab rats by their tail. "It's been a thousand years since I met the first of you Ever Afters, and you never fail to amuse me. You all think you're so important. Did you really think they could stop me, Brother? Did you think they could free you?"

But besides us five questers and the scary argyle man, the room was empty. Unless you counted that huge glass vial right behind me. The weird metal symbols embedded in the glass looked kind of familiar.

Either the very big man in argyle was crazy and talking to himself, or someone invisible was trapped in the jar. With magic people it could really go either way. "Come now, Brother. Do as I ask and join the queen."

As soon as the last word was out of his mouth, my stomach flip-flopped. He meant the Snow Queen.

"Wait. The same queen who poisoned my mom?" Ben asked.

"Yeah. Who wants to bet we just walked in on a recruiting mission?" Chase muttered.

"Any suggestions on how we might rescue Kenneth?" Ben asked hopefully.

Kenneth wouldn't let go of his sword. He kicked his legs, struggling to get free. I couldn't think of a plan that didn't involve fighting the argyle man, and that definitely seemed like a bad idea.

"Otherwise I'll find the ring you were making and I'll use it to bind you here forever, West," continued the man.

The glass vial rattled the way a rattlesnake shakes its tail, furious and waiting. Definitely something in there.

"All right. Perhaps a little shorter than forever," said the big argyle guy. "Centuries, at least. But after a few decades in one of those, I can tell you—the boredom will drive you crazy."

Lena's workshop—that was where I had seen a vial like that before. The argyle man must be the East Wind. The West Wind was in the jar.

Chase gulped. "We really have to get out of here."

"Kenneth." I didn't like the eighth-grade idiot either, but we couldn't just abandon him.

"The last time the East Wind and West Wind had a fight, humans called it the Great Tri-State Tornado of 1925," Chase hissed back. "Two hundred nineteen miles long, and six hundred ninety-five dead. That was in a *human* region, when they were trying not to attract attention. We want to be far away."

"Have you missed the part where the West Wind is imprisoned?" I whispered.

The East Wind picked up a regular-looking cardboard box and inspected its contents—wire-rimmed spectacles appeared on his face for theatrical effect. "It's in here somewhere. You were very clever, Brother, hiding it in plain sight."

"Don't just ignore me!" Kenneth kicked both legs toward the box and knocked it out of the East Wind's other hand. "I *am* going to kill you."

The box hit the ground, and bracelets scattered across the floor—wooden ones, and metal ones, and a jade one, and one made out of shiny, dark stone. No, they weren't bracelets. They were rings, just sized for a twenty-foot person.

"Stop that, little mouse." East gave Kenneth a stern little shake. Something popped, and then Kenneth's arm looked wrong somehow, near his shoulder. He screamed and dropped his sword. "Don't you know how easily I could bury you?"

You could see the power rippling off East, gusting over Kenneth. Their clothes flapped against their bodies. I couldn't see how we could free him, but I couldn't see how we were going to get the four of us out of there either. All the doors were at least fifty feet away and locked.

"Okay, Companions—this is the time for bright ideas," Ben said. "If you have some, just throw them out here."

"All of us winds could bury you, little mouse." East smiled down at Kenneth, and the wind in the room blew so hard that the discarded red rug flew back and slapped against the wall. I had to fight just to stay upright. "My brother here is as strong as I am—well, except for yesterday, when he cast off his strength and forged it into a ring. I just need to find it, and I'll be the strongest wind there ever was."

So we needed to find that ring first.

It will be the one that moves against the current.

I stared at the bracelet-size rings on the floor, searching for the one not moving like the rest.

"Somebody's quick thinking has to get us out of here," Ben added, "and I'll be honest. It won't be mine."

"Ben, seriously, if I had a bright idea, I wouldn't share it out loud," Chase said. "The bad guy can hear it too."

There. All the rings were slowly drifting toward the corner opposite East—except for one. Between an emerald ring and another forged from iron leaves, one slid straight toward the vial—toward me.

"It will be an inconspicuous one," said East. "The plainest of the lot. My brother was always old-fashioned like that."

This one had a single swirl etched into the silver. I picked it up, and as soon as the cool metal brushed my skin, it began to shrink.

East flung Kenneth away like an unwanted toy and turned to me. Wind hit me square in the chest, pushing me back a few steps toward the glass vial. "Little girl, you have something that belongs to me."

Behind him, Kenneth scooted over to the wall, clutching at his right shoulder.

My hand closed over the ring. "But it's not yours. You just said it's your brother's."

East didn't like that. Air gusted again and shoved me back so far I slammed into the glass vial.

"Bargain." Chase's eyes lit up. "It could get us out of here. I'll do it for you."

"Yes, girl. What is it you want? Your freedom?" said East.

If he had wrestled his own brother into a glass thing that looked like a giant rainwater gauge, then I seriously doubted he would keep a promise to me.

Only fire can fight fire; only wind can fight wind. I slid the ring on my finger.

Mia huddled up against the glass cylinder, like she was trying to hide behind it. Yep, not that smart.

"I would move, Mia," I said.

The East Wind caught on. He rushed me, but I spun as fast as I could and punched toward the vial. Glass shattered as soon as my fist struck, and the wind pressure in the room doubled—no, tripled. It lifted me off my feet and knocked me against the wall.

"Wonderful! Now we have a brand-new Great Tornado. No, a Great Hurricane. In one room—" Chase started.

Oh. East and West were fighting each other.

"Hey! There are kids in here!" Hopefully, the West Wind would feel enough gratitude to make sure we didn't all die.

I heard a scuffle. Then, for a half instant, a very tan, very big man held his argyle brother by the throat against the stained glass. One of the panes gave way. With an earsplitting whistle, both winds slipped outside, and the room was still.

The only sound for a moment was our heavy breathing and Ben retching up his breakfast.

"Don't worry," Ben said, in between heaves. "I'm okay. Just nerves."

"You know, if that's gonna happen every battle, you might skip the eggs at breakfast," Chase said, not without sympathy. "Oatmeal comes up easier. I speak from experience."

Mia had fallen to the floor, limp as a rag doll. I helped her up, scared that she might be a bloody mess, full of glass shards, but she didn't have a scratch on her. She just blinked up at me. "Is it over?"

"Um. No, I think it just moved outside," I said.

The stained-glass window had changed: Two winds wrestled each other, their bulging cheeks red with fury, their long, cometlike tails twisting together.

The gnome woman. Or, actually, the woman I'd mistaken for a gnome. She'd sent me here because she couldn't interfere with her sons. I guess that made her the winds' mother. Atlantis was so weird.

Chase marched to the corner where Kenneth leaned against the stone.

"I'm fine." Kenneth dropped his hand from his shoulder with a wince. His face shone with sweat.

"Your shoulder's dislocated." Chase fumbled through the front pockets of Kenneth's pack. Everyone knew he was searching for the ring.

"Stop." Kenneth tried to shove him off, but moving clearly hurt too much.

"Sorry, Kenneth." Ben wiped his mouth and stood up. "This isn't about you. This is about saving my mother. And I need four healthy Companions for that."

"See ya, man." Chase shoved the ring on Kenneth's finger. The eighth grader vanished with a shout.

Then, before Chase could even stand up, Darcy appeared with a crunch of glass, an arrow already notched in her bow, mouth gaping. She glanced around. "Oh. This is why Rapunzel told me to stand in the corner with my longbow. I thought she was just trying to freak out the witches."

"Hey, Darcy," said Ben.

"Hey." She took in the glass under her feet, and the hole in the window, and Mia trembling beside me. "So, no spring yet?"

"Whoa. You weren't here when I left," said a voice in the middle of the room.

West stood shirtless and barefoot in some glass shards. The only thing he wore was an unfortunate set of board shorts, orange and blue and very, very bright. With his long, tangled blond hair and his deep tan, he didn't look much different from a surfer. Except twice as big.

In the stained-glass window behind him, one wind figure with bulging cheeks stood triumphant, fists in the air. I guessed he'd beaten East.

But West must have looked sufficiently scary to freak Darcy out, because she blushed and stammered. "Uh, no. You see,

Rapunzel gave us these rings of return, which were really rings of exchange, and when Kenneth went back, we sort of switched—"

Speaking of rings, I pulled West's off—before he could ask for it back and see I was still wearing it.

"Rings of exchange?" West's face broke into a smile. "But they haven't been seen since Madame Benne's time. How did you manage five?"

Not exactly what I'd expected to hear from an extremely powerful dude, especially not one who had been trapped in a magic vial all day long. "Lena made them."

"You know Lena LaMarelle?" said West, surprised.

When he looked at me, I could kind of tell why Darcy had reacted the way she had. The room didn't actually fill with wind the way it had earlier, but his gaze was forceful. It left me unsteady, like I was still fighting my way through a gale.

He squatted down, peering at me with the same eager hopefulness I usually saw when Mom's fans asked for an autograph. "Can you introduce me to her?"

"Um . . ." I glanced at the others. It couldn't be safe to introduce my poisoned best friend to this guy. His brother had called us little mice.

West's gaze swung around, and I could breathe a little more easily. "Quest, I'm guessing? Why are there five of you?

"This quest is important," Ben said eagerly. "We came to see if you know where the spring for the Water of Life is."

West grimaced. "It's in the South—my brother's territory. That's all I know."

"Oh," Ben said, disappointed.

But Chase had studied a few more fairy tales than Ben had. He knew what to ask next. "Can you take us to him, then?"

"Not a good idea," said the West Wind. "South's in with East, who's not your biggest fan."

"Great," Chase said with a sigh.

"But I can make sure you reach the southern coast this afternoon," said West. "Save you three days' journey."

Ben grinned. "Deal."

"Well, wait until I finish," the wind said, uncomfortably. "I can't take you myself. I'll have to put you on the Fey railway."

"What about Rory?" interrupted Chase.

"Rory?" repeated West, confused.

Chase pointed at me with two hands. "Rory Landon? Girl with crazy punch action? The one who just freed you from centuries of imprisonment?"

"So you do know Lena LaMarelle," said West. "You guys are buddies."

It was news to me that people kept tabs on who my friends were. But maybe he had just heard what had happened up the beanstalk last year.

"I still have your ring." I held it out, hoping to distract him.

But he didn't take it. "That ring only accepts one user. You'll have to keep it now."

"What are you going to give her?" Chase asked West.

"Keep in mind: You probably won't be able to use them for this quest. I'll need to stay here recovering for the next four days, but three boons," said West, and Chase's eyes bulged in a way that clearly said, *Jackpot.* "All you'd have to do is to tap my ring three times and say my name. But no deal unless you introduce me to Lena."

"Wait. Can't we find out why he's obsessed with Lena first?" asked Darcy.

"Why?" repeated West, astonished. "Lena LaMarelle is the greatest inventor in living memory, or at least she will be. Aren't you obsessed with her?"

I couldn't wait to see Lena's face when she'd heard that. "But you already gave me the ring—"

"Rory, trust me," Chase said quickly. "This is how it works. You save the big powerful guy, and he grants you one, two, or three boons, depending on how dangerous it was. You'll want them. With the kind of trouble you get into, they'll definitely come in handy."

He probably meant my Great Destiny. I sighed. "Okay. Then thank you, sir."

West smiled, his eyes crinkling at the corners. But behind his back Chase gave me a big thumb's-up—like those three boons were the best thing that had happened all week.

10

est changed before he let me introduce him through the magic mirror. Not just into another outfit, but into a whole new body. The surfer was replaced with a tall slender man, clad in a pin-striped suit, pink shirt, and silver tie. He looked very distinguished, especially with the gray hair.

My jaw hit the floor, along with Ben's and Darcy's. Even Mia's eyebrows rose. Chase explained that West wasn't a person so much as a personification. He could pretty much change his appearance at will.

"The only limitation is that East and I have to be opposites. He probably looks like a young tobacco farmer right now," West said, straightening his tie. "Okay, I'm ready."

On the magic mirror Lena was extremely flattered when she realized who the dapper old man was. He wanted advice. Apparently, the ring I had used to smash through his prison was his first successful invention in two and a half millennia. He told her all about his many experiments-turned-explosions as he led us questers outside, grew eighty feet tall, stuck us into his suit pocket and rose into the air, flying low over the trees. West's voice boomed so loudly the pocket shook with every word—that made it impossible to figure out what he was saying as the forest slid by in a blur of green below us.

Chase leaned so far out of the pocket that I thought, kind of panicked, he might fall out. "When we're around the Fey, it's better if you guys don't speak. Not at all. Not even English. Half the Fey understand it. You won't know what'll tick them off."

Ben didn't look like he minded, and Mia was still too dazed to offer an opinion, but Darcy said, "Why? We're not at the Unseelie Court yet."

"We might as well be. A lot of Fey will be on their way to it. The last station on the southern line is about a half morning's flight to the court." Chase probably knew from experience. The thought would have weirded me out much more if West hadn't just swooped upward over an extra-tall tree.

"So you expect us to just sit there for the whole ride?" Darcy scowled, obviously not going to take part in any plan where she couldn't talk all day.

"No, just at the station and during boarding. We won't sit with them, but it could seriously suck if you insulted a Fey at the platform," Chase explained. "They view us as playthings, especially us Characters. They've been better since the war, but it'll be a miracle if we make it out of there."

I rolled my eyes. Clearly, Chase was trying to spook Darcy into shutting up.

"No, Rory—I'm serious. Going to the Unseelie Court will probably be the most dangerous part of the quest," Chase said, like he knew what I was thinking. "They might turn you into a statue. They might steal your voice, or scar your face. They might kill you outright, or they might set you an impossible task and then execute you when you Fail. You know the phrase 'like trying to find a needle in a haystack'? It came from the Unseelie Court. It was King Klarion's favorite task for humans who accidentally wandered through a portal. One hundred fifty-seven mortals died in the fifteenth century because they couldn't find a needle in a haystack."

I couldn't remember the last time I'd seen Chase so serious. Even during Lena's Tale, surrounded by man-eating giants, he hadn't talked like this. Atlantis had knocked all the wisecracks straight out of him.

Then the West Wind swooped down toward an empty clearing. My churning stomach forced all thoughts out of my head except the fact that I couldn't vomit in the pocket of an eighty-foot personification.

Darcy scooted as far away from me as the fabric would let her go, whispering, "You're not gonna hurl, are you? God, how did you manage the beanstalk?"

But when West touched down, she helped me out of the pocket and watched with concern while I had some quality bonding time with solid ground.

I couldn't see any sort of platform or ticket counter, but we weren't the only group waiting. When West landed, the other passengers all reacted in different ways: A small army of dwarves with silver chains braided into their beards turned their backs to us. A few witches did that cheer-squawk thing—this version sounded angry. Some goblins adjusted greasy wigs over their triangular ears and clanged the manacles that chained them together, looking hopefully over at West, but their jailer—a smallish Fey with slate-colored wings and armor to match—snapped at them.

West shrank down to a more manageable twenty feet and strolled over to the trees to finish talking with Lena. I wondered if we should stick close to him, if those witches might attack us when his back was turned.

Somewhere to our right, metal clanged on metal—Ben, Darcy,

and I jumped about a mile. I thought for a second that an actual fight had broken out among the passengers, but then I spotted them. Small figures leaped together, clashed swords, and sprang apart with an aerial sort of grace that reminded me of circus performers on silk ropes—impossible-looking tumbles and soaring sorts of spins.

Others stood in a circle around them, waiting for their turn. I saw delicate white wings, and ones that were grayish and stumpy like a moth's, and others as bright and intricate as stained glass. Fey kids. I'd never seen any, unless you counted Chase.

"Sword class," Chase said before we could ask. "A field trip so the students get experience fighting on a bunch of different terrains."

No wonder Chase always looked so good when he fought. He'd probably had way more years of practice, just like these two duelers.

One stumbled away, straightening quickly before he fell over on his little fairy behind. The fight paused. I wasn't sure why. It didn't look like the Fey kid was hurt.

Someone moved in the shadows, a full-grown fairy with slender light-green wings. He held something that looked suspiciously like a wand.

"Don't do anything, Rory. It won't help them," Chase hissed. I stiffened.

The Fey child waited with wide eyes, his slender tangerine-colored wings fluttering nervously, watching the grown-up Fey approach. The Fey instructor just kind of lightly slapped the kid on the shoulder with the stick. But the fairy child screamed, so full of agony that Ben sprang back and almost knocked Mia over.

"The Iron Hemlock method," Chase said quietly, as the

tangerine-winged kid trudged to the back of the class, his hand pressed to his shoulder like it still burned. "Same concept as the one behind invisible fencing for dogs. One jolt of pain to make sure you don't make the same mistake twice."

"But he didn't make a mistake. He didn't even fall down," Ben said, hushed.

"No talking," Chase said, with a significant look at the Fey jailer twenty feet away. "And the mistake was stumbling. Perfect form is important to the Fey."

He said this like it didn't matter—but this was how Chase had learned to fight.

He wasn't a good fighter because he wanted to be. He fought like the perfect Fey soldier because someone had electrocuted him if he tripped. And his mom asked him to go back there?

Horror washed over me.

They were so young. They looked like they could be in kindergarten. That one there, he was even sucking his thumb, clutching the sword to his chest as tightly as some kids held security blankets.

I took a step toward him, to do . . . something, but Chase shook his head.

Right. The quest had to come first.

Chase pointed behind me. "Train's coming."

I spun around, looking for the train tracks. I wanted to make sure they didn't leave the ground.

They did.

A vine as thick and leafy as Lena's beanstalk twined through the tree canopy, then stepped down through the branches and slid across the forest floor before climbing up again. West noticed and ambled back over to us. The actual train chugged in a minute later.

"Pumpkins? We're traveling by pumpkin?" Ben said, shocked.

A chain of them traveled along the vine like the monorail at Disney World—the one in front as white as a cauliflower, the one behind it a very pale yellow, and each one after it a little darker, until the sixth and final pumpkin—the caboose—which was such a vibrant shade of orange it seemed to glow in the trees.

"Oh! Is that the Fey railway? Let me see!" Lena cried from the mirror. Amused, West turned the M3 around so she could watch its approach.

"The Pumpkin line! It travels from north to south. The Apple line travels from east to west, and the Leaf line travels intercontinentally," she explained, as the pumpkins bumped down the branches to the forest floor.

As they slowed to a stop, you could see that these were hollowed out. If a luxury passenger train dressed up like a very artistic jack-o'-lantern for Halloween, it would look like this.

Lena happily told us that all of the human inventors of trains and railroads had been Characters. The Fey hadn't been very happy when humans had stolen their idea.

One Fey with turquoise wings, a uniform made of peacock feathers, and a snooty expression flew out to meet us, clipboard in hand, but most of the fairies sat in the first and second cars, still as statues in thronelike chairs. Long, slender branches fell from the scalp of the nearest Fey, almost covering the whole body underneath, even her wings.

The peacock fairy waved the Fey kids and their teacher on, and they all flitted up to the second car's roof with a flutter of multicolored wings.

"What—" I started, as the teacher paired up a copper-skinned Fey kid with a moth-winged one.

Chase silenced me with a glare. "They're going to practice fighting on a moving surface."

The Fey jailer stepped up next and pointed at the miserable-looking goblins. "Tithe evaders. Bound for the Muirland work camps."

I heard something behind the words—almost like an echo, but with a different rhythm. I didn't realize that Lena's gumdrop was translating for me until Darcy asked, "What did he say?"

"Shut it, Darcy," Chase hissed, and both the peacock conductor and the jailer scowled at us.

"Third car." The peacock fairy made a note on her clipboard, and after the Fey jailer and his prisoners left, she could no longer ignore the twenty-foot-tall personification looming over her. "Yes?"

"Full passage for five," said West. The peacock fairy narrowed her eyes, but if she was going to argue, she changed her mind the second West paid our fares with a sack of gold as big as Chase's head.

"I'll need their full names," said the peacock fairy.

My heart sank. Names have power. It's not a good idea to just say them out loud in public, but even worse, telling people my name usually drew stares and whispers. I braced myself for the blush that always came from being the center of attention.

It didn't come.

"Chase Turnleaf," said my best friend, and half the Fey in the first two pumpkins turned to stare.

Even the conductor's gaze snapped to his face. "Second-to-last car."

Normally, Chase would eat this attention up. He'd grin the smile that took up half his face and wave at all the people watching him.

Chase just walked down the line of pumpkins, face blank. He didn't seem to notice when a cat-eyed fairy hissed at him from the second car. He didn't even flinch when pixies swarmed around his head, close enough to stir his hair, as menacing as wasps, before darting back inside to watch.

We mere humans drew closer to each other. So much closer that someone stepped on the back of my heel.

Ben and Darcy exchanged a glance that clearly said, *Is that going to happen to us?*

West didn't pay any attention to how unpopular we were. He just put the M3 in my hand. "Take care, Rory. Good luck on your quest, Ben."

Then Ben took a deep steadying breath and stepped up to the conductor. "Benjamin McCrory Taylor."

"Aurora Landon," I whispered, right after him, and the peacock fairy barely batted an eye as she wrote it down.

I rushed past the pumpkins to catch up with Chase—the dwarves tugged their long beards at me angrily—and stomped up the steps to the second-to-last car.

"Characters," spat a green-skinned witch inside near the front. She and the other three green-skinned witches sitting beside her had the same stiff, matted gray hair, even the smallest one, who was bigger than the Fey children battling on the roof.

"Can't stand the smell of Ever Afters," snarled a squat, square-faced imp. Suddenly, I seriously doubted that this was a good idea.

But the train lurched forward. Out the window, West had grown eighty feet tall again to wave us good-bye.

"I can't believe you get to ride the Fey railway." Even through the M3, the jealousy was obvious in Lena's voice, as we followed Chase to seats in the middle of the pumpkin car, between the witches and the army of beard-pulling dwarves. "It's so hard for humans to get tickets."

I swung into the seat beside Chase, but he chose not to say anything about how he had ticked off a whole train of Atlantis citizens just by saying his name. He wouldn't even look me in the face. "Ben, we might want to bump up our trip to the Unseelie Court," he said.

"I thought we had three sunrises," Ben said, obviously not a fan of the idea, and I didn't blame him. I didn't want to see a whole court of people like the peacock fairy conductor either. "We've only had one."

"We do, but by dinnertime news about five human questers on the Fey railway will reach the Unseelie Court," Chase said. "It's better if we visit them before they decide to come looking for us."

"I guess. I mean, we'll be close, right?" Ben said. Chase didn't respond. He just stared out the window. "Hey, Lena? If it's okay— do you think I might talk to my mother? I didn't get to tell her good-bye yesterday."

Long family chats were clearly not what Lena had had in mind when she'd invented M3s, but it was impossible to tell Ben no—he looked too pitiful.

Then Darcy wanted to say good-bye to her brother, the fawn. Then Gretel gave Chase an update on which dwarf cities his father was visiting.

So I watched the green leaves blur out the windows as the train wound its way down the Pumpkin line, through trees and over streams. I tried not to think about how awkward it was to sit with this silent, serious version of my best friend.

Ben and Mia fell asleep in their seats on the opposite side of the aisle, Mia's dark head on Ben's shoulder.

Darcy pointed at them. "Are they, like, a couple?"

I shrugged. Probably not if Mia woke up and saw Ben drooling.

"I think the West Wind's more my style," said Darcy thoughtfully. "The surfer-dude version."

Chase and I both snorted at the same time.

"Jinx." Chase passed the M3, grinning a little, like he was almost back to normal.

"You know what I never got?" said Darcy, peering out the window and trying not to look embarrassed. "If it's on the Pacific Ocean, why name it Atlantis? Why not Pacifica?"

"It was originally on the Atlantic Ocean," Chase explained. "They moved it in the tenth century—when the Vikings discovered Canada."

"So, Rory, did West let you keep that ring?" Lena squealed.

I held up my left hand. I'd placed it on the finger that fit the best, the middle one.

"You have to let me examine it when you get back." But before I could tell her she got first dibs on all ring research, Chase interrupted, "Are you two going to yammer on all day?"

"Are we bothering you, Chase?" Lena said, lifting her chin. She coughed a little, though, which kind of ruined the tough act.

"Not me," Chase said grumpily. "Those witches keep looking this way. Either they think we look like dinner, or we're talking too loud."

Two of the staring witches had thumbnail-size warts on their noses in exactly the same spot. Maybe they were twins, or maybe they had both gotten in the way of the same unfortunate curse.

"Do you think they might work for the Snow Queen?" I asked, as quietly as possible.

"Doubtful. But we need to put it away soon. Rory, the only reason they don't have cell phone rules on the Fey railway is because they don't have cell phones on the hidden continents," Chase said.

I scowled. Even West had gotten to talk on the M3 before me. It was definitely my turn. "Since when did you become such a stickler for rules?"

"Since that Fey conductor came in and started glaring at you."

I turned to the door behind us. The fairy in the peacock uniform watched me, eyes narrowed, her turquoise wings vibrating with irritation.

"They actually do throw people off these trains, you know," Chase added. "It doesn't bother the ones who fly."

"I still need to tell Rory one more thing!" Lena said quickly, stressed out. So she meant one more *important* thing. I sincerely hoped it didn't involve my mother and my cell phone.

Chase gave us that *why are my friends such girls* sigh. "There's a luggage car back that way."

The dwarves watched me go, as I peeled back the giant green leaf that served as the door. One of them, a fierce dude with a black beard, met my eyes and gripped his pickax in a meaningful way. I rushed into the next pumpkin hastily, wondering if anyone else thought that the Fey had sent us to the car with the sketchiest crowd.

The baggage car was packed tight, but most of the room was taken up by two leather suitcases about the same size as an SUV. (Were there giants on this train? *Where?*) Everything else was squished up against the sides—copper-bound chests, ornamental tables, and a stack of rolled-up carpets (probably the magic, flying variety).

I wiggled through, sniffing, until I found an easy place to stand, just beside a bird cage with a gold-feathered wren inside. "Okay, Lena. I'm here. What is it? Is something going on with my mom?"

"No. I texted her last night, and she texted back that she loves you. But I don't know if it really was the witches," said Lena, so fast she coughed again. "I mean, you're not here. You haven't seen them. They're really upset. We had to give them their own wing in the infirmary, because they're always weeping and wailing and threatening to curse us."

That sounded like an exaggeration if I ever heard one. "Maybe it was just one of the witches. If only one did the poisoning, the others would have been just as surprised as the rest of us." My money was still on Kezelda.

"Maybe." Lena really meant probably not.

I sighed. "Okay, Lena—who do you think it was?"

"Well, besides the witches, there were only a few people in the kitchen—"

"Right. Me, Mia, and Rapunzel," I said quickly, slightly distracted by the fact I had a sneeze coming on.

At the last name, Lena nodded.

"You seriously think it was Rapunzel?" I'd thought we were back to *Mia is a spy* territory again.

"Think about it: The Director says that Rapunzel insisted on being assigned to the kitchens the day of the feast."

"She had a dream about it. The prophecy kind," I replied. "She told me after."

"And she didn't eat any of the pie," said Lena. "That can't be a coincidence."

A sneeze burst out of me, which was good—it looked like I was scowling because of that and not because Lena was accusing someone who had saved hundreds of lives on Friday.

"She told everyone as soon as she worked it out," I said. "If we'd listened to her—"

"She 'worked it out'"—Lena used air quotes here—"so late. Most people had already been served. And that warning, what was that? All she had to do was shout 'poison' and everyone would have stopped eating. Don't you see, Rory? That whole scene would've been the perfect cover. The best way to avoid suspicion is to cry foul first."

"Not perfect. Not if you think she did it." Then I sneezed again, which kind of messed up the sternness I was going for. I was tired of everyone misunderstanding Rapunzel for no reason. "Why would Rapunzel do something like that?"

"Well, who was in charge right after everybody got sick?"

"Then why wouldn't she poison everyone before? She's been at EAS for years." My eyes itched. I eyed the stack of wooden crates behind the bird cage, wondering if one of them held unicorn tails or something else I was allergic to.

"I don't know. To throw people off the scent? To store up good-will when she played the hero later?"

This didn't sound like Lena. She never said snotty phrases like 'store up goodwill' unless she was using her tinny, reciting voice. "Who told you all this?"

Lena opened her mouth and hesitated. "I believe it too. It makes sense."

"Lena—" I started.

"The Director." She knew this wasn't helping her case.

"The same paranoid Director who flipped out over your portal?" And then I sneezed three times in a row, so hard my ears started ringing.

"Whoa. Are you okay? Are you getting a cold or something?" Lena asked.

"I feel fine. Maybe this luggage is super dusty. Hold on." I slipped between a crate of iron shoes and a stone elf statue a tiny bit too detailed to be just a work of art. "Anyway, the Director—she's just—" I nearly knocked over a black cauldron and narrowly avoided breaking my foot. "Crackers. I mean, crap."

"She might not be wrong, Rory," said Lena in the slow, quiet voice she uses when she is trying to keep me from freaking out. "Rapunzel might not be trustworthy. Atlantis could be a wild-goose chase."

Irritation slid right into rage, and I couldn't really tell you exactly where it came from—the Director's persistence, Lena's mistrust, or that stupid heavy cauldron. "Well, it's not like we have much choice."

I was with Ben. Unless they had another way to save everyone, I didn't want to hear it.

Lena's chin jutted out. "Rory, don't just blow this off . . ."

I really didn't want to fight with her—not when she was sick, and I was so far away and we couldn't make up. I shoved the cauldron back upright and sneezed the most ginormous sneeze of all. Then I spotted the best excuse to change the subject ever. "Lena, there's a horse trapped in here."

Lena paused. "That explains the sneezing."

The horse was big. I mean, most horses tend to be on the large side, but this one seemed way too huge for this cramped car. His fur was black, and red streaks glinted where the sunlight slipped in through the windows. A quilt covered his back from shoulders to rump. Only one foot stood on the pumpkin floor. Three of his hooves were trapped in different things: the front left in a reed basket, one back leg in a cardboard box, and the other in a planter, dead leaves piled around it.

Then the beast looked at me and blinked slowly. It was the most miserable blink I'd seen in my entire life.

"Poor guy. He's really tangled in there. Lena, look—" I turned the mirror around.

"That sucks," Lena agreed. "But Rory—"

"Don't move, horse. I can't help you if you kick me in the face and give me another black eye." But the horse stood still as I bent and ripped away the cardboard box.

Through my sneezes, I could just barely hear Lena. "Rory, I know you're changing the subject. Honestly, you've gotten as bad as Chase—"

Before I could think of a good comeback (one that would almost definitely get us into a fight), a low, nickering voice said, "Free me."

"Wow. You're a *talking* horse." Whoops. That was actually a little insulting.

But the horse had decided he couldn't be too picky on the rescuer front. "Free me, or I shall spend my days as a slave."

"Lena, I have to go," I said to the M3. "I'll talk to you later."

"That's not—" Lena started.

But I slapped the case shut. If there was any possible way to hang up on someone with a magic mirror, I had just done it, and I felt kind of bad about it.

I shoved the heavy quilt off the horse's back. It hit the floor with a clink—something heavy had been sewn inside. Someone had clearly gone through some effort to imprison him.

"You're not . . . an evil horse, are you?" Eyes watering, I dug into the planter and loosened the dirt trapping the horse's hoof.

"I have done nothing wrong." The horse sounded stronger and kind of offended, but that didn't exactly answer my question.

Still, the poor guy deserved to be free. "Well, just don't kill anyone I like when you get out, okay?"

I was joking, but the horse said, "I swear."

As I struggled to break the reeds in the basket (they were thin but tough) and free the last hoof, the door to the baggage car ripped open.

Metal rang against metal. Great. Either a battle was going on, or the Fey kids wanted to practice fighting *inside* a moving train car.

"Rory?" Ben called.

"How do you feel about jumping off a train?" Grunting, Chase blocked a particularly heavy blow.

"Who ticked off the dwarves?" I called back.

"Not the dwarves—the witches," Darcy said. Her bowstring twanged and thwacked. "They said a Character was stealing their property."

I glanced up, suspicious. "That wouldn't be you, by any chance, would it?"

"My life is my own," the horse said, clearly feeling better. When he shook his mane, little burps of fire flickered at the ends, filling the car with the smell of smoke.

"Whoa. What was that?" Darcy asked.

I sighed. "Anybody have a knife?"

"Won't your sword work?" Mia glanced over my shoulder at the horse, head tilted.

"Tight space plus long sword equals stabbing wound," I said, annoyed.

"Here." Ben wiggled past the crates and slapped a Swiss army knife in my palm, handle first.

Chase managed to beat the witches back with the flat of his blade, and as soon as there was room, Darcy shoved the door shut and latched it.

"Did you seriously bring a pocketknife to the feast?" Chase couldn't decide whether to be impressed or to start teasing Ben.

Ben obviously expected the latter. He shrugged, uncomfortable. "Boy Scout."

"This door isn't going to hold them for long," Darcy said. On the other side of the leaf we could hear the witches' enraged shrieks and then a splintering thump. "I think they borrowed an ax from one of the dwarves. They're hacking through."

"This one is locked," Mia said from the door at the far end of the pumpkin. "We're trapped."

I sawed through the last of the reeds and sneezed. "Okay, you're free."

The horse whinnied and shook out his mane again, like he was getting rid of the cricks in his neck. The tight space seemed even smaller now that he could move.

I drew back, covering my nose with my shirt so I could breathe more easily. "Any ideas on how to get out of here?"

The horse calmly kicked out the wall with both hind legs. Leaf-smelling air blew in.

"A Dapplegrim?" Chase said in disbelief, spotting the horse. "Rory, you found a Dapplegrim, and you didn't tell me?"

"I didn't know—are you a Dapplegrim?" I asked the horse.

"In forty seconds the tracks will come to water—deep enough for frail human children to jump in without harm," said the horse. "I'll leave you. But I owe you a boon. Only one, since I would have eventually freed myself. If you should ever need my help, stamp your hoof three times and call me."

"Um, you know I don't have hooves, right?" I said.

The Dapplegrim wheeled around, scattered big piles of luggage, and leaped out into the forest. He landed at a gallop alongside the train.

"Did that really just happen?" I said, muddled with allergies.

"A Dapplegrim, and you didn't even know," Chase said mournfully, watching it swerve off into the trees. "Next time you have to come find me."

"Want me to swear?" I asked sharply.

But then several things happened at once: Ben took his pocketknife out of my hand and closed it. The door gave way and revealed three green, seriously angry faces. And the train began to cross a wide river, glittering in the afternoon sun, filling the baggage car with light.

"Time to go." Ben jumped out first. Mia dove after him.

"My bow's going to get all wet." Then Darcy hopped out too.

"Aurora Landon," said a witch. I guess people had been listening when I'd said my name to the conductor. "You have made an enemy of the Wolfsbane clan for life."

"Whoops," I said, doing my very best to sound sarcastic and not freaked out.

"Go bite your broom and get over yourselves," Chase told the witches. "You know the Dapplegrims can't be tamed. He was going to get out anyway."

The witches just raised their long, skinny wands. A spell fizzled in the air, but before it could hit me, Chase shoved me out the opening.

I slammed into the river so hard that all the air whooshed out of my lungs. Then the water closed over my head—sudden and cold and so full of bubbles I couldn't tell which way was up. Something tugged the straps over my shoulder, and I surfaced, too breathless to even cough. The carryall had dragged me back to air. Lena must have embedded a flotation enchantment in it.

Chase treaded water right next to me. "Well, Rory, you're on a roll with the boons. Four in one day." He didn't sound too happy about it.

"Oy! Are you guys going to swim all afternoon?" Ben shouted from the muddy shore. The forest behind him stretched out like a green blanket all the way to the mountains, the same peaks above the West Wind's palace.

"Me and Mia are safe!" Darcy waved. Little drops of water sprayed out from her hoodie sleeve. "Just in case you're worried!"

Chase and I struck out toward them. Pain flared across my side as soon as I reached forward. I faltered a bit, surprised, but it really wasn't that bad. I barely noticed it after I reached the riverbed and splashed the rest of the way to shore. Walking hurt much less than swimming.

Darcy shrugged off her sweatshirt and wrung it out. "I don't mean to rain on anyone's parade, but now that Rory got us kicked off the train, does anyone know how to find the Unseelie Court?"

Ugh. She was right. I *had* gotten us kicked off.

"We walk." Chase pointed downstream. "We're about a day away. Over the crest of that hill is a waterfall with a bridge, and then there's a stairway down to the shore. After that, it's a straight shot to the Unseelie Court. We're good."

"*We* are," said Mia coolly. "But is Rory? This is the second time she has cost us time we can't afford to waste."

I frowned. "What was the first time?"

"When you strolled straight into the West Wind's palace and got Kenneth hurt." Mia turned to Ben. "Maybe she should go home."

I stared at her. I mean, the whole quest she barely puts two words together, and her first whole sentences in hours are to try and convince Ben to send me back?

"Rory was also the only reason we were on the train in the first place." Chase glared at Mia, water streaming unnoticed down his arms. "Besides, it's one thing to get dropped off at a Fey railway station by the West Wind. It's another thing for five questers to show up unannounced. We might have had to fight our way out at the end station. I don't know if you've noticed, but nobody on this continent trusts us."

Mia shrugged delicately. Ben and Darcy definitely didn't look like they wanted to say anything now.

I was suddenly glad Chase was on *my* side.

It definitely hurt to walk with a wet, heavy pack banging into my ribs. I must have bruised them somewhere between the winds throwing me against the wall and jumping off the Fey railway.

Mia wasn't wrong, I thought as we walked. We only had a week to find the Water of Life. The only lead we had was the southern coast of Atlantis. It didn't take a genius to figure out we'd need more than a few days to search.

Maybe Ben wanted a fresh Companion. Someone who hadn't been in the kitchen when the pies were poisoned. Someone who wouldn't get us kicked off the Fey Railway for accidentally freeing a Dapplegrim. Someone who wasn't an enemy of the Wolfsbane clan for life.

Now that I was kind of injured, no one would blame Ben if he ordered me to put on my ring of return.

I was so focused on my thoughts that I didn't hear the crash of the waterfall or notice the ocean sparkling far below. When Ben stopped, I nearly tripped over Darcy's feet.

"That is the most gorgeous bridge in the history of mankind," Darcy said, gaping.

Where the river dropped off the horizon, a marble bridge arched over the falls. It was carved as delicately as lace, and in the mist, it looked gauzy and impossible, a mirage made out of moonlight—something too fantastical to be real.

"Feykind," Chase said. "A famous Fey architect built the Cala Mourna Bridge."

Just beyond the far side of the bridge were two posts—the top of the staircase. We must have had ten stories of steps between us and the sand.

Suddenly sick to my stomach, I was incredibly tempted to ask Ben to send me back. Getting out now would save me from the climb down.

Coward, said a voice in my brain. *It won't be fun for anyone. Be a team player. If you survive it, then the next Companion won't have to.*

Darcy ran up the gentle slope of the fairy bridge. "That view is amazing."

I followed her, but I wasn't interested in any view. I ignored the vomit-y feeling, stared at my sneakers, and concentrated on putting one foot in front of the other. Out of the corner of my eye, I could still see the waterfall shooting down into the ocean.

"We should probably have an offering. Even when it looks like no one is watching, the keeper expects some sort of toll," Chase told Ben and Mia behind me. He always liked freaking out the new kids. "Fey and goblins take hostages with them for that exact purpose. Even dwarves and witches usually carry a very pretty animal for tolls. Black cats and stuff."

"The witches sacrifice their own familiars?" Ben said.

I could practically hear Chase grinning. "There's no such—"

Underneath us came a deep and gravelly voice, like an out-of-tune tuba with rocks inside. "Who's that trip-trapping over my bridge?"

I whirled around.

Chase leaped back. A huge gray hand with cracked fingernails reached over the bridge railing and grasped at the air where he had been standing.

"Troll!" Darcy cried.

"Wait. This isn't a fairy bridge?" Ben asked.

"This troll adopted it," said Chase, drawing his sword. "The trolls love pretty things, but they're not very smart. Or creative. They can't make anything pretty by themselves. So they tend to steal things or conquer places and then call them their own."

"I'll take care of it." Darcy was in such a hurry to draw her bow that she fumbled. Her arrow clattered to the stone. "Wow. Real smooth."

A hulking shape swung itself onto the top of the bridge— between me and Darcy and the other questers.

This troll was about eight feet tall and four feet across, and his thick arms hung down to the stone. His eyes were tiny, his nose just two slits. He had a major underbite, and two tusks curved over his top lip.

Unfortunately, this troll had seen bows before. He swatted at Darcy first. She was too busy picking up her arrow to notice.

"Watch out!" I tackled her, and the troll's arm sailed harmlessly above us. Fortunately, my sword was sheathed this time. Unfortunately, my bruised ribs protested when we hit the ground.

Then the troll roared with pain and turned around, so I guess Chase had decided to stab the big guy to get his attention.

"Geez. How many fights does this make today?" I couldn't see Ben, but he sounded terrified.

"Only three," Chase said. "Rory, are you really going to make me protect the new kids all by myself?"

I hesitated. On the ground, Chase and I could take pretty much anything, but we were up really high. I didn't know if I could handle the height, *and* the troll, *and* the battle, *and* my pack banging into my poor ribs.

Well, at least one of those was easily fixed. "Darcy, take my pack, and cover us from that boulder."

"Good idea." Darcy grabbed the top strap and sprinted for the other side.

I drew my sword and turned to join the fight.

Then Mia did the bravest and stupidest thing I'd ever seen her do. She dove between the troll's legs.

The troll spun around before she even straightened up. He reached for her. Mia shrieked, cowering away, a second too slow. His fingers were just inches from her cheek. I sliced through the air between them, driving him back.

"Mean pointy," said the troll. No, I'm not kidding. And he stamped hard, faster than I expected, and pinned my sword to the marble beneath his foot.

"I can't shoot without hitting someone!" said Darcy from her boulder.

But the troll had turned his back a little. Chase shoved Ben past the fight. "You two go on ahead."

The bridge vibrated as Ben and Mia ran for the other side.

The troll raised his fist again—Chase didn't see the blow coming down on his head.

"No!" My sword was still trapped, so I did the only thing I could think of—I shoved at the troll's chest with both hands.

I felt the West Wind's ring work this time. A swift gust flickered over my left arm and blasted the nearest target. The troll flew back and hit the railing ten paces behind him with an enormous crack.

"Whoa!" said Darcy. "Rory, you need to teach me that Jedi trick."

But I scooped up my weapon, concentrating on protecting

Chase. The sword's magic tugged me across the bridge. It pulled my arm back.

The troll bent over the railing and stared at the fractures in the marble.

"Bridge!" You could hear the grief in his voice, like a child whose favorite toy is broken.

We had outnumbered him and destroyed his home. He never had a chance. "Sorry!" I said.

Then my sword thrust its blade forward. It would stab the troll in the back, kill him, I realized, and the idea was so startling that my hand uncurled.

I dropped my sword.

Not a great idea in the middle of a battle.

The troll turned around and kicked out with both feet.

Chase yanked me out of the way. "Rory, come on—we do not drop our weapons and apologize to the enemy."

Flushing, I snatched up my sword.

"That ring—you need to be careful what you do with your left hand," Chase said, his eyes on the troll. His sword was smeared with blood, just a little too orange to be human. As the troll lumbered to his feet, I spotted the slice on his calf—not enough to stop him, but it might slow him down. "The bridge can't take another blow. The Fey architect built it to look pretty. Making a strong structure isn't something fairies worry about."

The drop flashed through my mind—maybe a half mile of open air, separated from me only through a thin layer of sneaker and fragile marble. My mouth was suddenly so dry that my tongue stumbled over words. "Are you saying that this bridge is going to collapse under us?"

"Don't look at me like that. You're the one who smashed it,"

Chase said. "Maybe you should run across too, and let me handle this—"

I shot him a dirty look. He couldn't seriously think I would leave him.

The troll rushed us. Maybe it was my imagination, but with every heavy footfall I thought I heard stone cracking.

Horror locked my knees exactly where they were. I glanced back at the other three questers, at solid ground, at safety.

Chase stepped slightly ahead of me, like he knew my fear of heights had transformed me into a Useless Rory statue. An arrow thwacked into the troll, right where the neck met the shoulder, so quickly that it was like he'd sprouted a feathered branch below his left ear. Too fast to stop, he toppled toward me and Chase.

The hand not holding my sword shot out to push him away, but as soon as my skin brushed his coarse, grimy tunic, the troll's feet left the ground.

Crap.

"Rory!" Chase snapped. "What did I tell you about your left hand?"

The troll landed back-first against the nonsmashed railing. The white stone splintered. Cracks crawled under us. The troll's flailing arms knocked Chase over the side.

I reached out automatically. My hand caught his—

The troll fell past us, howling, and disappeared in the waterfall's mist, but Chase looked freakishly calm for someone whose feet were dangling over a ten-story drop.

"I'm sorry!" Darcy cried from the far side. "I'm so sorry."

—and before I could use the ring's strength to haul Chase back up, the bridge crumbled beneath my feet.

e dropped so fast my stomach scrambled up to my throat. Bridge bits fell all around us—big, jagged pieces struck me hard in my calf, my shoulder, my ribs—

Then, sliding into the waterfall, I couldn't see anything. Water roared in my ears, and my scream turned to choking. I might drown before I reached the ocean.

I clutched at Chase's hand—only to realize that my hands were empty. I had lost him.

I was going to die—

Someone seized me under the arms, and I could breathe again, I could see again. Waves crashed around colossal stones a hundred feet below my sneakers.

I groped around. I needed something to hold on to.

"Rory, stop squirming. You've still got your sword out, and if you injure me so bad I have to leave the quest, I swear I'll drop you here and let you swim to shore."

I froze. I didn't risk twisting upward to look, but only one person could sound that cocky this far off the ground. "Chase?"

"Two words, Rory: fairy wings," he said.

I would have felt a lot more relieved if we weren't still in the air. "Can we land someplace?"

"What? The wind's too loud. I'm only getting every other word. Hang on. I'll land." He steered us toward shore, so sharply that I forgot myself a second and kicked my legs. "Whoa. Relax. Flying is one Fey thing I'm really good at, but I'm not really big enough for passengers yet. Don't throw your weight around."

Great. I stiffened, straight as my sword. We wobbled again, but Chase recovered. "See?"

We glided around for what seemed like an excessively long time. The high cliffs on shore turned into shorter cliffs, and then to stony hills, and then to sand dunes. We passed several stretches that I could have sworn were completely acceptable landing spots.

"Head's up." Chase swooped lower and dropped me.

I was sure he meant for me to land on my feet, but my legs were numb with wind. I skinned both knees in the sand and then fell on my side, staring up at the sky. Everything hurt.

"I couldn't fly up to the top of the cliffs. You're too heavy. We had to land here. Did I lose you?" A winged figure loomed over me, and then Chase knelt in the sand and snapped his fingers in my face. "Did you faint with your eyes open?"

I shoved his hand away. "Yes."

"Sarcasm intact. Definitely alive," said Chase, grinning. "I don't think the other questers saw me. I waited until the waterfall blocked us before I caught you."

Of course he would care more about keeping his secret than me screaming myself hoarse. "The troll?"

"Drowned, I guess. Did you expect me to save him, too?"

I shot Chase a very well-deserved glare and spotted his wings. They rose up over each shoulder and extended past his head, slightly pointed—kind of like how I'd expected fairy ears to look. They fluttered nervously. Chase's face turned slowly red.

I had to press my lips together, but I didn't laugh and embarrass him more. "Well? Turn around."

I pretended not to be surprised when Chase actually stood up and did. The wings extended all the way to his ankles, as long as he was tall. And they—well, they didn't glitter, or shine, but they seemed to be made of light, like a hologram projection.

"How come I haven't seen them before this?" I asked.

"They're invisible unless I move them for longer than five seconds," Chase said, voice tight.

Then he'd probably perfected using them for four and a half seconds. "Is that true for all Fey?"

Chase snorted. "No. It's not even true for all halflings. Fey wings are normally forty percent physical and sixty percent magic. I just got the magic part. Believe me, that's much better than the other way around. Almost all the flying ability is in the magic."

"Why didn't they show up when we fell off the beanstalk? Did you see the flying carpet, or were you going to let us hit the ground?" I sat up. Pain shot over my ribs and ripped the air from my lungs. Not good.

Chase didn't notice, his back still to me. "I couldn't fly then. That's why I was so freaked out. All the flying muscles in my shoulder were torn up. My wings aren't physical, but I still have the same back muscles as a fairy—you know, adapted to flying. Now, if you had fallen on the way *up* the beanstalk, you would have been very impressed with how awesomely I would have caught you. I've always been good at flying. That and glamours and picking locks and Binding Oaths and—" He stopped. "Well, that's actually it."

I reached a hand toward Chase's wings and then stopped. I probably shouldn't touch them without asking. "They're pretty," I said finally.

"They're pink," Chase said, exasperated. They were—two shades lighter than salmon. I'd been trying not to mention it. That sword class for mini Fey would especially suck for a boy with pink wings. "They're supposed to get darker. You know, like your hair color as you grow up." Chase obviously counted on it.

"You know, they're actually more peach here," I said. "Right by your shoulder blades."

His fists clenched. The wings vibrated again. This was an angry flutter, not a nervous one. "That doesn't make it any better!"

"Yes, it does," I said. "That means it's already getting darker. You'll probably have a cool orange in a couple years. Flame-colored."

That cheered Chase up. "Well, nobody's going to see them until then. Nobody *else*."

Sometimes, I didn't like being the only one who knew Chase's secret. It was kind of a lot of pressure.

"Well, thanks for saving my life." I sheathed my sword, gritting my teeth against the pain.

"Good," Chase said. "Now hold on to that gratitude. I need to tell you something, and you can't bite my head off. We're twelve miles away from the others. I couldn't find a closer spot to land, not at high tide."

I pressed a hand to my sore ribs. Chase had told me to run before the bridge cracked. He knew that *he'd* be fine. He could fly. I just hadn't realized he'd had it under control. If I hadn't fallen too, he would've just flown straight back, made some excuse, and rejoined the quest.

Darcy had my pack with the M3, so we couldn't even remind Lena to text my mom.

I'd screwed the whole thing up. Again. Between getting us

kicked off the Fey railway and breaking the bridge, I'd probably cost us a whole day.

I suggested calling the Dapplegrim, but Chase said that boon was too awesome to waste. He still had his ring of return in his pocket, I pointed out. He could head back to EAS and explain what had happened, but Chase refused—if he left the quest, they might not send him back. Then I tried to convince him to fly off and tell the others where I was. I could stay in one place so they could find me again.

Chase rolled his eyes. "First of all, we still have two days to get to the Unseelie Court, and we're not that far away. Only about a three-hour flight. I mean a day's walk. Second of all, I'm not leaving you—not on a hidden continent, not at night, not alone. End of discussion."

That was an unexpectedly nice and terrifying thing to say. I would have come up with a great argument for that, but I got distracted. "Your wings just disappeared." Without warning, Chase looked like a regular, human kid.

"I told you they would. That's what happens when I don't use them for a while," he said, shrugging. "We'll just walk. If the others are keeping to the coast, and we're keeping to the coast, we're bound to run into each other. We'll reach them by midnight or so." He strode up the sand dune, slipping once on loose sand but catching himself with a flutter that made his wings visible. "As long as we don't run into trouble. By trouble"—he swung around to grin at me—"I mean bad guys. I can't believe you dropped your sword, by the way."

I followed along more slowly, step after painful step. "It was going to kill the troll."

"Yeah, so? What do you think we've been training for?" Chase said.

This *was* what we'd been training for. I'd been so focused on getting better I'd forgotten that.

Chase rolled his eyes. "You'll need to get over it sometime."

I hated that he was right. "I just want to get through middle school without killing anyone. That would be a really normal thing to want if I wasn't a Character."

Chase looked a little taken aback. It took him a couple seconds to change the subject. "Have I told you yet how awesome smashing the troll was?"

"Even though it broke the bridge?" I asked grimly.

"Minor detail." He pointed to the grove of pines we walked into. "Hit one of those."

"Why?"

"I wanna see. I'd do it myself, but the ring only lets *you* use it."

"It seems like a waste of a perfectly good tree."

"Please please please." He poked me in the shoulder with every word. He apparently thought I'd give in if he annoyed me enough. "You need to learn how to use that left hook anyway. Better a tree than my face."

"You shouldn't call your face a target. That tempts me." But I swung my fist at the nearest trunk, mainly to shut him up. My ribs were not happy when I connected. The tree cracked and fell.

Chase grinned. "Except for the way you punch like a human, that was the greatest thing I've seen all week."

"What do you mean I punch like a human?" He couldn't expect me to punch like anything besides human. It was a biological fact.

"You don't put any of your body weight behind the punch. You need to punch and kind of lurch with it—like you're going to do a shoulder roll."

"Does it matter how I punch if this ring gives me superman strength?"

"Well, first, you have two arms and just one ring." It amazed me how quickly Chase could go from goofball to teacher. "Second, I'm almost positive that the ring responds to the intensity of the blow. If you punch harder, it'll hit harder too. Try." He tapped the nearest trunk.

I did, tired of arguing now that the adrenaline was draining away. And if the other one broke, this one exploded. I squeezed my eyes shut against the splinters flying everywhere. Chase whooped.

"I think I've reached my tree-killing quota for the evening." My left hand was all scratched up. I could feel it.

"We'll see how bored we get later. But you know what this means?" Chase said. "We have to rework your fighting style. You've got the sword work down pretty well, but if you throw in your natural kicking skills and that kind of punch, you'll be unstoppable. If you had pulled a Mighty Snap Kick at Lake Michigan with just the right timing, you could have stunned the chimera and stopped it without tackling anybody."

I couldn't even think about the chimera without seeing Mia's head on the table. The dream was definitely bothering me. "Chase, what do you think of Mia?"

"Useless," said Chase with such disgust I felt kind of pleased. "I don't know why Ben asked her to be his Companion."

I told him what I'd dreamed. "Do you think I should tell her?"

Chase shot me the look he always gave me when I asked for advice—the one that Lena called the *why the hiccups are you asking me?* expression. "Some Characters get beheaded in their Tales."

"Which Tales?" Maybe I could list them for Mia.

"No idea," Chase said.

"Lena would know." But without the M3, I couldn't ask her.

"Yeah, well—Lena can't fly," Chase said shortly. "How many times have you dreamed it so far?"

"Two." It was darker in the trees. I stared at the ground to make sure I didn't trip over any roots.

"Then you don't need to worry unless you dream it again. Besides, it's really rare for someone to dream about someone's Tale besides their own. It could just be a regular dream."

"But last year, I dreamed about falling out of a beanstalk four times. That's how I knew to jump off."

"Glad you had a plan then. Other than dragging me down to my death," Chase said. I lifted my fist threateningly. He skittered out of the way, laughing.

I hoped it was a regular dream, but somehow I doubted it. "But it feels like the dreams that come true. You know. Kind of still. Focused. Not jumbled and confusing like regular dreams."

Chase shrugged. "The Fey don't dream."

"You mean, you've never dreamed of your Tale?" This would be news. Chase liked to brag about how he would have the biggest and best Tale ever.

"You have?" Chase said, clearly skeptical.

I nodded, smirking. I didn't usually have an advantage with Tale-related stuff.

"Oh," Chase said.

A stack of split wood stood in the next clearing, as tall as I was. A giant double-headed ax leaned against it.

Chase delicately kicked out a piece near the bottom. Then he kicked out another.

"That's probably a whole week of some poor woodcutter's work." Woodsmen were fairy-tale staples, just like fairy godmothers and big bad wolves.

Chase shrugged, kicking out a third. He flew up and landed on the top. "See? It's still stable."

Then the whole thing toppled, scattering logs down the slope.

Chase hovered, shocked, his peach-colored wings blurring behind him.

I burst out laughing and immediately regretted it. My ribs enjoyed laughing even less than smashing trees.

"Time to go." He landed at a half run.

I rolled my eyes. *Now* he was worried about the woodsman.

"I don't really dream, you know," he said. "I've only had one dream my entire life, but it gets longer and longer every time I have it."

"That's what happens in the Tale dreams," I told him.

Chase grinned, like someone had said he would get his very own quest for his birthday. "There's this table, in this house, with all these people, and then there's this cake, as big as a giant's palm. Candles are shoved in it, all over. Sometimes I try to count them, but on the top of the cake, someone wrote in blue icing, 'Happy birthday, Grandpa Chase.'"

Then I did trip over a tree root.

It was official. Of all the weird things Chase had told me that week, him telling me that he dreamed about being a grandfather freaked me out the most.

"I'm going to live to be an old man and die in my sleep." He had said that before, usually when our lives were in danger, but I had thought it was just him being cocky. Not once had I suspected that he believed it. "That's how I knew I needed to leave the Fey and live among humans. I needed to grow up."

The winds' mother was right. Chase had been a turncoat. I mean Turnleaf.

I could never make fun of him the same way again. Maybe Chase was an idiot sometimes, maybe he bragged more than he should, but he'd also made a very grown-up decision before I'd even reached first grade.

Thunder rumbled above us, but we couldn't see any lightning. We couldn't even see the sky. Too many giant pines in the way.

"That might put a damper on our plans." Then Chase clapped a hand over his mouth.

"Whoa. Corny much? I think Ben's rubbing off on you."

"I meant—we should figure out which way that storm is headed." Chase jumped up, and with two beats his wings carried him up past the trees. "I'm going to check it out."

So he left me alone with my thoughts. I hoped Lena had remembered to text my mom. I hoped it would take less than a day to find the other questers. And if we didn't find them, if we were lost on Atlantis for weeks . . .

Thunder cracked again overhead—much closer. "Chase! We really should find shelter. It would suck to get electrocuted."

He didn't answer.

I was alone in the woods after dark, on a strange hidden continent. I drew my sword, just in case nymphs from the pine trees I had busted wanted revenge. My ribs didn't like that. Wincing, I let the weapon dangle at my side. "Chase?"

All was quiet, except for the thunder.

If Chase had been flying around above the trees, he'd been the tallest thing around. Dodging lightning was probably impossible, even if he was a good flier. "Chase! Answer me!"

"Rory!" His voice was faint, behind me, and kind of strangled.

I whirled around, the hair on my arms standing up. In the gloom, a large wingless figure carried a double-headed ax over his shoulder. Iron Hans. Relief spread through me.

Rolling my eyes, I trudged down the slope. "Chase, I don't care if that ax was too good a prop to pass up. This is not the time for your scary Iron Hans impression."

But the man didn't grin, or laugh, or break the glamour like Chase would have. And when the lightning flashed, the man's pewter skin lit up. His features were more rugged than Chase usually made him, the jaw more square, the dark eyes more deep set. Just the way he stared at me, emotionless, waiting, freaked me out.

I slowed. "Chase, seriously, I'm going to try my new ring out on you if you don't stop faking."

"Is this Chase?" The figure lifted his other arm, the one not holding his ax. A tall, skinny boy dangled from his hand, by his belt. Chase's curls flopped into his eyes, his jaw slack. I knew it was real then—Chase would never create an illusion of himself that looked so scared.

If you ever meet this villain, you should turn around and run the other way. None of you are good enough to face him. That was what Hansel had said about Iron Hans. My feet stopped where they were.

If I attacked first, I might surprise him. But what good would that do against someone bigger and stronger than me? *No,* I thought, my thumb finding the ring, *not stronger.*

But how did you beat a man with metal skin? He was like a walking suit of armor. My blade would just glance off him.

Chase was too terrified to even speak, except for a breathy sort of "I— I—"

No, not "I." "Eye."

I sprang forward.

Iron Hans lifted the ax in a guard position, almost lazily. I bashed it out of the way with my sword, using all the strength in my right arm. Then I hurled my weight behind my other fist, aiming at the hand holding Chase's belt. Iron Hans had expected the sword slash, but the punch came as a surprise. Grunting slightly, he dropped Chase and stepped back unsteadily.

The sword's magic increased my speed—I swept my leg under his heel, tripping him. He slammed into the ground. I stepped over him, one grubby sneaker on the shaft of his ax, the other on his chest. My sword guided its point right to Iron Hans's eye, and I just held it there, resisting the blade's magic, its impulse to thrust.

"Chase?" I didn't risk looking away from the villain.

"Freaking Iron Hans. *Here*." If Chase was talking, he was fine. Whatever spell Hans had cast over him was broken. "And you beat him in like four moves. He's never going to live that down."

Iron Hans just stared up mildly, like it wasn't too unusual for a girl to be standing on his chest one wrong move, one *twitch* away from shoving a blade through his eye and into his brain.

I suddenly felt a little queasy.

I didn't want to kill him, not a man beaten and defenseless on his back. But what else could we do with him? He was an enemy. He'd killed almost fifty Characters in the last battle against the Snow Queen alone.

Rain started to fall, in fat, chilly drops.

"What would he swear on?" I trembled—holding my sword over Iron Hans's face really hurt my ribs. I hoped they thought I was shivering from cold. "If you did the oath and made him swear not to hurt us, what would he swear on?"

"I dunno. His life?" Chase obviously liked the idea.

You would have thought we were talking about the price of tickets on the Fey railway. That was how interested Iron Hans looked.

I shook my head. "Dying doesn't scare him."

"The enchantment he's under. The one that turned him from human into metal man," Chase said.

It was news to me that Iron Hans had been human, but the villain scowled. Chase had guessed right. "That one. Fast."

"Hear that, iron brain? You've got a choice—you can help us, or you can die. I'm not as nice as Rory. I *will* kill you. Got it?" I glared at Chase for ratting me out. Iron Hans didn't need to know that. "So, repeat after me: I, Iron Hans, swear upon the enchantment that binds me—"

The man's chest rumbled under my foot. "I, Iron Hans, swear upon the enchantment that binds me—"

"If I break the oath, then the enchantment will hold forevermore, and I'll never be human again," Chase said, and Iron Hans repeated this too, not even winded by me standing on him. "I swear never to harm the two people I see before me, Rory Landon and Chase Turnleaf, and not to bring harm to them by aiding their enemies through information or action. Furthermore, I swear to help them in whatever way is necessary."

Chase was pushing it with this last sentence.

Iron Hans repeated it too. But he also added, "But I shall determine for myself what is necessary, rather than follow any orders the children should have. In return, they must inform no one of my whereabouts."

Chase tensed up beside me, and I knew without looking that he was clenching his fists.

"Repeat it, or else the oath won't bind," Iron Hans told Chase.

Through gritted teeth, Chase muttered what Iron Hans had added and then he started swearing in Fey and in English so loud Lena would've whispered, *Oh, my gumdrops.*

"You can stop now, child," Iron Hans told me. "I won't hurt you."

"Yeah, let him up—he's harmless," Chase said. I jumped back, breath hitching slightly as I pressed a hand to my ribs. It didn't actually make them hurt any less, but the shuddering stopped. "We could have had a magic servant for life if he hadn't added that last bit, the stupid tricky bastard."

"I wouldn't want to do everything you said either," I replied. Chase would probably order Iron Hans to hop on one foot all day just because he thought it would be funny.

Chase ignored that. "I need to find my sword before it rusts."

"Where is it?" I asked, watching Iron Hans stand.

"Wherever it fell when he disarmed me." Chase stomped off into the woods downhill.

"The base of the maple sapling," said Iron Hans.

"See? He's still helpful!" I couldn't bring myself to sheathe my sword when I was alone with the scary metal bad guy. It wasn't just his reputation. He was so still. Except for his brown eyes, obviously wet and not metal, it was like turning around to find a pewter statue staring straight at you.

Cue pouring rain and awkward silence.

Then Iron Hans turned up the hill.

"Where are you going?" I asked, kind of accusing.

"I am leading you out of the wet. The boy will follow. The path is clear."

I couldn't exactly refuse. Shivering, and wincing with each step, I climbed up after him, through the trees to some rounded boulders and a small dark opening within them.

"You live in a cave?" Don't ask me why, but I'd always assumed that villains were big on castles, mansions, and gingerbread houses.

Iron Hans moved straight into the dark. I didn't have much choice. I stepped just inside. When lightning flashed again, I glimpsed simple wooden furniture: a bed, a chair, the table Iron

Hans stood over, and the cupboard open beside him. Minus the dark cave part, it looked kind of cozy.

I didn't know what to do besides hover around the entrance.

Most grown-ups I knew would have had something to say about two kids forcing them to help—something unpleasant. It freaked me out that he didn't.

"You should use that to dry yourself." Iron Hans pointed at a blanket-towel thing hanging from the peg beside me, light colored even in the dark. "You will never survive the Wolfsbane clan if you are ill."

"You heard about that, huh?" Chase stepped into the cave, water streaming from his hair.

I wiped my sword off and sheathed it. Then I eased the blanket off the wall and slowly rubbed it over my wet hair, wincing at the pain. Definitely a challenge, considering how hard my hands were shaking now. Well, all of me, really. My ribs hurt even when I held my breath.

"Enemies sworn on the Fey railway?" Iron Hans said. "All of Atlantis knows about it."

"I was afraid of that." Chase sighed. "Where's my blanket?"

"I have only one. Make a fire if you are cold. The wood is stacked behind the bed."

But no, Chase had lost the oath round. He wanted to win something. "You make the fire. It's your cave. We're your guests."

"I am busy with another task."

"It better be making us dinner," Chase muttered.

It was too much effort to intervene. I just dried a little faster.

"I am preparing a poultice for the girl's injury."

My head snapped up. So much for hiding it.

"You're injured?" Chase asked me, in a completely different tone.

"Just my ribs." I would have shrugged, but I knew that would hurt too. "I think I got slammed into one too many things today."

"Why didn't you tell me?" Chase apparently took it as a personal insult.

"That is the wrong question, Turnleaf," Iron Hans said. "The question is why you didn't notice."

Rapunzel had said almost the same thing just a few days ago. I hated that he reminded me of my friend. "Maybe because some big metal dude picked him up and started carrying him around like a piece of luggage."

Now Chase felt bad. "And you've just been fighting with broken ribs all day?"

"They are not broken. She could not move so quickly if they were. Cracked, perhaps. Severely bruised." Iron Hans carried a gauzy bandage, smeared all over with something that looked like spinach-artichoke dip but smelled like mint. "This needs to be wrapped around your ribs, herb side on your skin. Can you manage?"

I nodded, taking it with a wince. I didn't want him any closer.

"Let me!" Chase reached for the bandage.

"The fire will help her more," Iron Hans said sternly. I expected Chase to mouth off again, but he just swerved and started carrying wood to a blackened fireplace as Iron Hans turned back to his table.

Painfully, I lifted my shirt and pressed the herby stuff into my side. It felt uncomfortably cool for a second, like the shock of cold sunscreen on a sunny day, but then the pain eased, the throb subsiding. Tying the bandage tight after was a challenge, though.

As soon as I smoothed my shirt down again, Iron Hans reappeared, this time with a bowl of water, a jar of ointment, and some more bandage. "Let me see your left hand."

Chase looked up from the tiny flame he was feeding with dry leaves. "You had two injuries you didn't tell me about?"

"No, I—" I looked at my left hand to prove it, but even with the small light Chase's fire cast, I could see it more clearly—the split knuckle oozing blood. It was slightly swollen and blotchy with new bruises. "Oh. Well, this one doesn't count, because I didn't notice."

"Didn't notice." Chase blew the flame a little bigger and built a pyramid of twigs around it. "Defeats Iron Hans with two injuries, and didn't notice."

"You helped," I pointed out. Chase gave me a look that clearly said, *In what way was hanging by my belt helping?* "You said 'eye.' I would have never thought of attacking him that way if you hadn't suggested—"

Chase turned back to the fire, scowling.

Oh. He'd just been stammering.

Iron Hans dabbed at the bowl and cleaned my hand with brisk strokes. It was weird—his metal skin didn't yield at all. It was too hard. But it also had a rough, calloused texture, and the warmth of any other human.

He tapped the ring with one finger. The metals clinked. "This gives you the power of the West Wind. But you still have the body of a human girl. Your hand was not designed for the strength you now possess. You must remember that."

I knew he was right. It made me kind of sad. "Does everyone on Atlantis know about the winds this morning?"

"No." Iron Hans smeared ointment all over my hand. It smelled familiar. The ointment of the witch whose power is in her hair. I wondered how Lena was.

"Is it true that you have spies everywhere?" Chase asked Iron Hans.

"They are not spies, but I gather information from many sources."

"You wouldn't happen to know where the other questers are, would you?" Chase stood up, dusting off his hands.

"I might. After the rain clears."

"Right. No point traveling now," Chase said.

He wasn't sarcastic. That was a shock.

Iron Hans wrapped the bandage, winding the gauze all the way up and down my hand, which I thought was kind of excessive.

"How about the Water of Life? Could you find where that is?" I asked eagerly.

"No." Turning his back to me, Iron Hans started concocting something else, something so strong it made my nose run.

"Do you know someone who does know?" I asked.

"The Unseelie royals."

That was kind of good news. We were already on our way there. "Do you think you can get that prince to tell us?" I asked Chase.

He shook his head, obviously worried. "We'll need that just for permission to stay."

Maybe Chase could have squeezed the location out of the stupid prince if we'd gotten to the Unseelie Court early, if we hadn't gotten split up, if we hadn't gotten kicked off the train.

Panic snuck its way in. We might have been there right now, if I hadn't screwed it up.

"We heard that the spring is currently here in the South," Chase told Iron Hans. "Do you know if—whoa, Rory. What's with the pacing? Just because your ribs don't hurt anymore doesn't mean they're healed."

"I hope you aren't gonna bug me about my ribs for the rest of the quest." I couldn't keep still. I felt so useless, as useless as Mia, trapped here by a rainstorm, miles away from the other questers. Worse than useless. What if we ran out of time because of my mistakes? "Maybe we should go right now. Find the others."

Chase pointed at the sheets of water pouring down outside the cave. "If we go out in that, we could walk right off a cliff. That would really slow us down."

Iron Hans held something out to me—a dark liquid in a brown, clay mug.

I did *not* want to drink it. "What is it?"

"A sleeping draft," said Iron Hans.

"I don't want to sleep." I wanted to go find the others and run all the way to the Unseelie Court. I wanted to save everyone at EAS.

Iron Hans refused to take the mug back. "That poultice will not heal unless you are still."

Chase piped up. "So you can either stay up worrying all night and met the Unseelie Fey with sore ribs, or you can sleep. Wow, what a tough choice."

I shot him a dirty look. I swallowed the sleeping draft in three gulps and grimaced. It tasted like I always expected nail-polish remover to taste, sharp and surprisingly chemically coming from an iron dude wearing a tunic and leggings.

I passed the mug back, thinking fast while I still could. "Could I give the Unseelie prince my boons—like a bribe?"

"No, only Dapplegrim boons work like that, and Fael wouldn't want yours," Chase said. "And stop trying to get rid of your boons. Those things last for decades."

"Is there something else the court wants? Something we can trade for information?"

"Now you're thinking in the right direction." Chase came away from the wall, frowning at me. "Rory, maybe you should sit down."

My legs felt unnaturally heavy, and so did my eyelids. I couldn't keep them open—oh, and now my vision was growing dark. "Wow, that sleeping draft works fast." My words slurred together a little. Great. My tongue wasn't working either.

Chase caught my elbow. I sat down on something cushy. Someone threw the blanket over me.

"I'd say I'll wake you up for your watch, but that won't happen," Chase said.

I wanted to argue, but my mouth wouldn't move. Then, promising myself that I'd tell Chase off in the morning, I slid into sleep.

By the time I clawed my way back into waking, the storm was long over. The sun shone into the cave and stretched shadows along the earth floor; the breeze was warm. Morning must have been half over. Something was going *thwack-thwack-thwack* at the cave mouth in a very annoying way.

It took me a second to realize it came from Chase and the hatchet in his hand and the log he was splitting into fire-ready pieces.

"Are you seriously chopping wood?" I asked. The *at a time like this?* part was implied.

"Yep. Rory? You're up, right?" He shielded his face and squinted inside. "I can't actually see you. It's too bright out here."

"Can you stop? Otherwise, I might have to smack you over the head with that log," I told him.

"Go ahead. You'll put me out of my misery." He held it out, grinning. I sat up gingerly, but I was barely sore at all. "Feel better?"

"Yeah," I said. "Where is Iron Hans, anyway? And how long did I sleep?"

"Fifteen hours," said a deep voice just outside.

I jumped out of bed, my hand reaching for my hilt, but someone had taken my weapon away while I slept. My sword leaned against the wall, out of reach. "Geez, way to be creepy and not talk. I thought Chase and I were having a private conversation."

Chase hit the log one more time, and it broke apart. "Well, I knew he was there. He's been making me do chores."

Only an ancient metal warrior could make Chase split wood.

"There's a third one missing, isn't there? The one you call Lena?" asked Iron Hans.

I wished I could've seen his face when he said that, but when I walked out, he didn't look up. On an old stump, he sat still as a pewter statue, the sun glinting off his metallic skin.

He didn't feel like an enemy. I had faced enough of them to know—malice kind of radiates off them, so you go, *Oh, right—that person wants me dead.* Maybe it was the Binding Oath, but Iron Hans only seemed . . . mildly interested. And patient.

I still didn't want to talk about Lena in front of him.

"How about we go find the others now?" I had forgotten all about the bandage on my arm. Easing down to another stump, I unwrapped it slowly. The back of my hand was bruise-free, except for a tiny brown spot between the first two knuckles. "We need to get back to our quest."

"Others have found them," Iron Hans said in a low voice, like squat twisted imps were scurrying around doing his bidding. I tried not to imagine Ben's face when Iron Hans's evil minion showed up. "We can only wait."

"But how are we going to find them? We can't afford to just wait around all morning." We only had a day left before our grace period with the Unseelie Court ended.

"Rory, we're good," Chase said. "Iron Hans sent out an army of squirrels."

I paused. "Is that a Fey term Lena's gumdrop didn't translate?"

"No. His Tale was 'The White Snake.' He can talk to animals." Chase stacked the freshly split logs behind him. "According to the squirrels, the questers are following a road just up the ridge. They'll reach us in an hour. Technically we could meet them halfway, but then we would just have to walk all the way back."

So they had solved problems while I slept. That didn't happen very often. Everything might turn out okay after all.

I looked Iron Hans over. His light brown eyes looked too human in his very shiny, metal face. I had assumed villains showed up fully formed in our stories. It had never occurred to me that they might have Tales of their own. They might have even been Characters before they were villains.

"Everybody calls you the Snow Queen's strongest warrior," I told him quietly.

"I was once. I am no longer," Iron Hans replied, "but when you are as old as I am, your past actions follow you more closely than your shadow."

Now he really reminded me of Rapunzel.

Chase glanced between us. "Rory, he hasn't been in touch with the Snow Queen since the end of the war. He swore it on his enchantment earlier."

That made me slightly less suspicious.

"This Lena," Iron Hans pressed, "is she clever? Does she prefer to follow the rules?"

"How did you know that?" I glanced accusingly at Chase. He was too busy chopping wood to notice, or at least he pretended to be.

"You are not the only three to change the course of Character history," Iron Hans said. "There is a precedent."

"We haven't done anything," I said, but goose bumps popped up over my arms.

Chase grinned, perfectly delighted. "This is when you tell us why everyone talks about Rory, right?"

Iron Hans's eyebrows—a slightly blacker metal than the rest of his skin—rose. "You do not know already? Rory—"

Then he stopped, and it looked like he had swallowed his tongue. He looked just like Kezelda had when she had started to tell me something—only way less ticked off.

"Well?" Chase said, putting down the hatchet. "I order you to tell us!"

"Chase, he doesn't have to do what you say," I reminded him. "Besides, I don't think he can help it."

Iron Hans met my eyes, nodded once. Obviously, he hadn't gotten control of his tongue back yet.

"Are you cursed?" Chase said, interested. "You lose your voice every time you say Rory's name or something?"

"That's the dumbest-sounding curse I ever heard," I said.

"No, it's not. It stopped him from telling us whatever he was going to tell us."

"Is there an object located at your chapter?" The second Iron Hans had his voice back, he used it to interrupt the bickering. Lena would have done that too. "A silver cylinder, closed on the bottom, the top riddled with holes?"

"No," Chase said.

"Wait, you mean the magic saltshaker?" I said.

Chase stared. "How do you know about it and I don't? I live there."

"I saw it the day of the feast, right before I found out you—right before I met your mom," I said, kicking myself when Chase's face fell. "It's on a pedestal in a room full of enchanted statues. It was next to a statue in old-fashioned clothes, and his name was Husky, or Wolf, or—"

"Wolfgang Sebastian Bruhm?" asked Iron Hans.

"Yeah, I think so," I said.

"Wolfgang?" Chase repeated. "Did his parents hate him?"

"He was called Sebastian," replied Iron Hans, and the look on Chase's face clearly said, *That middle name isn't any better*.

I waited for Iron Hans to tell me how he knew the name, but he just stared out at the landscape, face smooth. I was pretty sure that was his thoughtful expression.

"Soooo . . . ," Chase said, impatient. "The magic saltshaker?"

"It's a Pounce Pot," Iron Hans said. I did not snicker, mainly out of shock that the words "pounce" and "pot" went in a sentence together. "Centuries ago, to help ink dry, you would sprinkle powder over the wet vellum. This one keeps secrets. It is enormously powerful."

"With a name like 'Pounce Pot'?" Chase thought Iron Hans was pulling a fast one.

"You write the secret, and the name of the person or persons from which the secret should be kept," Iron Hans said, "and over it you sprinkle ground unicorn horn from the Pounce Pot. It can keep one secret from one person their entire life. If someone tells, or tries, their tongue will rebel, as mine did now. If the secret is written, the person will lose interest, or perhaps the ability to read. Its adaptability is its power."

"What if we made Rory go hide over there?" Chase said sarcastically. "Could you tell me, then?"

"Mildred must have added your name as well, and Lena's, knowing that you are close to Rory," said Iron Hans. "The Pounce Pot can keep secrets from more than one person."

Chase turned to me, mouthed "pounce pot," and shook his head darkly.

"But for less time," added Iron Hans. "Not their whole lives."

That was only slightly comforting.

"How do you know if the Director used this thing or not? She might not even know it exists," Chase pointed out.

"Mildred knows about it. She went on a quest for it with Solange and Sebastian," Iron Hans said. "I helped them."

Yeah, I'd felt less bowled over when a dragon knocked me down last February.

"You're making that up. No way the Director went on a quest. That would be too far from her hairbrush." Then Chase went still—like he had just processed the second name.

I only knew one Solange. "The Director and the Snow Queen knew each other?"

"Solange and Mildred were the closest of friends," Iron Hans said. "When they were girls, Mildred read everything. She memorized rules and recited them. Only Solange could convince her to break them."

If EAS was looking for a traitor, wouldn't they suspect the villain's best friend? No wonder the Director was so eager to accuse Rapunzel. The best defense was a good offense, right?

I had serious doubts that the Director was actually behind it, but even poisoned and confined to her sick bed she would try to preserve her reputation. I couldn't wait to point this out to Lena.

"They called them the Triumvirate," said Iron Hans.

Chase's gaze met mine, and I knew he remembered what the Director had called us, too. This was why the Director thought I had convinced Lena to make the portal in EAS's courtyard. More evidence to tell Lena. Solange had probably convinced young, pre–Sleeping Beauty Mildred to do bad stuff—maybe even evil deeds, considering who Solange grew up to be.

"It was more common," Iron Hans said, "when lifetimes were shorter: The ties you made at eleven could forge the course of your life."

Was he talking about Solange and Mildred and the other guy? Or did he mean me, Chase, and Lena now?

"That's right, Rory. You're stuck with us." But Chase didn't look at me as he brought the ax crashing down on the log.

"Wow. That sucks. How will I ever manage?" I said, adding extra sarcasm, and Chase grinned back.

Part of me wanted to stop talking about this, like I usually did when we were talking about my Great Destiny or whatever it was. But a practical part—a *curious* part—knew I might never get this opportunity again: someone outside the Canon, someone who knew and *wanted* to tell me.

"What quest?" I wondered if villains had a Canon too—and a school, and a book like Rumpelstiltskin's.

"They defeated the Pentangle," said Iron Hans.

"The same Pentangle that King Navaire founded?" And when Iron Hans nodded, Chase actually looked a little pale.

Lena would have just recited off every fact she remembered about the Pentangle as soon as it came up. I missed not having to ask. "Uh . . . who?"

"He was the longest-running king the Unseelie Court ever had. Fey, obviously—and a tyrant. You couldn't sneeze in Atlantis without his approval. But that wasn't enough for him," Chase said. "He recruited four of his most powerful contemporaries—a goblin priestess, the last mage ever, a gnome seer, and the matriarch of a witch clan. With them he conquered almost all of the hidden continents. He was preparing to conquer the human lands too, before some Characters stopped him."

Suddenly, I couldn't stop myself from imagining some winged, crowned figure sitting in the Oval Office, telling the U.S. president what humans were and weren't allowed to do—the same way Madison told the KATs.

"The gnome seer was why they needed the Pounce Pot," Iron Hans said. "Solange knew they would never be able to reach Navaire if he realized his enemies were coming."

Oh. The Director hadn't started out evil and then switched sides. The Snow Queen had started out good. Solange had once been a regular Character, back when she was my age. Overwhelmed by her destiny, just like me.

My heart contracted in my chest, like it wanted to shrivel up and hide rather than listen to any more of this.

"Are you sure we're talking about the same Mildred?" Chase said. "Taking down evil Fey kings is something she'd mention."

"You cannot speak of the Triumvirate without mentioning Solange, and no one discusses that part of Solange's past," said Iron Hans, "but when she joined the Canon in the nineteenth century, she was widely heralded as a hero."

The Snow Queen was even part of the Canon. My heart shrank a little more.

I didn't want to know Solange had been a good guy once. I hated hearing that even more than I hated hearing I was just like her.

"So," said Chase, "you're saying that me, Rory, and Lena are supposed to defeat the Snow Queen and her minions the same way the Triumvirate defeated the Pentangle?"

Iron Hans was silent.

"You—" Chase started angrily.

"No, that's what he can't tell us," I said quickly, before Chase started shouting.

Iron Hans nodded. "Part of it."

"So now that Rory's here, you're all set to dump your old mistress and help us?" Chase said, clearly skeptical again.

Iron Hans's eyes suddenly turned as hard as the rest of him. "Solange was not my mistress. She was my friend."

Chase snorted. "You and the Director have great taste in friends."

But when Iron Hans had gotten out of his Fey prison, he hadn't gone to join the Snow Queen. He hadn't even spoken to her. He'd come out here to the woods. All he wanted was to be left alone. That was the only thing he had added to the Binding Oath—that Chase and I tell no one where he was.

Iron Hans sighed, like he didn't want to fight about it. "No one's story is ever the complete one. Soon after I helped them gain the Pounce Pot, Mildred's Tale began, and she slept for a hundred years."

Chase took another swing at the log with an extra loud thwack. "Tell me about the dude. He was the best fighter, right?"

Wow. Chase was being so subtle. I had no idea which one he wanted to be.

"Sebastian was the grandson of a Potsdam Giant. So he had a warrior's training," said Iron Hans.

Chase beamed. "Well, that definitely doesn't describe Rory, so it's got to be me—"

"How do you know I couldn't be the warrior?" It ticked me off more when Chase openly snickered. I ignored the little Kenneth-like voice in my head that said I was useless without my sword. "Don't laugh. Which one of us beat the metal dude yesterday?"

Chase rolled his eyes. "Yeah, and who dropped her sword and apologized to the troll for smashing his bridge? You've never killed anyone."

And I never wanted to. I'd told him so.

"Neither have you—" I started, but Chase looked at me sharply. I broke off and added something else to the list of things Chase had never told me. "Oh."

"The Fey forge their warriors very young," Iron Hans said, like he disapproved.

Maybe I didn't want to be the warrior anyway.

"And the third one?" I couldn't bring myself to say the Snow Queen's name.

Iron Hans looked me with his far-off thinking stare. "You are the glue, and the current."

Great. He had stopped making sense. Definitely like Rapunzel.

He must have guessed that didn't tell me much. "It was Solange who had the conqueror's heart."

I made a face. That didn't sound like me at all.

"What Tale did Sebastian get?" Chase said. "Tell me it was something with a Dapplegrim."

Iron Hans frowned. "That is the wrong question."

"You keep saying that," Chase said, swinging the hatchet again. "It's annoying. There's no such thing as a stupid question."

"You'll need to find your own path, Chase," Iron Hans said. "You cannot wait to be defined by your Tale."

"Yes, I can." Chase's face was on the red side, and I couldn't tell if it was because he was mad or because chopping wood was hard work. "I'm going to have the best Tale anyone has ever seen—"

"You should be more truthful."

And instead of flipping out at Iron Hans, Chase was silent, jaw clenched. I was definitely missing something.

"Tell her," said Iron Hans. Chase didn't say anything. "Do you still want the reward we discussed?"

Chase sucked in a huge breath. He turned to me. "You know the test for Characters?"

"Where you see something in a magic mirror?" What did this have to do with the Triumvirate?

"I saw the Tree, but being half throws everything off," Chase explained. "The Fey always see something in a magic mirror. The Director said I might never get a Tale."

My mouth fell open. I snapped it shut before Chase could comment.

Chase had always bragged about getting a great Tale. But I knew suddenly, from his half-defiant, half-hopeful stare, that he hadn't been trying to convince me and the other seventh graders. He'd been trying to convince himself.

What if he didn't get his Tale? What would stop him from leaving? He could grow up in more places than just Ever After School.

"Of course you'll have a Tale," I burst out fiercely.

Chase grinned.

"You don't have the luxury of waiting for your Tale, Chase," Iron Hans said. "You and you alone must determine your role in what will come." I wondered if he really wanted to sound so freaky, or if you naturally said stuff in a scary way when you lived for a thousand years.

"You don't know that." Chase's knuckles were white around the hatchet's handle.

But Iron Hans talked like he did know. "I know there may be no glory in it. It should not be glory you seek, no matter what you have been taught."

Chase gave him a long, hard, withering look, the kind that terrified the fifth and sixth graders, and sometimes the triplets. But he didn't say anything, which probably meant that he couldn't think of any way to argue.

"You're out of wood. You know where you left it," said Hans.

Chase burst into the air with a flurry of peachy wings—like he couldn't get away from us fast enough.

"Okay, here's what I don't understand," I told Iron Hans, mainly to lighten the mood. "How did you manage to get Chase to chop wood? Chase only does chores if a giant threatens to throw him down the beanstalk if he doesn't sweep to her satisfaction."

"He destroyed my winter's woodpile last night," Iron Hans said. "I offered him a boon if he would chop up the two trees you smashed to the ground."

"Chase would do anything for a boon." I ignored the fact that a thirteen-year-old would need more than a few hours to chop up two whole trees. "But I would have loved to see Chase's face when you told him to split firewood."

The corners of Iron Hans's mouth quirked up. "His exact words were, 'Don't you have any armies you need slain? I also kill a mean griffin.'"

The idea was too strange—it took me a second to recognize that Iron Hans was smiling. He liked Chase, even if he'd spent the last ten minutes chewing him out.

"I learned of Solange's misdeeds after the war, in prison—what she did to Chase's brother and to her own sister, and to so many others," said Iron Hans. "I will never enter another war. I no longer trust a side enough to kill for it."

"She had a sister? What did Solange do to her?" Images of torture and beheading flooded my brain.

Chase dropped out of the air, hugging a circular piece of tree trunk, mud splattered over both knees. "Duh. Stuck her in the tower. The Snow Queen played the witch in Rapunzel's Tale."

"Rapunzel?" It sank in slowly. "*Our* Rapunzel? She's Solange's sister?"

"Half sister, technically." Chase buried the hatchet so deep into the wood he had to wiggle it free.

I stopped breathing.

They looked similar. I knew that. I'd noticed it in the beginning, but I'd forgotten. They felt so different, the Snow Queen always cunning, Rapunzel always so sad.

A squirrel—with two metallic stripes of gold down its back—scampered into the clearing and up Iron Hans's leg. I stared at it, uncomprehending, as it chittered away. Apparently, Lena's gumdrop translator didn't cover animal speech.

When I took a deep breath, the air rattled on the way down, and Chase looked so startled I wondered what my face was doing.

He stepped closer, hatchet in hand. "Rory, you really didn't know? You didn't even suspect?"

I shook my head, too shocked to trust my voice. I *should* have suspected.

Iron Hans looked up from the squirrel. "I am sorry to rush you, but the human questers are a quarter mile north of us. They tried to outrun their enemies, but they have been attacked. They are fighting for their lives." His warm brown eyes met mine, mournfully. "They are losing."

e didn't have time for a proper good-bye. Or for any of my questions, and definitely not time for answers. I yanked the smelly bandage off my ribs and strapped on my sword belt. "Bye, Iron Hans. Thanks for all your help."

Chase buckled on his own sword. "Rory, he had to help us, remember? We made him take an oath."

"Then maybe we should apologize, too," I said.

"Go." Iron Hans pointed toward a ridge lined with firs. "There. That is where you must run."

Of course it was uphill. I took off at a sprint. At least we weren't carrying our packs.

"See ya, Iron Hans!" I heard Chase call, right behind me. I was panting within ten seconds, but Chase said, "Are we going to tell people about metal man?"

"Is this a good time to talk about it?" I asked, annoyed at how out of breath he wasn't. "Our friends are in trouble. Besides, the Binding Oath won't let us."

"The oath only keeps us from telling people where he is, not that we met him," Chase said. "Anyway, I don't know if you noticed, but our friends are almost *always* in trouble. As soon as we handle the fight, they'll ask us where we've been all night."

I was so sick of keeping secrets. Keeping track of what I could talk about was exhausting.

"If the Canon finds out, they'll send my dad to track him down," Chase said. "Dad will have to kill him. Iron Hans is that dangerous."

That would probably end worse for Jack than for Iron Hans, but I couldn't tell Chase so.

"It would be a shame for him to die just because we found him. And he likes you, Rory—he told me you have to be as tough as dragon scales to fight with your ribs that bruised."

We ran up the ridge, along a narrow path probably made by deer or goats or the Atlantis equivalent. My foot found a loose rock, and when I stumbled, Chase caught my elbow and hauled me up. Wings fluttered, but I didn't see them.

"Fine," I said. Iron Hans had been really nice for a famous villain. "But we're telling Lena."

Chase grimaced. "You want to tell the biggest Goody Two-shoes in the whole seventh grade? Iron Hans is doomed."

Sounds drifted through the trees: metal clanging on metal, and a human girl's scream.

I pushed myself faster. "Lena needs to know what he said about the Triumvirate, and she'll want to know where we heard it."

Chase was quiet, except for a rasping *shink* as he drew his sword. "Let me do the talking when they ask. You're not very good at lying."

We reached the top of the ridge just about the same time my thighs started burning so much I thought they would combust. I spotted the EASers first—three figures defending someone on the ground. Crooked metal limbs dove down at the questers, red leaves flapping.

Trees, I thought, watching their gnarled black roots creep along the ground like inchworms, dragging their trunks along lurch by lurch. *Trying to kill us.*

Another witch forest, and this one was moving.

"My arrows are useless!" Her face sweaty with pain, Darcy sat behind the others. It seemed like a stupid thing to do—until I saw that her leg was bent in a nauseating way. She couldn't get up, not with a broken leg.

An iron branch shot forward. Someone—Chatty?—swung a spear like a baseball bat, so hard that the tree swayed and almost fell.

"Geez. It *is* always the quiet ones," said Chase.

Another figure drew closer to Darcy's tree—Ben. Darcy was the best fighter among them, but arrows couldn't hurt metal trees. They were in serious trouble. The sword's magic tugged me across the ridge at an even faster sprint than before.

"Did you guys miss us? I get the feeling that you did." Then Chase leaped onto the nearest witch tree and stood where the trunk split into branches.

Ben straightened a little. "Chase?"

"At your service," Chase said. "When did Chatty get here?"

"Yesterday. Lena walked us through how to send Rory's ring of return back without her. She cried a lot, mind you, but Chatty still showed up. Kenneth is still healing, but she's supposed to come and replace—" Ben started. "Look out!"

Another witch tree—this one with a giant slash on its trunk— plunged three branches toward Chase, but he jumped out of the way. The crooked limbs of both witch trees tangled together, so tightly that the metal squeaked.

"See?" Chase said. "More mobility, but absolutely no brain. Not so scary."

It took me slightly longer to catch up, but I was there in time to see a squat witch tree take a twiggy stab at Ben. My sword parried, and the deflected blow shot straight into the forest floor and stuck.

"Rory?" asked Ben.

I waved over my shoulder, too breathless to answer.

"Watch out!" Ben said, as the scarred tree whipped a limb at Mia's head. Mia was busy with a witch tree with a silvery-looking trunk, blocking branches right and left. She was pretty efficient for someone who hadn't even attended one of Hansel's training classes yet.

I stepped forward, ready to protect her, and the runner's high disappeared.

I didn't think anyone else noticed—there wasn't time. I just snap-kicked the limb from the scarred tree away, one twig an inch from Mia's hand.

When the squat witch tree swung a branch at Ben's head, my sword's magic flared again, and I shoved Ben six inches down. The branch sailed harmlessly over his hair, the momentum of the swing spinning the tree all the way around.

I stared at my sword. Its magic had hiccupped. Just for a second. Just while I was defending Mia. I wondered if I'd given away Chase's secret and broken the Binding Oath.

The scarred witch tree lashed another limb at Mia. This time she dodged. The limb sailed toward my nose, and I was so stunned, Chatty had to shove me out of the way. Then she gave Mia a reproachful look that clearly said, *Even a new kid like you could have blocked that, easy.*

Mia clearly didn't mind if I got hit.

Suddenly I knew. The sword's enchantment wasn't wearing off.

It only worked if I really wanted to protect the person I was defending. I just didn't like Mia enough to keep her alive. I was a sucky warrior *and* a terrible person.

"Run, you guys. Seriously." Darcy would have been a lot more convincing if she hadn't been sweaty with pain.

"We're not leaving you here to die," Ben said, and Chatty nodded.

"Don't be stupid," Darcy said grumpily. "They're metal trees. It's not like they can be killed. Once you get tired, those branches will get past your guard, and you'll die. And so will everyone else back at EAS."

She had a very good point. The battle was more evenly matched with me and Chase there, but there wasn't much human kids could do against killer trees, except run. Running was how we'd gotten away last time. "We'll make a sling," I suggested, turning aside a whip-thin branch aimed at my face. "We'll carry Darcy out of here."

Mia shook her head. "No matter how far we run or how fast, they catch up. They've chased us from the beach all the way up here."

So moving metal trees were more of a challenge.

The scarred tree smashed three branches down at once, scattering our line. I jumped back and nearly lost my balance when I glimpsed the huge ravine behind Darcy's boulder. The twenty-foot-wide crack stretched down and down and down, until you could barely see the jagged rocks and tiny waterfall winding its way through the bottom.

I swallowed hard, overwhelmed by the sudden urge to vomit. *Ugh. Not another battle around heights.*

"Head in the fight, Rory!" Chase shouted.

My eyes snapped open. "We need a plan, Chase!"

"What makes you think I don't have a plan?" Chase ducked out of the way of a swinging branch and pointed back to a black mass of metal tree limbs. It had four trunks. He'd managed to get all the witch trees with the same *dodge at the last second* trick. "I tangle them all together. You make sure everyone else is safe. We questers go on our merry way while the trees spend all week trying to get loose. Simple."

"Oh." Ben straightened up, obviously feeling better about the whole situation. "Brilliant."

"Exactly. Simple, but brilliant," said Chase, grinning. Then Chatty hit my shoulder and pointed again at the clump of trees Chase had defeated.

They were untangling themselves.

"I hate to break it to you guys, but there's a hole in your plan," Darcy said.

The four trees stood apart now, but even worse, with the rustle of red leaves and the earsplitting squeak of black metal, the roots slithered out of the ground and twisted themselves into two separate, near-identical pillars—I mean legs. And the branches twisted into two arms, complete with knotted fists. Perfect for smashing Characters with.

Worst of all, even though the trees didn't have faces, even though they didn't have *heads*, they whispered one word with voices like dead leaves crackling underfoot: "Aurora."

"The Snow Queen," I whispered, because I could only think of one bad guy who could do this. "She found us."

"Oh," said Mia. "I was going to guess that the Wolfsbane clan caught up to us."

That made more sense, actually.

One of them lunged forward and punched.

"Chase!" I shouted, but he'd already leaped back.

"Okay. Now we need a new plan," Chase said, frustrated.

Another tree ran forward. It wasn't very fast, its root legs were too stumpy, but it raised a hammerlike fist dotted with blood-red leaves.

Mia pulled Ben away, up the path, farther from the edge. Chatty hooked her arms under Darcy's and pulled. Darcy cried out as her broken leg slid over the ground.

The tree punched toward me. I blocked with my sword. A mistake. The blade flew from my hand and skittered to the side, stopping inches from the ravine.

I knew I was faster than the tree—I could grab my sword—but Chatty and Darcy had barely budged. They'd be smashed instead. I couldn't leave them.

The tree struck again. I pulled a Chase and dodged at the last second. The metal fist swung through the empty air beside me instead. The tree tipped forward, off balance and perilously close to the edge of the ravine, and I put two hands against its trunk and shoved.

It shot through the air and smashed against the rocks so hard it flattened against them, all bent out of shape.

"Wow," said Darcy.

I stared at my left hand, at the West Wind's ring on the middle finger. I ran a little farther away from Chatty and Darcy, scooping up my sword and sheathing it on the way. "I'm Rory Landon! Me! Rory right here!"

The trees all turned at once, like they'd been waiting to hear my name. Then they staggered toward me on their stumpy legs.

"I don't think I like your plan!" Chase said.

I stood as close to the ravine as I dared, less than three feet from the edge, and watched the trees run closer and closer. Twelve feet. Eight. The closest one tried to clobber me, but I ducked.

The trees were five feet from the edge. That had to be good enough.

Aiming carefully, I punched the way Chase had taught me. My fist connected.

Pain flared over my left knuckles.

The tree I'd punched knocked into the one behind it, straight back toward the ravine.

That was all I had meant to do, but the trees had stupidly come at me too close together. All three tumbled like bowling pins and rolled over the edge, tangled together. They smashed into the boulders below.

I made myself step closer to check, but the trees were still. The West Wind's ring had knocked all the magic out of them. I waited for someone to tell me off for setting the Wolfsbane clan on us, but the other questers were just staring at me.

"Geez, Rory," Chase said. "Three trees with one punch. I need to stop ticking you off."

I didn't feel ticked off. I felt like I'd almost broken my hand. I was really glad I hadn't needed to shove all three into the ravine one by one, which had been my original plan.

"Hear, hear," Ben said.

That broke the tension.

"Did you just say 'hear, hear'?" Chase asked. "What decade do you think we're in?"

"You can't say stuff like that without a smoking jacket, and maybe a cigar," said Darcy, sitting on the ground, her leg broken.

"Guys, it's time you all knew—I'm a huge dork. I hope we can still be friends." Ben grinned, only slightly sheepish, and then he threw up beside Darcy's boulder.

"I'll think about it," said Chase, looking a little worried about him.

"We thought you were dead, dummy." Darcy tried to sound irritated, but her voice shook. "You guys fell, and we were so high up. It was all my fault—I shot the arrow at the troll, and made it so angry . . ."

I didn't know what to say.

"Nah, I think it's safe to blame Rory and her bridge-breaking skills," said Chase. "Luckily, one of us happened to have a spare boon from the West Wind."

"The West Wind got there really fast . . . ," said Mia. "And why didn't you just have him fly you straight back up to us?"

Ugh. Mia was always really logical at all the most annoying times.

"Didn't think of it." Chase was much better at lying than I was. "We figured you guys would head this way, and if we wandered around for long enough, we would find you."

Ben wiped his mouth. "Well, Darcy, your Companionship has been a real pleasure, but we should probably return you now. Your leg needs looking after." Ben moved toward the carryalls, and now that we were talking about broken bones, both Darcy and Chase went suddenly pale.

Chase hated bones—you couldn't even mention them without him breaking into a cold sweat. He changed the subject, like he was hoping no one would notice how freaked out he got. "Good news, though—we ran into a friendly Fey on vacation. She said the Unseelie royals know where the spring is. You know, for the Water of Life."

Hope flared across Ben's face. "And we're close to them, right?"

Chase nodded. "About a day's journey."

Ben placed a ring of return in Darcy's hand. Her lip trembled as her fingers closed around it. "Bring the Water home, you guys. I would have poured it straight into Bryan's stupid little fawn mouth if I could have."

"Of course we will—" started Ben, but Darcy was already gone. In her place appeared one of my least favorite people.

"I thought you were dead," Kenneth told me, obviously disappointed.

"I thought your arm was broken," I shot back.

"My shoulder was just dislocated. Good as new now." Kenneth turned to Ben. "You're running through all the good fighters, man."

"Can we eat? Where's the Lunch Box of Plenty?" Chase's appetite always astounded me. "Me and Rory haven't eaten anything since yesterday."

Rapunzel had sent Chatty and Kenneth because there wasn't anyone else left to send. Kenneth told us that all the remaining healthy Characters had left. Their parents had found out about the poisoning and ordered them home. Only Jenny and Rapunzel were left at EAS to tend to the others. Jenny couldn't leave—she was in charge of Hansel's practice dummies, which Lena and Melodie had converted into an army of nurses.

Then Ben asked how everyone was doing. Kenneth just grimaced.

When I called Lena on the M3, her tears fell on the mirror and blurred her image. She only cried this much when she felt awful, like the time she'd come to EAS with the flu and botched a batch of M3s. I felt about five million times guiltier, wishing that I had realized they would all think we were dead.

"Sorry!" The mirror filled with Lena's purple sleeve as she wiped it dry. "I mean, I was hoping. Rapunzel kept saying you were alive, but the Director was so sure."

Chase popped his head over my shoulder, his mouth full of chicken nuggets. "Hey, Lena—I'm still alive too."

"Hi, Chase," Lena said with a weak, watery smile.

But Chase had seen the tears. He hastily backed away to the Lunch Box of Plenty. Ben and Kenneth were still pulling handfuls of potato chips from it like it was a regular snack bag.

"Did you see his face?" Lena giggled. She almost sounded like her normal, healthy self, but then she coughed hard—like she'd choked on something.

"Are you okay?" I'd wanted to ask whether or not Rapunzel was really Solange's sister, but suddenly this seemed like a much more pressing question.

Lena nodded, her hand still over her mouth. She held up a finger and unwrapped a cough drop.

"Well, Companions, we better skedaddle." Ben stood up, wiping the grease off on his jeans.

"'Skedaddle'? Where do you *get* these words?" Chase asked.

Mia volunteered to scout ahead, and when Ben asked who wanted to go last and watch our rear, Chatty raised her hand, holding up a whistle—since she couldn't exactly yell for help.

We marched down a switchback trail that led to the sandy beach. I stared into the mirror, watching Lena's coughing fit subside, mainly to avoid looking at the drop.

"Your mom called a few times," Lena said apologetically when she could speak again. Her voice was hoarse. "You have four new voice mails. I've been texting her back, pretending to be you, but she's starting to sound kind of . . . upset." Lena was being nice. I'm sure Mom had started threatening to show up uninvited on Lena's doorstep.

"Thanks. Just to warn you, it might get a lot worse," I said.

Lena sighed. "I should probably let you go. I'm due for another dose of ointment in a minute. Jenny will kill me if I miss it."

I was officially worried about her. "Lena, we'll get the Water for you."

She smiled briefly, but she still looked tired. "I know you will. Bye, Rory."

I closed the M3 cover and pushed it back in my pack.

Rapunzel was on our side. I was sure. Pretty sure.

But no wonder the Director had been so desperate to stop us. To her it would seem like a fool's errand: The Snow Queen poisons almost everyone at EAS, so the healthy kids follow her little sister's orders? Leaving the sick in Rapunzel's hands, unguarded, so she could finish the job?

But why didn't anyone suspect the Director?

I glanced around to ask the only person I could think of—Chase. I could hear him whooping down the beach.

He ducked past Kenneth's outstretched sword and slapped the back of his opponent's legs with the flat of his blade. Enraged, Kenneth stood-stock still in the middle of the beach until Chatty and I nearly caught up with him. Then he charged Chase with everything he had, his sword raised high. Chase disarmed Kenneth, tripped him, and tapped the back of his skull lightly with the pommel of his sword.

Kenneth glanced ahead. Mia hadn't turned around once. Then, still stomach-down in the sand, he must have said something amusingly murderous, because Chase and Ben fell over laughing. As Ben helped Kenneth up, Chase scooped the fallen sword out of the sand and passed it back, saying something—probably explaining exactly what Kenneth had done wrong.

Chase liked them. He especially liked the way both eighth graders listened to his every word, even though he was supposed to be younger.

If it hadn't been for me and Lena, and if it hadn't been for the Beanstalk Tale and the mysterious destiny I couldn't shake, he would probably have hung out with these guys.

Stupid of me to worry about Chase leaving EAS. He didn't have to go anywhere to stop being my friend. It wouldn't be the first time. Just ask Adelaide.

If we didn't find the Water of Life, I would lose Lena, too. I could be alone.

I caught Chatty staring at them over my shoulder. "Weren't you supposed to be watching behind us?"

Chatty raised one eyebrow and pointed to herself innocently, as if to say, *Who me?*

"We'll switch." If I had to watch out for attacking trees, fairies, or witches, I might not think quite so much.

Until nightfall, I was sure that a bad guy would jump out at us from behind every tree, thicket, and boulder. But the scariest thing that hopped out of the forest that afternoon was a beige-and-gray rabbit. Delicate antlers sprouted up between its ears.

I stared at it, wondering if Atlantis animals could do glamour.

At the time, Ben was telling Chase about the storm the night before, how they had found shelter in a seaside cave, how Chatty had stood at the cavern mouth, tossing pebbles into the ocean. "Seriously. She just stood there, skipping stones and getting soaked until the storm stopped. We asked her if it was some magic from her chapter, but she . . ."

Beaming at the attention, Chatty shrugged, all the way up to her ears.

"Right, she did that, and—oh, my God, a jackalope," Ben said, spotting the creature. Chatty jumped, eyebrows up high, and the movement scared the little guy so much it scampered back into the woods. "Dude, those are real? My grandpa has one of them on his wall."

"It's a witch specialty," said Chase. "They bred them for bridge tolls, like the black cats."

"Could the witches be tailing us?" It was the first time Mia had spoken since the attack. "The Wolfsbane ones?"

The thought hadn't occurred to anyone else. Mia was apparently much smarter than she wanted us to think she was.

"Now we need to worry about witches, metal trees, *and* spying jackalopes?" Kenneth shot a dirty look in my direction. I flushed. "No wonder this Tale needs five Companions."

"If Darcy were here, I could have sent her to hunt it down," Ben said thoughtfully. "But we don't have any long-range fighters left."

So we moved on. If we were being followed, it wasn't a great idea to wait for them to catch up.

We walked until the sun set, and then all through dusk. The beach widened, and Mia led us down a path through the middle of the dunes. Each of my sneakers picked up enough sand to fill a playground.

Waves roared. A couple of them soaked my jeans. No one spoke.

The twilight deepened. Ben tripped for the third time, scrambled to his feet, and dusted the sand off his shirt. "I'm good. No worries."

I called up to the pack leader. "Hey, Mia—we should probably stop. We're not going to get there any faster if someone sprains an ankle."

Chatty nodded so vigorously she swayed and stumbled into the dunes. Her wince made me suspect that her feet were covered with blisters.

Ben looked at Chase. "How far are we from the Unseelie Court?"

"About an hour and a half walk down the beach, and then a long climb up a stone stair. Not that far. It could suck in the dark, though," Chase said, thinking. "Three days, so that's until noon tomorrow. We might as well make camp for the night."

I called first watch since I had gotten a ridiculous amount of sleep in Iron Hans's cave the night before, and Chase volunteered to help. Then he called first dibs on the Lunch Box of Plenty, because he had first watch. Clearly, he'd had an ulterior motive.

I found a boulder to watch from. The sea breeze was even gustier at night, almost chilling, and too loud for us to hear anything but waves and wind. We would have to rely on sight to see bad guys.

"Here." Chase passed me a slice of pizza dripping with pepperoni grease. "Eat it fast, or I will."

I took a bite. "Why does everyone suspect Rapunzel, but not the Director?"

Chase gave me a weird look, like he couldn't believe I would still be thinking about this when I had food in my hand. "Binding Oath. The Director swore on her life to do everything in her power to stop Solange."

"But they were friends."

"Not anymore. Solange killed the Director's husband right in front of her. Like seventy years ago," Chase said. "Revenge is a pretty powerful motivator."

I made a face. "Do you think we'll find it? The spring, I mean?"

"Yeah. That's what we're here for, right? We'll find out where it is from the Unseelie, and we'll be fine." The *duh* was implied in Chase's voice.

"But what if they don't tell us?" I said. "The southern coast is hundreds of miles long. We'll run out of time before we find it, or some witches will—"

"Rory, you're trying to be logical about this. It's a Tale." Chase took another bite, and I realized he had three pieces of pizza stacked on top of each other. Gross. "Bad stuff is supposed to happen. Then someone turns a bad thing into a good thing and saves the day. That's how it works."

That wasn't all that comforting. I wanted a solution. I wanted to know everyone would be all right.

He put his pizza stack on his leg, not caring that the grease was seeping into his jeans, and picked up his sword. "Anyway, I still say you're going to need to kill things eventually, but here's how you can win a fight without it: You can either bash people with your Left Hook of Destruction"—he tapped the West Wind's ring—"or the Mighty Snap Kick. Or, because you have this nifty sword, you can use it. Either hit with the hilt or smack 'em with the flat part of the blade. I would try to knock them out or, uh, break their legs"—he shuddered here, probably picturing a femur fracturing, and hurried onward—"to get them out of the fight. Got it?"

"Yeah." He was so good at this. I wondered if he enjoyed

teaching Kenneth and Ben more than teaching me—if he would rather have students who didn't feel bad about killing trolls, who could become real warriors someday.

"Good. Other people's lives depend on it. Probably mine. So finish your pizza. We'll run through some drills. Your sword should adapt to your new fighting style. Just . . ." Chase looked stern, but it was hard to take him seriously—a stringy piece of mozzarella hung from his chin. "Don't drop your weapon in the middle of a fight again. If nobody is covering you, it could be bye-bye, Rory."

I shoved the rest of the pizza in my mouth and stood up to practice jabbing, banging, and knocking with my hilt.

I didn't think I would be able to sleep at all when Kenneth and Chatty relieved us two hours later. I was sore from my shoulders, down to my fingertips.

But the dreams came anyway. Nightmares of Mia's head on a marble pedestal, her dark hair combed out, white silk spread underneath. A dark door covered in frost, a delicate snowflake with a scrolling S under its handle, and something terrible waiting behind it. My mother telling me I have to call her back, because Kezelda's familiar—a jackalope named Amy—is worried about me. My father at the LAX airport, demanding to know where I've been for three days—not noticing that standing in line at the taxi stand behind him are all green-skinned witches. And then my alarm, on my nightstand at home, ringing shrilly to tell me that it's time for school, spring break is over, Lena's dead, it's all my fault, and I can't even tell my mother what happened—

When I opened my eyes, the alarm continued across the dark beach—except it wasn't an alarm. It was Chatty's whistle. It cut off mid-blast. A Fey in glossy green armor plucked it out of her mouth.

"Turnleaf, did you miss us?" A Fey kid sat on Chase's chest. Moonlight gleamed on his breastplate, Chase's bulging eyes, and the dagger he held to my friend's throat.

I swiped at the Fey kid with my left hand. He tumbled into the air like a bug I'd flicked off my arm.

I reached beside me, where I'd left my sword the night before, and my hand closed on only sand. Chase and I both sprang to our feet before the Fey kid could stretch out his wings and right himself.

But another Fey knight had my weapon, and three more had pinned Ben, Chatty, and Mia. Two held Kenneth, who cursed and thrashed. Three more Fey knights were waiting to pounce. The Fey version of a Viking longship had been dragged ashore, its golden sail hanging loose, billowing in the breeze, the sun just peeking over the water behind it. That was how the Fey had reached us, but it didn't explain why they were here and holding us hostage. They couldn't wait a couple more hours to see us?

The Fey kid glanced at the others hurriedly, clearly making sure the knights hadn't noticed I had hit him. "You're no longer welcome here."

Chase swept a bow, unexpectedly graceful. He'd probably learned it via the Iron Hemlock method. "Prince Fael. I've come on Canon business. We were just on our way to see you."

The breeze drew sudden goose bumps on my skin.

The Unseelie prince had come in person just to mess with some EASers? I scanned the Fey knights, trying to figure out which one was royal.

The Fey boy tut-tutted. "You know as well as we do that your Director has only negotiated for three at a time. You have three persons over that allotment."

The *kid* was Fael? He didn't look any older than Kenneth.

"And our quests have run into very bad luck on Atlantis recently." Chase's face was blank in the gray light. "The Canon thought it best to send more Companions this time. We planned to arrive this morning at the Unseelie Court for approval of our number as the treaty requires."

"Your Director negotiated for three sunrises, Turnleaf," Prince Fael said, not even trying to keep the glee out of his voice. "You're about two minutes too late."

No way. Using fancy language against us was so nitpicky.

Chase's face didn't change, but his body flinched. So, it was true, and he didn't know how to get us out of it.

"I would love to kill you for the transgression, but I believe the punishment your Director approved was seven years' imprisonment," continued the Unseelie prince.

Seven years? We didn't even have seven *days* before the ointment ran out.

We were only a tiny bit behind schedule. If only we hadn't gotten stuck fighting the witch trees yesterday, or gotten separated crossing the troll's bridge—

Oh.

It was all my fault. The questers would have reached the court in plenty of time if I hadn't kept screwing up.

"What's going on?" Ben asked, and I remembered he didn't

have a gumdrop translator. The other questers didn't have any idea what Chase and Fael were saying and I didn't want to be the one who had to break it to them. "Is Chase using his favor to ask where the spring is?"

I shook my head. Never mind getting permission for a six-person quest. Now Chase needed to use that favor just to keep us out of prison.

"I apologize, Prince. I meant to ask—how is His Royal Majesty, your father? I think he would agree that a little extra time isn't worth seven years of imprisonment." Chase still sounded polite, so maybe most people would've missed it. But I'd heard it long enough to know: Smugness crept into Chase's voice. "We were always fond of each other. I'm sure that the king and I would have a great deal to catch up on."

The prince's face darkened. He obviously didn't feel like letting Chase blackmail him first thing in the morning. "You presume too much upon us, Turnleaf. You have betrayed your heritage, and now you seek to ingratiate yourself with our king, our loving father. How like you, Turnleaf, to show such *spine* here, the land where our ancestors' *skeletons* are buried, but we have a *bone* to pick with you."

"If you'll just give us—" Chase started, but then he went rigid.

"We know why you have turned your back on us and all that the Fey have offered you," spat the prince. He was doing something to Chase to keep him from negotiating anymore. "After all, who would choose to be a substandard Fey when he could pass himself off as an extraordinary human?"

Sweat gathered at Chase's temples, both fists clenched. I had to do something.

He'll fall under enchantment, Rapunzel had said. *You'll know when. Skin-to-skin contact is best.*

I grabbed Chase's elbow.

Suddenly, a closet was cast over me like a nightmare, or an ancient memory. The spell had spread to me.

No, not a closet. I recognized that smell—like earth and rot and chalk. I was in a crypt. Shelves rose up all around me, and each one housed a skeleton, the bones of its arms bleached white and crossed over its rib cage.

I couldn't even feel the sand under my feet. The enchantment was so strong, even spreading secondhand.

Panic thrummed in my chest. I couldn't stop myself from grabbing the silver grate on the door and rattling it so hard that chalky dust rained down from the shelves all around me.

But the fear felt distant. It came from Chase.

They were fairy bones. I noticed that with the detached part of my brain. You could tell, because they had spokes poking out of their shoulder blades where their wings were supposed to go. Lena had shown me that during her Tale—when we'd gotten stuck in a giant's bread box, right after Chase had freaked out.

I got locked in a tomb for three days, Chase had said then. *You'd be scarred too.*

Now Chase couldn't even talk about bones without shuddering. Fael had caused that—a teenage fairy prince terrorizing a five-year-old.

"Stop it, you petty—" I shouted, but someone shook me before I could finish telling Fael what a bully he was.

Then the vision vanished. I knew that Chase was out of the crypt too, because he was staring at me, his hand on my shoulder.

Great. I'd forgotten Fey Etiquette 101 and almost insulted the Unseelie prince.

"Interesting." The prince's wings hummed, and he flitted upward. His dark eyes glittered—the only hint he was angry. "They were all so meek; I never suspected that one of them had a mouth on her. Ori'an."

The boulder he'd been sitting on detached itself from the beach. A stone statue of a huge, ugly man, with a silver chain clanking around his ankles and tusks coming out of his mouth. A troll! No, he had gritty, cementlike wings.

I didn't get a chance to run. The stone troll fairy picked me up, squeezing me so tight all the air escaped my lungs. If Iron Hans hadn't healed my ribs, I would have screamed in pain.

"And then there were five," said Chase. I tried not to think about my legs dangling above empty air, or estimate how far away I was from the sand, or pay attention to how much the troll fairy's breath smelled like rotting garlic. "That's closer to the allotted number. Will you grant us safe passage now?"

My head whipped toward Chase. He couldn't have said what I thought he said.

The prince's eyes narrowed. "So, you wouldn't mind if we killed this girl, squeezed her to death right in front of you?"

Chase glanced at me. His face shot ice down my back. He looked . . . bored. I had seen him angry, cocky, hopeful, wry, impatient. Bored was new. Bored was too much like the stupid, bullying prince.

"If you want." Chase sounded bored even talking about my *death*. "But personally, I'm more interested in finishing our negotiations."

If I'd had any more breath left, it would have whooshed out in a relieved sigh. That face was a bargaining tactic.

It is nearly impossible for a human to get exactly what they want in Fey deals, Rapunzel had said.

Not a problem, I told my panic. Chase wasn't totally human.

Fael frowned, suspicious but unsurprised. "I could never allow you to simply walk away. You understand. We Unseelie have a reputation to maintain. We can't be known as being needlessly helpful."

Chase nodded, like this was reasonable. "But you're missing a great opportunity by imprisoning us questers. I'm sure there's something out there you would like to send us after."

I slapped the giant rock fairy's thumb to let him know he was holding too tight, but he only squeezed tighter.

Eagerness flickered across the prince's face. "Only one could go. The rest would have to serve as hostages."

"Fair," said Chase. "As long as we get to choose which quester."

Right. Because it would be all over if the Fey wanted to send Mia.

"I choose the object. You won't find out what until an agreement has been reached," said Fael.

"Naturally. And the chosen quester must have access to all resources we brought to Atlantis. For the full period of the quest."

"You understand that this will render the Unseelie agreement with your Director null and void," said Prince Fael lazily. "If you fail, I'll be free to kill whoever I wish."

Seven years in prison, or sending one person on a second quest and risking everybody else's life?

Chase nodded, considering it, his face smooth. "Yes. I'll need to run it past the other questers first, of course."

Fael waved a hand, which must have meant okay, because Chase looked significantly at me and the stupid rock fairy and added, "*All* the other questers."

Fael sighed. "Let her down, Ori'an."

As Chase went over to explain things, Ori'an lowered me down, and sand became my new favorite thing in the world. I walked over to the others on shaking legs.

Chase finished explaining just as I reached my pack and unzipped it.

"Chase, you suck at negotiating," Kenneth said, and Chatty looked just as horrified.

I pulled out my M3. "Lena," I whispered. Her face appeared almost instantly. She had bags under her eyes that hadn't been there the night before. She opened her mouth, but I put my finger over my lips.

"If it was your mother, what would you do?" Ben asked Chase.

Lena caught on fast. She pulled out a pen and paper to take notes.

"Imprisoned, we definitely won't find the Water of Life in time," Chase said grimly. "We still have a shot if we add a second quest."

"Then that's what we do," Ben said.

Chase turned back to Fael and switched back to Fey. "We'll take it. What do you want us to find?"

"The scepter of the Birch clan," Fael said. He could speak English. Then he smiled, obviously relishing the way Chatty covered her face and Chase went pale.

"The what?" Kenneth asked.

"I feel generous today. I'll tell you everything I know about its whereabouts: Iron Hans traded it to the king of the Hidden Trolls," the Unseelie prince told the other questers. "That court is located in one of the largest cities on your continent, where no Fey would deign to tread."

"The Hidden Troll Court that hasn't been seen for the past hundred years?" Kenneth said, furious. "That one? There's no way we can find that."

"It's in Los Angeles," Chase said. "That's what the Fey and the Canon think anyway."

That didn't make me feel any better. L.A. was kind of a big, crowded place.

Fael smiled wider. He knew it was impossible to find. He expected us to fail. He thought we'd just given him permission to kill us all.

"I know where to look!" Lena burst out. Her image bobbed in the mirror, and the infirmary background blurred. She was running.

"What is that?" Fael pointed down at my M3.

"One of the resources we brought to Atlantis," Chase said, with all his usual smugness.

Lena coughed, a hacking that sounded like it scraped the inside of her lungs, and then the M3 showed me a glimpse of fancy, leather-bound volumes. She was in the EAS reference room. A book thumped against a table, and Lena flipped through the pages. "Okay, the EAS encyclopedia on trolls doesn't really list a location for the Hidden Troll Court. It's just a riddle: 'In the land of sun and silver stars, / where all that is gold and not gold glitters, / the ugly ones live in the land of stories, / false for the chosen few, but for most, greater than real,'" Lena read. I could hear her pen tapping against her notebook.

"Oh," I said, ever so slightly more hopeful, but the other

questers slumped a little. Ben rubbed his eyes and blinked hard, like waking up more would solve the riddle for him.

"In Troll, it rhymes," Lena told us. "Now, I can do a scrying spell, but with that much area, it will take a lot of dragon scales and about a week. It would help if we could to narrow it down."

"What's that sidewalk? With the stars and the handprints?" Kenneth asked.

"The Walk of Fame?" Ben said eagerly.

They were totally on the wrong track. "No, it's not that. It's a movie set. An abandoned one, probably." Someone would have probably noticed a bunch of trolls if it was an active one.

Kenneth blinked at me. "Movie set."

"Are you sure, Rory?" Ben asked.

I nodded. "'Land of stories' makes me think some sort of entertainment. 'Silver stars'—Hollywood. 'False for the chosen few'—that would be all the film people who work behind the scenes, but everyone else gets sucked into the illusion."

"Oh, my gumdrops," Lena said, wide-eyed. "It's so obvious."

I shrugged, face hot. I didn't like the way the other questers were staring at me. "Hollywood is kind of in my blood."

Something clicked for Ben. "Oh, Rory *Landon*."

"The scrying spell will only take about an hour now." Lena was moving again. Past her, the M3 showed blue sky and then the ceiling of the workshop. "Rory, we need to figure out how to explain to your dad why you're coming to L.A. after all. I think Gran can handle that—"

"Wait—who said Rory was going?" Kenneth burst out.

I was about to agree with him, for the first time ever, but the others had turned to me too.

"Well, Mia and I are out," said Ben, "because we can't fight a whole court of trolls. Chatty's out, because she can't talk. Kenneth would probably lose his temper—"

This was too much responsibility. "So send Chase."

"What are you going to do, Rory? Tell your dad you can't visit, and then ask him if he can cart a complete stranger around L.A.?" Despite what he said, Chase obviously wished he were going instead. "Besides, I really doubt His Unseelie Highness over there would let me go."

It was really up to me. I struggled to breathe through the huge knot in my throat.

Through the M3 I could hear Lena opening and closing cupboards— grabbing what she needed for the scrying spell.

"I suppose I should tell you: You have twenty-four hours," Fael said, and I froze, hoping I hadn't heard him right. The only thing worse than searching for an impossible-to-find Hidden Troll Court and stealing a scepter was doing it with a time limit.

"Wait," Kenneth said. "That's not fair. You can't just start changing the rules."

But Chase's gutted expression said that Fael could. "Forty-eight hours—"

"She can have that long, if she wants," said the Unseelie prince. "But every dawn that scepter isn't in my hands, I'll kill a hostage. I'll start with that one."

Fael pointed at Mia. I felt extremely relieved. I *was* a terrible person.

"Thirty-six hours—" Chase tried again.

"Turnleaf, you fail to comprehend the situation. You are my prisoner, and I am no longer required to keep you alive," Fael said, his mouth curling even more. Chase went still. I knew he was going over the whole morning again, trying to think of everything he had forgotten to ask for. "The time for negotiation is over. Unless you would rather reject our new understanding. Then I can just kill all six of you now."

"I don't think," Chase said in an extra-loud voice, "that we'll be able to talk our way out of this. We better just cooperate."

I stared at Chase, almost positive that the Fey had abducted my friend and glamoured one of their knights to impersonate him. The word "cooperate" did not exist in Chase's vocabulary.

"I have a better idea." With a roar, Kenneth rushed at Prince Fael with both fists raised. Two Fey knights had the eighth grader's arms twisted behind his back and his face pushed in the sand before Kenneth had even gone two steps.

Chase stepped closer and whispered, "Go to L.A. I'll try to arrange a jailbreak on this end, but you need to concentrate on getting that scepter."

Chase, master of diversions and brilliant backup plans.

Getting the quest back on track wasn't all up to me. I could move again.

"I'll do it." I dug around my pack until I found the ring of return. Then I turned to the Fey knight holding my sword—shorter than the others, with gleaming clawlike nails. I reached for it.

"I never said anything about you taking your sword with you," Fael said lazily.

I was not heading to some troll court unarmed. "Yeah? Well, I never said anything about bringing you the scepter in one piece. If you want that to happen, I'll need my sword—and I'll need to be able to reach Chase through this mini magic mirror at all times."

"Oh, snap," said Kenneth. One of the fairies holding him shoved his face harder into the sand.

Scowling, the Unseelie prince gestured. The silver-clawed Fey knight passed me my sword.

But I didn't have time to feel triumphant.

"Rory." Ben looked at me, and I remembered his poisoned mother, Lena's five-minute coughing fit. "Hurry."

I nodded, heart in my throat, and slipped the ring on.

Gran got in touch with your dad. She said we had a family emergency, and we had to send you to L.A. He seemed pretty excited. You have an hour and a half before your flight is supposed to land." Lena looked much worse than she'd seemed through the M3. Her face was haggard, her eyes half-lidded, the bags under them bigger and more purply than before. I'd been stunned for a few seconds when I first found her, eyes glued to her scrying spell, in the back of the workshop. When she'd hugged me hello, she'd smelled like cough drops. This was usually the moment when she had some brilliant idea, but she looked at Melodie. "Now, we need to get you back to Atlantis in twenty-four hours . . ."

The golden harp said gently, "So we'll need a temporary transport spell to the beach where the questers are."

"Right," Lena said, relieved.

She hadn't been able to think of the next step. That was how bad she was feeling.

"Do you have any sand on you? From that beach?" Melodie asked.

I opened both hands. To my surprise, my right palm was covered in a fine layer of it. Lena drew a beaker out of her pocket and scraped a few grains off. Then she shuffled around the workshop, pulling dried herbs and a jar of powdered dragon scales out of a cupboard. She even walked like she didn't feel well, bent slightly forward like an old woman.

"Can I do that?" I asked.

"No." If I hadn't been looking at Lena when she said it, then I would have sworn the voice came straight from Jenny. "You need to worry about the scepter and about what you'll tell your dad when you leave to go back to Atlantis. Now shower."

I didn't even try to argue. I came back when I was clean and L.A.-ready, as close to looking like I'd just climbed off a flight as I could look, but Melodie was the only one in the workshop.

The golden harp lifted both arms toward me. "She's in the ballroom."

"And she didn't take you with her? Did you guys have a fight?" I asked, trying to lighten the mood. I picked her up and wove my way back through the tables to the door.

"She can't pick me up anymore, Rory." Melodie's golden chin wobbled. "And don't you dare tell her I told you, but she'll be bedridden soon."

Bedridden, from a tiny taste of Fey fudge pie.

"How do we make her better?" I stepped into the courtyard. "Besides, you know, the Water of Life."

"Make her sit still." Melodie sighed. "But you know how impossible that is."

Telling Lena not to move was like telling Chase not to eat—it only made them cranky. Besides, I needed Lena's help to save the others. I'd never get to the Hidden Troll Court and back without her help.

I pushed open the door to the ballroom infirmary. It smelled like burned cheese—like the ointment juice. The patients were all so still. For one horrible second I thought that someone had finished the poisoning job while we were gone, but then I heard people breathing, some more raspily than others.

"Rory, these are the healthiest ones," Melodie said, much nicer than usual. "The bad cases are farther in."

One of Hansel's practice dummies, an evil fairy, held out a spoonful of something to a boy, who stiffly slurped it, grimacing with pain. Kyle Zipes. I hadn't recognized him at first—his skin was ashen, his lips almost white.

Melodie tugged on my sleeve and pointed. Ellie. Her lips were white too.

"Lena asked about the Hidden Troll Court and went back to the workshop," Ellie said before I could ask. Kelly had crawled into the same bed, and Ellie stroked her daughter's hair. Puss-in-Dress sat sphinxlike on top of their pillows.

Beside their bed, reeking, was Rapunzel's flask of giant ointment juice, less than a third full. There wasn't enough of it to fill a milk jug. That couldn't be all we had left. It didn't seem like enough to last through Friday.

The golden harp threw her hands in the air. "This is why it's so much easier when she keeps me in her satchel." She was trying to lighten the mood too—for Ellie's sake.

Poor Melodie—she'd been here the whole time. She'd watched everyone get sicker and sicker.

"Melodie, these practice dummies follow anyone's orders, right? Even yours?"

"Yes," Melodie said, clearly not sure where I was going with this.

"You. Come here." I pointed at a witch practice dummy, friendlier-looking than the others. When it was close, I passed the golden harp over. "Melodie, this dummy will be your legs, and you'll be

Lena's hands. Let her boss you around. Maybe she won't move around as much."

Melodie nodded, her face brightening slightly. When she ordered the friendly witch dummy back to the workshop, Ellie explained Jenny needed to know that I had commandeered one of their nurses, and pointed me deeper into the infirmary, past the sleeping Director. Her blond hair fanned out perfectly from her pillow, her hands clasped over her stomach.

Only a few beds were occupied in the next section. I stood and stared. I knew the person in the closest bed was Rumpelstiltskin—he was the only Character at EAS as short as a fifth grader and as wide as an adult—but his skin was so blue. His lips were almost black, and it looked like someone had drawn spidery vines across his hands, over his face.

"The final stage of cockatrice poisoning," Jenny said grimly, appearing beside me. "We have to feed him some of the ointment every fifteen minutes, just to keep him alive."

It was so much worse than I'd thought.

I wanted to shout at the top of my lungs, *I'll save you!* just to break the silence above all these beds. I'd find that scepter and get it back to Prince Fael.

Someone else screamed first, so loudly that it echoed down the hall. "I won't die here!"

Apparently, this had happened before. Most people just rolled over and pressed their pillows over their ears. Jenny and I hurried down the row of beds.

The witches had an entire room to themselves, ringed off by a curtain and guarded by huge troll dummies. Past the curtain, two evil fairy dummies held the raving witch down, while Rapunzel struggled to tip a potion into her mouth.

The witch shoved the medicine goblet away, and I recognized her: Kezelda.

"What would you do," she shrieked, trying to twist free of the dummies, "if your mother had been killed by a Gretel, and your grandmother killed by a Gretel, and your great-grandmother, and your great-aunt, and four of your cousins? Wouldn't you want revenge too? Would you be so tempted to kill a Gretel that you would let one into your gingerbread house? Wouldn't you want to change your family's fate?"

It sounded like she was trying to justify the poisoning. But from the look on her face, I would say Kezelda was just as terror-stricken at finding herself near death as everyone else.

"We have to keep them sedated," Jenny explained to me.

It couldn't have been the witches.

No, I told myself. It couldn't have been *all* the witches. Because if it wasn't the witches, then who could it have been?

Rapunzel tried again to push the medicine past Kezelda's lips. Remembering why I'd come, I told Jenny that I'd assigned a dummy to Melodie.

"Good. Thanks, Rory," Jenny said.

At my name, Rapunzel looked up, and a little weariness lifted from her face. She handed off the medicine and came to hold both my shoulders, smiling. "I knew you were not dead. I was not sure how you could be saved, but too much of the future I have seen contains you. How did you survive?"

The real answer wasn't something I could say in front of sick Characters. "Um—" I glanced back at the door, hoping she would take the hint.

"Yes, I could use some fresh air," Rapunzel said smoothly, leading me back outside. I waved to Jenny and trotted after her.

The bed-bound patients watched us leave, staring so hard that I felt my face burn. I wondered if they suspected Rapunzel like Lena did.

"Did Chase use his wings?" Rapunzel asked when the door closed behind us. We were alone in the courtyard. I nodded, trying to figure out a graceful way to bring up what I really wanted to talk about. Rapunzel smiled wider, a laughlike catch in her voice. "Interesting. That child is extraordinary. His Fey gifts are weak by fairy standards, but he uses them so masterfully—"

"Are you really the Snow Queen's sister?" As soon as it burst out of me, I wished I could take it back.

The shock on her face faded, and then she reminded me of Chase on the beach, negotiating with Fael when Ori'an was about to kill me. No, she looked exactly like the Snow Queen—Solange's carefully composed, chilly expression. "Yes."

I had expected her to say no, it was just a rumor, the Director had misunderstood. But now a new feeling crept in—the same guarded watchfulness I felt when Madison and the KATs walked into homeroom.

Rapunzel was the grown-up I trusted most at EAS. What could I do without her?

"Aren't you going to say anything?" I snapped, frustrated. Rapunzel *always* said something. Sometimes it didn't make any sense, but it still helped.

"I don't know what else there is to say," Rapunzel said, not looking at me. "She is my sister. We share a father. Her mother was a French noblewoman killed in the Revolution. Mine was a peasant Character with mermaid ancestry."

"What was she like?" But that wasn't what I really wanted to know. "How do you feel about her?"

"I love my sister," Rapunzel said, and I couldn't believe she used the present tense. "She was the witch in my Tale. She was my whole world for my first fifteen years. But my sister is gone—the Snow Queen is heartless. I love a ghost."

I couldn't stand listening to her talk about Solange like she was a good person. The Snow Queen had deceived Iron Hans. She had killed Chase's big brother. "You aren't telling me anything useful."

"You sound like Mildred, Rory," Rapunzel said wearily. I recoiled. That was definitely an insult. "My life was not designed to provide information to you, or the Director, or the Canon. The beginning of my life was manipulated toward one end only: an immortality I never wished for. Solange sliced my neck when she cut my braid away. She left me, bleeding, in the path of the Rapunzel before me. The previous Rapunzel gave me her apple and brought me into the Canon. Else she would have watched me bleed to death."

"But you didn't have to take it," I reminded her.

"I was pregnant. My twins," Rapunzel said shortly, almost impatiently. "Is this what you wanted? Does this tell you a thing you didn't know about my sister?"

She had never mentioned kids before. She looked about sixteen, so it never crossed my mind. "Why—why would she do that?"

Rapunzel sighed, and her temper gusted out too. "Solange believed she was giving me a gift. She believed I would thank her and stay beside her forever. When I did neither, she punished me."

"What happened to your, um, twins?" I asked, worried that they were part of the Snow Queen's punishment.

Rapunzel shrugged, fresh pain in her face. "They were born. They grew up. They lived their lives, had their own children, and they died. Centuries ago now."

Chase might have told me I was being gullible again, but Rapunzel's grief felt real. "You truly did not know? All this time?" she asked.

I shook my head.

We were quiet for a moment.

"I can say nothing to make you trust me." Rapunzel spread both hands palms up between us. "That decision must come from you. Regardless, you must arrive in Los Angeles in ten minutes. But I would ask the mother of the four winds what happened the night Iron Hans escaped from the Unseelie Court."

"Oh," I said, a little stunned by how quickly we had moved from tragic backstory to this-is-what-you-need-to-know-to-survive-the-next-few-days mode. "Okay."

Then Rapunzel disappeared back into the ballroom infirmary. She didn't say anything else. She didn't even wish me luck.

Across the Courtyard, the workshop door creaked open, and Lena spotted me. "Rory! Where the hiccups have you been? We only have nine minutes left, and it'll take me four to explain how to do this spell."

I didn't want to go. I didn't even want to cross the courtyard. I wanted to go find a quiet corner and try to process at least one thing that had happened that morning before I had to go face my dad. Everything was happening too fast.

But I jogged over and picked up my luggage, hoping that my dad would be too busy to notice that it didn't have any airline tags attached to it.

"Another new carryall." Lena pushed a neon-green backpack to me as soon as I was close. I tried not to notice how she was leaning heavily on the courtyard wall, too weak to stand up straight. "Put your sword in here, so nobody asks questions about it. A new magic mirror and your cell phone are already inside. Your battery died, by the way. The transport kit is in here too. And some water bottles. They're magic. They'll contain the water of life's essence. Now pay attention," said Lena, still in Jenny mode, as I unbuckled my swordbelt, "because you're going to need to do this for yourself after you find the scepter in the Hidden Troll Court." She showed me what looked like a baby food jar of greenish-gold paint. "First you need to find a doorway. It can be to a closet, anything, it doesn't matter, but isolated is probably better. Then you need to paint this solution on the frame, including the floor."

We faced a familiar-looking green-and-white-striped door. "I thought this was the door back home for you, to Milwaukee."

She pulled a brush out of her back pocket and began painting. "It is. This spell will reroute the portal to L.A. for you, and once you're gone it'll revert back to normal. I have to go to the library across the street from this exit. I have the coordinates for the Hidden Troll Court, but I need to get an actual street address. Can you believe we don't have Internet at EAS?"

She was still moving around too much. "Can't someone else go? You should probably rest—" I started.

Lena scowled hard at the doorway she was painting. "Who would we send? Melodie with a practice dummy? That won't attract attention."

Obviously, Melodie's efforts to keep Lena still were met with Lena's usual stubbornness. I backed off. I wasn't sure if I could handle both Rapunzel and Lena almost yelling at me in one morning.

"Anyway, this is just a temporary portal spell," she said, with a very Lena-like gleam in her eye. "It's only good for one transport. It's basically disposable, so the Director can't get mad."

The paint smelled like sulfur. The greeny-gold stuff must have been ground-up dragon scales.

"Okay. Make sure there's an unbroken line all the way around. If there's a gap in the paint, the spell won't work. Next, you put the jar and the paintbrush down, right on the painted stripe on the floor." She did so. "Then you need to activate the magic with the actual spell."

"What's the—?"

She hushed me. "'Up and down, left and right, lead me out, out of sight. Keep me and mine safe from plight; please ignore how this line's trite.'"

If I hadn't understood Fey, it would have just sounded like a rhyming singsong. It might have even sounded impressive, but with Lena's magic translator I caught every single ridiculous word.

"I wrote it down for you so you don't have to memorize it." She shoved a printout toward me and noticed how I pressed my lips together to keep a very Chase-like snicker from escaping.

"I'm so sorry, Lena—" I said.

"It's okay. You can laugh." She was already grinning. "I know it sounds stupid—I'm not great at rhyming anyway, and Melodie said it *had* to rhyme. So I tried that last line out of desperation, and it worked. All my spells are a little bit silly. I guess it can be my trademark."

I grinned back. She reached for my hand. I thought at first it was just to squeeze it, to be encouraging or something, but she peered at my new ring curiously. "West told me it has a half day's worth of his strength. It'll run out of magic eventually, but do you have any idea how much he can blow, lift, smash, and carry in twelve hours?"

"It breaks trees, you know." *And all the bones in my hand,* I almost added. There was so much I wanted to tell Lena, but no time.

Lena's watch started beeping.

She gasped. "The spell! You have to go! You only have a minute left."

"Is it ready?" I stared at the dark doorway. "Shouldn't it glow or light up or something?"

Lena put her hands on her hips. "That flashy stuff is a waste of perfectly good dragon scales. Now go."

Then she pushed me. I stumbled through, my luggage rolling behind me. The sulfur smell was replaced with exhaust. The sun was brighter and hotter. A plane engine screamed overhead, scarily close, and four impatient drivers honked their car horns at the same time.

LAX. I'd made it.

Rory! Perfect timing! I was going to risk a parking ticket to come find you." Hearing Dad's voice, I searched the crowd for his face. Since my cell phone was dead, I'd just wandered around in front of the baggage claim, hoping Dad would just show up. "Here, honey!" A flicker of movement to my left, and there he was, waving, his grin ginormous. The first person I had seen all day who wasn't holding my friends hostage, or being held hostage, or poisoned, or nursing poisoned people.

"Dad!" I broke into a sprint, and when he opened his arms, I crashed into him.

"You've gotten so tall. What happened to my little princess? Let me look at you." His dark hair ran in a thousand directions, like he'd been running his hands through it for a while, maybe stuck in traffic. His gaze lingered on the left side of my face. "My gorgeous girl. I'm so glad you decided to come." He squeezed me so hard he half lifted me off the ground, and I laughed.

It was disloyal of me—with all the work Lena had done to get me there, with everyone depending on me to save them—but I wished that I could have been there for a real visit. I wished I'd chosen to spend spring break with him instead of at EAS. I hadn't realized how much I'd missed him.

"Well, you're in trouble. Your mom has called me three times since Lena's grandmother told her you were coming here."

Doom.

I hadn't thought of Mom all morning.

Dad took my luggage. "She made me get you a new charger, and you're supposed to call her as soon as I have you."

Scratch the traffic theory. This explained Dad's hair.

"No, it's okay, Rory." He squeezed my shoulder. A blue SUV was parked in the no-parking zone. He held the door open for me. "She's just a little overprotective. She doesn't realize that you're a grown-up young woman of twelve."

He threw my duffel in the back of the car, as I hurriedly plugged in my phone.

The glorious homecoming quickly went downhill from there.

"You understand why I'm angry, don't you?" Mom asked as Dad drove up the ramp toward the highway.

I braced myself. "Yes. Because I didn't call when I promised to call."

"That's only part of it. Your cell may have been dead, but it's not the only phone in North Carolina, is it?" Mom snapped. I had seen her get this kind of mad with Dad, but never with me. "I can't believe I had two calls from Lena's grandmother this week, but none from you. Texts don't count."

"You have?" Lena or Jenny must have recruited Mrs. LaMarelle's help for me.

"Yes, that was the only thing that stopped me from flying down south to find you."

"I'm just surprised. I thought she would be too worried." Lena's gran had to be the toughest woman in the history of grandmothers. "Lena's—um, sick."

"Yes. Lena's grandmother explained there was a family emergency," she said. I waited for her to ask, *Sick how?* She was too mad. "But you're back in L.A. You have a charger and plenty of signal. No more excuses. We'll talk about this more when you come home."

I cringed against the seat. The upcoming lecture would be epic.

Mom paused. "I worry, because I love you so much. You know that, right?"

"Yeah," I said quietly. She had told me this about a thousand times, and every time, it made me feel guilty.

"Maggie, five minutes is over in one minute," I heard Amy say. Then her voice got a bunch louder, like she'd leaned toward Mom's phone. "Rory, I'm sorry about your friend, but you lost a lot of trust points." If Amy sounded that mad, Mom had been super freaked out.

Guilt made me extra polite. "Yes, ma'am."

"I love you, sweetie," Mom said finally. "Don't forget to call me tomorrow, please."

Hopefully, by tomorrow evening I would be back in Atlantis. Maybe I could find a sand dune with reception. "Okay. Love you too."

By the time I got off the line, Dad was on his phone—I could tell by the dopey smile on his face that he was talking to his girlfriend. I caught the words "casting call" and "Nuthatch Studios." Since Dad, as a director, never had to suffer through casting calls himself, this was a very bad sign. Either he was having a maybe-I-should-dabble-in-acting crisis, or it was for me. I'd known something like this would happen if I visited him.

As soon as he hung up, I asked, "So . . . Is there something you wanted to tell me?"

"So . . ." Dad mimicked me with a teasing grin, but when I

didn't smile, he sighed. "Well, I cleared my schedule when I found out you were coming—except for one meeting. There's this film I want to work on. Their first director just dropped out. We're supposed to talk about it today. It shouldn't take too long."

I made a face. I doubted I could sneak away from a meeting full of studio people. "Could I stay in the car?"

"You could." He glanced at me, his gaze hitting just to the left of my eyes. "Or you could go to a casting call for the film. They need a child actress for a flashback scene. It would be great if I could reach out in a different way . . . ," he started. I shook my head, arms crossed. "God, you look like your mother when you do that. It's terrifying."

I stopped. I didn't have any right to be mad. I'd told so many lies to my parents, I was having trouble keeping them straight.

"I already told Klonsky you might stop by," Dad said. That did make me angry. "That's the casting director. Please, Rory—it's not a very big role."

"Wait, where is it?" Lena's voice piped up. I jumped forward and started digging though my backpack.

"Same building as the Nuthatch Studios offices." Dad gave me a weird look. "Are you throwing your voice, princess? It's kind of creepy. Cool, though!" he added hurriedly. "In case you're planning to take up the underappreciated art of ventriloquism."

My hand closed over the mirror.

Lena hadn't figured out how to text on an M3. Instead she had scrawled a note and pressed it against the screen: *Go. Nuthatch is right by the entrance to the Hidden Troll Court. I'll give you better directions when you get there.*

Well, at least I wouldn't have to catch a cab to a sketchy part of town. "I'll do it," I told Dad quickly.

"Really?" He sounded so delighted that I hated having to trick him. He talked all the way through the drive—about the film, and how he'd always wanted to work with such-and-such actor, and how the script had made him want to cry, and how it had made Brie actually cry. Meanwhile I bit my fingernails, plotting out excuses that could separate me from Dad and imagining giant trolls lurking behind tour trams.

When we reached the studios' parking deck, I reminded him, "It's just a reading, Dad. Try not to get your hopes up." I climbed out of the car and whispered to my M3, "We're here."

Lena held up one finger, scribbling a note.

"Of course not. Thank you, by the way, for agreeing to do it." Then he opened up the trunk and yanked out my duffel.

"Why do we need that?" I asked, hiding the magic mirror behind my back.

"I thought you would want to change before your reading. Maybe brush your hair." Dad's gaze flickered to the left side of my face again, and I wondered if I'd missed some shampoo in the shower or something. "No one in the world can walk off a plane without looking a little rough around the edges." Dad led me past a workshop dedicated to making props and a row of trailers.

We were halfway to the giant beige office building before I spotted her—red curls, heart-shaped face, wide eyes that widened more when she spotted us. Standing, she smoothed her airy green dress over her hips. She was obviously in costume—something glittered on her face, and a carnival mask dangled from her wrist.

Brie Catcher. I had better things to do than make small talk with Dad's girlfriend right now. Like find a Hidden Troll Court. And steal a scepter.

"Hi! Rory! I'm so happy to meet you!" Brie extended her hand toward me. I wondered if she always gave every word its own exclamation point, or only when she was talking to kids under the age of sixteen. "I could barely eat anything all morning I was so excited."

I took her hand and almost forgot to shake it. "Hi."

"Hi." She smiled. Very brightly. She obviously bleached her teeth. "Actually, I'm not much of a breakfast person anyway, so don't feel bad about me not eating."

"Do you have a lot of coffee instead?" She certainly talked like she'd drunk about fifty espressos.

Now Dad looked at me sharply. "Rory—"

"I'm sorry. I didn't mean it bad," I said hastily, but Brie Catcher laughed—kind of loud.

"You're funny. Your dad didn't tell me you were funny," she said. "You have a casting call this afternoon?"

"Yeah, we were going to see if we could borrow your dressing room for a sec, but . . ." Dad squinted at the left side of my face. "Rory, do you have a black eye?"

I covered it up with my hand. That was what he had been staring at. I'd totally forgotten about it. I struggled to remember what lie I'd told Mom. "I walked into a baseball. I mean, a game of catch—"

"It looks a lot worse in direct sunlight." Dad frowned. He was deciding whether or not he could take me out in public.

I looked down. I couldn't think of anything to say.

"Rory, let me see," said Brie, and I turned to her automatically. "Oh, that's nothing. It's not even swollen anymore. I once got a really black eye before an audition—a little sister for some sitcom. I think I'd wiped out on a treadmill or something. But I still got the part. The casting people said it made me look spunky."

That made up Dad's mind for him. "Okay. Now, the office is right down the way. The waiting room's marked. You want to get dressed and meet me there, or did you want me to wait for you?"

Brie opened the door to her trailer, and Dad set my duffel inside. This was one of those situations where the grown-up is acting like you have a choice, but really, it's very clear what he wants you to do. "I'll meet you there."

Dad grinned and kissed my cheek, then Brie's. "Still on for a late lunch in a couple hours?"

Brie nodded. Waving good-bye to my father, she said, "Want to come in? You'll have to ignore the mess."

There *was* a mess—dirty coffee mugs on the counter, and a table scattered with scripts and magazines, and a comfy-looking love seat buried under discarded sweaters, purses, and jeans.

I pushed a few shoes into the corner so I could open my duffel.

"Yeah, I'm kind of a slob. Those are all my clothes, by the way. I'm usually a little bit nicer to the wardrobe the studio gives me." She pointed to a rack against the far wall, where lots of dresses hung, just as airy as the one she had on. She peered into my duffel and pulled out a shirt with a glittery smiley face. "Ooh, what about this red one?"

I'd known her for two minutes, and she already thought she could dress me. Not that I cared too much. I carried it in behind a folding screen, scarves hanging from one corner.

"Yay! I mean, you don't have to, but I love red. I usually can't wear it very much—with my hair."

Wow. Dad's girlfriend was really a talker. At least she wouldn't hear me when I whispered into my M3. "Ready?"

It's really close, Lena's next note said. *500 yards or less. I'm trying to find the lot number for you.*

I sighed and changed.

"Should I not have picked one for you? I talk a lot," Brie said. "My friends tell me that I just say whatever pops in my head, and it's almost true. I say almost everything I think, and right now, I'm thinking that I do talk too much."

She paused, probably to let me speak. I couldn't think of anything to say. I just walked out and kind of smiled awkwardly.

She smiled back. "Want to borrow my hairbrush? So you don't have to look for yours?"

"Yeah. Thanks," I said. She beamed as she passed it over.

I stood in front of the mirror. I hadn't brushed my hair since I'd gotten to Atlantis. I hoped Brie wouldn't notice how long it would take me to get out all the tangles.

But Brie was busy folding the clothes piled on her chair. With her long, pretty fingers, she made even that look elegant. One of the magazines—something Madison had read out to me—had said that she had a "goofy glam appeal," and now that was all I could think about. She had an old Hollywood sort of grace, but she managed to make whatever she did seem silly and fun—whether it was walking down the red carpet, or jumping on a little kids' bouncy castle, or talking to her boyfriend's daughter.

I turned back to my reflection, so she wouldn't catch me staring. The black eye was almost healed, but when I tilted my head and caught the sunlight, the bruises were a lot easier to see. Yellow-green. Ugly.

The only thing that could make her look uglier is a black eye, Madison had said.

Suddenly, it was hard not to notice how big my chin was.

"You know, I can take care of that, if you want," said Brie. "The bruises are so light they'll be invisible under a little makeup. I mean, I think you're striking enough to pull off a teensy-tiny black eye like that, but you need to do what makes *you* feel comfortable."

"That would be great, actually," I said, relieved. At least Dad wouldn't look at me like that again.

"Yay!" Brie pointed to a cushy chair beside a mirror lit up with lightbulbs. The little table under it was covered with eye shadows, lipsticks, and makeup brushes. Rings, earrings, and necklaces glittered in a cup. She pulled up a stool next to me, dug a sponge out of a side drawer, and sat. With a concentrating sort of frown, she dabbed some skin-colored goo on my face. "Did you want to do mascara, lip gloss, and that whole shebang?"

I couldn't stay that long. "No, I should probably get to the casting call—Dad probably already told them I'm here—but thanks for offering."

Brie's sponge stopped patting. "God, Rory. You're such a good kid. My sister and I were such little terrors when my dad was ever with somebody, whether it was serious or not."

Uh-oh. The conversation was shifting in a more dangerous direction, and there was nothing I could do to stop it.

"Is it okay with you? You know, it would really help if you gave us permission."

I couldn't believe Brie would ask *now*. I mean, they had been dating for almost a year. Maybe she was warning me they were getting serious.

I must have given her a weird look, because she added, "I mean, not permission, exactly, but you know what I mean. I wouldn't say we need it, because I think you'll eventually warm up to the idea. I really believe we can make each other happy. But knowing that you were okay with it, we would both feel better." She looked at me with an expectant, hopeful look, and guilt did jumping jacks in my stomach.

I couldn't think up a response. Especially not one that would get me out of the trailer so I could go find the Hidden Troll Court.

"Can I have more than ten minutes to think about it?" I half smiled, hoping that it would sound like a joke. Maybe this talk could be steered into less intense topics. "It's been kind of a long day. Long week, actually . . ."

"Why? Do you mean the flight?" asked Brie, brushing some powder over my cheek. "No, your friend is having a family emergency. Is everything okay?"

My heart panged. Mom and Dad hadn't even asked. They assumed that nothing was really wrong.

Brie Catcher was going to be harder to fool than my own parents.

"Oh, no. It's not, is it?" Brie said, sounding worried. "Did you want to talk about it?"

"I should probably get going soon, if you don't mind," I said quickly. "Otherwise Dad might come looking for me."

"Right. Of course." She straightened and put the powder down. "Well, your face is all set. I'll see you for lunch later, though. I'm really excited about it."

You could barely see the bruises. The only hint that I had a black eye was a deepish line running down the side of my nose. Even Madison couldn't find anything to make fun of.

Brie wasn't a bad person. She couldn't help that I had way too much going on to deal with her, too. "Me too. Thanks for this," I added, tapping my cheek lightly.

"You're welcome." She smiled tightly—like she wanted to say more, and like *not* talking was a little painful.

I grabbed my duffel, just to make sure I wouldn't have to come back and get trapped in a trailer with my dad's girlfriend again.

Then I waved a little and slipped out the door and down the alley toward the offices, relieved about my escape.

No wonder EAS and all its weird magical escapades had seemed kind of normal after a while. My regular life was pretty bizarre. Most girls my age would have been thrilled to meet Brie Catcher. They would have been thanking their lucky stars and glitter eye shadow for a chance to try out for a part in a movie. Madison would sacrifice the KATs for a chance to do both.

But most girls my age didn't have to keep a bargain with a fairy prince.

I squeezed my duffel through the doors and followed the sign that read CASTING CALL.

A few hopeful child actresses and half the mothers looked up when I shouldered my way into the waiting room. My face flamed.

I wished Lena would hurry up and find the lot number.

A door opened at the far wall. A woman with a severe-looking bun stood in it, holding a clipboard. "Jenkins and Johnson."

Two girls—one with long brown hair and another in an extremely pink dress—stood up and disappeared after bun-and-clipboard lady.

Good. They were going in alphabetical order, and they were only at *J*. Judging by the number of people waiting, I had maybe eight girls ahead of me. Plenty of time for me to leave, find the Hidden Troll Court, steal a scepter from a bunch of trolls, and get back.

I glanced round the room, wondering if I'd gone to school with any of these girls before I moved, but I didn't see anyone I recognized. Well, the one shredding a flyer between her hands looked exactly like Madison—

Oh, my God, I thought, as the girl looked up and my gaze shot down to the duffel under my feet. It was Madison. *Crap.*

She had definitely recognized me, too. She straightened up and squared her shoulders. I resisted the urge to touch the makeup on my eye. Great. *Now* I was officially nervous.

"Rory!" hissed the magic mirror in my hand.

I slung on my carryall and marched out, leaving my duffel behind.

"Sorry!" I whispered to the mirror, as soon as I ran out into the sunshine.

Lena waved aside the apology, as I dodged some women dressed like Jane Austen—extras in some sort of period piece. "I figured out what was taking so long. It's in the Shed."

"What shed? Like a costume-production workshop?"

"No, the lot's name is the Shed."

"Um . . ." I'd never heard a lot being called something like that. I glanced up at the sign, the one that said 16 to 20 were to the right and 21 to 25 were to the left. "All these lots are numbered."

"Exactly! So this lot must have been built and taken over before there were so many of them," Lena said happily, like this was helpful information.

I stepped over to the wall so a tour tram could drive by. "But which way am I supposed to go?"

"No, Rory—it no longer exists! That's why it's hidden! It's the most brilliant thing ever! Either the trolls have one smart person, or someone else came up with the design."

The excitement was too much for Lena. She started coughing so hard that she fished in her pocket and unwrapped a cough drop.

"Lena, saying something doesn't exist doesn't help me," I told her, kind of freaked out. "We need the Hidden Troll Court to exist. We need that scepter."

"In 1924 the whole studio burned down, right?" Lena

explained, kind of hoarse. "It's like the carryall backpacks. You burn down a space into its essence and you incorporate it into the backpack. Same deal—the trolls did the same thing with one of the lots. That's why everybody knew it was in L.A., but no one could find it."

"Wow, Lena," I said, impressed. "Only a genius could make that connection."

"Well," Lena said, "I've also spent a lot of time with carryalls recently. Now you just need to find the external container—the thing that's like the actual backpack part of the design."

"Oh," I said with a sinking feeling. Looking for something a lot smaller than an abandoned lot might slow us down.

"According to my scrying spell and Google map calculations, it should be right next to lot sixteen," Lena said, and I jogged right, searching. "You should be able to see it from there. And it'll be pretty—I don't think the trolls can help themselves."

I found lot 16 and flattened myself in its doorway. I scanned the area, but all I saw was the back lot, which looked like an empty neighborhood: a small bakery, a law office, a brownstone with a short flight of steps leading up to the front door, a fountain attached to the side—

"What about that?" I flipped my M3 around so that Lena could see the three-foot statue backed up against the wall—a young couple doing a tap number. Water spewed from their outstretched jazz fingers into a basin about the same size as a plastic kiddie pool.

"Yes!" Lena said. Two set designers gaped at me as their trolley passed, one almost dropping his staple gun.

Blushing, I noticed the plaque as I got closer:

Jane Olivier and Marty Thomas lost their lives in a studio fire on July 19, 1924. The tip-tapping steps and real-life love of this married dancing couple will always be remembered in such films as Love Knocks Only Twice and The Man in the Green Tie.

That was actually kind of sad—both the lame movie titles and the fact they'd died. "It's a memorial."

"Rory, look at the water!" she whispered.

The bottom of the fountain was a mosaic of blue and orange tiles, patterned like flames. With the water moving over them, they seemed to flicker. "Cool optical illusion, but um . . . Oh!"

For an instant I glimpsed something else: a garden full of hedgerows, and sweeping gravel paths, and topiaries—very French, pre-Revolution. Between two topiaries lurked a hulking shape that had recently become familiar: thick legs, wide shoulders, tusks curving out of its mouth—a troll.

"I think you have to go through," Lena whispered.

Gulping, I pulled out my sword—in case I got rushed by twelve trolls as soon as I landed. "Just jump in?"

"Yeah. Bend your knees, though—I'm not sure how far the drop is," Lena said nervously.

If I broke my leg down there, I would be all alone, surrounded by enemies and unable to run. I stepped up on the rim. I wished that Lena and Chase could have come with me.

I squeezed my eyes closed and jumped. Water shot up my nose and splashed over my smiley face shirt.

"Is everything okay?" Lena said, kind of panicked.

"It didn't work, but besides that, yeah, I'm fine." Across the alley, two security guards rolled by on Segways. I froze. It didn't matter how uncool they looked. If they caught me playing in the memorial fountain when I was supposed to be at a casting call, I would still get into the kind of trouble written about in Madison's magazines.

"Okay," Lena said, disappointed. "I'll do a little more research."

I wondered how many girls had tried out while I was gone. I might still have time to change before it was my turn. Trying to climb out, I slipped again, banging my knee and soaking the other side of my shirt.

"I'm going to head back," I said. Lena nodded, already leafing through one of her books.

My shoes left tracks down the alley. Awesome.

I slipped inside, down the hall, and into the waiting room, shivering under the AC. Head after head in the waiting room turned to stare at me as I unzipped my bag and avoided looking at Madison.

My cheeks flared. At least we had found the court. For the first time all morning, getting the scepter seemed slightly less impossible.

I stripped off my sneakers and my socks. They *were* looking kind of awful. They were stained brown with Atlantis mud, and the rip at the ankle had gotten bigger somewhere between Iron Hans's cave and here.

Inside my bag, the pretty orangey ballet flats Mom had given me glittered.

I pulled them out and shoved my feet inside. *Amazing*. They did actually make me feel a little less like a wet mess. Especially when I caught the girl next to me glancing at the sequins. Now for a shirt.

"Landon and McDermott," said the bun-and-clipboard lady, just as I reached down for my discarded sneakers. "This way, please."

No way. They couldn't have waited three more minutes until I was dry again? I'd just have to pretend I wasn't there. I would tell Dad I'd been in the bathroom.

Madison practically skipped across the room. "McDermott here."

The bun-and-clipboard lady scowled down at her clipboard. "Where's Landon?"

My classmate pointed straight at me. "Right there, ma'am."

I froze.

"Well? Come on, Landon. Quickly. No time for cold feet," said bun-and-clipboard lady. I didn't have any choice except to dump my sneakers in my carryall and follow Madison.

As I passed the bun-and-clipboard lady, I dripped on her a little. She looked up, finally, kind of stunned.

Then, when I joined Madison McDermott in a small circle of light, my classmate smiled her triumphant smile, and dread weighed down my middle.

Besides the stage area, the rest of the room was dark. I wished I could run off and hide in it.

"Is this some sort of gimmick?" asked the only person in the room wearing a suit—a stout woman with a severe-looking part in her hair. She sat at a table, a few feet away from the light. The casting director, Klonsky.

I glanced around and realized that Klonsky was talking to me. "N-no."

"Dripping wet, a black eye," Klonsky snapped. I touched my face. All the makeup Brie had painted on must have come off. "Did you get into an accident or something? Are you trying to prove how dedicated you are?"

I shrank away. I couldn't think of any excuses except that I had jumped in a fountain on my way to the Hidden Troll Court. "No."

Madison stood at my left elbow. I wished any of the other kids had been called with me—anyone except the one person I would have to see again. Next Monday's homeroom would suck so much more than usual.

"Then is this some sort of joke?" Klonsky's eyes flashed even from the dim area. The bun-and-clipboard lady should have warned me that she was this type of casting director—the kind who lost it if you were rude. "This isn't a comedic role. You're not pretty, or talented, or charming, or famous enough for us to overlook this disrespectful behavior."

I thought nothing could make me feel any worse, any smaller, but someone moved in the shadows just behind Klonsky—a man ran his hands through his hair. I couldn't see his face, but I recognized the gesture. My father.

"There's nothing appealing about you," said Klonsky. "You're a waste of my time."

And Dad never said a word.

They made me do the reading anyway.

Later I remembered holding a sheet of paper in my hand and hearing words sail out of my mouth. I remembered how Madison glowed. I remembered clinging to the hope that Dad would interrupt and say that I was his daughter, that no one could treat me like that, and that he was taking me home.

I remembered not crying, not even when we finally finished, or when Klonsky pointedly thanked Madison for her time, but not me, or when I shuffled back into the waiting room, face hot, and bent over my luggage to find some dry clothes.

In the bathroom, changing, I racked my brain for something I could tell Dad. But my rebellious mind just tried to puzzle out why he hadn't stood up to the casting director.

He was waiting for me when I came out. All he said was, "Did you do it on purpose?"

"No." My nose prickled just under the bridge. I was three seconds away from crying. If he asked what happened, I would tell him the truth—about EAS, and the quest, and the Hidden Troll Court. I would show him the fountain as proof. I would lift up the car with the ring.

It didn't matter if he freaked out and locked me in my L.A.

room. I had the ring of return. If I could get back to EAS, Lena could get me back here.

But he didn't ask. He didn't even look at me as he grabbed my duffel and walked out the doors. I followed him to the parking lot, so focused on wishing Dad would turn around and hug me that I didn't recognize the redheaded figure leaning against his car, munching on something.

Brie waved when she saw us, with that super-bright smile. She had changed out of her costume and into jeans, a flowery blouse, and a ton of dangly necklaces. "I'm so hungry. If I hadn't found this apple, I might have fainted."

Oh, no. I couldn't go to lunch right now. I needed an excuse to return to that back lot, and it had to be a good one.

Brie glanced between us. "You two have a fight?"

"No," Dad and I said at the same time—except I said it kind of resentfully. I would have preferred having a fight. At least then Dad would be talking to me.

"Rory, did you take a shower? And what happened to your backpack? I could have sworn you had a backpack," Brie said.

My carryall with the temporary transport spell, with the ring of return, the M3. I'd left it in the bathroom where any child actress, cleaning crew, or studio exec could take it. I had to go back for it, but Brie was way more interested in asking questions than in getting answers. She didn't even pause for breath.

"Did the casting call today not go well or something?" she continued.

"Kind of an understatement," Dad muttered, as Brie took another bite. Her extremely long, extremely skinny fingers were almost spidery. Even the ginormous diamond on her hand was wider than her ring finger—

I choked a little on my own spit.

Dad was engaged. Brie Catcher was going to be my stepmother.

"What?" Brie followed my gaze, and then, with an embarrassed grin, she covered the huge diamond with her other hand. "Oh. I know. Someone in the ring department told Eric that bigger is always better, but—"

"I hadn't gotten a chance to tell her yet," Dad whispered to Brie, in a voice almost too low to hear. He didn't even seem sorry about it.

"But you said you would tell her when you picked her up." She turned back to me. Her eyebrows pinched together. "And we talked about it in the trailer. I said it would be nice to have permission, and you said—"

"You didn't say you were engaged," I whispered, throat dry. "You weren't even wearing a ring."

"I take it off when I'm in costume," Brie said slowly.

I tried to remember all the Tales that had stepmothers in them. There were too many to count. There were too many lame ones to count.

I didn't want a stepmother, especially not one named after a stupid smelly cheese.

"Rory, are you okay?" The concern in Brie's voice was real. I wished it hadn't been, because then I would have had reason to hate her.

My nose prickled under the bridge again. "I left my bag in the bathroom." Before either of them could answer, before Dad even looked up, I sprinted into the building, down the hall, and into the bathroom.

My carryall was where I had left it, propped under the sink.

I locked the door behind me and checked all the stalls to make sure I was alone. I needed to talk to Lena.

I scooped the M3 out of my carryall's front pocket. "Hello?"

"You got away," Lena said, relieved. All the coughing had taken its toll. Her eyes were bloodshot, and her shoulders kind of drooped. "I've got three options that might get you in."

Maybe I could spare five minutes, though, just to get it off my chest.

But her image was replaced by Chase's: His blond curls were muddy. A new red welt on his forehead promised to become a pretty serious bruise. "So . . . I have good news and bad news."

"My M3s can do conference calls?" Lena seemed kind of impressed with herself. "Chase, how did you do that?"

He rolled his eyes. "Oh, it was really hard. I picked up the magic mirror and started talking. Anyway, bad news is the escape attempt failed." He lifted up his arms. Both wrists were encircled by heavy manacles of tarnished Fey-tempered silver.

"What? You tried to escape?" Lena asked.

Right. I'd never filled her in on what Chase had whispered to me right before I'd left Atlantis.

"Yep, and Fael—I mean, His Highness the Royal Prince of the Unseelie Court—" Chase added hastily, for the benefit of someone just beyond the mirror's frame—"well, he was kind of expecting it. But the good news is we didn't get roughed up too bad. Although there was one hairy moment when Ori'an was going to step on Ben's head, elephant execution style, and burst it like—"

Lena shuddered. "Stop. Just stop."

I knew what Chase was trying to say. The questers would be watched even more closely than before. They wouldn't be able to escape on their own.

It was all up to me. I didn't have time to be upset.

"Your sympathy is simply overwhelming, you guys," Chase said.

"I'm sorry. Did you want sympathy or rescue?" Melodie asked from over Lena's shoulder. "Because we've been working on the second one."

"At least tell me good things are happening on your end?" he said.

"We found the entrance," Melodie said proudly, like she'd helped.

"We got a little stumped getting through," Lena said.

I took out my phone and started a good-bye text to my dad: *I'm sorry*.

But what else could I say that wouldn't make him blame himself? I didn't want to make him even angrier than I already would, running away like this.

Are you sure about that? asked a vengeful little voice inside me.

Tears filled my gaze. I blinked them back, annoyed.

I couldn't save Chase and Lena, and everyone else, if I let myself get really upset. I couldn't give in and wonder why Dad hadn't told me he was engaged, why he hadn't asked me how I felt before he proposed, why he hadn't interrupted that casting director—

I shrugged on my backpack. "Stay quiet until I say I'm alone. Okay?"

I opened the door slowly, but no one was waiting for me this time. I ignored the pang in my chest and crept down the hall, away from the double doors that opened toward the parking lot, away from Dad. I slipped out a side exit, where a child actress was crying so hard her hair stuck to her tear-and-mascara-smeared cheeks. Her mother gave me a sharp look that clearly said, *Move along*.

"Sorry," I whispered. I checked each way for passing trolleys, and then I hurried down the alley toward the back lot. It was empty except for a skinny boy wearing neon orange sunglasses, carrying an armful of bowler hats. The back lot was totally abandoned, but

I kept an eye out anyway. You never knew when an angry father or a security guard on a Segway would come by.

"Okay. I made it." The fountain's mosaic rippled and showed me a glimpse of hedges again. "What's next?"

"Try 'open sesame' in Troll," Lena said.

"No, really," I said, half-annoyed. Too much was at stake for us to be joking around.

"No, she's right. I've heard that too," Chase said. "Trolls aren't smart enough to remember passwords, so they use the classic ones."

"So close your eyes, picture a troll, and say it," Melodie said huffily.

I tried it, and instead of words, a weird gurgling noise came out of my mouth instead. I was smart this time. I checked by hand before I tried to jump through. My fingers brushed the mosaic immediately. "Didn't work. What's the next one?"

"This one is a little tricky, because it's technically a spell," Lena said. Great. Spells. Something I sucked at. No wonder she sounded worried. "But it's a really common one. It's basically the Fey trick for picking magical locks."

"'Break what was whole, crack what was smooth, open what was shut,'" said Chase in Fey.

"Exactly. You say that, and then you'll need to throw in something that has power," Lena said. "I wish I'd thought to pack you some dragon scales, but I think one of your water bottles would work."

"Perhaps more than one. The stronger the lock, the more power is necessary," Melodie added.

I unzipped the carryall and shoved my arm in, all the way to the shoulder, and felt around. I pulled out a cylinder with a metal cap, with symbols embedded straight into the glass—a miniature version of the West Wind's prison.

"Here goes nothing." I repeated the spell and let the water bottle go. It didn't splash. It didn't clink to the bottom of the mosaic. It completely disappeared. So did the tiled flames. All I saw was the maze of hedges. "I think it worked."

"Yes!" Chase pumped a manacled fist in the air.

I glanced over my shoulder. A trolley rushed by an alley over, but I didn't see any security guards. I didn't see my dad.

No one had come after me. I pulled my cell phone out of my pocket and finished the text: *I'm sorry. I have to go back. I can get to the airport on my own. My friends need me right now.*

It wouldn't matter if Dad got this right away. He might not even check the bathroom. He would try to head me off at LAX.

He would be so worried. Mom would scream at him, probably, when he told her that he had lost me. This wasn't the way he and Brie should spend the beginning of their engagement.

But I ignored the lump in my throat and pressed send. "You guys ready?"

"Yep," said Lena.

"All systems go," Chase added.

I took a deep breath and jumped.

I braced for another splash, but it never came. I didn't even feel wet, and when my heels struck the ground, so hard I stumbled, my clothes were as dry as they'd been on the surface.

"Ow—no broken bones," I told Lena hurriedly, before she could freak out, "but still—ow."

A palace stretched out in front of me—white marble with huge, shining windows and gleaming cherub carvings, gilded gates, and windowsills. I'd fallen through the fountain onto the set of a Marie Antoinette movie—with trolls.

The ceiling was smeared with decades-old soot. We were

definitely inside some sort of ancient, almost-burned down studio lot.

The trolls streamed out of the palace in ragged armor, their spears and axes and swords glinting under a giant lamp. Fifty of them, at least. It would have scared me a lot more if I hadn't noticed one thing.

"Chase, why didn't you tell me that the Hidden Trolls were so short?" No matter how fierce they looked, or how sharp their weapons were, they only came up to about my waist.

"I didn't know," Chase said. I could practically hear him rolling his eyes. "It's the *Hidden* Troll Court, Rory. Nobody has seen them for a century."

The trolls surrounded me, fifty feet or so short of pricking distance. Some of them looked nervous to be confronted by a giant seventh grader like myself. "Who knows what the sceptor looks like?" I asked.

"Like a birch tree," Chase said. "But silver and about two and a half feet tall."

I dashed up onto the nearest white bench to get a better view. In the clearing beside me, a human mannequin stood on display, garbed in a gold robe with a funky geometric pattern. In the next clearing, a pair of shoes—red low heels with bows—glittered on its own pedestal. Another space boxed off with hedgerows had a pair of towering emerald doors standing open in the middle of a grassy space.

But no scepters in sight.

That was when the trolls decided to attack.

"Geez, Rory—hold still," Chase said. "It's hard enough to see on this itty bitty screen."

"Fighting now, just FYI." I disarmed the half-size troll who ran up first and stabbed at my shoulder. "If I stay still, I'll lose blood."

The hollow feeling in my chest eased. Maybe I didn't know what to do with a new stepmother, but *this* I could handle.

I turned aside an ax with my sword. I snap-kicked at a bunch of spear shafts—knocking one out of a troll's hand. I winced when I put my foot back down, feeling a new bruise. I wished I'd thought to change shoes. These flats didn't protect the top of my foot the way my sneakers did.

"How many trolls have you killed so far?" Chase asked eagerly.

I frowned. "Guess."

At least seventeen more trolls ran up behind the bench. They really weren't very smart. They kept knocking their comrades out of the way trying to get to me. And they kept injuring each other. One with wrist guards broke the nose of his neighbor with a crack so nauseating that it probably would've given Chase nightmares.

"Okay, fine—how many did you knock unconscious?" When I didn't answer, Chase said, "Rory, come on. This is not a good time to become a pacifist. We're not there to watch your back. Do you want to win this fight or not?"

"I just want to grab the scepter." With my left hand I snapped the handle of several battle-axes like toothpicks. "Beating up a bunch of little trolls doesn't exactly appeal."

But I did accidentally knock a few out. A troll with a gauntlet and a sword snuck up behind me and spooked me with a quick stab at my neck. I managed to knock the blow aside and punched at his face without thinking about it—he flew back, taking three of his fellow soldiers with him. They didn't get up again, but more than one groaned.

"Whoops," I said, panting. The trolls backed off slightly, kind of freaked out, I guess, by the super strength. My hand hurt, but first

I checked the mirror I'd been holding, looking for cracks around Lena's worried face. "I don't think I messed it up—"

Chase emerged in the M3 suddenly, pointing, "Rory, behind you!"

I whirled around, expecting a super-huge troll with a mace or something. But two clearings over, beyond those ruby red slippers, something silver shone in the fake sunlight.

"They just left it out there in the open, where anyone could steal it," Chase said, clearly delighted about it. "How stupid can they be?"

"Well, they don't have many visitors," Lena said. "Besides, I'm not so sure that's it."

I eyed the paths of the garden, memorizing the way.

The short truce was definitely over. The trolls stepped closer, but they weren't looking at me. I mean, they were, but not at my face—they stared at my feet with a freaky gleam in their eyes.

"Lena, are you even wearing your glasses?" Chase asked.

"Yes. But it doesn't look like a scepter to me."

Something pricked my left elbow. I turned aside just before a spear jabbed me. I smashed the shaft with my sword hilt, and it broke with a very satisfying splintering noise.

"Wanna bet?" Chase asked Lena.

"You guys—we're not making bets while I'm fighting for my life."

I vaulted off the bench and dashed out of the clearing.

"Yes, we are," Chase said. "So, how about it, Lena? If I win, you'll give me one invention of my choosing."

The trolls stumbled after me, but slowly. Sprinting past the fan's pedestal, I congratulated myself on my clean getaway—until I spotted a helmeted troll hiding among some rosebushes.

"Whoa!" I lifted my sword to deflect his battle-ax, but instead, the troll dove at my legs.

I fell, not expecting a tackle. I skidded so hard my shoulder dug a groove in the grass, but I squirmed out of the little troll's grip pretty fast.

"You okay, Rory?" Lena asked, slightly panicked.

"Yeah." Two steps later I snatched up my sword from the grass. I didn't notice I had lost a shoe until I glanced back. The troll hugged it close to his chest, his squarish fingers stroking the gold beads.

"I—I don't think I can concentrate on a bet right now," Lena said, kind of apologetically.

Another troll caught up, but he didn't come after me. He snatched at his comrade's hand—at my shoe. The helmeted troll didn't appreciate that—he punched the newcomer in the stomach.

I didn't question it. I just ran.

I ducked into the circular patch of manicured grass, close to the silver thing Chase had pointed out, and found something disappointing. "You guys, this isn't it. I mean, it's a scepter, but not *the* scepter."

I turned the M3 around so they could see. On the pedestal sat a skinny wooden rod with a globe at the top. It had been painted silver, glass jewels glued to the side. A tag—yellowed with age—fluttered from a string. I turned it over and read, PROP USED IN FILM PRODUCTION OF KING LEAR, OCTOBER 1939.

"A decoy," Lena said with new respect. "Oh, they definitely have someone helping with their security system."

Chase didn't mention he'd lost his bet. "So, we move on to plan B: Run around until you find it."

I hurtled over the hedge and back onto the path. A bunch of trolls ran after me, slowed by their short legs and heavy armor. I tore across the gravel, wincing at the sharp little stones pricking my bare foot. I glanced at the pedestals as I passed them: a ruffly hoop skirt, a bent spoon, an Olympic medal that was obviously fake—the gold paint had rubbed off on one edge.

"I'm not seeing it." I tried not to panic. I'd almost run all the way back around to the weird trolls fighting over my shoe.

"Okay," said Lena slowly. "So they must have hidden it. Can you take one of the trolls aside and see if you can get any more information out of him?"

"Oh, yeah—brilliant idea," Chase said. "I bet if she says 'please' and 'thank you,' the other forty-nine trolls won't kill her."

"Give her a break, Chase. She's not feeling well." I swerved around a corner and sprinted down the next path, wondering what the heck was so special about my shoe?

I mean, it was pretty, but—

I slowed.

No. It was more than just pretty. It was a Hollywood artifact.

So was the fake silver scepter. So were the red slippers. The *ruby*-red slippers from *The Wizard of Oz*. Most of the garden's treasures were human-made—a museum to old Hollywood. It could have just been a coincidence that everything here belonged in old movies, considering where the Hidden Troll Court was located. Or maybe not.

I stopped in the middle of the path.

I tugged off my remaining shoe and faced the rest of the Hidden Trolls. "Wait!"

They stopped hurtling toward me, their eyes not on my sword, but on my shoe. I took that as a good sign.

"What are you doing?" Chase asked. "If you wait for them to catch up, you'll lose your advantage."

"Do you understand me?" I thought I heard myself speaking troll, but maybe I was just so out of breath I was rasping without Lena's translator. "Somebody nod if you can understand me."

Two dozen tusked troll faces bobbed up and down.

"I want to make a trade. This shoe for the scepter of the Birch clan." Okay, so that trade sounded idiotic. I had to make it sound more appealing.

The trolls were silent, but at least one of them made a face. His tusks were capped with gold and blue gems. That must have made him the troll king.

"What's Rory saying, Lena? All I hear is grunting," Chase said.

"She's trying to negotiate," Lena said.

"It's really nice," I added, feeling ridiculous. "Designer, I think. It makes an appearance in *Whose Heart Is Mine?*, a movie that comes out next spring. Maggie Wright wore them."

Several soldiers gasped, and every troll eye in the room snapped to the shoe in my hand, as if searching for the imprint of the famous actress's foot. For the very first time in my life, I was happy to find out that someone—a whole army of someones, actually—was a fan of my mom.

"All I want is the scepter of the Birch clan," I said.

A couple of trolls glanced from me to the palace. I could think of only one reason why not-so-smart soldiers would look there. That had to be where they'd hidden the scepter.

"Rory," Chase said. "There's no way they're going to trade. If they want the shoe, they'll just kill you to get it."

He was right.

So I threw the shoe as far as I could behind the trolls. Half the trolls spun and chased it, but I didn't wait long enough to see if they would fight over it too. I whirled around and dashed up the palace steps.

Past the elegant white-and-gold door, you could see all the plywood, beams, and rusted nails that held the set together.

Here was another row of pedestals, this time with weapons: a slender samurai sword that glowed faintly green, a golden bow and arrow with rubies on the quiver, a beautiful spear with geometric patterns inlaid into the shaft.

But no silver scepters.

"It's not here, either," I said disappointed.

Five trolls clattered inside. The one with gold-capped tusks pointed—not at me, but at a door I hadn't noticed behind the bow and arrow pedestal. "There," the troll king said. "Before she reaches it."

That was where they kept the scepter. And I was closer.

I leaped. My fingers closed around the door handle, and I glanced back just in time to see a troll's spear sailing straight for my chest. I jumped aside, and it hit the door so hard it gouged out a chunk of wood.

I threw the door open and dove through.

From all sides, mirrors reflected and fractured me—twenty, fifty, a hundred times over. I couldn't open my eyes without seeing myself in pieces—an elbow here, a ponytail there, both back pockets, my shoulder, my ear, a single hazel eye, one giant chin.

"What is it?" Lena's curiosity was on a rampage even now.

"Mirrors." I flipped the M3 over, so she could see.

The light was dim. I looked around for a light switch or a chandelier or torches but I didn't see anything. The ceiling above me was just more mirrors.

"Rory, trolls are after you," Chase said. "Don't just stand there with your back to the door."

I whirled around. The door was covered in mirrors too, so it took a second for me to find the dark rectangle outlining it. I would have loved to wedge something under the doorknob, but unfortunately there was no handle from this side.

"Remember," Chase said. "They can only come through the door one at a time. Between your sword and West's ring, you can handle that."

My heart thudded, my grip on my sword sweaty. My face, reflected back to me a hundred times, was on the red side, some hair plastered to my forehead. The glass was cool against my bare, dusty feet.

After a minute I lowered my sword slightly. "I don't think they're coming."

"You're alone in a room with the scepter you're trying to steal," Chase reminded me. "Of course they're coming."

But the door didn't open.

Maybe they'd tricked me, and this *wasn't* where they kept the scepter—the trolls didn't seem smart enough to fake me out, though. Maybe this weird mirror place had another entrance, and they were running to cut me off.

Or maybe whatever was in here with me was too scary for them, scepter or no scepter.

I straightened up. "Okay. I think I'm going to start looking. The sooner I find the scepter, the faster I can get out of here. Who thinks I should take the time to put on my sneakers?"

"Yes!" Chase said, sounding horrified. "No fighting without shoes!"

I fished them out of my carryall, tugged on my socks, and laced my sneakers up, still wet. I put my M3 away for good measure. If I dropped it, I might never find it again.

"Great, now I can't see anything," complained Chase.

The trolls still didn't come. I couldn't hear anything except the scuffle of my own feet, echoing out and out, taunting me from every direction. Wherever I was, it must have been pretty big.

"This has to be the creepiest place I've ever been," I whispered, stepping forward.

"Creepier than the Glass Mountain?" asked Lena.

"Yeah," I whispered. "At least in the Glass Mountain I knew what to expect."

"Try looking at the ground," Lena said. "That's my brother's trick for fun houses."

I looked down and certainly hoped my nostrils didn't normally look that big. "No good. Even the floor is a mirror."

I squeezed my eyes shut, tired of looking at myself. All the reflections were too disorienting.

"Let me know when you run across a troll," Chase said.

I tried again, but as soon as I opened my eyes, I spotted the Director. "Wait, there's something else here." I wouldn't have exactly said she was a welcome sight, but she was vastly preferable to staring at three of my chins. I walked closer.

"The scepter?" Lena asked.

"No."

The mirror ahead showed the infirmary, the Director awake now and propped up against the wall. "A terrible, terrible idea," she told Hansel and Gretel. "I'll acknowledge that she has clever and talented friends, but what has Rory Landon ever done by herself?"

I was offended. I'd just fought my way past fifty trolls on my own, hadn't I? And—

I couldn't think of anything else.

"How could we send her with so much at stake?" the Director continued.

My heart constricted, as Hansel and Gretel nodded. I'd been so busy fighting in the Hidden Troll Court that I'd forgotten for a second what might happen if I failed.

"Well . . . ?" Chase asked impatiently. "What is it?"

"The Director, in the infirmary." I didn't want to tell them what she had said. Then I smashed into something hard and cool. "Ow. I think I hit a dead end."

"You mean, you're in a maze . . . ?" Chase said.

Lena gasped. Learning this excited her so much that she started to sound like her regular unpoisoned self. "Yes, a mirror vault! Hold on! I'll set up a scrying spell to guide you through. I've read about these."

"Oh," Chase said, quietly. "The Unseelie Court has one too."

"Now we know who helped the trolls with their security system," said Lena. "The goblin priestesses from the Temple of Mirrors set them up. They must have owed the king of the Hidden Troll Court a boon, because they only build a mirror vault maybe once a century."

"Only people with royal blood can walk through the mirror vault without activating the magical traps. The goblin priestesses set it up that way," Chase said, sounding uneasy. "That's why they're not following you. The troll king probably doesn't want to fight you all on his own."

"Or he thinks the vault will stop you for him," Lena pointed out.

"Great. We've cleared that up. Any tips for getting through one?"

They were quiet. They didn't know anything cheerful.

"Ooooh!" Lena said suddenly. "The scrying spell is up. And I can kind of see—no, I do see all the walls. Rory, I see you! Go left. Walk slowly," she added as I turned. "I'll tell you when you need to go right."

I stepped forward, hands stretched out in front of me so I wouldn't smack into anything again.

"Keep in mind that whatever you see is designed to stop you," Lena said. "It's basically a big, fancy security system."

"Whenever a thief gets caught in the Unseelie mirror vault— dwarves, trolls, witches, Characters—they come out crazy," Chase said, and I froze. "The Unseelie knights keep straitjackets beside the entrance."

"You didn't need to tell her that," Lena snapped.

"Hey. We're not doing her any favors by keeping secrets," Chase said.

"So," I said, hating how my voice squeaked, "nobody's really broken into one?"

"Iron Hans, the night he escaped from the Unseelie prison," Chase said.

I didn't know if that made me feel better or worse. Iron Hans was a lot more impressive than I was.

Up ahead, on my right, another scene flashed among the reflections. This one was a hotel room, a nice one, and perched upon the scarlet comforter with glossy magazines was Madison McDermott.

"Now it's a girl from my school in New York," I said. "Not a Character."

"What's she doing?" Lena asked.

"Talking on her cell phone."

Madison smirked as she flicked through the pages. "Yeah, I know—Rory Landon showed up to the casting call. It was sooooo perfect, Katie." Ugh. Was the vault seriously going to show me every single mean thing people had said about me that day? Was that how it would try to stop me? "Everything I ever told her was so true. Klonsky—this big-deal casting director—said it too, and even her dad didn't argue. She's no one special without her parents."

I *knew* that she would say something like that. But all the hurt from the casting call rushed back and welled up in my chest. I took deep breaths until my nose stopped prickling.

"Right in three more steps!" So Lena couldn't hear Madison through the M3. That was one thing to be grateful for.

Letting my right hand trail along the mirrors, I swung around the corner as soon as I felt an opening. I was hoping that it would change—that the mirrors would be replaced by something else— but I just faced another kaleidoscope of ankles, elbows, chins, noses, chunky lips, and my t-shirt's sleeves.

"Just keep going, Rory. You're about halfway to the next turn," said Lena.

I nodded, distracted. I wondered if I would have to live through what Klonsky had said again too, if I'd have to watch my dad agree with her.

"Left here, Rory," Lena said.

I turned and stepped forward, but my shoulder smacked into something hard, smooth, and cold. My gasp of pain echoed through the cavern behind me, to each side, and far, far above me.

"Other left!" Lena said anxiously.

"Sorry." I spun around and strode down the turn.

"Keep it together, Rory."

"Shut up, Chase," I said automatically.

"I . . . didn't say anything." Now Chase sounded really nervous.

I swallowed hard. That meant I was hearing voices again.

Up ahead, another scene flickered across the mirrors. It took up the whole left wall, so I couldn't really look away. Waves crashed on the Atlantis beach. Fey knights circled around the imprisoned questers. No one was wearing manacles. This must have happened earlier today, before they tried to escape. Chatty stared out to sea, Mia slept, and the boys clustered around a game of cards. The M3 sat on the rock beside Chase.

I didn't want to hear what the questers would say behind my back. I needed to focus on saving them.

Ben slapped a card on the pile. "I wish Rory hadn't suggested we make camp last night. We would have gotten to the Unseelie Court in plenty of time if we hadn't stopped."

I'd forgotten that was me.

"This one's a straight shot for a while," said Lena through the M3. "But don't run or anything. They might put obstacles up."

"Okay." My throat ached, a much worse sign than my nose prickling. It only happened when I was about to cry really hard.

"Well, I wish she hadn't smashed up the troll bridge," Kenneth said. "We lost a whole day there."

"I wish she hadn't freed the Dapplegrim on the Fey railway," Ben replied.

I didn't want to listen, but I couldn't make myself stop.

"Plus there was the surprise ambush from those stupid Wolfsbane trees," Kenneth added.

Ben shook his head. "Her sword and her ring don't make up for the fact that she's a walking disaster."

"Great choice in friends, Chase," Kenneth said.

Chase would defend me. He had stood up for me in front of the Snow Queen. Of course, he'd do the same with kids only a year older than us.

"Yeah, well," said Chase uncomfortably, "there's not exactly a wide selection in the seventh grade."

No. Don't say that.

"If I may extend such an invitation," Ben said, "you're always welcome to hang out with us eighth graders."

Chase's face lit up. Of course he would jump at the chance. They were guys, and besides, they were closer to his real age than Lena and I—

My sneaker found an uneven ridge of mirror, one I didn't see, because it reflected twin images of my ponytail. As soon as I stumbled, I threw both hands out to catch myself. But that was a mistake too—the ring on my left hand was too strong. I smashed through the fragile mirror, and the cavern filled with the tinkling of broken glass.

God. I *was* a walking disaster.

"Rory!" Lena cried.

"I'm okay." But I wasn't. Something warm and wet filled my palm. Blood. I was cut somewhere.

"What happened? What is it?" Chase sounded pretty panicked for someone who was only hanging out with me and Lena until someone better came along. "Did the troll king decide to come after you anyway?"

"No, calm down—I just tripped." The cut started to hurt, and that helped me think a little more clearly. "Lena, I still need to go straight, right?"

Lena paused, retracing the maze. "Yeah."

I couldn't listen to many more of these. *I should really put my hands over my ears.* But then I wouldn't be able to hear Lena's directions.

One more scene emerged from the clutter of sneakers and big chins, a mirror filled with round tables. At one of them, a couple held hands across the violet tablecloth. Brie stared at Dad as he twirled a spoon in his soup.

I cringed. I couldn't hear this one, not right now. I hurried down the path between the mirrors, hoping to outrun whatever was coming out of Dad's mouth.

"Rory, what is it? Do you see something?" Lena asked.

"A skeleton?" Chase said, hushed.

My voice was thick, my cheeks wet. I was already crying, and

Dad hadn't said even anything yet. "Lena, just tell me when to turn."

"There's still a hundred yards to go," Lena said.

"You're right, Brie," said Dad's image to my right. "Rory didn't turn out like I hoped. But we can have other kids."

One sob escaped before I could slap a hand over my mouth, and the noise echoed all around me.

"Was that you?" The idea obviously freaked Chase out more than the skeleton.

"What's wrong? What did you see?" Lena asked.

"It's okay." A hiccup-y sob crept into the middle of the sentence. My eyes were full of tears. I rubbed them away quickly and strode forward, hugging my bloody left hand to my chest so I wouldn't accidentally break anything else.

I'd suspected that Dad didn't need me in his life—hadn't wanted me for a while now.

"Rory, talk to us," Chase said.

If I couldn't talk without crying, I wouldn't talk at all. I had to find the stupid scepter.

Ahead and to the right I spotted the long, elf-size tables, the furnaces full of fire salamanders, the golden harp gleaming on top of Lena's workstation, and my friend bent over a book.

"Oh, my gumdrops," Lena breathed.

"Don't gumdrops now. Do something," Chase snapped. "I'm in manacles, so it'll have to be you."

"Rory, look at us. Take the mirror out of your pocket!"

But her voice blended with the other Lena's. "I know Rory's not as smart as me. But sometimes I wish she was just a little quicker. I mean, it just gets so tedious having to explain things all the time. Can't she do her own research?"

No wonder my dad hadn't stuck up for me, didn't want me—I was worse than useless.

I stopped, just for a second. I couldn't help it.

No. These were just words. Was this really worse than fifty armed trolls? What was the point of crying?

My steps were slow, but at least my legs moved when I told them to.

Walking out of earshot of the Lena-in-the-mirror scene, I pulled the M3 out of my pocket. I licked my lips and tasted tears.

Chase looked horrified. If he'd been on the fence about whether or not he should be my friend, seeing me cry was definitely making the choice easier.

"Lena?" I don't know what I would have said or asked, but when her image replaced Chase's, I saw the pillow behind her—recognized the gilded woodwork on the sky blue wall behind her. "Are you in bed?"

"You're crying," Lena said, pulling the M3 closer. "You have to tell us what's wrong."

"Lena, you're in the infirmary," I said.

She couldn't deny it. Melodie leaned toward the M3, enthusiastically nodding her golden head.

"Yeah," Lena said with a small cough, clearly not happy about it. "But I've got everything I need to help you here. Look."

She reached toward the M3. Her palms filled the screen for an instant, and the bottom dropped out of my stomach. Dark gray lines crept up her hands. The final stages of cockatrice poisoning. Pretty soon she would be as bad off as Rumpelstiltskin.

Lena tilted the M3 toward her table. The golden harp stood above books, dragon scales, various herbs, and the bowl of water that held the scrying spell.

Melodie wrung her hands. "Hi."

If I stayed here crying, wasting time figuring this out, we would run out of time.

I didn't care what Lena had said about me. She didn't deserve to die.

"Lena, I need you to draw a map of the maze and mark the fastest way to the center. Then I need you to leave it flat on top of the mirror." I knew I'd said the right thing when Melodie smiled.

Lena's chin jutted out. "But I can—"

"I hear stuff that you guys can't. I need to plug up my ears." I drew my sword, sliced my shirt, and ripped off a strip. I cut away two bits for my ears and used the rest of it to bind up my bleeding left hand. "I won't be able to hear you anymore when you give me directions."

Her face fell. She reached over to her nightstand for a pen and paper.

I'd hurt her feelings, and a part of me—the part of me furious at her for calling me stupid when I was trying so hard to save her—was kind of glad. I *was* a terrible person.

Chase came back, scowling. "You won't be able to hear anything else, either. The troll king could ambush you."

I couldn't meet his eyes right then, so I concentrated on tying the bandage one-handed. "This is the only way. You need to sign off too, Chase. If you keep talking, you'll cut in on Lena's signal, and I won't be able to see the map." And then he could hang out with his new friends as much as he wanted.

Chase's face closed. "Okay. Mirror, mirror, go to sleep, they'll leave a message after the beep." His image disappeared.

Lena didn't look too happy either as she sketched. It took her an excessively long time and I nearly had second thoughts—the maze must have been bigger than I thought. Then she finally finished her drawing and turned it facedown on top of the mirror.

"We'll be back soon, Lena." But if she said anything else, I didn't hear it. I'd already stuffed the torn scraps of shirt in my ears.

Checking the map, I found the next turn and followed it. I wasn't exactly surprised to see a scene of Lena and Melodie in the ballroom infirmary up on my right, but I definitely didn't want to hear what Lena had to say about me now. I clapped my hands over my ears, humming as I ran past.

A big improvement.

Even with Lena's map, I hit about a thousand dead ends. The mirrors were too confusing. I only saw a few more scenes—one of Chase on a dark beach, and another of my dad at his car, and one of Rapunzel speaking to someone through an M3, but I didn't stop to torture myself anymore. I didn't know how long the maze took. The mirror vault messed up my sense of time. It felt like only thirty minutes or so, but by the end of the maze, my feet throbbed. My shoulders ached under the straps of my carryall, and my eyelids scraped over my dry eyes every time I blinked. Hours must have gone by.

Finally the path widened and funneled out to a door made of black marble. Four statues stood guard at the columns—the regular kind, not the enchanted kind. They wore golden outfits somewhere between togas and dinner gowns, their shaved heads held high, their ears and their noses sticking out from their skulls in perfect triangles, their skin dusted with gold. They were at least two feet taller than me.

The goblin priestesses. They had to be. But they just seemed so . . . dignified. Most of the goblins we ran into were a lot seedier. These were a whole different kind of intimidating.

And as glad as I was not to see more mirrors, I still drew my sword. With the night I was having, something worse than this vault might be waiting on the other side.

I opened the door.

The closet space inside was empty except for two things—a pedestal and the two-foot-tall silver birch tree sitting on top, glinting in the moonlight.

I picked it up cautiously, expecting a trap, but the scariest thing that happened was me almost dropping the scepter of the Birch clan on my foot. It was a lot heavier than I had expected.

Well. That part was easy.

Touching it, I'd expected to feel triumphant, or at least relieved. Hollowness gnawed at my insides.

We had the Birch scepter, but that only solved one of our problems. We needed to force Fael to tell us where the spring was. We only had three days left to find the spring—not enough time to just go searching.

I lowered the scepter gently to the floor and sheathed my sword.

I pulled the T-shirt bits out of my ears cautiously, but I didn't hear anything except how hard I was breathing. I slipped the M3 onto the pedestal. "Lena?"

The map disappeared, and then the M3 showed a picture of Lena—not as she was when I'd seen my best friend last, but healthier, happier. *Hello! I'm not here right now, but please leave a message and I'll get back to you via mini magic mirror as soon as I can. Thanks! Bye!*

She was either asleep or I'd hurt her feelings so bad she didn't want to talk to me until I had the Water of Life for her.

Easing my carryall over the scepter, I sighed and tried again. "Chase?"

"Rory? RORY?" His eyes were humongous. Sand stuck to half his face.

"It's okay," I said, showing him the silver tree inside my carryall. "I got it."

"You have to put it in his hands. Fael said—" A gauntlet arm reached for Chase, but he wrestled away from it. "He's taken us to—"

Two more hands came into the picture—with a piece of silk stretched between them—and gagged Chase.

Another mistake. I'd told Fael I would need to be able to reach Chase at any time, but I hadn't said Chase had to be able to talk back when I spoke to him. I wondered how long it had taken Fael to figure out that little loophole.

"It doesn't matter." I reached into my carryall and felt around all the glass bottles until I found the baby food–size jar. "I'll take Lena's temporary transport spell back to the beach, give this dumb scepter to Fael, and everyone will be fine."

But Chase still struggled—while I carefully painted the frame attached to the marble door, when I set the bottle and brush down carefully on the floor stripe, and even while I read the spell from the paper Lena had written out for me.

I didn't realize what he was so upset about until I stepped through the doorway and onto Atlantis sand. The sky was charcoal, and greenish-gray waves lapped the abandoned beach.

Prince Fael had taken the questers somewhere else.

And by the looks of things, I had less than an hour to find them before the sun rose.

I couldn't believe this night wasn't over already.

I sighed and rubbed my face, trying to think where they'd go, worrying about how much time I had.

"Prince Fael took them back to the Unseelie Court."

Hearing the voice, I almost tripped and fell face-first in the sand.

On top of the closest boulder sat a small, hunched old woman, her nut-brown face lined with a thousand wrinkles—the mother of the four winds. Either she was following us around or she felt a little bad for having enchanted me without my permission. In the gloom, I couldn't quite see her expression. "The Turnleaf told the other Ever Afters that you had made it inside the Hidden Troll Court. The Fey overheard. The Unseelie prince was so looking forward to killing someone that he relocated to his throne room, where you could never reach him before time ran out."

So Chase's bragging had given us away. Big surprise there.

"How long before daybreak?" I asked.

"Little more than a half hour," she replied.

Chase had said we would walk for a while, and then climb some steps, but I was pretty sure he'd said it would take longer than thirty minutes. "And how long does it take to get to the Unseelie Court from here?"

"It depends on how you plan to travel." That was a hint if I'd ever heard one.

The West Wind was out. He'd said he would need four days to recover from that glass vial.

I only had one other boon left. I stepped onto a flatter bit of sand, trying not to think about what would happen if this didn't work. I stamped my left foot three times and whispered, "Dapplegrim."

The beach was still.

I missed Chase, master of the brilliant backup plan.

"Give him a moment," the mother of the four winds said. "Five minutes is usually standard. You Ever Afters grow more and more impatient with every generation."

"Sorry." I rubbed my face again. All the adrenaline from the Hidden Troll Court had worn off long ago, and my thoughts were processing much more slowly than normal. "This isn't an insult or anything, but why are you here?"

"I owed Rapunzel a boon," she said.

"She asked you to meet me?" That didn't make any sense. If Rapunzel knew that Prince Fael would move the questers, she could have told me herself back at EAS. Or through the M3.

"Given a choice," the winds' mother said, "I would have repressed the vault's magic to spare you the blood, tears, and broken glass. The goblin priestesses and their magic are bound to me. What they see, I see."

My face burned. She must have watched the whole thing. "What stopped you exactly? You thought my day needed to suck a little more?"

"Rapunzel believed you would benefit from the mirror vault," she replied.

Ugh. Rapunzel was Solange's sister through and through.

"What did you learn when you faced such doubts, child?" said the mother of the four winds.

I hoped she didn't expect me to thank her for reducing me to a sobbing bloody mess on the maze floor. "Walking and crying at the same time can end in broken glass."

The winds' mother narrowed her eyes in a way that clearly said, *I don't have to help you if you're going to be a sarcastic little snot.* I sighed. "You still need to conquer the Unseelie prince," she said. "Ask me the question Rapunzel gave you."

"Um . . ." Despite everything, I thought back. I didn't want Rapunzel as my enemy. I still wanted to believe she was helping me, but setting me in that maze . . . "She said to ask you what really happened the night Iron Hans escaped."

"The priestesses' magic reveals the fears and desires of anyone who passes in front of their mirrors, and the Unseelie prince entered the Unseelie vault the night Iron Hans escaped. We learned three secrets." The winds' mother grinned. You could see goblin in her smile.

"Prince Fael stole his father's key to accomplish a childish prank. He locked a half-Fey child in the tombs of their ancestors," she continued. She obviously meant Chase. "To taunt the Fey child, the Unseelie prince threw the key away from him, over the wall to the beach below. But the king's key can open any lock in his court. It must not be misplaced. It must not be missed. When Prince Fael summoned the key back to his side, as only Unseelie royal can do, the key did not come. A chipmunk had found the key, picked it up, and carried it between his teeth down to his master in the dungeon. That is the first secret: Fael gave Iron Hans the key that opens all Unseelie locks, the one that set Iron Hans free."

Oh. Nice. But I didn't know what to do with that secret—besides maybe tell Chase.

"Iron Hans went walking—in the small hours before dawn, when fairy revelers are in bed. He searched for his ax. He kept to the shadows. He discovered the Unseelie prince lying asleep and covered Fael's mouth with his iron hand. 'Return my ax to me,' Iron Hans told the sleep-muddled prince, 'or I will kill you.' That is the second secret: Prince Fael was the only Fey who saw the prisoner before Iron Hans left the court that night, and Prince Fael raised no alarm."

I didn't have time for long-winded stories. The gloom had lightened to gray, a few shades darker than Rapunzel's hair. The sun was coming up. I glanced past the winds' mother, searching for a giant horse thundering across the beach. Maybe I should try stamping my foot again.

"The Unseelie prince did not want to die, but he could not give Iron Hans his ax. The war trophy had changed hands many times since Iron Hans had been defeated. The Hidden Court trolls now kept it in their Hall of Fallen Warriors," continued the winds' mother. That must have been the name of the room of pretty spears, and bows, and swords. I was still waiting for a point to this story. "Prince Fael pleaded for his life. He would give Iron Hans anything except the ax. He would give him something the Hidden Court trolls might trade for. He would give Iron Hans the scepter of the Birch Clan."

I snapped to attention. "Wait, Prince Fael *gave* the scepter to Iron Hans?"

The winds' mother nodded deeply. "That is the final secret. That night, the Unseelie prince entered the mirror vault just before dawn. Because he is of royal blood, the goblin priestesses could not invoke their magic to stop him, but they could read his fears. The first two secrets, if revealed, might strip the prince of his rank, but to freely give away the scepter of the Birch clan, the symbol of his family's power . . . Fael would be banished from the Unseelie Court. He would be deemed a Turnleaf, shunned by all Fey."

This was the blackmail we needed. We could make Fael tell us where we could find the Water of Life. We could make him *take* us there.

If I could just reach the Unseelie Court before the sun rose, everything might be okay. Everyone might live.

I sneezed unexpectedly, and with a leap of joy I whirled. "Dapplegrim."

The horse thundered down the beach, flames flickering at the end of his mane. He trotted to a stop directly in front of me, even more massive than I remembered. I sneezed again.

"You know, I find it insulting that you have this response every time we meet," said the Dapplegrim.

My eyes itched like crazy. "I'll be out of your hair forever if you drop me off in front of the Unseelie prince before the sun comes up. Can you?"

"Simple," said the Dapplegrim, with a trace of scorn.

No wonder Atlantis was so dangerous. Everybody who lived here was so touchy.

I turned to the mother of the four winds. "Mind if I borrow your boulder?"

She just smiled. I scrambled up behind her, and the Dapplegrim sidled closer so I could clamber up his back.

"Remember, Rory," said the mother of the four winds, while I looked for a bit of mane I could hold without crispifying my hand.

"Doubts can conquer a person more quickly than an army. If you know yours, you can conquer them instead."

I couldn't think as far ahead as conquering. I just wanted to get them out of my brain. I slid a leg over the Dapplegrim's back. "Was it real?"

"Of course it was real," said the mother of the four winds. "Check the wound on your hand if you believe you made it all up."

"No, I mean what everybody said; did they actually—" But I couldn't finish the question. As soon as my behind settled on the Dapplegrim's back, he sprang forward.

I decided that I would rather get singed than fall off. I clutched two fistfuls of mane and squeezed my eyes shut against the fiery horsehair flapping in my face. The Dapplegrim galloped so fast that the world slid by in gray. Sea spray filled my mouth as the Dapplegrim splashed through wave after wave. My clothes were soaked in minutes.

I opened my eyes only in snatches. The sun was rising. We would beat it. We had to.

After my fifty-seventh sneeze, I spotted a dark gray structure set atop a cliff. Its muted green banners danced in the breeze. "There!"

"Draw your blade." The Dapplegrim's voice was ragged. Even he was out of breath. I wondered how far we'd gone. "Knights guard the top of the stairs. I could fight them, but it would slow me."

"What stairs?" Then, unsheathing my sword, I spotted the narrow ledges barely a hand's length wide, winding up and up. A giant horse couldn't possibly gallop up that. "Crap."

It doesn't bother the people who can fly, Chase had said.

"Slice me, and I will throw you from my back—boon or no boon," said the Dapplegrim. It took true talent to sound that intimidating when you were wheezing.

His hooves struck the stone steps with a jolt so hard I nearly dropped my weapon. I tangled my fingers deeper in his mane and sneezed again. My teeth clattered as the Dapplegrim hit each stair.

We were too high. I was going to throw up. I couldn't throw up. The Dapplegrim wouldn't carry me to the top then, and I'd never make it in time.

"Open your eyes, human."

I did, staring upward so I wouldn't have to see the drop. The gray sky was threaded with gold. The sun had almost risen.

Closer now, I could see the structure better—how dozens of trunks twisted together to form walls, towers, and turrets. Those green banners blowing in the wind weren't cloth. They were actually hundreds of thousands of leaves.

Right at the front, two massive oak trees formed an arch two and a half stories high. Between them, two huge doors barred the way, made from vines woven in angular loops and swirls.

Two figures guarded the arch. Each wore black armor, and each had leaves hanging down its back where hair should have been.

Only two. I could handle two.

I concentrated on protecting the Dapplegrim's sweaty flanks, and my sword's magic flared.

The one on the left threw his spear at the Dapplegrim's heart. The horse dodged it, as the guard on the right slashed. I locked my hilt guard with his and yanked. His blade spun out of his hands. The Dapplegrim reared—I squeaked a little, groping for a better hold—and kicked the huge doors open.

He galloped through. The hall's ceiling was so low I had to duck my head against the Dapplegrim's.

I sneezed again, and then we reached the throne room.

Fael was on the dais, his eyes as big as dragon scales. The questers sat beside him, in chains.

Chase sprang to his feet, so fast his manacles jangled. "It's about time, Rory!"

Fael's knights stepped out of the shadows. Etched leaves gleamed on their armor. They edged closer to the Dapplegrim until I unzipped my carryall and tugged the scepter out.

"No! You could damage it!" someone shouted.

The knights stopped. They stared at the scepter the same way the trolls had stared at my shoe.

When the Fey made no further move to stop us, the Dapplegrim trotted in the rest of the way. I glanced over the questers. Kenneth and Mia had just woken up, but besides a new bruise on Chase's head and Kenneth's split lip, they didn't look hurt.

An orange sky shone through the windows. Dawn. We made it.

"So . . . ," I said slowly, sheathing my sword. "I got it."

"Very good." Fael had recovered enough to lounge against the throne again. He was trying to seem uninterested, but his eyes never left the scepter. He was relieved to have it back. "Unfortunately, I said that the scepter needed to be in my *hands* before dawn, so one of your number will lose their life."

Unbelievable.

What an evil little coward Fael was. He'd never done anything besides hide behind his daddy's throne, tricking people, *tormenting* them. Chase was worth a thousand Faels.

"No. No more tricks." I slid from the Dapplegrim's back, scepter in hand. Nose running, clothes covered in magic horse fur, I marched up the dais. I grabbed Fael's hand from under his chin—the prince nearly fell over in shock; the whole court gasped behind me—and I stuffed the silver tree into it.

The Dapplegrim had apparently decided he was done. His hooves clattered against the stone floor on the way out, but I didn't turn around to watch.

"You dare to touch the Unseelie—" Fael began, outraged.

"Save it." I lowered my voice. "I know what happened the night Iron Hans walked out of here. I know how he got his hands on the scepter."

Horror and rage washed over his face. I knew I had him.

"This is what is going to happen." I pointed at the lump of questers. They couldn't hear me—they were too far away. But they were all on their feet, staring. Chatty's hand was clutching Ben's arm. "Like we agreed before, you're going to let them go, because you got your scepter back. That includes removing the manacles, by the way. And unless you want me to tell this whole court what I know about how Iron Hans got this scepter, then you'll have to take us all to the beach beside the Water of Life spring. And we need to get there safely by sundown—no excuses, no funny business."

"Do you have any idea how far away we are?" the Fael snapped.

"You're the Unseelie prince. I'm sure you can work something out. And," I added in a flash of inspiration, "we're going to do a Binding Oath. You can swear on your life or on your claim to the Unseelie throne, your choice. If you do these things, then I will swear only to tell Chase, and no one else."

"You'll tell *no one*," Fael said, eyes narrowed.

I was way too exhausted for him to intimidate me. "I'll tell Chase, and he'll swear on his life that he won't reveal it to anyone unless you give him the kind of trouble you gave him yesterday."

The prince opened and closed his wings absently. "You drive a hard bargain, Rory Landon."

"I'll get what I want, Your Royal Highness." Then I sneezed

again. Geez, I would have traded Lena's Lunch Box of Plenty for a lint brush.

"Turnleaf!" Fael beckoned Chase with one finger, and tossed something to the closest Fey guard. Keys—they clinked against the knight's metal glove as he caught them.

Chase did pretty well. He didn't look surprised at all when I explained how Fael was going to take us to the spring, and under what conditions. He just nodded, like this had always been our plan. When we swore the Binding Oaths, he managed to look serious and not smug.

Fael stopped me just as I started to tell Chase the three secrets. My fists clenched, thinking he was going to try and weasel out of our bargain again, but he just whispered, "Let our words die outside this circle of three; let their ears close up, their eyes not see."

"Fey spell," Chase explained, before I could ask. "Makes it impossible to eavesdrop."

"You may proceed," said Fael sullenly.

When I finished telling Chase, he didn't exactly gasp—he just breathed in kind of sharply.

The Unseelie prince sprang to his feet. "Knights, ready the royal ship. We're sailing the Ever Afters south."

We would reach the spring by nightfall. I was so relieved I almost sat down in the middle of the Unseelie throne room.

The thing no one mentions about staying up all night, especially if you stay up all night stealing some scepter for a Fey prince, is that you're completely useless the next day.

My brain had turned to stone. No thoughts could get through; they just made my head feel heavy.

The knights led us out of the throne room, around the corner, and down a long corridor, where the palace was waking up. Fey ladies and noblemen raised a few eyebrows when they opened their doors and saw Ever Afters paraded past them. One Fey with dots on her face covered her mouth and stifled a gasp, but I was the only one who noticed Chase clasp her hand quickly, barely even pausing before hurrying on. I think Lady Aspenwind knew her son would never forgive her if she made a scene and outed him to Ben, Kenneth, and the other EASers.

She didn't follow us—she just watched as Prince Fael led us down a stairway. I don't remember much else except that the steps were made of interwoven branches, stripped of bark by a thousand scuffing feet. I was busy trying not to fall down the stairs face-first.

A cavern opened at the bottom of the steps, its stalactites hanging gilded from the ceiling. Underneath them was a harbor—strange ships connected to long, ornate docks. A large yacht with five masts, carved and painted to look like a life-size blue whale. A tiny skiff with a spiderweb sail. The sky was blue and clear outside the cave mouth.

Chase turned to me as soon as the Fey knights were busy with the boat. His eyes were huge, but he contained his smirk. It was too small for the Unseelie prince to find insulting. "Well, it has to be said—you definitely know how to make an entrance."

There's not exactly a wide selection in the seventh grade. I couldn't ask him if he'd really said it.

Chase's tiny grin faded. I'd taken a second too long to respond.

"I would crack an awesome joke right now if I'd had more sleep," I said finally, but he didn't talk to me again after that. He just handed back the M3 I'd lent him. He was probably wondering if I was going to cry again.

As soon as we got on the boat that looked like a Viking long-ship, Chase started burning off last night's adrenaline by climbing every inch of rigging, sliding up and down every rope. It also had the added bonus of getting him away from the Fey on deck—and me.

Ten minutes later we glided over the ocean, the water rushing underneath in a funnel of sea foam. If you hadn't been able to tell it was a fairy ship by the fancy gold deck and the pretty blue stone inlaid in the rail, maybe the enormous odd sails would have tipped you off. They were shaped like outstretched fairy wings. Apparently, the boat could sail itself, because eleven Fey knights stood at attention at the railing. The twelfth and biggest fairy, Ori'an, was lying down in the middle of the deck.

Fael sat on a low chair covered in silk, his fingers drumming on his knee, clearly not pleased.

The Atlantis cliffs stood high and white and stark in one direction and the sea stretched out endlessly in the other, gilded with the sun. Every once in a while we could also spot a scaly rump of something swimming beside the boat. Apparently, the dolphins here came in turquoise, emerald, and violet.

I leaned against the mast, trying not to show how much I felt like hurling.

At least I wasn't as bad off as Ben. He threw up nearly as often as Fael glared at me, but if anybody could seem cheerful while being violently ill, it was Ben. When Chatty handed him a glass of water from Lena's Lunch Box of Plenty, pointing a finger at it sternly to remind him to rehydrate, he grinned and hugged her around the shoulders with one arm. I'm not sure that I would have appreciated being so close to vomit breath, but Chatty beamed back.

They were so relieved. We all were. Things were going smoothly for once.

But the contented sleepy glow of being extremely proud of myself had worn off. My shoulders ached with tension. Rounding the next bay, I even caught my hand gripping my sword, like a sea monster might raise its scaly head at any second.

It got harder and harder not to think about life after we reached the Water.

I already knew that Mom wouldn't be sleeping tonight. Mom and Amy would be so worried. I wasn't so sure about Dad.

Well, there was nothing I could do to fix *that* problem. I couldn't even ask Lena to send them a text to tell them I was okay. She still wasn't answering her M3. I'd already checked.

I wished I could nap, like Kenneth and Mia, but I didn't want to dream on a boat where a bunch of Fey could see me have nightmares.

Something was going to go wrong. I'd dreamed of Mia's head

sitting on a marble pedestal, clearly separated from her shoulders. I had seen it three times. And she deserved to know.

Especially since she couldn't rely on me to protect her, considering how my sword's magic had hiccupped during the last witch forest battle.

I crossed the deck quickly. There was absolutely no way to be sneaky about it on a boat, especially one full of bored fairies. A few knights glanced at me. Fael narrowed his eyes like I was up to something that would embarrass him.

Curled up on his side, facing the coil of rope Mia had stretched out on, Ori'an opened his gray eyes and stared. Without blinking. Yes, it was safe to say that Ori'an had won the creepy award.

"Mia." I crouched down beside her.

She didn't jump, or give me a *what's your problem* glare, or squint like the sun behind me was too bright. But Kenneth, who had been sleeping on the deck just beside her, did all of the above.

Mia just looked at me, like she hadn't been asleep at all, like she had been lying there awake, waiting for me. Her eyes were bluer than the sky behind her. "Yes?"

"I—" I got even more flustered. "I've had a dream about you. Three times. Your head is always on this table."

She blinked at me. Clearly, it didn't register.

"And it's not attached to your body," I added hesitantly, preparing to reach out and comfort her if tears came next.

For a second she didn't process that either. I wondered if the Director hadn't covered dreams in her orientation.

Swearing, Kenneth drew his sword like the beheader would jump out from behind the sails. "I'll protect you, Mia. Don't worry."

Mia's lips slowly curled up into a small, tight smile. "Thank you for telling me, Rory Landon."

Goose bumps rose up on my arms, ones that had absolutely nothing to do with the sea wind.

I had been avoiding Mia. It wasn't just the dream or how quiet she was.

Something was off about her. Who reacted so calmly when someone basically said, *I think your head's going to get cut off?* Scratch what I'd said about Ori'an. *Mia* had won the Creepy award.

Chase dropped from the rigging and landed beside me with a thump. "Kenneth, how idiotic can you get? Put that sword away." Kenneth opened his mouth like he would argue, but then Chase added, "The Fey aren't exactly in the best mood. You could start a fight if they think we're going to commandeer the ship."

Every fairy eye was on us. They didn't have their hands on their weapons, but a tense sort of readiness had replaced their boredom. Kenneth hastily sheathed his sword.

Mia being awake caused a stir too. Apparently, Ben thought he could get some quality time with her in between bouts of vomiting, because he started over. Chatty watched him go. Then she pulled stones from her pocket and started skipping them out to sea with the intensity of target practice.

Ben obviously didn't notice how upset Chatty was. "Mia! How do you feel? I'm as sick as a dog."

Chase leaned closer to me. "You had to tell her?"

"I dreamed it a third time. Right before they came," I said, jerking my head toward the Fey knights.

He didn't tell me off for adding another complication, like I thought he would. Either the crying fest the night before had freaked him out, or he felt crappy for talking bad about me while I was saving his life. "Do you remember what it looked like? The room in the dream?"

I couldn't believe I hadn't thought of that before. Your dreams could only help you if you looked for clues in them. I shook my head, frustrated.

Fael looked our way again, scowling. Clearly, he thought we were plotting against him. He was just a self-centered little brat. I wondered how the Fey knights felt about following the Unseelie prince, and whether or not Chase—if he had stayed with his mother—would have grown up to be one of them.

"I just had a thought," I said. Chase glanced up. "In a year or two you'll be older than he is. I'm pretty sure you're already taller."

I didn't say Fael's name on purpose, in case the Fey overheard, but Chase understood anyway. That tiny smirk returned, and a second later he was climbing up the rigging again.

And, staring up at where he hung from a rope near the crow's nest, so high that the wind would rip away sound before it could reach the deck below, I realized what he was doing up there: He was laughing, completely delighted with how things had turned out between him and the Unseelie prince.

My chest squeezed. If we did go our separate ways after this quest, I'd miss him so much.

We reached the spring when the sky blushed with sunset. I'd thought that the directions were vague—I mean, two crossed pines somewhere next to the sea on a continent ringed with beaches? But you recognized it as soon as you saw it: The pines were as big as redwoods, and they weren't just crossed—their trunks twisted together in the middle.

"Geez, X marks the spot," said Chase. "Way to be obvious."

"I have fulfilled my part of the bargain," said Fael. "It's your turn now."

"I bargained to get us on the beach," I said shortly. "We're kind of far away."

"'To' was your exact word," said Fael smugly, and I fought the urge to throw my carryall in his face.

"Still, good for your first negotiation," Chase said without sarcasm. He was still being freakishly nice.

"But," said Mia, "how will we get to shore?"

Chatty looked at me, rolled her eyes, and climbed up on the railing. Then, with a graceful dive, she slipped under the ocean's surface and came up seventy feet closer to the beach. Her strokes were so neat that from this far away you couldn't even tell she was wearing a pack.

"Looks like we're going for a swim." I climbed up on the railing and held on to the nearest rope. "Everybody else go first." I didn't trust Fael not to try something. Maybe he had been planning that the whole way. Maybe his pouting face was the same as his plotting face.

Ben, Mia, and Kenneth splashed into the ocean behind me.

Chase was thinking the same thing. "Please don't attack us when we leave the boat. It's already been kind of a long day."

"We will sail to the Unseelie harbor," said a knight. "We have been called back. Our king has come home, and he wishes us to return his boat as soon as possible."

Nope. That was definitely Fael's pouting face. He knew he'd probably be grounded for joyriding in Daddy's boat.

"Awesome. Well, tell him hey for me." The knight gave the Turnleaf a look, like no one had ever told the Unseelie king hey. With a grin, Chase dove off.

"I won't forget this, Rory Landon," the Unseelie prince said, like this was supposed to scare me.

"Good." Maybe then he wouldn't mess with Chase again.

Then I jumped out of the boat. Luckily, it was only a twelve-foot drop.

The water was searingly cold, and the salt stung the slice on my left hand under the bandage. With the flotation spell in the pack, it was easy to stay above water. All I had to do was propel myself toward the beach, but I'd never swum so far in my life.

Chase waved both arms at me from the sand. *Yeah, I see you,* I thought, not sure why he was shouting. He couldn't expect me to hear him with all these waves crashing around me.

But the sea tugged at my jeans and sucked me backward. I glanced back at the Fey ship—Fael would figure out some sort of spell to stop me. But the Fey vessel was already gliding away.

So this was just an ordinary current—the Pacific Ocean kind? The kind that drowned people?

I swam even faster—*too* fast. I splashed so much I choked on the sea.

A hand closed over my wrist. Chatty, treading water. She widened her dark eyes pointedly, with a very small smile, as if to say, *Chill out, Rory. I've got you.* I copied her and treaded water, trying not to panic even when the current dragged us out farther and farther.

Then she wrapped one arm across my shoulders and towed me back—parallel to the beach. When I tried to help paddle us to shore, she slapped my arm and shook her head. It would have been humiliating if I hadn't been so tired. She wouldn't let me move until we could touch the sandy bottom. We stood up together, and Chatty stumbled forward, her breath hissing through gritted teeth.

I grabbed her shoulder, steadying her before she could fall over. "You okay? Did you cut your foot?"

She shook her head, eyes squeezed shut, clearly still in pain.

"Lean some weight on me, if it helps," I said, helping her toward the beach.

It was nearly dark. I heard Chase before I saw him. "A rip current."

Chatty and I splashed the rest of the way out of the water. I spotted the others.

Mia had apparently swallowed half of the ocean. Kneeling in the sand, she delicately spat it all back up.

Ben wrung out his T-shirt. "Right. Nobody had almost died in a while. We were starting to forget what that felt like."

"That was my bad," said Chase, as Chatty and I trudged up the beach toward them. "I knew we got off too easy. Fael must have stopped the ship right in front of the rip current."

Chatty shook her head so violently that drops of water flicked off her dark hair and all over one side of my face. When she was sure everyone was looking at her, she pointed her thumb at her own chest.

"You think it was your fault? Because you jumped off the boat first?" I guessed.

"You guys, everybody survived—thanks to Chatty's excellent lifeguarding skills," Ben said tiredly. "We're a team. Stop worrying about what was whose fault, and let's eat something."

Ben decided not to pass through the X-marks-the-stop gate until morning. Chase and Kenneth told him that was stupid, but Ben held firm. He wasn't going to jeopardize the mission when we were so close. We were all tired. It was dark. The path up to the spring was rocky. We could all break legs, and—as Ben pointed out—he couldn't afford any more injured Companions.

"I'm injured." I didn't really want to admit this, but if I didn't,

Kenneth would point out the giant no-longer-white bandage on my hand. "I cut myself in the mirror vault. You can send me back—"

"Can you still walk and fight?" Ben interrupted. I nodded. "Then you're staying. You're the reason we got here with two days to spare. You'll see it through to the end."

I grinned, almost smug with happiness, and to hide it I slung off my pack and started searching for my sleeping bag. We set up camp as close to the giant crossed pines as possible. My eyes drooped as Mia and I searched the beach for firewood.

Chase broke out the Lunch Box of Plenty, and everybody teased Ben when he ordered what looked like weird purple mush in the dim light beside our pizza, chicken fingers, and hamburgers. "What can I say? I have a highly cultivated palate," he said, snagging a fork from the lunch box. Then Ben put his arm around Mia's shoulders, and she kind of leaned in to him, smiling. Clearly, being held hostage by a fairy prince had helped their romance.

Chatty blew her whistle and motioned that she would take the first watch. Then she stomped up the beach, her feet hitting the ground so hard she threw up little fountains of sand with each step.

I inhaled my grilled cheese in three and a half seconds and called the last watch. I got dibs because I'd been wandering a mirror vault while everyone else had been sleeping last night. Then, as Ben assigned watches to everyone else, I crawled into bed and fell asleep to Chase and Kenneth arguing about who got to order dessert from the Lunch Box of Plenty first.

I thought I would be too tired to dream, but I was wrong.

Mia's head looked perfect and delicate on the marble pedestal, her lashes casting long, spiky shadows over her cheeks. Her black hair shone in a smooth river, cascading down her neck and over the table. Her arm lay beside the pedestal—the side that should have been attached to her shoulder was covered with white silk. Dread knotted in my chest.

I glanced back. His face white, his eyes huge, Chase was clutching a glass door with a single snowflake etched near the doorknob. He pointed at the table.

I turned. Mia's eyes cracked open, her lips curling.

Gasping, I sat up. There were the stars, piercing through the black sky in unfamiliar constellations, and there were the huge pines twisted around each other. There was Chase sleeping on my right.

Heart hammering, I wrestled myself free of my sleeping bag and walked down to the water. I sucked in big drafts of fresh ocean breeze and tried to wake up enough to think.

Beheading hadn't killed Mia. I shuddered all over again. Who would have guessed that a severed head staring at you could be way creepier than having it cut off in the first place?

In some Tales, you could get chopped up into little bits and brought back to life with magic. I must have read them, but I couldn't remember what they were.

Maybe that's why Mia hadn't freaked out when I told her. Maybe she already knew she would get that kind of Tale.

Smiling about it seemed excessive, though. That snowflake symbol etched into the door could only come from one place—the Glass Mountain. I didn't know how Chase, Mia, and I had gotten there, but considering how close we were to the spring, I sincerely hoped we would manage to get the Water of Life back to EAS *first*.

Just a few steps from the water, Chatty was throwing pebbles into the sea. Letting off steam, I guessed, but then I spotted elegant, short-haired heads bobbing in the waves, their tails curling up out of the water behind them, scales catching the moonlight.

Mermaids.

They didn't seem too disturbed by the fact that some girl was chucking pebbles at them. They just sang a few notes, and Chatty paused. Then she threw pebbles again: two stones, which skipped once. One stone, skipping four times. Four stones that skipped twice.

A mermaid sang a warbling note back.

"Oh. Are you talking with them?" I asked. Wherever Chatty was from, their chapter had to be right next to the water if they taught their Characters to speak Mermaid.

Seeing me, the mermaids dove under, their tails making great splashes.

"Whoops, sorry about that. I didn't think they would mind another Character—" But then I saw her face. The tears on her cheeks glinted as brightly as the mermaids' scales. "Whoa. What's wrong?"

But either she didn't want to tell me, or she couldn't figure out how to explain it, charades-style. She covered her face with her hands, one of them fisted around a dagger. I hadn't even known she carried one. I guessed she took guard duty very seriously.

I didn't know what was wrong, but the tears were kind of freaking me out. Maybe I had been hanging out with Chase too long. "It's okay. I'll help you."

She hugged me swiftly then, pressing her wet face into my neck. I was missing something. It nagged at me as I hugged her back, but unfortunately, my mind had decided to shut down for the night.

"How about this?" I said. "I'll take the rest of your watch, and you can get some more sleep. That'll help, right? Everything feels better in the morning."

Chatty wiped her eyes and smiled ruefully.

"Who had the next watch after you? Mia? Kenneth?" Chatty nodded. "Okay, I'll wake up Kenneth next. You go to bed."

And she went.

I never even suspected that I should worry about that dagger.

What Chatty really was never even crossed my mind while I kept watch, pinching myself again to stay awake, or when I gave in to the sleepiness and woke Kenneth, or when I fell back into my sleeping bag, snoring practically as soon as I touched it.

Then I woke to Kenneth shouting, "No!" Chatty was crouching over Ben, the dagger's small blade pressed to the new kid's throat.

The sky behind them slowly brightened from indigo to a silvery sort of yellow.

When Ben gulped, staring up at Chatty, the knife's edge parted the skin on his neck. Blood sank into it a breath later—a short red line right below his Adam's apple. Chatty just moved the blade back a fraction and smiled, one eyebrow quirking up at him as if to say, *Ben, you big, clueless dummy*.

She wasn't going to really hurt him. She was just getting his attention.

But the prankster in Chatty definitely enjoyed watching him squirm, especially since he kept ignoring her for Mia—

Suddenly, I knew exactly what was happening—exactly what I hadn't been able to figure out a few hours before.

I reached into the front pocket of my pack. Chatty didn't seem to mind. She didn't even take her eyes off Ben.

"Wake up, Chase. Now," I said.

Chase didn't bother to open his eyes. "What? Did Chatty draw on Kenneth's face with a permanent marker last night? Because I say we let her."

"Idiot. She has a knife," Kenneth said, shaken. Chase bolted upright.

My hand found the M3. "Lena! I need your help!"

She had to answer this time. I couldn't remember the exact wording of Chatty's Tale without her.

"Chatty, whatever it is," Ben said nervously, "we can talk about it." She scowled at him, reminding him she couldn't speak. "I mean, we'll help you. We'll get you what you need."

Mia was the closest to them, but she just lay in her sleeping bag, watching.

Lena appeared in the mirror, rubbing her eyes. She sounded just like one of those talking dolls when their batteries start to wear out—unnaturally slow and crackly. "What is it?"

"Quick, Lena. What do the Little Mermaid's sisters tell her about the knife?" I said.

"Um . . ." Lena dropped her hands, and I saw her face. Ice splashed down my spine. Her lips were turning black, just like Rumpelstiltskin's.

"Wait, pass me to Melodie." If Lena got any sicker, she would fall into a coma and never wake up.

Lena gave me a dirty look. "I'm fine. 'We have given our hair to the witch, to obtain help for you, that you may not die tonight.'"

"Wait. You're a mermaid?" Chase asked Chatty.

Chatty nodded vigorously. Her smile was so delighted you would have never guessed she was holding a knife to someone's throat.

"'She has given us a knife: Here it is; see, it is very sharp. Before the sun rises, you must plunge it into the heart of the prince.'" Then a cough overtook Lena, a wet hacking deep in her lungs.

My throat ached with sympathy. I shouldn't have asked. It was killing her. "Please, Lena. Let Melodie."

"I have the book, Mistress," said the golden harp anxiously.

"The prince?" Ben glanced at Chase and Kenneth. "The guy who married the wrong girl?"

"Guess who." Chase pointed down at Ben's and Mia's interlaced fingers. I hadn't even noticed. Blushing, Ben dropped Mia's hand. "Chatty, Ben's chest is a little lower down."

"Whose side are you on?" Ben asked.

"Don't you see?" I said. "She's not actually going to do the spell. She just wanted us to figure it out."

Chatty removed the knife from Ben's throat and pointed to me, nodding again.

Ben covered his neck and scrambled out of the way.

Melodie must have found the right passage: "'When the warm blood falls upon your feet they will grow together again and form into a fish's tail, and you will be once more a mermaid and return to us to live out your three hundred years before you die and change into the salt sea foam.'"

Sea foam. I knew she was going to turn into *something*. I shoved the magic mirror toward Chase and hurried across the campsite, to the Lunch Box of Plenty.

"Bowl," I told it fiercely. "Big widemouthed bowl."

"'Haste, then; he or you must die before sunrise,'" continued Melodie. Lena coughed.

Chatty sighed, glancing up at the sky for the first time. I fumbled with the latches on the lunch box. The Little Mermaid straightened and took a few steps back toward the water.

"'Our old grandmother moans so for you that her white hair is falling off from sorrow, as ours fell under the witch's scissors.'" Melodie said.

The lip of a metal bowl appeared inside the lunch box, and I pulled it out with both hands. Apparently, the lunch box couldn't supply any dishware without putting food in it. Oatmeal bounced in the bottom as I ran.

"'Kill the prince and come back. Hasten—do you not see the first red streaks in the sky?'" Gold glimmered on the horizon, but, smiling, Chatty looked straight at Ben and tossed the dagger into the sea. The water turned red where the blade plopped in, like the ocean was bleeding.

"'In a few minutes the sun will rise, and you must die.'"

"You die?" Ben took a step closer.

The sun climbed above the cliffs beyond us, red blazing around it. One eyebrow quirked up, Chatty blew Ben a kiss. Then in her place was a Chatty-shaped statue, made out of a substance like soap bubbles, almost the same color as dirty snow, but slightly greener.

Before it started to fall back into the ocean, I shoved the bowl under it—the fastest scoop of my entire life.

For a few seconds the only sounds were Lena's coughing and a crackling noise like tiny bubbles popping, as the sea foam formerly known as Chatty collapsed slowly over the oatmeal.

"So what happened exactly?" Lena said hoarsely from the M3, and Chase started to explain.

"How did you know, Rory?" Ben asked.

I hugged the bowl to my chest. I'd thought catching her would make me feel better. I explained about the mermaids the night before, and about Chatty skipping rocks, and the dagger. "I promised to help her."

"And you didn't wake us up and tell us about it?" asked Mia.

"I don't want to hear any accusations out of you, Mia," I snapped. "I'm onto you. You're the fake."

"There's no need to call Mia names, Rory," Ben said, a little bit mad.

"Don't you get it, Ben? Mia never saved your life during the griffin fight," I said. "*Chatty* did. She saved you when she was still a mermaid, and Mia took the credit. That's how the Tale goes. Mia lied to you, to all of us. She's evil."

Mia blinked at me. Infuriatingly calm again.

"Not necessarily," said Melodie from the M3. "In most Little Mermaid Tales, the fake isn't actually bad. She was just in the right place at the right time. Taking the credit is usually an accident."

"How do you *accidentally* take credit?" I said.

"Rory," Ben said, like a warning. "Is that true, Mia?"

Mia looked down at the sand, her beautiful hair falling over her face. She had perfected the *look* of being innocent. Ben wouldn't even be mad.

"Or did you just not have the heart to tell us?" Ben's voice softened. "I mean, I just assumed it was you. You were the only girl around with long, straight, dark hair, and it happened pretty fast."

"I wanted you to like me so much. I'm sorry." Mia hadn't even come up with her own excuse. She'd just let Ben create one for her.

"It's okay," Ben said, so eagerly that I hated him as much as Mia for a second.

"It's *not* okay." I shoved the bowl of sea foam under their noses.

Ben looked ashamed, but he sounded firm. "Rory, I understand you're upset. I'm upset too." *Not upset enough,* I thought savagely. "But we can't afford to start fighting now. We have to work as a team. This is bigger than us."

I refused to let it end this way. Chatty deserved so much better.

"Chase, I need one of the water bottles from my carryall." I must have seemed pretty intense, because he didn't argue. He just stuck his head in my pack to look.

"Why?" asked Lena from the M3. "Rory, what are you doing?"

I didn't know exactly what I would do, but it involved keeping Chatty safe until I could figure out a way to save her. "Magic turned her human. Magic turned her into sea foam. Magic can bring her back."

My hands shook, and I put the bowl down carefully in the sand so I wouldn't drop it.

"Rory, this is how 'The Little Mermaid' is supposed to end—" Coughing interrupted Lena again. When she covered her mouth, I glimpsed her hands—the black vines had almost reached her fingertips.

I couldn't stand to lose her, too. "Lena, please go back to sleep. We're almost there. We'll be back with the Water of Life soon."

Lena stopped coughing and nodded. She was feeling too weak to protest, to even say good-bye. The M3 went blank.

"She knew what she was doing, Rory. Chatty knew she was going to die," Chase said, but he handed me a water bottle anyway.

"Chatty," Ben repeated. It was clearly sinking in—how much she'd given up to help him. Knowing how long he'd feel guilty made me feel slightly better. "That's just what we called her. We don't even know her real name."

Breakfast was a silent activity. Mia broke a muffin into smaller and smaller pieces. Ben gnawed absently at a bagel. Only Chase and Kenneth attacked their egg sandwiches with any enthusiasm. Chase was worried—he kept glancing my way. He didn't come over while I spooned Chatty into the water bottle, but when Kenneth muttered something I couldn't hear, Chase told him, "Leave her alone, Kenneth."

Maybe Chase and I still were friends after all.

By the time the others had finished packing up camp, I'd slid the last spoonful of the Little Mermaid in the bottle—oatmeal and all. Even the tiniest bit of forgotten sea foam could turn out to be a fingernail or an earlobe or one of Chatty's teeth.

Chase brought me my carryall and approached with caution, ready to run away at the first sign of tears.

I pushed the water bottle inside. "Don't worry. I'm not going to cry."

But I definitely felt like crying. I took deep breaths to calm down as we all assembled in front of the huge X-marks-the-spot pines.

It was my responsibility now to turn Chatty back. I didn't know if I could do it.

Giving Chatty a footbath in Ben's blood couldn't be the only way to save her. That was just the sea witch's way. She wouldn't blab about other solutions. That would be bad for business—

"Rory, now would be a good time to look up," Chase said beside me.

Underneath the arch, you could see the path, covered with stones and boulders—a straight rocky staircase to a cliff above. All we had to do was walk through the legs of this humongous pine guy bending over us.

"Oh, my god," I whispered.

The X-marks-the-spot trees weren't just a gate. They were the guardian's limbs, each leg about as big around as a door, each arm as big as my bedroom window, with huge hands furry with pine needles. A head sat where the trunks twisted together. It was human-size, which explained why we hadn't noticed it in the dark the night before.

"Just FYI, getting lost in thought on a hidden continent is a bad idea," Chase said.

"Shh! Don't attract its attention!" I hissed.

Chase snorted. "It's a little late for that."

The humongous pine guy bent toward Ben, who stood bravely up front. Now that it was closer, we could see the head better—a man with tiny gray eyes, matted dark blond hair in half-unraveled braids, a mustache with moss growing on it.

"I will never smash any more innocent baby trees again, I promise," I whispered, covering West's ring, and Chase valiantly tried not to laugh.

"Well?" asked the humongous pine guy. "What do you seek?"

Ben's voice was surprisingly steady. "The Water of Life."

"Not the Talking Bird? Or the Tree of Beauty?" said the pine guy.

"Um, no." Ben glanced back at us, unsure. "I don't know what those are."

The pine guy squinted at us Companions with mild surprise—like he'd just noticed us. Maybe he was nearsighted. "Usually, questers arrive one at a time."

"Do we have to separate?" Ben said, obviously hoping the answer was no.

"You may pass together, if you wish. I will give you the same advice I give the single travelers," said the pine guy. "Climb to the top of the slope. The path is so full of stones you will hardly find places to step. It will feel as if every stone in the world mocks you. Do not turn your head to the right. Do not turn your head to the left. If you can continue on, paying the stones no heed, you shall reach the spring. Few have returned."

"Those other people couldn't deal when *rocks* teased them?" Kenneth said. He obviously had no idea what we were getting into.

This was the rock version of the mirror vault. This morning was just getting better and better.

"Beware." The giant pine guy straightened up. When he stood

at his full height, his face was too far above our heads to see. It was easy to pretend that he was just a couple of trees.

"That's our cue," said Chase cheerfully.

"I think we should travel in pairs," I said.

"Really? The buddy system?" Kenneth said. "This isn't kindergarten."

I glared at him. "This will probably suck. We don't know for sure what's out there." Not to mention I didn't think I could survive this alone twice.

"I'll go second," volunteered Kenneth. "Without a buddy."

"Yay. Rear-guard duty," Chase said unenthusiastically.

The climb wasn't easy. If you guessed wrong and placed your foot on an unstable rock, you had to scramble to a steadier one before you slid backward. I tried to tell myself that with the heights and all, it was a good thing I couldn't look behind me. But the steepness was the real problem. After a few minutes, the only person who wasn't out of breath was Chase, and I strongly suspected that he was cheating and using his wings. I heard a flutter every now and then.

"I take it back," said Kenneth, panting. "I definitely feel mocked by these rocks. They're saying, 'You're gonna fall, sucker.'"

"What?" called Ben, from way up front. Of course he didn't turn around. "I can't hear you guys."

A few minutes later we didn't even think about talking. I didn't know about everybody else, but my thighs were mocking me too. They were saying something like, *This is the magical StairMaster of doom. You will never reach the top.*

Chatty should have been there. It wouldn't have mattered if she'd been out of breath. She would have started a cheerleader clap—something to distract us from the climb.

"Did anybody else hear that?" said Kenneth, half freaked out and half ticked off.

Right. Quest, I reminded myself firmly. *Concentrate.*

"No," said Chase. So, the rocks really would start talking in a second. I didn't look around to check if the stones had faces in them.

"I heard my brother. You seriously can't hear him?" Kenneth said. "Older guy? Not a Character. Plays football for Notre Dame."

"What's he saying?" Chase asked.

Kenneth hesitated. Obviously nothing he wanted to share "He said—"

"Don't look—" I said, too late.

Kenneth whirled around to his right, both hands fisted at his sides. "Come here and say that to my face, Denton! I'll—"

We were behind him, so even looking straight ahead, Chase and I could see it happen.

"Crap," Chase breathed, and my chest squeezed. Kenneth was gone. In his place stood a boxy stone—dark gray and flecked with mica.

Then I heard something. Not Kenneth's brother, Denton.

Madison.

What an ugly loser. No wonder your dad didn't stick up for you. He knows how uncool you are. He's too good for you.

Chase stiffened. He'd heard something too.

"We'll figure something out for Kenneth later," I told Chase. "Just keep climbing."

And now Dad's whisper. *You're so embarrassing. I wish you had never been born. Brie and I will have more better children. Much prettier and more talented. We don't need you.*

My breath hitched, but honestly, the mirrors had sucked much more.

It had been so much more detailed. The goblin priestesses had really known what would hurt the most—what would stop me. They—

The goblin priestesses had been trying to *stop* me when they'd had me in the mirror vault.

Those scenes didn't have to be real. They just needed to be believable.

To make sure, I asked, "Chase, did you ever tell Kenneth or Ben that there aren't a lot of kids to be friends with in our grade?"

"What? No," Chase said, distracted by whatever he was hearing. "Way to be random."

"It's not real," I reminded myself softly. The stones must have been enchanted to tell us our worst doubts, just like the mirror vault. It was all in my mind.

This was why Rapunzel had enlisted the goblins. She wanted me to know that what the stones said wasn't true. But I was the only one here who knew that.

"You guys, it's fake, okay?" I called up the path to Ben and Mia. "We're all hearing something different, but it's not real! The stones are making it up!"

"What did you say, Rory?" Ben shouted back.

Chase wasn't listening. He had stopped. He couldn't resist anymore. He needed to see who was talking to him like this.

Without looking, I reached out and grabbed his face to keep his head from turning. One of my fingertips found something wet.

"Oww." He sounded like he had a cold with my hand squeezing his nose. "Thanks, Rory. I didn't need that eye or anything."

"Whoops! Sorry!" I lifted the poking finger. "But don't look. It's not real."

"I'm just glad that you didn't use your Left Hook of Destruction." But he grabbed my hand off his face and held on to it, too tight, crushing my knuckles together. Then he took a deep breath and shouted, "Ben, Mia! Hold hands! The enchantment can't work right if you're holding on to someone else!!"

Up ahead, Ben and Mia didn't hear us. They just kept going. I had figured it out too late. We'd already lost Kenneth. If we lost Ben, we couldn't get the Water. The quest would Fail.

The rocks picked up on my guilt immediately, weaving it into the spell.

Now I heard Iron Hans. *You are useless, child. You can't protect anyone. You're doomed to lose everyone who ever cared for you.*

My nose started to prickle, just under the bridge. No, I refused to cry. Not again.

It doesn't matter how long you train, how much you improve yourself. You'll lose them anyway, just like you lost your brother to the Snow Queen.

But I didn't have a brother.

Chase was supposed to hear this. We had managed to screw up the spell!

As a Fey, you were vastly inferior. That was Fael. *But do you think you are anyone special even among the humans? Your father doesn't think so.*

I didn't want to hear any more.

We clambered past Kenneth, the boxy rock. I didn't step on him, but there wasn't much else I could do for him right then. Far above us, Ben and Mia climbed together, and two steps later they disappeared. Either they had turned into stones, or they had reached the top.

If he believed otherwise, he would not leave you so often, needled Fael's voice. *Will your human friends enjoy your company so much if they find out you have been tricking them? Or will they react like Rory? She has grown more and more distant since she met your mother. She has barely spoken to you since she returned from the Hidden Troll Court.*

But I hadn't talked to him much because I thought he liked Kenneth and Ben better.

Lena and I talk about you all the time. If it wouldn't have turned me to stone, I would have glared at Chase right then. The Rory in his brain sounded insultingly close to Madison.

Oh, my God. If I was hearing the Rory in his head, did that mean he was listening to the Chase in mine? My face had been sweating already, but now it felt like I'd landed headfirst in a pile of flaming phoenix feathers.

"We're almost there," I said quickly, hoping to distract him. I climbed faster.

Without your dad, you're just a kid waiting for your Tale to start, just like everybody else. But I had actually said this a year ago, back when Chase and I were enemies. He'd gotten so angry, and now I knew why.

Only a few more steps to go. Past them the sky yawned—blue and cloudless.

Except yours won't ever ever come. You're just some useless halfling. It's only a matter of time before we drop you.

I would never have said that. I would never have even thought it. He was one of my best friends.

I couldn't stop myself. I squeezed his hand, too stunned to feel very embarrassed anymore. Did Chase really worry about something completely untrue?

We heaved ourselves on top of the last ledge. Staring straight ahead, I spotted a tree—a really big tree, bigger even than the pine guardian at the bottom, and two figures lying on the ground, gasping for air.

"There. At the grass. That's where the voices stop," Ben wheezed, pointing.

Chase and I hurried onto the plush, ankle-high grass, dropping hands the second we were safe. He wasn't looking at me, either. He had definitely heard stuff too. Great.

"That sucked so much more than I expected," Chase said. I was too out of breath to do more than nod.

The tree—which I guess had to be the Tree of Beauty—looked more like seven trees together, the branches ducking in and out of each other, swirling cyclonelike into the sky. Each leaf was a fresh-looking green, and the bark was a silvery sort of white. Up at the top I caught a glimpse of fuchsia tailfeathers. Apparently, the Talking Bird didn't want to talk to *us*.

But there among the Tree's roots, bubbling up with a cheerful gurgle, was the spring. The Water of Life looked pretty ordinary, actually, trickling down a granite trough into a small pool.

It would all be over soon. We would fill up the water bottles, slip on the rings of return, heal everyone, and be safe. Within an hour, within *half* an hour.

"What happened to Kenneth?" asked Ben wearily, like he already knew the answer.

"He's a rock," Chase said. I don't think he would have sounded so upset over it if Kenneth could hear him.

"I don't know what you're concerned about," Mia said quietly. "To change him back, we just sprinkle a little of the Water of Life on him. It's in the original Tale."

"Oh," said Ben. He and Chase grinned at each other, relieved.

"Wait, how do you know?" I asked, pretty sure she had made it up to comfort us.

"Well, let's not waste any time then," Ben said. "Rory, did I hear you mention earlier that you have some water bottles?"

Lena had given us at least a dozen—way more than we needed to give a few hundred poisoned people one sip each. I think she was hoping to have some Water left over for experimenting. I handed over my pack, feeling extremely uneasy for someone at the end of a successful quest. "Seriously, Mia—how did you know? Rapunzel didn't tell us that."

She shrugged delicately. "I read the Tale."

From this spot on the plateau, right next to the pool, you could see what was on the other side of the tree—a clear, rounded structure, tall as a lone peak, glinting in the sun. The Glass Mountain. I had never seen it from the outside. It was colossal. The trees only reached a quarter of the way up. Plenty big for the Snow Queen to hide something. Even though it was leagues and leagues away, the hairs on the back of my neck stood up.

Chase noticed where I was looking. "Been there, done that."

I hadn't told him what I had learned in my last dream. He didn't know we were going back to the Snow Queen's prison—us and Mia. But if we went now, what would happen to Ben?

"No, not from there," Mia said, bossy like she had never been bossy before, as Ben unscrewed the first water bottle and dipped it into the pool. "The Water of Life is more potent near the spring."

"Oh, okay." Ben got up and knelt at the top of the trough.

"And how do you know that?" I asked.

"Same team, Rory." Ben finished one bottle and started the next. "We can all play nice for a few more minutes."

"I will personally help you chew her out when we get back to EAS," Chase added.

But I'd figured out Chatty was a mermaid too late to save her, and I'd figured out the rocks too late to help Kenneth. I wasn't going to make the same mistake again.

"No. I need you to explain," I told Mia. "You shouldn't know that. You're the newest Character here."

Ben dipped another water bottle in the trough. "You sound kind of jealous, Rory."

"I don't care what I sound like." I did care, though—just not enough to stop.

I stared hard at Mia, who blinked back calmly. Was she a halfling pretending to be a human Character, like Chase? Was she a spy?

Ben's next bottle glugged as it filled.

Finally, Mia said, "Lena told me. When you were in L.A."

"No, she didn't. She doesn't like you," I said, even more suspicious.

"Are you sure?" asked Mia. "Maybe she wants new friends."

That might have worked. Before I'd gone to the Temple of Mirrors, and walked up this staircase of talking stones, I might have wondered if Mia was smarter than I was, if Lena liked her better than me. "Yes, I'm sure. Lena told me so, and she's a terrible liar."

The corners of Mia's lips turned up slowly, the same creepy smile I remembered from the dream.

"Mia, you didn't have the magic mirror when Rory was gone," Chase said carefully. "I didn't let it go all day. Lena couldn't have told you anything."

Stowing the second-to-last water bottle in the pack, Ben stood up. He narrowed his eyes, thinking.

She rushed him. I thought we had been safe—Chase and I had been closer to Ben than she was—but I hadn't realized how fast she could move.

Ben stumbled back a few steps, arm raised to block off a tackle. But Mia didn't tackle him. Her dress ripped, and white silk unfurled from her shoulders with the *shink-shink-shink* sounds of a knife being sharpened. Chase and I were still a few steps away when something clicked inside the silk, and a giant hang glider snapped into place, rising straight from her back.

Then she snatched up the strap of the pack that wasn't attached to Ben's shoulder, dragging him, the carryall, and all the bottled Water of Life off the plateau. Chase and I stared dumbly after them, as Mia's hang glider sailed straight to the Glass Mountain.

"Of course we're going after them," Chase told the West Wind. "I can't believe you're even asking."

I let him do all the talking. We were about a mile above the ground, zooming fast enough to outstrip small airplanes. West's shoulder *felt* solid under my sneakers, but this guy was made of air—he could disappear into tiny molecules at any second. It might not even matter how hard I held on to his ear.

I'd called him almost as soon as Mia and Ben were gone. Kenneth obviously couldn't come with us, so I had filled my pockets with enough plateau dirt for a temporary transport later. When West landed beside the Tree of Beauty, I barely recognized him. Today he wore jeans, squarish black-framed glasses, and a T-shirt that read I AM THE COMPUTER WHISPERER.

As soon as we explained what we wanted, West lifted one of us to each shoulder and gusted over toward the Glass Mountain. He also tried to talk us out of it, which—I was almost completely sure—was not part of the boon.

"Can't you at least call for reinforcements?" West told us.

"We don't have our mini magic mirrors," Chase said. They were both in the pack Mia had stolen. Next time we would have to remember not to store them all in the same carryall. "We're on our own."

"I could take you back to your homes," West said hopefully. "If this Mia has gone ahead of you, the Snow Queen will know you're coming. You surprised her last time, but no one has ever escaped her when she was prepared. You won't survive."

I was tired of grown-ups telling me what had never been done before. People told us that all the time, and then we did it. "Look. Lena's poisoned. Almost every one at EAS is dying. We have to save them. So if you don't have anything helpful to say, I think you should stop talking and fly faster." Then I shut my mouth so I wouldn't pull a Ben and throw up.

Chase didn't say anything. I was sure his face clearly said, *He can still step on us as soon as we get there, it doesn't matter how many boons he gave you.*

But West just sighed. "God, I love humans. You're just so . . . earnest. It's a shame you guys don't live longer."

The Glass Mountain was twice as big now as it had seemed from the plateau. I could see a dark rectangular opening in the front, at ground level. An open door.

I guessed Mia had already gotten there.

The same thing must have occurred to Chase. "So should we rescue Mia, too, or just Ben?"

"Where were you ten minutes ago?" I said, almost positive he was joking. "She's a bad guy."

"No, this could be a blackmail situation. The Snow Queen could have her family or something," Chase said. "We won't know until we talk to her."

"I thought you didn't like her either!"

"No, I said she was useless. *You* said her head gets cut off," Chase reminded me. "Does it seem like a good idea to chop off the head of your minion? Even the Snow Queen doesn't have enough of them right now to waste any."

My gut told me that Mia was not on our side, but I didn't want to argue about it. "So we rescue Ben definitely and Mia only if we get a good opportunity. It might be too late."

"Two minutes left. I see two squadrons stationed outside— one of wolves, and one of trolls." I thought West was telling us this as a substitute for "last chance to turn back," but then he added, "I can get you past them. I'll hide you somewhere in the maze of rooms."

"Great. Rory, you go in front and focus on covering me," Chase said. "It's easier for you to fight more than one villain when your sword kicks in."

"Got it." I probably should have drawn my sword too, but I would have had to let go of West's ear first. Wasn't ready for that yet.

"I can't get you out, though," said the West Wind apologetically. "Don't tell anybody, but even *I'm* afraid of Solange."

"We have rings of return. We can use those," I said.

"Rory?" West said hesitantly.

I was sure he really would tell me to go home while I still could. "Yeah?"

"Are you wearing my ring? You're bruising my ear."

"Sorry!" I loosened my death grip a fraction.

"She's afraid of heights," Chase explained. "You should have seen her when she broke the Cala Mourna Bridge."

"Really?" West said, interested. "Then I guess I shouldn't do this." He dipped at probably a hundred miles an hour. My stomach lurched weightlessly.

"Don't!" This was payback for bossing him around.

Up ahead, two long rows of black wolves (armed with giant

yellow teeth) stood to attention in front of four rows of trolls (medium-size, armed with spears in front and swords behind, complete with hockey masks). I was twice as grateful that Chase and I didn't have to fight our way through fifty bad guys.

"Trust me." West dipped lower and blew, flattening both the wolf and troll squadrons as easily as blowing out candles on a birthday cake. He gusted past the heavy, dark doors, and then we were inside. I glimpsed long panes of frosted glass dividing the floor into rooms, and then West deposited us gently in a sitting room with red-and-gold sofas.

Almost immediately I tasted sweat on my upper lip. I'd forgotten how hot the Glass Mountain was.

"I'll try to throw them off your trail," West whispered. He gusted away noisily, banging doors open and shut on the other side of the mountain.

"Great boon. Seriously," Chase said.

"Shhh." I listened hard. One wolf howled, a few corridors away, and a troll grunted out orders—assigning pairs to search down each hall. "They're looking for us, but only in teams of two. We can fight two."

"How convenient." You could hear Chase's grin in his voice.

But instead of my friend, a troll smirked at me, tusks curving around his lower lip. My sword was out in a flash, and just as I started to swing, the troll held up both hands and said with Chase's voice, "Rory, it's me. I cast a glamour over us. It even has a scent to fool the wolves."

I lowered the sword. "Oh. Good idea."

Troll Chase shrugged. Behind his hockey mask his eyes were still blue. "The Snow Queen will sense it right away, but it should buy us some time."

"We better start searching, then." In the glass door my reflection was faint, but it was still pretty weird to see a troll reaching for the door when I told my hand to move. Outside, the hallway was empty except for side tables that looked like they were carved out of blue gemstones.

Chase followed. "I need to tell you something."

"Do you really think this is the best time?" I whispered, hurrying down the passage.

"Yeah, I do, actually. The stones on the way to the Water, the ones that sounded like me—"

This was not a topic I ever wanted to bring up again. My cheeks went hot. Hoping the blush didn't show through the troll glamour, I peeked through a doorway—nothing in there but low couches.

"Last year, on my birthday, Amya asked me if I wanted to come back and live with her," Chase said. "She was going to ask the Unseelie king if it was okay, and she could probably have done it. He gives her pretty much whatever she wants, because of Cal. And I was thinking about it. Dad was never around."

Chase was lonely. That's what he really meant. "You had Adelaide. And the triplets." I stopped to check another door. Couches. These had gold clawed feet. What was with the Snow Queen and couches?

"Shut up—this is my story. And they don't actually know me that well." He sucked in a deep breath. "But I didn't do it. And this year she asked again, and I wanted to say no right away. That got me wondering what the difference was between this year and last year. And the only thing I could think of was you. I mean, I'm sure it's not the only reason," he added hastily. "But things were better after you came."

This was, by far, the nicest thing he'd ever said to me.

I stopped and looked at him. "Are you telling me this because you think we're going to die?"

Even through the hockey mask I could tell he was scowling. "I think Mia heard what the stones were saying to us."

"But she wasn't touching us," I said, kind of panicked. "It doesn't work without skin-to-skin contact! We didn't hear what the stones said to them."

Chase shrugged. "She's a magic spy. Listening spells are the first thing you learn. Even Dad knows a few. But Mia heard. Lena, or the stone that was supposed to be Lena, said the thing about wanting new friends. She'll use it against us. The Snow Queen likes to mess with your head."

The worst villain ever knew all my worst fears. Fantastic.

"That's actually really smart of you. I'm impressed." It was easier to say that than tell him how grateful I was.

Troll Chase pointed two thick thumbs at himself. "Grew up with fairies. They invented mind games."

I really didn't want to admit this, but— "I never minded that you're half Fey. But I care that you didn't tell me. And I care that I didn't notice." He'd lived a whole different life before I was even born, and I'd never even suspected. "I feel like a sucky friend for not noticing. But the actual Fey bit—that's actually pretty cool, like finding out you have superpowers."

Troll Chase's face twitched around his tusks, and I thought he was trying hard not to smile. "Are we done?"

"Done," I agreed. "That was really awkward. Let's not do that again."

"Unless our lives depend on it."

"Yeah, unless our lives depend on it." But even then I would think twice. It was so much harder to talk about feelings with Chase than it was with Lena.

I peeked inside another room. Eggs the size of my head rested on the wall's wicker shelves, cushioned in loose feathers. A bonfire crackled in the middle of the room; even bigger eggs nestled inside the flames.

"Hatchery," Chase said. "For ice griffins and dragons."

I closed the door quickly. "I think I preferred the couches."

In the four halls we searched, we only ran into one troll partner team. They saw us, grunted, and jogged right past us, their spear butts striking the floor in rhythm. "Told you I was good at glamours," Chase whispered, once they were gone.

Then, just when I started to worry that we would find the Snow Queen before we found Ben, we got lucky. I pushed open a door and spotted something neon green sitting on a couch with embroidered snowflakes. I sprinted across the room and picked up my carryall. "Yes!"

Rolling his eyes behind his hockey mask, Troll Chase stepped into the room. "Way to check for traps, Rory."

I unzipped the pack. "It looks like the bottles are all still here."

"So we really should suspect a trap, then."

I didn't see anything unusual about this room except that it had a second door, and a worktable just beyond it.

My stomach lurched.

Mia was in pieces upon the table. Only her head and one arm were visible. The rest of her body lay like lumps under the white silk of the hang glider, cut apart at almost every joint.

Chase noticed and gagged.

Her eyes were still closed. She wasn't dead, though. Reminding myself of that made it easier to think.

"Okay, if Mia's here, then Ben probably is too." I started looking.

"One dismembered body isn't enough for you?" Chase said, clearly grossed out.

"But he can't be. We would have seen him already," I said.

"Should we gather Mia's parts together?" Chase said, not help-ing me search for Ben. "Because I'm definitely going to let you take that job."

Besides the sofas, and the two marble-topped end tables, and the workstation, the only other thing in the room was a small, round paper weight, resting on the couch's arm.

"Rory," Chase whispered.

I had seen the same kind of paperweight in the Snow Queen's office the year before. So it didn't completely shock me to see Ben inside, shrunk down to the height of a toothpick, his face contorted with pain.

"Rory!" Chase said, as I picked up the paperweight.

I turned, annoyed, just in time to see Mia's eyes open, her lips curling into a smile. Then the parts under the silk moved on their own, drawing together. An arm attached to a lumpy torso and tugged off the cloth covering to reach for a leg.

Beware the doll, Rapunzel had said. "Chase, she's a puppet."

"Then where's the puppeteer?" Chase hissed, so freaked out that he dropped the troll glamour.

The Snow Queen was the puppeteer. Solange had been acting through Mia all week.

The second arm hooked back into the second shoulder, the sil-very shoulder hinges clearly visible under Mia's tank top. The tips of her wooden fingers had folded away to reveal slender blades.

I ran, grabbing Chase on the way out. "It's official. We won't be rescuing Mia this afternoon."

"What about Ben?" Chase said, as we hurried down an empty corridor.

"I got him. Just don't ask me how to get him out." I passed Chase the paperweight.

"The Water of Life?" he said. "It's basically pure magic. It should unravel most spells, just by overloading them."

I fished inside my pack for a bottle and spilled some Water of Life over the glass.

Lena could have listed off a thousand reasons why overloading a spell was a bad idea. She would have been right.

The paperweight exploded, showering us with tiny shards.

"Owww," I said. "Does anyone else feel like there's way too much broken glass in this Tale?"

Ben lay on the floor, normal-size. "Rory? Chase? What happened? Last thing I remember, some strange lady touched my forehead with her finger, and Mia—where's Mia? Is she okay?"

Chase helped him up. "Brace yourself, Ben. Mia's a bad guy."

"No . . . ," Ben said, clearly too bleary to process this.

"What? Her stealing the Water of Life and dragging you into the Glass Mountain didn't tip you off?" Chase said.

I rolled my eyes. "Find your rings of return so we can get out of here."

"Stupid Rory," sang Mia, somewhere behind us. "Rings of return don't work in the Glass Mountain. What if the evil queen found one and used it to escape?"

Crap. I slipped mine on just to make sure, but she wasn't just trying to trick us. "Put them on anyway. They'll take us straight home as soon as we get outside."

Mia appeared at the end of the corridor, her elbow joints glinting metallically in the sunlight. Even her perfect face looked different—hinges shone around her mouth. "You have to reach outside first. This prison only has one exit."

We fled in the opposite direction. I ran with my pack in front of me, my hand digging around for an M3.

Ben turned to Chase, wounded. "You failed to mention that Mia was a bad guy *and* not a real person."

"Right. She's a doll. She's been wearing the best glamour I've ever seen. You had a crush on a puppet," Chase said. "I bet you feel stupid now."

"Wow. Last time I ever look for sympathy from you," Ben said. He learned fast.

"We need a way out of here," Chase said.

"No kidding." I flipped the magic mirror open. "Lena! I mean Melodie! We need a scrying spell! We're lost in the Glass Mountain. Can you find us a way out like you led me through the mirror vault?"

"Right. Rory, you handle the escape plan," Chase said. A wolf leaped through a doorway, its teeth nipping at my friend's throat. Chase ducked and drove his sword into the beast's heart. "I'll cover our fronts. Ben, keep an eye on Lady Pinocchio."

"Lay off, Chase," Ben snapped.

"Lena, she—she can't come to the mirror right now." Melodie flipped her M3 over so I could see Lena: On top of an infirmary bed full of rumpled sheets, she frowned in her sleep, a tiny line between her brows. Her lips had turned so black it looked like she was wearing Goth lipstick. The vines snaking over her face had thickened so much they showed up through her brown skin.

Worst of all, I could hear her breath rattling around in her throat, even through the mirror. She sounded like a car engine with a broken muffler.

She wasn't just sick. She was dying.

Chase paused at a fork in the hall, looking at the three paths ahead. "Which way?"

But Mia reappeared behind us, snowflake-shaped throwing stars in each hand. She launched them at our heads.

"No time." Ben shoved me and Chase down the middle path, out of the way, and the throwing stars buried themselves in the wall's frosted glass, throwing out spiderweb cracks in each direction.

"What happened, Melodie?" I breathed. "We talked to her just this morning. That couldn't have been more than three hours ago."

"She snuck away from me and Jenny. She ran to the library to see if Chatty's Tale showed up in Rumpelstiltskin's book, and a nurse found her there an hour later." Melodie flipped the mirror back around. Golden tears beaded along her jaw. "She's woken up a few times since then, but she can't talk. Rapunzel says—" And Melodie's face crumpled.

"What does Rapunzel say?" Iron bands closed around my heart.

Chase tried to lead us left, but four trolls guarded that corridor. We ran right.

The harp pressed fists into her eyes. "She says Lena has an hour, tops. Jenny called Gran in."

Even though Lena had only eaten one bite, she'd run around a lot—just as much as Jenny and Rapunzel. The poison must have worked its way through her whole body. "But why would Lena do that? Didn't she know she was getting worse?"

"She so wanted to help you, Rory," Melodie said, and the iron bands grew tighter. "She wanted to be involved even though she couldn't be there. She was afraid that you would stop needing her, and that she wouldn't be invited on the next quest. Now she won't ever get the chance."

I'd been so stupid, worrying about whether or not Lena wished I was smarter. I hadn't once wondered how she'd felt, left behind, watching us through the M3. "There's still ointment juice left, right? Give her the rest." We had the water. The other poisoned people could hold out.

"Her body is too weak to even break down the ointment now. It's too late."

This was happening. It was real now.

Melodie's tears clinked onto the mirror, leaving a blob of gold on the corner. "She could've been an even better inventor than Madame Benne, and we're going to lose her."

"Will the Water of Life still save her?" I asked.

"Yes, but what difference does it make?" snapped the golden harp. "The Snow Queen has you trapped."

If we didn't get out of the Glass Mountain right now, Lena would die.

"No. Not yet." I was coming out of this Tale with both my best friends. I had to.

We tried to turn left, but trolls in hockey masks marched forward. We tried to turn right, but Mia blocked the way, hurling a few more throwing stars.

"No, Rory. You're surrounded and outnumbered," said the harp.

Five more trolls appeared behind us. This had to be an organized effort. They were herding us down this hall in particular, toward the door at the end. It was the only one made out of silver, not glass.

"You three will die soon," Melodie said. "And Lena will die too. And before the week ends, this whole chapter will be wiped out. The Snow Queen has won."

"I'll be there in less than thirty minutes," I promised.

I had to think.

What was at the end of this hall? Where would the Snow Queen's servants want us to go? The dungeons?

A troll jabbed a spear at us from the next opening we passed, and Chase intercepted it too quickly for me to see. His sword came back orange with troll blood.

No, not the dungeons. Even villains don't install fancy doors on the way to their dungeons.

The scrying-spell idea wouldn't work, but last year the Snow Queen had wanted Melodie to escape. The harp had to know *something* we could use. "Melodie, is there anything else helpful you can tell me about the Glass Mountain?"

"There's only one entrance," she said acidly. "One singular way in and out."

"We know that, Melodie. Rory asked for something helpful," Chase said, as we ran. The silver door at the end of the corridor drew closer and closer.

That ticked the harp off even more. "The Glass Mountain is a variant of the same spell that imprisoned the West Wind, the one embedded in those water bottles. It contains a person's essence. The heat interferes with the Snow Queen's magic. She has a tenth of her usual power."

Ben shoved me and Chase again, and I collided with an end table so hard that I felt a bruise forming on my hip, red hot with pain. A few silvery throwing stars whizzed by, inches from our shoulders. Mia had gained on us again.

"The Snow Queen shouldn't be able to touch the actual structure. She probably can't get closer than a yard or so," said Melodie.

Mia was twenty feet behind us, and the silver door only forty feet away. There were no openings left ahead of us—there was nowhere else to turn. *Now* we were trapped.

Whatever was behind the silver door, we were about to find out.

"Her magic will disintegrate as soon as she casts a spell upon it," Melodie added. "If a servant breaks the outer wall for her, it will re-form in one-point-one seconds, too quickly for her to reach the barrier and get out. The only way to break it is to pull every single silver Fey symbol out of the glass at the exact same instant—"

"Dude, Melodie," Chase said. "Minions listening."

"—and there are thousands upon thousands enclosed in the glass," Melodie continued, like he hadn't spoken. "If it were possible, then the Snow Queen would have done it by now. It was made by Madame Benne. It is the best prison ever invented. Is this what you wanted to know?"

My hand was on the silver doorknob. I was actually kind of surprised when it didn't electrocute me or anything. It wasn't even locked.

"Yes," said Mia, seven feet behind us. "There is no way out but for the way you came in, and we will never let you reach it."

I threw the door open, and the boys dashed in behind me. White silk covered the walls from floor to ceiling, making the room almost cold. And in the back stood a high-backed silver throne—seated upon it was a tall figure with skin the color of slushy snow, strawlike blond hair, and glacier-pale eyes.

Of course. No need for dungeons. Her servants had chased us straight to her.

"Rory, all this effort to get away," said the Snow Queen in her musical voice. Goose bumps formed on my sweaty skin. "I am hurt. It is as if my guests don't wish to talk to me."

Mia stood in the doorway, three silver snowflakes in each hand. She didn't attack. She was just blocking our escape route. Clearly, the Snow Queen was in the mood to chat.

Seeing that nobody was hurling any throwing stars at us, Ben bent over, wheezing.

Solange smiled. Her teeth seemed almost transparent, like they were made out of ice. "It is nice to have guests. You cannot imagine what my life has been like, Rory Landon. I have been locked in here for decades. Every thought has been of my escape. Every message has been of my return. Every action has worked for my triumph. I have been working toward this end since before you were born, Rory Landon, and you know the day will come soon."

I did know. Remembering it usually filled me with the same mindless terror as heights, but now, with her seated just a few feet away, I had two thoughts:

She hadn't used any magic yet. She probably needed all her power to keep Mia up and moving.

And she was enjoying this. We could use that.

"Melodie, why would the Snow Queen hang her throne room with white silk?" Chase asked.

"It reflects all the sunlight back through the glass," Melodie said automatically. "Lessens the greenhouse effect. Keeps the room colder and her magic stronger."

"Ah, you have the golden harp on the line," said the Snow Queen. "Let me have the magic mirror. If she tells me all I wish to know about the Glass Mountain, perhaps I'll give her enough Water to spare her mistress."

The Snow Queen was lying. Solange would never let any of the Water out of her sight.

Melodie's eyes widened. "Yes, I'll—"

Frustrated, I slapped the mirror face down on my palm. "Mirror, mirror, go to sleep; they'll leave a message after the beep."

There. At least Melodie couldn't tell the Snow Queen any more.

Chase jumped up, an inhuman seven feet, and slashed a wide gash in the white silk. Then he yanked on it, ripping it down. More light flooded in, through the thick wavy glass of the prison's outer wall.

Bright green grass started just a few feet away, right on the other side of the glass. I could see the plateau with the Water of Life on the right, and on the left, mountains rose up in jagged peaks, wearing snowy white caps.

We had to get out there.

"A futile effort." The Snow Queen leaned her head on her fist with a lazy smile. "It will take at least ten minutes for the room to warm. More than enough time for me to kill you."

"Every little bit helps," Chase said, with a tiny grin, ripping the last of the silk away from the wall, but he was scared. His shoulders had gone stiff.

"Wait," said Ben. "I don't know what's happening."

"Ben, meet the Snow Queen." Chase pried the M3 out of my hands. I'd forgotten I was holding it. "Geez, Rory, don't break it."

Ben's face, his whole body, was frozen. I knew that feeling, where terror had locked every joint rigid.

Solange nodded deeply. "A pleasure."

Chase flapped the M3 open and closed nervously, muttering something to himself in Fey. Probably cursing.

"Now, how would you prefer to die?" said the Snow Queen. "I will take requests."

"Peacefully. In my sleep. At a ripe old age," Chase said, and Solange actually laughed. Her face changed. She looked so much younger.

We had to keep her talking. I jerked a thumb toward Mia. "How long were you inside her?"

The Snow Queen's lips curled up very slowly, and I realized how many times I had seen that same smile on Mia's face. "Rory, are you trying to distract me with all your little questions? I have used that trick myself."

Okay, so this was an obvious plan. I willed my face not to move.

She sighed. "But I will play along. I have been bored for decades, and I'll probably be bored again after I kill you. The spell that animates my lovely doll can respond to most situations without my direct involvement. I only saw with her eyes and spoke with her lips when something interested me. Clever, Rory, but not clever enough. How heartbreaking. To realize what Mia was, an instant too late. Lena would have caught it by the second day."

She was trying to make me feel stupid, but it was a mistake to mention Lena. It only made me more determined to get out of here. "But how long exactly were you in her?"

Solange narrowed her eyes, like I was doing a bad job entertaining her. "That is the wrong question, Rory." I flinched. I guess I knew where Rapunzel learned that saying. "I'm disappointed. If I were in your position, I would want to know about much more than Mia."

"Fine," I said. "Tell me about your sister."

"Oh, dearest Rapunzel," said the Snow Queen. Her good mood was back. "My most loyal servant. I left her behind in the Canon to be my eyes and ears. You see, Rory, I always knew you were coming. I always knew that someone would come to take my place. Rapunzel offered to stay as long as it took for you to arrive, the girl they think will destroy me. She offered to befriend you. It was her idea to poison you as soon as you trusted her. I'm delighted that she managed to poison everyone else, too."

"You're lying." I knew it as soon as it was out of her mouth.

She might have convinced me if she'd mentioned Mia in that plan.

The Snow Queen smiled like this idea was too delicious not to share. "Yes, I am. But this is still what Mildred will believe."

An echo whispered around the room, and I couldn't place it until Ben shuddered and said, "Please stop."

She didn't stop. I watched Mia, her puppet, say all the Snow Queen's words with her. But Mia spoke so softly—we could have never guessed that they had the same voice. "Mia poisoned you all, right under Rory's and Rapunzel's noses. The blades on Mia's fingers hold the poison. It was a simple matter of changing the glamour slightly as Mia and I chopped up the chocolate for the Fey fudge pies. Now, since you will die here, Rapunzel will take the blame for it."

No, we wouldn't die.

"After all," the Snow Queen added, "you didn't even tell Melodie what Mia was before you cut off all communication with your Chapter. Rapunzel is the only suspect. Well, besides the witches, and all the witches are disposable."

She will attack you with words, Rapunzel had said.

Well, that was obvious, especially after the mirror vault and the staircase of talking stones.

I just needed more time. My mind raced back over what Rapunzel had told me the day we left. The part that hadn't come true yet, that would get us out of here.

"Why do you want the Water of Life?" I asked.

"Who doesn't?" she replied. "Next question."

Chase took over distracting duty. "Tell us how you and Rory are alike, then."

"You—" But then Solange made the same expression everybody

made, like she'd swallowed her tongue. Fury crossed her face. She didn't like losing control any more than the Director did.

"Two words, Snow Queen: Pounce Pot," Chase said gleefully. "I just wanted to see if I could get you to shut up."

Where others see a wall, or a mountain range, you see an escape.

The snowy peaks gleamed through the glass. Rapunzel had meant *this* wall. This was the way out.

On the other side, the rings of return would take us back to EAS. If we could just smash through, we would have an exit for approximately 1.1 seconds. Even the Snow Queen couldn't reach us that fast.

And I just happened to have a new ring that specialized in smashing.

"You are nothing compared to me, Rory." The Snow Queen had apparently gotten her tongue back, and she sounded extremely happy about it.

Good. She hadn't noticed I finally had a plan.

"Guys," I whispered, "I think this Tale needs more broken glass."

Ben stared at me like I'd lost my mind. "What?"

Chase understood. He glanced at the wall over my shoulder, sighed deeply, and shoved the M3 in his pocket.

"I will kill you today, of course, but I was to be your future. I was the direction your life was headed," said the Snow Queen. I thought she was just confirming my Destiny, but then she added, "You would have become me, if you had lived."

The idea hit me like ice injected straight into my bones, but my left hand curled into a fist. A new breeze rippled over my arm.

Chase grabbed my other hand and Ben's shoulder, and he gave me a look that clearly said, *This is going to hurt, and I blame you.*

Then the Snow Queen was on her feet. "No!"

I punched through the wall of the Glass Mountain. A hundred thousand clear slivers fell over us like confetti, and I dragged us through.

23

We tumbled to the ground. The grass burned my knees. Through the new slices in my jeans, tiny new cuts welled up red—like a rash of paper cuts. I looked up.

The Tree of Life's branches stretched across the sky. We were back. The courtyard hadn't even changed. Waves lapped the Tree's roots, and sea breezes rippled through the leaves.

I ripped my pack off and unzipped it.

Ben moaned, clutching his shoulder. "I think I've been shot. Can you say you've been shot when you get hit with a throwing star?"

Chase's face had the same paper-cut rash. "I got him, Rory. Go save Lena."

Then, a bottle in hand, I sprinted across the courtyard. I threw open the door to the infirmary. Hundreds of faces turned to me, but none of them were Lena's. "Melodie, you little gold dummy, scream if you're right next to Lena!"

"YOU MADE IT OUT OF THE GLASS MOUNTAIN A SECOND TIME?"

The voice came from the row on the right, eight beds down. Then I spotted Lena, lying way too still, her breath rasping way too loud. I leaped across the room in three strides and knelt on her cot, unscrewing the lid and pouring a quarter of the bottle into her open mouth.

"She doesn't need that much," Melodie said, disapproving.

The snaky vines under Lena's skin disappeared. Her lips grew pink again. Then she sat up, choking, raising her hands to her mouth. The Water of Life dribbled through her fingers. "Oh, no—I just wasted so much of it. If I could have just spit it into a cup—"

I grabbed her by both shoulders and hugged her so hard that the wet spot on her T-shirt bled a wet spot on mine. "Lena, why wouldn't you stay in bed? I told you to rest."

Those aforementioned hundreds of faces stared at us from the beds stretching out beyond her, but then a voice from the ballroom door made everyone turn away.

"Mother?"

Ben held a water bottle in both hands, searching the faces just like I had.

"Benjamin!" A few beds beyond Lena, Mrs. Taylor sat up weakly.

Every eye in the infirmary watched him as he sprinted down the hall.

"Hello, Miss Rory. You better have a little Water of Life yourself." Lena's grandmother sat right next to us, an apron over her rumpled navy suit. She would have looked like she was just politely welcoming me inside for dinner—if she hadn't had tears in her eyes.

I obediently took the tiniest sip possible from the water bottle. The stinging paper-cut rash immediately cleared up, and some glass fell from my left forearm and clattered to the floor.

Lena frowned at the dime-size pieces. "Rory, sometimes I think you're way too tough for your own good."

Wiping her tears away, Mrs. LaMarelle stretched across me and squeezed Lena's hand. "I take it you had some trouble with the quest?"

"No more than usual." Grinning, Chase strolled into the infirmary, his arms full of Lena's special bottles. My neon-green carryall hung from his shoulder. "Okay, which of you nurses want to take these off our hands? They've got Water of Life in them. Fresh from the spring."

The whole room perked up. The practice dummies clanked forward to take them. Mrs. LaMarelle stood to help and took the golden harp with her.

Jenny brought the eyedroppers. "Everyone needs three drops each. That's what Gretel says."

Ben unscrewed the water bottle and helped his mother sip from it anxiously. Mrs. Taylor's color immediately returned, but as soon as she put on her glasses, she paled again. "You're covered in blood."

"Just my clothes, Mother." Then he turned to the bed beside him, where Darcy stroked her brother's spotted back. The fawn was apparently too sick to lift his head from her leg cast. "For you, milady Darcy."

Trembling, Darcy took the bottle and carefully poured a little water into Bryan's mouth.

One second he was a sleeping fawn, and the next he was a boy hastily covering himself with a blanket before we could recognize what body part that big shock of skin belonged to.

"You couldn't have waited until I got clothes?" Bryan asked his sister. His hair was the exact same shade of brown as his fawn fur had been. "I'm never going to live this down."

Almost every Character in the infirmary laughed, and for the first time ever, I saw Bryan blush.

We were still missing something.

Then Jenny passed by, staring into her bottle. "Is the Water of Life supposed to look like breakfast?"

No, we were still missing *someone*.

I snatched the bottle away from her. "This one has Chatty."

Ben and Chase suddenly looked a lot less smug.

"No, wait. I have an idea." I grabbed an eyedropper and the Water of Life I had used to heal Lena. "You coming?"

"I'll be back soon, Mother," Ben told Mrs. Taylor, who looked kind of shocked to be abandoned so soon after her miraculous recovery.

"Now?" Lena glanced at the iron practice dummies moving from bed to bed with their eyedroppers.

"Didn't we all just escape certain death?" Chase said.

"Now. We have only about three minutes before the Director gets healed and takes over." I pointed at the exit.

They followed me to the shore outside, and I knelt in the sand. The Water of Life had worked on Ben's enchantment, and on Bryan's. As long as mermaids weren't completely different from humans, it might just work for Chatty.

"You guys are covered in glass." Lena brushed a fine, clear powder off my shoulders. "What did you do? Punch through every wall in the Glass Mountain?"

I filled up the eyedropper. "Not all of them."

"Just the outer one," said Ben.

"Oh," Lena said, impressed and jealous. "I can't believe you guys went to the Glass Mountain without me. Again."

Chase grinned. "That's the last time Rory and I visit the Snow Queen without you, I promise."

"Yeah, you could have definitely taken my place," said Ben.

"Here it goes!" Unscrewing Chatty's lid, I held the eyedropper over the top and counted out five drops. It started to steam. "Lena, quick—good or bad sign?"

"Pour it! If she re-forms inside, she could get hurt!" Lena dumped out the bottle before I could tell her how hard it had been to spoon Chatty in there the first time.

But a mermaid splashed headfirst into the waves, her powerful cobalt tail lashing out hard. Ben fell over. I couldn't tell if he had actually gotten hit or if he was just surprised.

Then Chatty sat up in the shallows, still wearing the faded green T-shirt she had been wearing that morning. "Look! I'm not dead! Or sea foam!" She pressed both hands to her face, checking to make sure she still had two eyes, two lips, and a nose. A beige glob came away with her hand. She sniffed it delicately. "Who thought I needed an oatmeal facial?" Then she spotted Ben, who was staring at her tail. She dove under with a little "eeep."

"Right," Ben said. "Well, I wouldn't want to see me either."

"I was going to ask her for some of her hair," Lena said, so disappointed that I knew she'd wanted to use it for spells.

But Chatty came back up, her face clean. She was fine. She wasn't even missing any body parts.

"Hey," said Ben.

"Where's Mia?" Chatty asked, clearly not happy with him.

Ben wiped his palms on his bloody jeans. "Turns out she's evil."

Lena gasped. "She was?"

"Puppet. Controlled by the Snow Queen," explained Chase swiftly.

"I knew it. She kept snooping in my workshop," Lena said, like this was an obvious sign of villainy.

"Oh." Chatty tried not to smile and failed. Then she looked

exactly like she did right after she had pulled some sort of prank. "Well, then."

"So," Ben said awkwardly, "have I said I'm sorry yet?"

Chatty cupped a hand behind her ear. "Could you repeat that? Mermaids are kind of hard of hearing."

I grinned so wide my cheeks hurt.

"I'm sorry," Ben said louder.

"Dude, she's messing with you. Mermaids hear fine," Chase said, and Chatty stuck her tongue out at him.

"I have a question," Ben said. "What's your real name?"

"I have fifty names. It's a mermaid thing." She rolled her eyes. "But my sisters call me Sherah."

"I'm not calling you anything but Chatty," Chase said.

"See if I answer," the mermaid shot back.

We were safe. I sat back on my heels, my hands twisting in my shirt to hide how much they were shaking. We were *more* than safe. We had saved EAS.

Relief turned my bones to liquid, and I breathed out slowly.

Lena saw my face. She hugged me so hard her shoulder pressed into my windpipe. "It's okay now, Rory."

But I was barely listening. The door to the infirmary banged open. The Director glided out, clutching a bathrobe around her as elegantly as a fine silk coat. You could tell by the tilt of her chin that she felt better, and that she was back in charge.

"Take her to the dungeon," she told the Characters coming out behind her.

Then Hansel and Stu walked out, fully recovered too, ushering Rapunzel between them. This time Rapunzel didn't struggle. Her head hung low, her hair trailing over the ground like a cloak, picking up stray leaves.

She looked so defeated. She looked so different from her sister. It was suddenly hard to remember why I'd suspected her in the first place.

"We'll hold the court-martial next week, once things have settled down," the Director added.

"Oh, right," said Chase with a deep sigh. "We need to sort this mess out."

"Hey!" I ran across the courtyard. "You have the wrong person!"

Rapunzel looked up slowly. The circles under her eyes were so dark it looked like she was the one with the black eye, not me. But she still smiled a little. "Rory, you will listen: The one they call Chatty, she—"

"We took care of her. Check this out. Hey, Chatty!" Chase waved back toward the water.

"I told you! I'm not answering to that name!" Chatty shouted back.

"See?" Chase said. "The Little Mermaid swims again."

"Wow. The Tales are changing," said Stu, but he was looking at me when he said it. "They're combining now."

Oh. He meant that *I* was changing them.

"Rory, yes, you and your friends have been heroic once again." The Director sounded kind of irritated about it. "And your loyalty to Rapunzel is touching, but I'm afraid that there are certain schemes at work that you can't possibly understand—"

I clenched my fists. "I think I understand pretty well, Director. I'll understand better after I break that Pounce Pot. You remember the Pounce Pot, don't you, Director? You, Sebastian, and Solange went on a quest for it?"

Lena gasped. "What?"

The Director paled, very slightly, and Chase groaned. "Not now you won't. Since you brought it up, she'll move it someplace we'll never find it."

"Mildred, I have told you, time and again," said Rapunzel softly. "The children will always find a way to learn what concerns them."

"Silence. You are still a suspect," the Director snapped.

"No, the Snow Queen planted Mia here to poison everyone," I said again.

Hansel was apparently having trouble following this conversation. "The new kid?"

"The one who isn't here to defend herself?" the Director said wryly.

Chase nodded. "She was a puppet with a very fancy glamour on her."

"The Snow Queen was acting through her," I said. "Sometimes she was inside Mia, and sometimes I think she was on autopilot, so she seemed kind of off."

The idea clearly terrified Lena. "That's very complicated magic."

"But you don't have any evidence?" The Director had no intention of taking us seriously.

"You have three witnesses—" I started, furious.

"Actually, we do. But Lena needs to get it off this." Chase pulled out an M3, the same one he had been messing with in the Snow Queen's throne room. I thought he'd just been muttering to himself, but—

"It was a spell? You were recording?" I asked Chase. "That's brilliant."

Chase grinned. "I have my moments. Many of them, actually."

Lena glanced at the grown-ups, clearly embarrassed. Then, flipping the mirror open, she whispered in Fey, "Please, please don't be botched. Come on, mirror, it's time to watch."

The Snow Queen's face appeared on the screen. "Oh, dearest Rapunzel," said Solange's image, and Rapunzel herself flinched. "My most loyal servant."

During her sister's speech, Rapunzel had the look on her face that she got sometimes around the Director: not defending herself, not smug—just stubborn. I had thought before that it was the look a teenager gives her mother, but it wasn't. Rapunzel looked at the Director the way Chase, Lena, and I dealt with Jenny. We did whatever we had to do to get her off our backs.

All Rapunzel wanted was to get out of her sister's shadow.

"You see—" the Director began indignantly, as soon as the Snow Queen got to the part that went, "I'm delighted that she managed to poison everyone else, too."

"Wait for it," Chase said.

"You're lying," the M3 said with my voice.

"Yes, I am. But this is still what Mildred will believe," said the Snow Queen's image happily. "Mia poisoned you all, right under Rory's and Rapunzel's noses."

Wearily, the Director gestured to the two guards. Hansel had already released Rapunzel, but Stu took a little longer, too distracted by the magic mirror to notice that the Director had called off the arrest.

"Sorry." The Shoemaker hurriedly dropped Rapunzel's elbow, dragging his eyes away from the M3. "I've never seen her before."

"She's scary," Lena whispered, huddled up against me. She had never seen the Snow Queen either. "The way she looks at you, and talks . . ."

"She draws your attention and holds it," said Rapunzel solemnly. "And next she draws your devotion. Her words sear themselves in your memory. That is why she is so dangerous." She looked straight at me. "Her words are often her most destructive weapons."

Yeah, I knew what she meant now.

"Turn it off. I've seen enough," said the Director, so sharply that Lena hastily whispered the off spell and surrendered the M3 into Mildred Grubb's waiting hands. "I'll review it later. Now we have more pressing matters."

"Ben's other Companion," Rapunzel reminded me quietly.

"Kenneth," I said quickly. "He's a rock right now. On the staircase leading up to the spring."

"We will send Jack. Where is Jack?" The Director said sharply. "Our champion should have been here to defend us during this dark time."

Sarah Thumb came winging out on Mr. Swallow, who landed on the Director's shoulder. "He still doesn't know we were poisoned. You wanted him to continue on his dwarf city tour, so no outsider would suspect anything was wrong. We can call him back."

"Yes, the danger is past. Call him back. Jack can go. He'll need two rings of return—"said the Director.

"And the Water of Life," Chase interrupted. "Mia said the Water of Life would break the enchantment. I mean, the Snow Queen said it through her puppet," he added uncertainly, "so it might be true . . ."

"No, that's right," said Lena.

"If we must send a second quest to retrieve a fallen Companion, our champion is more than equal to the task," the Director said smoothly.

"Did you guys think to get some dirt?" Lena asked me.

From my pocket I pulled out what I'd grabbed while we'd waited for the West Wind.

"Perfect! Give me five minutes and I'll make a transport." Then Lena noticed the Director scowling at her. The transports had been so helpful that I had completely forgotten that Lena was supposed to stop experimenting. Her shoulders hunched up, the same way they did before Jenny told her off. "They're disposable now, Director. They only have enough magic for a one-way trip. It's not a real portal."

"Fine. Lena shall do this spell. Stu, you shall shadow her and make sure it's suitable." The Director was so good at giving orders that she could change direction in just a few seconds. "Chase and Rory, you'll come to my office. You shall give a full report on the events of the week, so that I may debrief Jack when he arrives."

"Actually, Rory should probably go home," Sarah Thumb said. "My bed was right beside the infirmary phone. Her mother has been calling every half hour."

My stomach sank to my toes. I was going to be in so much trouble.

"Chase, then, to my office." The Director crossed the courtyard in long strides.

Chase obviously thought he'd gotten the suckiest task. He stomped after her.

"And then we'll do that thing," Lena whispered, cupping her hands so I could drop the Atlantis dirt into them. "The thing we talked about before the feast."

I stared at her, drawing a complete blank. "The feast was a really, really long time ago, Lena."

"Not for me," the Shoemaker said with a rueful grin. "I feel like I just lay down in the infirmary two seconds ago. I slept more getting poisoned than I have in the past year."

"The party," Rapunzel said with a tiny smile. "Chase's first."

"Surprise birthday party!" I said.

"But after the transport spell," the Shoemaker said.

"Okay, going." And then Lena sprinted across the courtyard toward the workshop, equal to any Kid Olympics runner.

I grinned. She was feeling better.

"God, does that girl operate at anything other than top speed?" Stu muttered, following her. "Lena, maybe you should take it easy. You've been poisoned all week."

And then it was just Rapunzel and me. I remembered how I had acted the last time we were alone together, and I squirmed with shame.

"Is she mad at you because you took over while she was sick?" I asked, watching the Director sweep past the amethyst door into her office, Sarah Thumb and Mr. Swallow on her shoulders and Chase following behind.

"I upset her the day we met, centuries past, and I have found other ways to upset her in all the years since," Rapunzel said. "But my relationship with the Director is my problem, as is my relationship with my sister. You should remember this even if the Director and Solange tell you otherwise."

So she wasn't mad at me. I felt twice as guilty. "Rapunzel, I'm really sorry I didn't trust you."

"Rory, you do not need to apologize. It is natural of you to suspect those closely associated with a villain who has tried to kill you many times," Rapunzel said. "In fact I should apologize to you. If I had been aware that no one had told you, I would have explained long ago."

So we had both been standing here feeling guilty about the same thing. "I was totally sure you were the bad guy when the mother of the four winds said you told the goblin priestesses to amp up the mirror vault."

Rapunzel's eyes lit up, flattered. I guess that was later than she'd expected. "You understand why I asked them to do this, don't you?"

"Yes. So I could tell everyone else the stones weren't real." I didn't mention that it obviously hadn't worked for Kenneth.

Rapunzel drew her hair over her shoulder and began rebraiding it. "No. I assumed that you would need no help among the stones, because I had seen you stop Chase from turning his head. But I knew that you would face Solange and speak with her. It is dangerous to listen to my sister."

I'd kind of already known that. Madison was the same. It was just a lot harder to dismiss whatever the Snow Queen said. She acted so sure. She spoke so confidently you questioned everything you knew.

"She would have stopped me if I hadn't survived the mirror vault first," I said.

"Yes. But just as we all have wishes that drive us, we all have doubts that hinder us. Not just you. Not just Chase and Lena," Rapunzel said. "Everyone. Even Solange."

"The Snow Queen has doubts?" Then I bit my tongue, worried that Rapunzel would think I was pumping her for information again.

"What did she want from you, Rory?" Rapunzel asked.

"She wanted to stop me from stopping her," I whispered.

Rapunzel nodded. "But you did stop her. Having once been a hero herself, she knows the strength of them." Was she really saying what I thought she was? That the Snow Queen was afraid of me? "Unfortunately she will try again."

The idea made me feel so tired, so defeated already. I closed my eyes for a moment. How much had Solange learned about us, spying through Mia? How much had I given away?

Rapunzel dropped a cool hand on my head. "Rory, you have done much, and you are becoming known as someone who makes the impossible possible. You freed the West Wind from a being much stronger and more powerful than you. You retrieved the scepter of the Birch clan. You created happy endings to several different Tales—Ben's, the Little Mermaid's, Bryan's. You stormed into the Unseelie Court and forced its prince to do your bidding, something the Fey will never forget."

I winced. "I guess I didn't make us any friends, huh?"

"You are assuming that Fael is popular in the Unseelie Court," Rapunzel said, smiling. "But Rory, you are fast becoming a legend in your own right—at a very early age, just like my sister."

The Snow Queen had tried to kill everyone at EAS, and I'd stopped her. With Chase's and Lena's help, I'd been a match for her at least twice in my life, but was that actually something to brag about?

I was the direction your life was headed, she'd said.

"Rory?" Rapunzel said.

"If I stop her the same way she stopped Evil King What's-His-Face, what'll stop me from becoming just like her?" It scared me to hear my voice shaking.

Rapunzel smiled her tiniest smile. "If it had been Solange in the mirror vault, if she had heard Sebastian and Mildred say what you heard Chase and Lena say, she would have turned back. Solange would have let her friends die for betraying her, but you wanted to save yours more than you wanted them to love you."

She said this like it was some sort of big truth, but I didn't get it. "So?"

"So you will never become a villain like the Snow Queen. It's not in you," Rapunzel said. I wished I could feel as sure as she sounded. "I know I cannot convince you to trust yourself, this will be the desire that drives your life. But beware: Some will not believe you when you declare that you will grow up to be Rory and not Solange the second."

I guess Rapunzel understood this more than anyone.

"But some will." Rapunzel touched my left hand, where I was unconsciously twisting my new ring. "Myself, Chase, and Lena especially."

That did make me feel slightly better.

"I just want to bring everybody through the war safely," I whispered.

"Please don't wish for that," Rapunzel said, stricken. She must have seen me lose someone.

I couldn't think about that now. Not yet.

She hesitated, and then added, "No one else will tell you this, so even though it is not my place, I will: You have done well. I am proud of you. I am proud of the person you are becoming."

To my embarrassment, tears rushed to my eyes before I could even decide if that statement made me feel awkward or grateful. "I'm sorry. I keep crying. I don't know what's wrong with me."

I sincerely hoped Chase wouldn't see. I was turning into *such* a girl.

"You are tired," Rapunzel said gently. "You have survived much. But you must remember what you have accomplished. Your parents' worry will trouble you, because you love them. They will not understand."

Mom and Dad were going to be furious. And Amy—she would be the worst of all. I had no idea what I could tell them. "I should have told them the truth a long time ago. Explaining would be so much easier if they knew."

"Perhaps," said Rapunzel. "Or perhaps you would still be convincing your mother to let you return here. Perhaps you would not have become Ben's Companion, and his Tale would have Failed. Your actions saved Lena's life today, and the lives of hundreds of others."

It was strange—to think that lives depended on me. Or on whether or not Mom let me come back to EAS, actually.

"Believe your father when you speak to him next. Now prepare yourself." I looked up, sure that Rapunzel was about to tell me something else helpful and scary about my future. She just smiled. "For the party. Your time here today is short, but I will be here when you return."

I took the fastest shower in the history of EAS.

Then, while Lena set up in the courtyard, I ran around inviting as many newly healed people as possible. I had just slipped the final and most important element of our surprise in my pocket when I ran into Lena and her grandmother in front of the ballroom-infirmary door.

"Now Miss Rory, it's about time for you to go home," said Mrs. LaMarelle. "I told your mother that Lena's appendix burst, and you came back to wait with us in the hospital. I promised to put you on a plane as soon as we were sure Lena would pull through."

For thirty minutes, being busy had kept the guilt at bay, but now I was pretty sure I was the worst daughter in the entire universe.

"Please, Gran," Lena said.

Mrs. LaMarelle shook her head. "I don't approve of lying, you know, and I certainly don't plan on breaking any promises."

"But remember that super-secret project?" Lena whispered.

"You can't expect me to keep track of all your super-secret projects, honey," said Mrs. LaMarelle fondly. "You have hundreds going on at one time."

"You remember this one." Lena stood on tiptoes to whisper in her ear.

"We won't be together again for another month or so," I added. "You've been on the phone with my mother. I bet she told you that I'm going to be grounded."

"Hmm," said Mrs. LaMarelle thoughtfully. I held my breath as she inspected the brooch pinned to her lapel. It looked like a *B* with three lines through the bottom—Madame Benne's symbol. "Well, Ellie and I will need about forty-five minutes to get the portal to the airport all set up and, say, another ten to get your mother on the phone. If you promise to come with us as soon as we fetch you, with not even one more excuse, I suppose it's all right."

"You'll have to keep that promise. Gran's promises are like Binding Oaths. You pretty much die if you break them in my house," Lena said.

I grinned. "Promise."

Mrs. LaMarelle shooed us away. Lena and I sprinted under the Tree of Hope, to the table where the golden harp and all the other seventh graders waited, plus a few eighth graders. Even Adelaide had come, but as soon as she saw me, she told Daisy again, "They must have made a mistake. Chase would've told us if it was his birthday."

The triplets had managed to dig up some cone-shaped party hats. Kyle offered a fourth one to Paul Stockton, who replied, "I am not putting that on my head."

"I will." Bryan reached over Paul's shoulder. Someone had given him some clothes, but he still hadn't taken off his spiked collar. He put the hat on, tucking the elastic strap under his chin. "Ah, hands. I'll never fail to appreciate opposable thumbs ever again."

"You know, if I'm going to have human friends, I need a spell that gives me legs when I want them." Chatty had dragged herself up onto the beach as close as she could, her tail shining blue on the sand. "Not the sea witch's, though. Every step feels like a stab in the foot, and you turn to sea foam after only a week? Not worth losing my voice."

"Yeah," Darcy said, looking as horrified as I felt. "You got ripped off."

Chatty smirked a little. She obviously enjoyed freaking people out as much as Chase did. "It would be nice to jump out and yell surprise, though. When is Chase getting here?"

"Any minute," I said. "Ben's bringing him."

Then Chase burst out of the guys' bathroom and into the court-yard, yelling back over his shoulder, "Ben, I get it. We bonded in Atlantis. I think you're cool too, but if you follow me into the little dudes' room one more time, I'm going to—"

I held up one finger, then two, then three. At the same time, we all screamed, "SURPRISE!"

Chase whirled around. Open-mouthed, he took in the partygo-ers, the streamers hanging on the tree, the banner that read HAPPY (BELATED) BIRTHDAY, CHASE!, and the cake on the table.

"Oh, good," said Chatty. "We surprised him anyway."

Ben nudged Chase closer to the rest of us.

"I—" Chase looked a little bit like Iron Hans had when the Pounce Pot had kicked in. "I don't know what to say."

"Say we'll have cake first," Kyle suggested.

"It came out of the Lunch Box of Plenty, so it's poison-free," Darcy said.

"Oh, thanks. I'm totally in the mood for cake now," said Bryan.

"There are no presents!" Lena clearly felt like she needed to apologize for this up front. "But only because we've been stuck in the infirmary all week. We'll do better next year."

"Okay." A smile grew on Chase's face, more ginormous than usual.

"But we have cake!" Grinning, I pulled the birthday candles out of my back pocket and began decorating that cake with thirteen candles. So enthusiastically that I broke the first one. "Whoops."

"And I invented a game." Lena opened a box of long, skinny sticks that looked suspiciously like wands. "At least I think I invented it. I've never read about magic laser tag before. I set it up in the obstacle course—the one that looks like a dwarf city behind the silver-and-granite door."

"Magic laser tag?" Paul said so scornfully that I considered uninviting him.

But about five other boys dove for wands at the same time. "That is your best invention ever," said Kevin.

Chatty sighed. "I wish I had that spell for legs *now*."

Chase stared up at the banner, grinning in a dopey sort of way. Speechless. I'd never thought I would see the day.

"Can we keep it in the fake dwarf city forever and play it at all birthdays?" Kyle asked Lena eagerly.

"I doubt it. The Director doesn't exactly know about it yet," Melodie said, and Lena shot her a look that clearly said, *Why are you telling them that?*

"A once-in-a-lifetime event." Ben snatched up a wand and sat on the sand next to Chatty, who made a valiant effort not to look too pleased. "It will be epic."

"Are we going to sing now or later? I'm hoping Melodie knows a spell for lighting these candles, because I couldn't find any matches." I was kind of focused, so I almost had a heart attack when Chase gave me a hug.

Chase never did hugs. In fact, he usually shot me and Lena

weird looks when we hugged each other. For a second I thought something serious was going on. Like he was going to tell me he didn't want any cake.

But then he let go, grinning. "You did this, right? You're the best."

"I just had the idea," I said, slightly weirded out. "Lena did all the work."

"And me," Melodie said.

Then Chase hugged *Lena*. "You're both the best."

"And me," Melodie repeated, but apparently Chase had reached his hug quota for the rest of the year. He just gave her a slightly dorky high five and grabbed the nearest wand. "Okay, someone explain what laser tag is, because I'm going to kick all of your butts."

I only had time for one and a half games before Lena's gran came. Everybody at the party protested when she ushered me over to the Door Trek portal, so it was really easy for me to keep my promise not to complain. "Gretel cast a spell over your parents and her mother's assistant to help them believe the story, but—" Lena's gran said.

"I know. Expect trouble." I checked my jeans pocket to make sure Lena's spare M3 was still there. She had given it to me after magic laser tag, telling me she wanted to make sure we could stay in touch even if my cell phone got taken away.

Mrs. LaMarelle opened the ruby door. "Rory, I need to thank you. You saved my grandbaby's life, and I'm sure it won't be the last time."

I half smiled. Something else to remember when I got to the other side of this portal, Mom cried, and Amy shot me her thin-lipped glare of doom.

With a deep breath I stepped through. I came out in baggage claim, the little one in the upstate New York airport nearest the house Mom was renting. I knew they'd be there, so I searched the crowd. They would probably be standing right at the bottom of the closest escalator, anxiously watching every person come down and discussing how they would never let me leave my room again.

But it wasn't Mom and Amy waiting. It was Dad.

His hair was going in a thousand different directions—definitely stressed, but then he would have to be, if he was taking time away from his work to pick me up from the airport across the continent. He wouldn't have come all this way just to yell at me, I was pretty sure.

Suddenly, I felt smaller even than Sarah Thumb, exactly how I had when that casting director had been yelling at me. *Hundreds of lives today,* I reminded myself firmly as I walked over. *What Klonsky said doesn't matter at all.*

But of course it didn't. Klonsky was a stranger. It was what Dad *hadn't* said that made me want to cry.

He didn't notice me until I was close enough to grab his arm. As soon as he looked up, though, he threw his arms around me. "You're okay."

I nodded against his shoulder, kind of wanting to squirm out of his grip, but I didn't. I didn't want to hurt his feelings and make him even madder at me. So I just kind of hugged him back awkwardly.

Then he stepped back and looked me in the face, so I could see how serious he was. I braced myself.

"If there were an award for worst dad in the world, then I definitely got it this week. Don't even try to deny it." Actually, I was so stunned I was speechless, so Dad just plowed on ahead. "I whisk you off to a casting call you don't want. I just sit there, dumb as a stump, when Klonsky yells at you. Then I spring a stepmother on you without even telling you first."

"I didn't mean to embarrass you at the casting call." The excuse came quickly now. "I . . . fell in the memorial fountain. I was running around to find a signal so I could call and check on Lena, and I just slipped. I didn't have enough time to change—"

"Rory, forget about that. I don't care about the movie." Dad took my duffel and steered me outside. "I told them to take me off the project."

"You did?" Dad had never dropped a film before.

"Of course I did," he said, surprised. "Do you think I would want to work on it now? I can't even think about it without feeling ashamed of myself."

It was slowly starting to sink in. Dad wasn't mad at me. *He* felt bad.

"Here. Take a look at this." He slipped his phone out of his back pocket, pushing a few buttons to pull up a video.

I recognized the stage area of the casting call. I turned away, chest tight. "I really don't want to see this, Dad."

"No. I mean, please? It's part of my speech," he said. "This is your audition clip."

Watching myself stammer wasn't exactly appealing, but I looked anyway. I couldn't bear to lie to him *and* disappoint him after worrying him for two days.

He pushed play, and the Rory on-screen was . . . well, she was fine. Her voice sounded kind of weird, but not shaky. But I felt again exactly what I had felt then. My nose prickled. The tears were coming back.

"You were good, Rory. Better than most. You weren't rattled at all. Just like your mom," Dad said softly.

If he meant my acting talent, he had just edged into the sucking-up portion of his apology. "Even if I don't look upset—"

Dad nodded. "Right. You're just like your mom. I could never tell when she was upset either. And me, I just froze in there. I couldn't believe anyone would lose their temper like that with a kid, and then my mouth just wouldn't move, and you seemed like you were okay. I mean, at least until we got outside," he said, running his hands through his hair again. We headed through the automatic doors to the parking lot. "I did finally tell that Klonsky woman to go to hell, but don't tell your mother that, please. At the time I was just so stunned, you know?"

"It's okay," I said automatically. He seemed so shaken.

"It's *not* okay," Dad said, so loud that a few people waiting for cabs looked over at us. "I told Brie, as soon as you went to the bathroom for your backpack, that I thought I'd screwed up. And she basically told me I'd done the worst possible thing anyone could ever do to a seventh-grade girl. I made you feel like you weren't important in my life, right? Like you didn't matter?"

I just nodded, throat aching, because I was pretty sure that Dad would handle me crying even worse than Chase.

"That is never, ever okay, Rory. Nobody should make you feel like that, especially not me," Dad said, and then it looked like *he* was going to cry. "I had to come see you. If I didn't, if I left it like that, you would probably never speak to me again, and nobody would blame you. I was really wrong. You're the best thing—no, not thing. But you're the best of everything I've ever done, and I'm so mad at myself for making you feel like anything less."

I was really crying now, possibly harder than I had in the mirror vault. Dad stopped, right in the middle of the parking deck, and held me even though we were probably in danger of getting run over.

"You're what I'm most proud of every second of every day, and I'm so sorry," he said softly.

Maybe you never really outgrew bullies. Maybe Dad wasn't that tough.

But he loved me. And he was trying.

I took several breaths, slow and deep. "I'm glad you came, Dad."

"Me too," he said, relieved.

"And I'm sorry I left L.A. without telling you first." I still felt guilty about that part.

"Yeah. What was that?" He asked, suddenly angry. "You just hailed a cab and booked a flight all by yourself? And I get to the airport and none of the airlines have any record of Rory Landon. If you ever run away again—"

He stopped, shoving a hand through his hair. I stared at him, and he looked a little taken aback too. He'd never yelled at me like that before. Of course, I had never done anything to deserve it before either.

I wished I could say it would never happen again. "I am sorry."

"I'm not perfect either, so I'm going to leave the yelling to your mom. But you're just a lot more independent than any twelve-year-old has a right to be. Don't tell your mother I said that either." Dad pressed the button on the rental-car keys, and something beeped several rows over. "There we go. Anyway, honey, the good news is that when I told your mom what I did, she aimed all her anger at me instead of you. It's totally my fault. You should be okay."

I wiped my face with my sleeve and gave him a look. We both knew I would never get out of this without punishment.

"Mostly okay?" Dad tried. "More okay than you might have been if I hadn't talked to her?"

I nodded. "I'll give you that."

"You'll give me that," Dad repeated with a wobbly sort of grin. "We've reached the age where you give me stuff. The next ten years of your life will be rough on me, I can tell. Here." He pulled something white out of his pocket and handed it to me.

"Since when you do you carry tissues?" I blew my nose.

"Since Brie." He said it so simply, like she dated a whole era in his life. He said it the way I said, "Since EAS." "She has the worst allergies of anybody I ever met. It's safer for everyone if I carry tissues, believe me."

He paused, and I knew exactly what he was going to ask next. "Does it bother you that I'm marrying her?"

It did bother me a little, to be perfectly honest. But the only reason I could think of was that I didn't want a Tale with a stepmother in it. Of course, Brie Catcher didn't seem like wicked-stepmother material. "Not really. I think—well, keep in mind that I only had maybe ten minutes around her, but I think I like her."

I liked that she told Dad the truth. She couldn't help it. She probably told everyone the truth. I liked that she made him see other people a little better. I liked that she made him happy.

Grinning again, Dad unlocked the car. "Then do you want to be my best man?"

"Depends on whether or not I have to wear a tux," I said, kind of shocked, and I didn't even realize it was a funny thing to say until Dad started laughing.

Dad was right about helping on the Mom front. As soon as we got out of the car, Mom ran out and held me, just like Dad had at the airport. Dad was clearly the bad guy—even though they tried to be civil, all the glares went to him and not me.

Then we sent Dad back to the airport—he had a red-eye flight so he could catch a morning meeting in L.A. He was really glad of an excuse to get away, but he asked me to think about being his best man. He offered to list me as "best daughter" in the program, if I wanted.

I could tell by the way Mom smiled—very politely, like someone kind of crazy had just asked for her autograph—that she didn't like the idea. But I said I would think about it.

Then Mom and Amy ushered me inside, and a weird period of pseudo grounding began. They couldn't pin me for leaving L.A. without permission, at least not completely, so I got a brief lecture on how I really needed to call when I promised I was going to call. I got only one week of no TV or Internet, plus an extra-early bedtime for two weeks.

But they didn't give me any privacy. They even made me leave my bedroom door open all night, like they expected me to run away again as soon as I was out of sight. That first evening, I was just so tired I fell into bed and slept for the next fourteen hours straight. But it got old really fast over the weekend. And Mom kept staring at me—half-wary, half-concerned. I tried not to let it bother me. I'd probably looked at Chase like that when I'd found out I didn't know him as well as I'd thought I had.

Then, on Monday, Mom and Amy both took me to school. Usually, it was just one or the other. That was the first sign of the new routine. The car was silent and tense, and I spent the whole drive frantically trying to remember if I'd had any homework.

Amy parked in front a good half hour before homeroom. The school was basically deserted. "Okay, kiddo. We'll pick you back up at three thirty. Right here."

"Three thirty?" I repeated blankly, bookbag in hand. They normally picked me up closer to dinnertime.

"We worked out a special schedule for the rest of the shoot," Mom said, extra brightly, turning around in her seat to look at me. "I get done at three, every day. Just in case you need to talk."

Oh. Mom thought I was rebelling against her busy work schedule.

Nobody mentioned EAS, but I saw the trick. If they were picking me up as soon as the bell rang, then there was no need for me to go to a special after-school program. It wasn't a punishment if Mom just wanted us to spend a little more time together.

It was going to be even harder to get back to EAS than I'd thought.

"Okay," I said hesitantly. Arguing at this stage wouldn't help.

"Good," Amy said with a tight smile.

"Have a great day at school, sweetie," Mom said.

We were all being so polite. That was worse than the new no-privacy rule.

But Rapunzel was proud of me, and Lena's gran was grateful.

I climbed out and wandered through the empty halls. The vice principal did a double take when he saw me, like he couldn't believe any kid would show up so early the first day after spring break. Even Mrs. Lapin wasn't in homeroom yet, but I sat down anyway, suddenly very lonely.

So instead of checking on that homework situation, I took out my M3. "Hello? Anybody out there?"

Lena's face popped up, a spoon halfway to her mouth. "Rory! Getting poisoned must make you really hungry. This is my third bowl of cereal. How did it go with your parents?"

"Weird, but okay." It was nice to speak with someone who wasn't mad at me.

Then Chase's image cut Lena out. I hadn't expected him to be waiting beside *his* magic mirror. "But you can't come back for a while, right?

"I think I'll have to spend at least a month convincing them." Actually, maybe two.

"A month?" Chase repeated, annoyed. "Do you know how much training you can lose in a month?"

"Rory," Lena said, serious now, "did Iron Hans really say that I'm like the Director?"

"Chase, you told her?" I thought I would have to bribe him just to bring it up.

"Because I'm not so sure that it's a compliment," Lena went on, worried. "I mean, I don't have to follow rules all the time. Right?"

Chase, very wisely, didn't say anything.

"Well, if you're exactly like the Director, that makes me exactly like Solange.".*You would have become me, if you had lived,* the Snow Queen had said. I shuddered.

"I plan to be about a million times cooler than that dumb Sebastian guy," Chase said. "Nobody's going to turn *me* into stone."

"If we're really a triumvirate," Lena said, as if she were extremely doubtful on this point, "then we're actually the third one. Madame Benne, Maerwynne, and that Dapplegrim guy were the first."

"That Dapplegrim guy?" Chase repeated. "His name was Rikard Longsword."

That cheered me up. Maerwynne seemed okay.

"Rapunzel told me to tell you hi, by the way. Thursday, after you left," Lena told me. "That's how I knew I needed to keep the M3 next to me."

"She told me I needed to tell you what Iron Hans said while

you were sleeping," Chase said. "Here it is: 'Stop making so much noise, or you'll wake her.'"

I rolled my eyes. "I'm sure it was more important than that."

"He said something like . . ." Chase frowned so hard it looked like it hurt. "'When the battle comes, you three must all play your parts, and when the war runs its course, the world will be forever changed.'"

Lena made a face. "Change isn't necessarily bad."

Chase snorted. "Tell that to the Director."

I noticed I was twisting the West Wind's ring nervously around my finger, and stopped. "I would settle for just not smashing things accidentally."

"Training," Chase said. "That's what you need."

"No, she needs a glove that helps her control the magic." You could practically see all the invention wheels turning in Lena's brain.

I laughed. "Or maybe I just need to get used to having this on my hand."

Voices rang out in the hall. I really hoped it was Mrs. Lapin, but they sounded too young.

"Someone's coming," I whispered reluctantly.

"Oh, okay! Bye!" Lena started chanting the off spell.

"See you later!" said Chase.

I snapped the M3 covering closed just two seconds before Madison, Katie, Arianna, and Taylor filed in. Each one carried a glossy magazine, and I knew that my picture was in at least one of them. I wondered if it was at the airport or the studios.

I waited to feel slightly nauseated with dread, but I didn't. I just felt . . . resigned. I was ready to get this over with.

They flipped pages at their desks right across from me, just like they always did, and the room filled with the sound of crackling paper.

"You'll never guess what happened to me over break," Madison said.

"What?" said Arianna.

"I went to this casting call on Tuesday, and this one girl—the director's daughter—was expected to land the role." Madison shook her perfect hair back. "But when she showed up . . ."

"Bad haircut?" Katie asked.

"Bad teeth?" Taylor asked.

"Bad breath?" Arianna asked.

I looked at her—really looked at Madison—for the first time in a long time. She had a zit on the side of her nose, and concealing makeup caked on around it. She was no Snow Queen. She was just a kid, just like me.

"All these, and more," said Madison. "She showed up dripping wet—"

No, I didn't just want to get this over with. I wanted to put an end to this whole thing before Mrs. Lapin showed up.

"I don't know what's bothering you, Madison," I said lightly. "All I did was make you look good. You should be thanking me."

Madison's superior smile faded a little bit. I wasn't following her script, and it obviously threw her off. "And your dad . . . I mean, her dad, this director—"

"My dad and I had a long talk after that," I said sharply, "and it's none of your business. You should stop wasting your allowance on those magazines."

The KATs glanced from me to Madison uncertainly, not sure what they were supposed to do now. Madison's mouth hung slightly open.

Definitely not the stuff of nightmares and goblin-induced visions.

"Did you get the part?" I asked, a little bit curious.

Madison looked hurt, just for an instant. She hadn't been called back, and she *had* wanted it.

She clearly had her own doubts to conquer.

Mrs. Lapin clunked in, her clogs hitting the linoleum with big thumps. She smiled at us, but she had a much larger mug of coffee in her hand than usual. "Hello, ladies! How were your breaks?"

"Busy," I said, because the others didn't speak up. "And kind of stressful. But I found out that I'm getting a new stepmother."

"Ah," said Mrs. Lapin with blank brightness. Mom gave me that look sometimes, on Sunday mornings, when I overloaded her too much on her day off.

Someone knocked on the classroom door, and Mrs. Lapin hurried to open it.

Across from me, the other girls didn't seem to know what to do with themselves. One of the KATs started folding the pages of her magazine to make a fan.

"New student," said a grown-up outside.

"There must be some kind of mistake," said Mrs. Lapin. "You can't be assigned here. I'm only supposed to have girls."

"It's the long eyelashes. They make me look like a girl," said a familiar voice, and I whirled around. Chase popped his head in and waved. I was too surprised to wave back. "Hey."

I had no idea what he was doing here, but I definitely wasn't complaining.

Madison perked up, like she did when the captain of the eighth-grade soccer team walked by. "Hi."

"I was talking to Rory, actually." Giving Madison and the KATs a weird look, Chase slipped past a dumbfounded Mrs. Lapin and fell into the desk beside me. He must have come through the ruby door across the street. "Hey. It's later, just so you know."

"What?" I said, still stunned.

"I said, 'See you later,' like two minutes ago. It's 'later.'" Chase had obviously been planning that for a while. Ben's corniness *had* rubbed off on him.

"I'll just . . . go visit the office to sort this out." Mrs. Lapin left the room, giant coffee mug in hand.

I leaned forward so the others couldn't eavesdrop. "What are you doing here?"

"I always wanted to try out regular school." I knew that by "regular," Chase really meant "human." "Lena's trying to come too. But her grandmother thinks switching schools will be disruptive for her education, and Melodie keeps telling her that even though she can make the temporary transports, it's a waste of perfectly good dragon scales."

For me. That was why they were doing this. They didn't want me to feel alone. Even if I lived to be as old as Iron Hans, I would never find friends better than Chase and Lena.

"So?" Chase stretched out his legs under the desk and crossed his ankles. "Good surprise or bad surprise?"

"Good surprise. Definitely good," I said, so happily that Chase grinned back. Life at school was about to get a lot more awesome.

ACKNOWLEDGMENTS

I'm not going to lie: writing this book was epic, and it absolutely wouldn't have been finished if I didn't have certain people in my life. Special thanks goes to:

Joanna Volpe, my wonderful agent, and Danielle Barthel, her savvy assistant, who both read the very earliest drafts more than once and gave me great feedback (which is no mean feat, considering that back then, this manuscript was about a hundred pages longer than it is now). Just so everybody knows, the people of New Leaf Literary are, in general, totally awesome.

Courtney Bongiolatti, my first editor, who suggested a big plot shuffle, which was as brilliant as it was terrifying. Julia Maguire, my new editor, who took over seamlessly and dove straight into a big, complicated manuscript without even missing a beat. I couldn't have asked for a smoother transition! Karen Sherman, my copy editor, who saved me from publishing many embarrassing mistakes, including misspelling the name of Rory's new stepmother about fifty times. Chloë Foglia and Cory Loftis, who wowed me with the cover a *second* time. ☺ And everyone else at Simon & Schuster Books for Young Readers, you guys have my undying gratitude for working so hard to share *The Ever Afters* with the world.

ACKNOWLEDGMENTS

Angela, my dear—I'm sorry for BBMing you a thousand complaints about various deadlines. I know you were busy planning your wedding. Thank you for always encouraging me to take a break and calm down. Mom and Dad—thank you so much for hanging in there with me. This book was fueled by a million hugs, and most of them came from you two. To the extended Trenkelbach and Randol clans, I'm sure that a big portion of my sales comes from you guys—either from your own purchases or through your word of mouth. You guys are the best, and I feel incredibly lucky to have such a supportive family.

Last but not least, *Of Witches and Wind* is all about how surviving middle school is so much easier when you have great, caring, loyal friends. Angela, Dana, Ems, Kaitlyn, Katie, Martha, and Will—I hope y'all know I'm talking about you.

Don't miss the latest tales of

THE EVER AFTERS!

The wolves might not have attacked if we had left right after school. If we'd headed for Golden Gate Park on time, they might never have sniffed us out.

Of course, I wanted to hurry for a completely different reason. I squinted up the hill. Half of our classmates had clustered behind my best friend, trying to convince him to borrow their skateboards.

"We don't have time for this, Chase! We need to get to EAS!" I told him.

Even thirty feet away, with a giant homemade ramp on the sidewalk between us, I could see Chase rolling his eyes. "Trust me, we won't miss the tournament," he said. He knew how much I wanted to wipe the smug look off a certain sword master's face. "This'll just take two minutes."

"What's the deal with that Ever After School?" asked the freckled kid who sat behind us in pre-algebra. "You, Rory, and Lena go every day."

You could tell by the way he said it: He thought eighth graders going to day care was the lamest thing since kids started bringing their teachers apples.

Ever After School wasn't day care. It was a program for

fairy-tale Characters-in-training. I'd been going for about two years, my other best friend Lena for a little longer. Chase *lived* there with his dad.

But we obviously couldn't tell that to a kid who didn't know magic was real. I hadn't even broken that news to my parents yet.

"It's awesome. That's all you need to know," Chase said coldly. "Hey, Rory! Move, or I might land on you."

Sighing, I trotted halfway up the steps to our school, Lawton Academy for the Gifted. It wasn't that foggy today, but the sky was gray, the clouds close.

The door opened behind me. Lena came out wearing yellow rain boots, a yellow raincoat, and a waterproof backpack over her shoulder. "Ready! I—" Then she stopped. "Oh, hold on. I forgot my umbrella."

She rushed back in, and I sighed again.

All I wanted to do was get to EAS, sign up for a duel with Hansel, and kick the sword master's butt. I'd been fantasizing about it for months—no, *years*. During my first sword lesson, Hansel had told us, *You have no idea what you might be up against. You would all be dead in two moves if the war hadn't ended. Especially you girls.* When I'd told him that we might grow up to be even better than him someday, he'd just sneered at me.

Well, today was the day I'd prove it.

But I couldn't do that if we missed the whole tournament. EAS only held it every three years, and it would end in an hour and a half. Plus, we had a pretty long walk ahead of us—four city blocks and the whole Golden Gate Park before we even reached the Door Trek door. If I lost my chance just because my friends were too slow . . .

No. Never mind. I still remembered how much school sucked before Chase and Lena started coming with me.

Because my mom's job made us move every three or four months, I'd been the new kid more times than I could count. I'd gotten used to it. Most of the time, it was just lonely.

Then, one morning last spring, Chase had shown up in my homeroom, and Lena had arrived the week after that. I hadn't asked them to come. My family had moved twice since then, and both times Mom had dragged me to a new school. Chase and Lena had been there too—even if they had to enchant every teacher, secretary, and computer to get themselves into the school's system.

Skateboarding and excessive rain gear were no big deal. I definitely had the best friends in the whole world, magical or otherwise.

"Rory! You're not looking!" Chase called.

I turned back to the top of the hill. "If I watch, can we do a warm-up match when we get to EAS?"

"Only if I hear a big round of applause." Chase hopped on the skateboard and rolled down the slope. He didn't brake or even take a few turns like the other boys had. He just barreled full tilt for the ramp.

The door squeaked open again, and a second later, Lena clutched my arm. "He's not even wearing a helmet!"

The skateboard's wheels clattered when they hit the ramp. Then Chase sailed off the end, way too high, and he grabbed the front end of the board. Gravity dragged him back down, and he hit the sidewalk smoothly. The boys rushed down the hill after him, cheering.

"I thought you were going to fly straight into traffic!" Lena told Chase. He just swerved to a stop right in front of us and grinned expectantly.

But I didn't have good news. "That jump wasn't human," I said, and his face fell.

Chase was half Fey. He had wings, which were invisible most of the time, and he couldn't resist using them to show off. It hadn't taken him long to figure out that he was a natural on a skateboard and that regular kids were a *lot* easier to impress than Characters and fairies. He always asked me to watch, so I could tell him if he overshot.

"About eight feet too high, I think," I added gently, and Chase nodded.

Lena looked at me funny, not getting it. She didn't know that Chase's mom was Fey. I'd tried to convince him to tell Lena a hundred times. She was the smartest person I knew. She was eventually going to figure it out, and then she would probably be furious with us for keeping such a big secret from her. But Chase refused.

So, except for all the grown-ups, I was the only Character at EAS who knew.

The boys reached us, and every single kid was begging Chase to teach them how to get that much air. His grin immediately reappeared.

Lena and I exchanged a look.

"We'll meet you at the crosswalk," she told him, and we skirted around the crowd, down the sidewalk, to the street corner. We knew from experience that Chase liked to bask in our classmates' admiration for a while, but when he noticed we were leaving without him, Chase broke away and caught up.

I stared at the crosswalk signal and willed it to change. Underneath it, a college student in a red sweatshirt was chatting on her phone. Her enormous black dog stood higher than her waist, and it didn't have a leash. It turned toward us, its eyes glinting yellow.

Chase looked at the bank sign clock over Lena's shoulder. "Wait. Is it really three twenty-two? Registration for the tournament ended at six fifteen, Eastern Standard Time. I totally forgot."

Seven minutes ago. I froze. He'd spent weeks helping me train. He *knew* how important this was. I couldn't believe he'd—

"Rory, he's messing with you," Lena said.

Chase laughed. "April Fool's!"

He loved April Fool's jokes. He'd also tied my shoelaces to my desk in English, stolen Lena's textbook in math, unplugged all the computers in the computer lab, and cast a glamour over our chemistry experiment, turning the sulfur bright blue. Our teacher had a hard time trying to explain that one.

I rolled my eyes to hide my relief. "I can't believe I fell for that."

The light changed, and we hurried across the street. The giant black dog sniffed at us as we passed, its ears pricked forward. We turned down the hill, the park very green ahead of us.

"*I* can. You're taking this tournament way too seriously," Chase said, obviously trying to sneak in one last lesson before we reached EAS. "You're never going to beat Hansel if you don't loosen up. Getting all nervous is going to make you stiff. It'll slow you down a fraction."

"No, Rory—you're going to do great," Lena said firmly, but she was just saying that to be a good friend. She was more of a magician than a fighter. "You'll beat him easy."

"I hope so," I said.

I'd been watching Hansel for two years. I knew his habits. He always fought with a broadsword, and he always finished duels in one of two ways: If he wanted to lull his students into overconfidence, he struck high with a one-handed strike, then low, faked a blow to the left—and *always* left; I think he had an old injury that made him a little slower coming from the right—stepped inside the kid's guard, and disarmed them. If he just wanted to get the duel over with quickly, Hansel switched to a two-handed grip, locked swords with the student, and kind of leaned on the crossed blades until the kid either buckled or freaked. *Then* he did the disarm. I'd never seen him end a fight any other way—not even with his advanced classes.

Chase and I had run through both scenarios until I was sure I could outmaneuver Hansel. All I had to worry about now was if the tricks I planned would work on an opponent bigger, stronger, and heavier than Chase. And more experienced. And not nearly as likely to go easy on me.

Right. I wasn't worried at all.

The street was full of traffic. Some smoke wafted toward us, and Lena waved it away, shooting a glare at the driver who'd rolled down his car window for a cigarette. He didn't notice. He was too busy turning up the radio.

". . . a frightening case of misreporting," said the announcer. "The incident in Portland was not an April Fool's joke. Those children *are* missing. The mass kidnapping is still under investigation, and the authorities have yet to name any suspects."

Mass kidnapping sounded serious. So serious that my worry-wart mom would probably want to see me as soon as she heard about it. *That's fine,* I thought, walking even faster, *as long as I have my match with Hansel first.*

We stepped into the park, and the trees closed over our heads. Pine smells replaced exhaust. Tourists passed us on their way to the exit, see-through ponchos over their I LEFT MY HEART IN

SAN FRANCISCO T-shirts. No other humans were in sight, but two huge dogs sat beside the trail ahead. The dark gray one with white paws tilted its head at us and whined, but the brown one nipped its ear. Golden Gate Park had some weird strays.

Suddenly Chase flinched. "Did I just feel a raindrop?" He hated the rain, especially getting his wings wet. He told me once that they itched while they dried.

As I pulled up my hood, Lena shook her umbrella open, happy to be prepared. "I can share!"

"We'll just hurry," Chase said, practically running down a sidewalk lined with benches. "It's not bad yet."

My eyes landed on a puddle forming on the concrete ahead, the perfect revenge for earlier. I grinned. "Lena, are you thinking what I'm thinking?"

She spotted it a second later. "Yep!"

Lena and I ran up to it, bending our knees dramatically. Catching on, Chase sprinted out of the splash zone.

We didn't jump.

"April Fool's!" I said, and Lena and I cracked up.

"Hilarious, you guys." Chase turned onto the next trail.

"Ooooo, I see," I teased as we veered toward the bridge. We always crossed Stow Lake and followed the path around the island. Lena was sure gnomes had built and hidden a colony between the waterfall and the gazebo. She was hoping to find one of their hats for an experiment. "You can dish out the April Fool's jokes, but you can't take—"

Three enormous dogs stood on the bridge, blocking our path. I stopped in my tracks, wondering how they'd caught up to us so fast.

"I've seen those dogs before." I was sure they were the same ones—the black one from the crosswalk, the older brown one, and the little gray with the big, white paws. All three triangular faces turned toward me in unison, pink tongues hanging past long teeth, and the hairs stood up on the back of my neck.

Lena squeaked and ducked behind a tree so she could unzip her backpack.

"Crap." Chase thrust his arm in the front pocket of his carryall—the one Lena had designed specifically for easy access to weapons—and drew out his sword.

If these two started freaking out, then we had a battle coming. So I started searching my backpack too. Somewhere in there was my sword, but since my carryall was the older model, it didn't have the convenient sword pocket—my sword could be anywhere.

"Rory, those aren't dogs!" Lena whispered. "They're wolves."

I could tell from the way she said it that these weren't the regular, endangered variety. The Snow Queen sometimes made wolves for her army, transforming criminals to create a soldier with the intelligence of a human and the teeth and claws of an animal.

Magical creatures sometimes snuck into human areas, like the bridge troll we'd once caught in Boston, but I had the awful feeling that these wolves had been waiting for us.

"At least there are only three of them—" I started, trying to make myself feel better.

Behind us, something howled, and a half dozen other wolves joined it, including the ones on the bridge. Forget the hairs on the back of my neck. Every hair on my body stood up.

"Looks like you're going to get that warm-up fight after all, Rory," Chase said.

But they weren't attacking. The three furry guys on the bridge hadn't even moved, except for the younger one, who tilted his head a little. Maybe they were here for some other reason. "So, what do we think? Did one of us just become the new Little Red Riding Hood?" I asked.

Lena shook her head, kind of apologetically, like she knew how much I hoped that was true. "I think one of us would have to be wearing red for that."

"The Snow Queen just sent something new to kill us," Chase said. "You know, since dragons, ice griffins, and trolls didn't work."

I'd been afraid of that. The Snow Queen liked to send her minions to kill Characters.

She especially liked trying to kill *us*. This was the second time her forces had ambushed us out of the blue. In February she'd sent a squadron of trolls after Lena at home. Luckily, Chase and I had been visiting. We'd managed to fight them off and transport Lena's whole house to EAS's courtyard.

"We've never been attacked in public before." I stuck my head half in the carryall, determined to find my sword.

"First time for everything," Chase said. "We have company. Four more wolves at two o'clo—*Watch out!*"

I looked up. The big black wolf had run forward, snarling seven feet away. Chase raised his sword to defend us, but he didn't notice the little gray one running at us.

Neither did Lena, who was busy tucking a baby food jar labeled 3 into her raincoat. When the gray wolf leaped, teeth bared, I shoved Lena down with my right hand and swung out with my left.

The punch connected with the wolf's muzzle. It sailed back

thirty feet and hit the lake with a splash so big that lake water doused the top of the bridge. Whoops. Definitely overkill.

I was still getting used to the silver ring that gave me the West Wind's strength. I hadn't learned how to totally control all that power yet, but at least I had gotten better at not smashing stuff accidentally.

The little wolf didn't surface. His brown pack mate on the bridge howled, probably calling for backup.

"Thanks." Lena peeked inside my bag, pulled out my sword, and pressed the ridged hilt into my palm. "Remind me to put a hook in here for your sword belt."

"We need to get out of here, before the rest of them catch up," Chase said, as Lena and I slung our carryalls back on. He sprinted down the path along the lake, not even looking twice at the pile of black fur he'd left behind.

My stomach squirmed. Chase killed bad guys so easily, and I knew he wanted me to do the same. But I couldn't imagine killing one the way I slayed dragons and ice griffins. These wolves had been human before the Snow Queen enchanted them. I didn't want to go home knowing I'd taken a life, without being able to tell my mom why I was upset.

Something snarled at my elbow. I spun and crashed my hilt between the eyes of a small red-brown wolf. It fell, legs sprawled out in all directions, its breath whistling through its black nostrils. It didn't get up.

Knocking a wolf out with one blow felt pretty satisfying though.

"We need a doorway," Lena said, huffing just ahead. "We're not going to make it to the Door Trek door."

She was right. The director of EAS frowned on temporary-transport spells, but for emergencies, Lena had premixed some paint with just enough powdered dragon scale to magic the three of us back to EAS. This definitely counted as an emergency.

"What about the museum?" Chase said.

"In this rain?" Lena asked, incredulous.

"It'll probably be filled with tourists right now," I agreed. "We need to look for a shed or a public bathroom or something."

Lena read the sign we sprinted past, her hands on her glasses to keep them steady. "Or the Shakespeare Garden!"

Chase snorted. "You want to go *there*? What'll keep the wolves away? The flowers or the poetry?"

"No, the fence has a *gate*," I said. "Where is it?"

Lena double-checked the sign. "Oh," she said in a small voice. Then she pointed at the far side of the lake.

"You mean, back *toward* the wolves?" Chase said, obviously not a fan of the idea.

But Lena was right on this. "We need a door frame. It's better than losing time searching for one."

"Time's not the issue." Chase said. "Wait, are you still afraid we'll miss the tournament? I was *joking*."

A wolf howled in the distance, and we all turned to stare in that direction. All we saw were trees.

"There's probably more than one," I said.

"Lena, can you check?" Chase asked.

We ran up the path. *His* way, unfortunately. Since he had the most fighting experience, he was used to taking the lead during attacks.

Lena fumbled inside her jacket and pulled out a fabric-covered square—her mini magic mirror. This was an improved one.

Since the first walkie-talkie M3, she'd added a video recorder, a flashlight, texting capabilities, and most recently, a radar for bad guys.

"Lena?" Chase said, sounding impatient.

"It's a lot harder to read when I'm running! Wait, just a—" Before we rounded the corner, Lena gasped and threw out both arms. Chase and I skidded to a stop. Four wolves stood shoulder to shoulder across the trail, growling. White teeth gleamed in their black gums, gray fur bristling around their necks. The second pack had outrun us.

"Rory!" Chase grabbed a fallen branch from beside the trail, hacked some vines to free it, and tossed it to me. I passed my sword to Lena, so I could catch the branch with both hands. The wolves plowed forward. I swung. A gust of wind built up over my left hand, and then the branch connected. Three wolves whooshed backward. With a crunch of broken glass, two hit a car parked thirty yards away; the other smashed into a tree as big as the one in EAS's courtyard. It slid to the ground, leaving a canine-shaped scar on the tree bark.

It whimpered, its forelegs bent in an impossible direction.

Lena handed my sword back. Chase had taken care of the fourth wolf. Red spilled into the fur above its heart. With his sword, he pointed at the injured wolf beside the tree. His blade was covered in fresh blood. "Are you going to finish that one off?"

I scowled at him but didn't answer.

I tried to explain it to him once. As much as I loved EAS, being a Character wasn't easy. It forced me to do things I would have really liked to leave to the grown-ups. Because I had to, I would face off with the Snow Queen and her minions. I would keep Chase's secrets from Lena, and even lie to my family, but I drew the line at killing. Not forever, of course—I knew I'd need to kill enemies *eventually*, but it could wait until high school.

Maybe I hadn't explained myself all that well, because Chase had only replied, "Waiting won't change anything, Rory."

He still bugged me about it too. And *only* me, even though I knew for a fact no one else in eighth grade had slain anyone besides beasts, like dragons and ice griffins. Even Lena, who had been in almost as many battles as me and Chase. It drove me *crazy*.

Chase rolled his eyes. "Come on, Rory—"

Lena sprinted back the way we'd come, cradling the M3 to her chest. "Tell her off later, Chase. More are coming, and one of them is *really* big."

Chase wheeled around too. "Better to take on two than five."

We dashed around the lake again. It was pouring now. The ground was soggy, and mud splattered up the back of my clothes.

Lena led us down a sidewalk between the road and some trees. Three cars passed, and I really hoped it was raining too hard for the people inside to notice that Chase and I both had swords. The path opened up, and I saw buildings—one was big and boxy, another had a lawn and glass bubbles on its roof. Between them was a sunken courtyard.

Chase wiped the rain out of his eyes. "Last call for the museum."

"I don't think so." A very big group of tourists, all with cameras, stood under the awning. *They* saw the swords. A few even took pictures.

I turned away, shielding my face, and dashed down the stairway to the courtyard. The last thing I needed was someone recognizing me and selling the photo to some tabloids. I could see the caption now: DAUGHTER OF HOLLYWOOD ROYALTY CARRIES WEAPON INTO GOLDEN GATE PARK, WOUNDS ENDANGERED WOLVES.

The courtyard was full of bald-looking, knobby trees. Their leaves had barely started growing in, so it was easy to see the wolves stream down the steps after us.

Lena glanced down at her M3. *"Eleven*. Oh my gumdrops. Oh my gum—"

"Don't panic," Chase said. "We've faced worse odds than this."

"When?" Lena asked. "Because this is looking pretty bad."

Near the museum, someone screamed. We looked back.

An enormous wolf trotted down the steps, easily four times as big as the others. The rain had soaked its black fur, but you could see red-brown streaks running down its sides—exactly the same color as dried blood. When it saw us looking, it howled so loud that it rattled the concrete under my sneakers.

Sometimes villains are so bad that you recognize them instantly, even if you've never seen them before.

Ripper. As in Jack the Ripper, the serial killer who was famous in Victorian London even before the Snow Queen made him a wolf. He had held the Big Bad Wolf title for one hundred and fifty years.

He'd never been captured. He'd never been defeated. He hadn't even been *seen* since his mistress, the Snow Queen, had lost the last war.

"Scratch what I said about panicking," Chase said in a tiny voice.

"Is that who I think it is?" Lena squeaked, starting to slow down. "Oh my—"

It didn't matter. We still needed to get of there.